THE TOY TAKER

Luke Delaney joined the Metropolitan Police Service in the late 1980s and his first posting was to an inner city area of South East London notorious for high levels of crime and extreme violence. He later joined the CID where he investigated murders ranging from those committed by fledgling serial killers to gangland assassinations.

Find Luke Delaney on Twitter: @lukedelaneyuk

Also By Luke Delaney

Cold Killing
The Keeper

THE TOY TAKER

LUKE DELANEY

HARPER

Harper
An imprint of HarperCollins*Publishers*
77–85 Fulham Palace Road,
Hammersmith, London W6 8JB

www.harpercollins.co.uk

This paperback edition 2014
2

First published in Great Britain by HarperCollins*Publishers* 2014

A catalogue record for this book
is available from the British Library

ISBN: 978-0-00-748614-4

This novel is entirely a work of fiction.
The names, characters and incidents portrayed in it are
the work of the author's imagination. Any resemblance to
actual persons, living or dead, events or localities is
entirely coincidental.

Set in Meridien by Palimpsest Book Production Limited,
Falkirk, Stirlingshire

Printed and bound in Great Britain by
Clays Ltd, St Ives plc

MIX
Paper from
responsible sources

FSC
www.fsc.org

FSC™ C007454

DEDICATION

To my Mum – Mary.

I grew up in quite a large family, my siblings and I being close in age and none of us angels. We were a nightmare at times and just feeding, clothing and keeping us clean must have been exhausting and stressful, enough to push a mere mortal over the edge. But to this day I can't remember Mum ever being angry with me or even telling me off much. All I remember is feeling safe and loved when she was there. I could have done with a kick up the backside from time to time, but I think Mum felt we'd take enough hits and knocks as we grew older, and saw her role as being the one to give us sanctuary when we needed it – and we did.

It would be wrong of me to give the impression she was soft though. She's intelligent and tough, and razor sharp – a legacy of being the only sister with three older brothers growing up in the industrial northeast. She used her toughness to protect us when we were younger: she was the buffer between us and the big bad world – mine in particular, I think. She'd occasionally bunk me off school on a Friday, and we'd head into the city centre where I'd watch patiently while she bought *yet more* cushions, my reward being a slap-up lunch in a café. They were the best Fridays ever!

As my childhood gave way to the teenage years she remained the brick I anchored myself to, dispensing words of wisdom in a never-ending supply, picking me up when I was down, encouraging me when I was ready to quit, slipping me (and my pals) a few quid when she could so we could buy some smokes and the occasional pint, feeding me (and my pals) at the drop of a hat, advising me (and my pals) of how to fix our broken hearts when girlfriends left us for boys with cars.

One day, as I was miserably nursing an aforementioned broken heart, she said something that has stuck with me ever since: *Being miserable is a conscious decision and a waste of life. Every minute you sit there being miserable is a minute of your life you'll never get back. In a blink of an eye you'll be as old as I am now and you'll regret wasting these minutes like you won't believe.* Wise words indeed.

Sadly Mary lost the one and only love of her life a few years ago – my dad, Mike. She's struggled since then, understandably. They were together for nearly fifty years – loyal and loving to the last. Not easy losing the love of your life, but she remains a beautiful and formidable lady.

For everything she's done for me, my siblings and my dad, Mike, I'd like to dedicate this book to her.

For Mum. For Mary.

God bless.

1

The street was quiet, empty of the noise of living people, with only the sound of a million leaves hissing in the strong breeze that intensified as it blew in over Hampstead Heath in north-west London. Smart Georgian houses lined either side of the deserted Courthope Road, all gently washed in the pale yellow of the street lights, their warming appearance giving lie to the increasingly bitter cold that late autumn brought with it. Some of the shallow porches added their own light to the yellow, left on by security-conscious occupiers and those too exhausted to remember to switch them off before heading for bed. But these were the homes of London's affluent, who had little to fear from the streets outside – the hugely inflated house prices ensuring the entire area was a sanctuary for the rich and privileged. Higher than normal police patrols, private security firms and state-of-the-art burglar alarms meant the people within slept soundly and contentedly.

His gloved fingers worked quickly and nimbly as he crouched by the front door, the small powerful torch – the type used by potholers, strapped to his forehead by an elasticated band – provided him with more than enough light to see inside the locks on the door: two deadlocks, top and bottom, and a combined deadlock and latch in the centre. His warm breath turned to plumes of mist that swirled in the tubular light of the torch before disappearing into the night, making way for the next calmly expelled breath. He'd already unlocked the top and bottom deadlocks easily enough – a thousand hours of practice making the task simple, but the centre locks were new and more sophisticated. Still he remained totally calm as he gently and precisely worked the two miniature tools together, each of which looked similar to the type of instruments a dentist would use – the thin wrench with its slightly hooked end holding the first of the lock's pins down as the pick silently slid quickly back and forth until eventually it aligned all the pins in the barrel of the lock and it clicked open. It was a tiny sound, but one that in the emptiness of the street made him freeze, holding his breath as he waited for any reaction in the night that surrounded him. When his lungs began to burn he exhaled the dead air, taking a second to look at his watch. It was just gone three a.m. The family inside would be in the deepest part of their sleep – at their least likely to react to any slight sound or change in the atmosphere.

He inserted the slim hook wrench into the last remaining lock and once more slid the pick through the lock's barrel until within only a few seconds he felt the pins drop into their holes and allow him to turn the barrel and open the lock, the door falling open just a few millimetres. He replaced the tools in their suede case along with the other dozen or so lock-picking items, rolled it up and put it into the small plastic sports holdall he'd brought with him. He added the head-torch, then paused for a second before taking out the item that he knew was so precious to the little boy who waited inside – the one thing that would virtually guarantee the boy's cooperation – even his happiness.

He eased the door open and stepped inside, closing it behind him and silently returning the latch to its locked position. He waited for the sounds of an intruder alarm to begin its countdown to the wailing of sirens, but there was none, just as he all but knew there wouldn't be.

The house was warm inside, the cold of outside quickly fading in his mind as he stepped deeper into the family's home, heading for the staircase, his way lit by the street light pouring through the windows. Their curtains had been left open and lights strategically left on in case little feet went wandering in the night. He felt safe in the house, almost like a child himself once more – no longer alone and unloved. As he walked slowly towards the stairs that would lead him to the boy, he noted the order of the things within – neat and tidy, everything in its place except for the occasional toy scattered on the hallway floor, abandoned by the children of the house and left by parents too tired to care any more. He breathed in the smells of the family – the food they had had for dinner mixing with the mother's perfume and bathtime creams and soaps, air fresheners and polish.

He listened to the sounds of the house – the bubbling of a fish-tank filter coming from the children's playroom and the ticking of electronic devices that seemed to inhabit every modern family's home, accompanied by blinking green and red lights. All the time he thought of the parents rushing the children to their beds, too preoccupied with making it to that first glass of wine to even read them a bedtime story or stroke their hair until sleep took them. Parents who had children as a matter of course – to keep them as possessions and a sign of wealth, mere extensions of the expensive houses they lived in and exotic cars they drove. Children they would educate privately as another show of wealth and influence – bought educations that minimized the need for parental input while guaranteeing they never had to step out of their own social confines – even at the school gate.

More discarded toys lay on the occasional step as he began to climb towards the boy's room, careful not to step on the floorboards that he already knew would creak, his gloved hands carrying the bag and the thing so precious to the boy. His footsteps were silent on the carpet as he glided past the parents' bedroom on the first floor, the door almost wide open in case of a child in distress. He could sense only the mother in the room – no odours or sounds of a man. He left her sleeping in the semi-darkness and climbed the next flight of stairs to where the children slept – George and his older sister Sophia, each in their own bedrooms. If they hadn't been, he wouldn't be here.

He reached the second-floor landing and stood still for a few seconds, looking above to the third floor where he knew the guest bedrooms were, listening for any faint sounds of life, unsure whether the family had a late-arriving guest staying. He only moved forward along the hallway when he was sure the floor above held nothing but emptiness.

Pink and blue light from the children's night-lamps seeped through their partially opened doors – the blueness guiding him towards George, his grip on the special thing tightening. He was only seconds away from what he'd come for. He passed the girl's room without looking inside and moved slowly, carefully, silently to the boy's room, easing the door open, knowing the hinges wouldn't make a noise. He crossed the room to the boy's bed that was pushed up under the window, momentarily stopping to look around at the blue wallpaper with white clouds, periodically broken up by childish paintings in the boy's own hand; the mobile of trains with smiling faces above the boy's head and the seemingly dozens of teddy bears of all kinds spread across his bed and beyond. He felt both tears of joy and sadness rising from deep inside himself and swelling behind his eyes, but he knew he had to do what he'd come to do: a greater power than he or any man had guided him this far and would protect him the rest of the way.

He knelt next to the boy's bed and placed the bag on the floor, his face only inches away from the child's, their breath intertwining in the space between them and becoming one as he gently began to whisper. 'George . . . sssh . . . George.' The boy stirred under his duvet, his slight four-year-old body wriggling as it fought to stay asleep. 'George . . . sssh . . . open your eyes, George. There's nothing to be afraid of. I have something for you, George. Something very precious.' The boy rolled over slowly, blinking sleep from his narrow eyes – eyes that suddenly grew large with excitement and confusion, a smile spreading across his face, his green eyes sparkling with joy as he saw what the man had brought him – reaching out for the precious gift as the man's still gloved hand stroked his straight blond hair. 'Do you want to come to a magic place with me, George? A special place with special things?' he whispered. 'If you do, we need to go now and we need to be very, very quiet. Do you understand?' he asked smiling.

'A magic place?' the boy asked, yawning and stretching in his pale blue pyjamas, making the pictures of dinosaurs printed on them come to life.

'Yes,' the man assured him. 'A place just for the best, nicest children to see.'

'Do we have to go now?' the boy asked.

'Yes, George,' the man told him, taking him by the hand and lifting his bag at the same time. 'We have to go now. We have to go right now.'

Detective Inspector Sean Corrigan sat in his small goldfish bowl of an office at Peckham Police Station reading through

CPS reports and reviews of the last case he and his team had dealt with – over six months ago now. Initially they'd all been glad of the lull in the number of murder investigations coming their way, but after six months, and with the paperwork for the last case already tidied away, they were growing bored and restless. They watched and waited as the other murder teams across south-east London continued to work on the everyday, run-of-the-mill murders that kept them in the overtime that meant they could pay their mortgages on time and maybe even save enough for an inexpensive family holiday. Sean's team were beginning to feel the pinch and even old, experienced hands like Detective Sergeant Dave Donnelly were struggling to find increasingly creative ways to justify the need for them to work overtime.

Sean momentarily glanced up and looked into the main office where half his team casually sat at desks and computer screens, the usual sense of urgency plainly not there. He knew he and they were being kept for something special, but if this went on any longer he'd have to speak to Detective Superintendent Featherstone and ask him to toss his team something, even just a domestic murder – anything to keep them gainfully employed. He gave his head a little shake and looked back down at the report on his desk from the CPS detailing the case against Thomas Keller – kidnapper and murderer of women, and the man who'd so nearly taken Sean's life. He rubbed his shoulder. It still ached, even after three separate operations to try and remove all the shotgun pellets Keller's gun had put there.

As he read the psychological report that detailed some of the abuse Keller had suffered as a boy, abuse that occasionally mirrored his own childhood, he struggled to work out how he felt about the man. He knew he didn't hate him or even resent him, and decided he just felt overwhelmingly sorry for him. But he felt sorry for his victims too. No one had come out of the Keller case a winner.

Despite being completely immersed in the report, he still sensed a change in the atmosphere of the main office that made him look up and see Featherstone striding across the office, all smiles and waves, as if he was on an American presidential campaign. Sean puffed out his cheeks and waited for Featherstone's inevitable arrival, his large frame soon filling the doorway as for some reason he bothered to knock on the open door before entering without being invited and slumping heavily into the chair opposite Sean.

'Fuck me. Freeze brass monkeys out there,' was his opening gambit. 'Nice and warm in here though. Wouldn't want to be stuck at an outside murder scene too long today.'

'Morning, boss,' Sean replied, his voice heavy with disinterest once he realized Featherstone wasn't about to hand him a much-needed murder investigation. 'Anything happening out there?'

'Nah!' Featherstone answered. 'Just thought I'd drop by and tell you myself.'

Sean frowned. 'Tell me what?'

'Now don't get too pissed off, but I had a call from the Assistant Commissioner a couple of hours ago.'

'And?'

'One of the top bods at the CPS called him and told him they wouldn't be trying to get any convictions for rape or murder against Thomas Keller or any other type of conviction for that matter. They're going to accept a plea of manslaughter on grounds of diminished responsibility and then he's off to Broadmoor for the rest of his natural. I thought it best if I tell you personally. I know what he did to you.' Sean involuntarily grabbed his shoulder. 'How is the old shoulder, anyway?'

'It's fine,' Sean lied, 'and I'm neither pissed off nor

surprised. Keller is what he is. I don't care how he ends up behind bars just so long as he does.'

'He can talk to all the other nutters in there.' Featherstone smiled, but stopped when he realized Sean wasn't returning the sentiment. 'Anyway, that's that job put to bed, so I suppose you'll be needing something to keep the troops busy. Idle hands and all that.'

'Right now I'll take anything,' Sean told him.

'Can't allow that, I'm afraid,' Featherstone said. 'Assistant Commissioner Addis is adamant you and yours are to be saved for the more . . . well, you know.'

'Yeah, but this is south-east London, not Washington State. It could be years before another Keller comes along.'

'Indeed,' Featherstone agreed. 'But what if you covered the *whole* of London and, sometimes, if the case merited it, beyond?'

'How can we investigate a murder in deepest-darkest north London if we're based in Peckham?'

'Which rather neatly brings us on to my next bit of news – you're moving.'

'What?' Sean almost shouted, drawing concerned looks from the detectives eavesdropping in the main office. 'Where to?'

'Where else? The Yard, of course.'

'Scotland Yard?' Sean asked, incredulous. 'Most of my team live in Kent or the borders of. How are they supposed to get to the Yard every day?'

'Same way everyone else does,' Featherstone told him. 'Train, bus – you can even drive if you have to. The Assistant Commissioner's bagged you a few parking places in the underground car park there. Best you pull rank and reserve yourself one.'

'This is not going to go down well,' Sean warned him.

'Nothing I can do about it, and nothing you can do about

it,' Featherstone replied, his voice hushed now, as if Addis could somehow overhear him from his office high in the tower that was New Scotland Yard. 'Mr Addis is determined to keep you for the special ones: murders with strong sexual elements, especially ones involving children; murders showing excessive violence and body mutilation, and missing person cases where there are strong grounds to believe a predatory offender may be involved. You get the drift. Addis put the proposal to the Commissioner and he agreed it, so that's that. They feel we've been getting caught out by not having a specialist team to investigate these types of cases, so they decided to create one and you're it.'

'Meaning,' Sean offered, 'when these high-interest, media-attracting cases don't go quite to plan they've got someone ready-made and in place to blame?'

'You may think that, but I couldn't possibly comment,' Featherstone replied. 'Let's just say you don't get to be the Assistant Commissioner of the Metropolitan Police without learning how to cover your arse.' Sean just pursed his lips. 'Anyway, your new home's on the seventh floor, Room 714. Used to be the Arts and Antiques Team's, until Addis decided they weren't offering value for money any more and sent them back to division – half of them back to uniform. Wonder how they're feeling this morning – walking the beat in some khazi somewhere freezing their nuts or tits off. A warning to the wise – Addis is not a man to piss off.'

'What if I say no?' Sean suddenly asked. 'What if I say I don't want to do it?' Images of his wife, Kate, flashed in his mind, smiling and clutching her chest with relief as he told her he'd quit the Murder Team.

'And what else would you do?' Featherstone answered. 'Go back to division and rubber-stamp search warrants, oversee endless dodgy rape allegations? Come on, Sean – it would kill you.'

'Flying Squad? Anti-Terrorist?'

'They're plum jobs, Sean. You know the score: everyone leaving a central or area posting has to go back and serve time on division before getting another off-division posting. And like I said – just in case you weren't listening – Addis is not a man to piss off.' Kate's smiling face faded to nothing. 'Besides, this is where you belong. I'm not blowing smoke up your arse, but seriously, Sean, you're the best I've got at doing this – the best I've ever seen, always one step ahead of everyone else, sometimes two steps, three steps. I don't know how you do what you do, but I know you can use it to catch some very bad people, and maybe save a few lives along the way.' Sean said nothing. 'What's done is done. Now get yourself and your team over to NSY and set up shop. Your new home awaits you.'

The discussion over, Featherstone stood and walked backwards towards the door. 'We're done here. I'll drop in and see you in a couple of days, see how the move's going. Who knows, you might have a special case by then. Just what your troops need to take their minds off being moved – and you too. Good luck, and remember, when you make it to the Yard be careful: Addis has eyes and ears everywhere. Loose lips sink ships.'

With that he turned on his heels and was gone, leaving Sean alone, staring at the space he'd left. A special case, Sean thought to himself. Such a neat, sterile way to describe what he had seen and would see again: women and men mutilated and abused before death finally claimed them. What would be next?

Celia Bridgeman checked her watch as she searched through the under-the-stairs cupboard for her training shoes and realized it was almost eight fifteen a.m. She needed to be at the gym by nine a.m. At thirty-five it was becoming increasingly difficult to maintain her sleek figure, no matter how little she ate; the hairdressers by ten thirty a.m and then she had a lunch date with some of the mums from school at twelve thirty p.m; grilled chicken salads, no dressing, all round. At least the nanny was here to get the kids fed and dressed and off to school, even if her soon-to-be-sacked cleaner was late again. She found her trainers just as she heard footsteps above her rattling down the stairs, at which she pulled her head from the cupboard in time to see her six-year-old daughter jump the last three stairs into the hallway. She flicked her perfectly dyed blonde hair from her face and spoke to her through straight, shining white teeth. 'Sophia, have you seen George yet?'

'No,' Sophia replied, sounding more like a teenager than a six-year-old. 'He's probably playing with his toys in his bedroom – as usual.'

'Yeah, well he's going to be late for school.'

'Nursery, mum,' Sophia corrected her. 'George goes to nursery, not school. Remember?'

'Don't talk to me like that, Sophia and go and tell Caroline what you want for breakfast.' Sophia tossed her head to one side to show her dissatisfaction and headed for the kitchen, her mother's genes already shaping her face and body for a life at the top table. Celia pursed her lips and shook her head as she watched daddy's little princess swagger towards a health-conscious breakfast before looking at the flights of stairs above her and calling to the heavens. 'George. Stop playing with your toys and come and get breakfast.' She waited for an answer, but none came. 'George.' Again she waited. Nothing. Caroline, the nanny, had arrived while she was still in the shower. Perhaps she'd already fed and dressed George? She looked at her watch again, the increasing concern she was going to be late for the gym urging her to speak to Caroline and save herself a trip up

11

two flights of stairs. She followed Sophia's route to the kitchen and found the nanny slicing apples and bananas for her daughter's breakfast. 'You should have some toast or something as well,' she reprimanded her.

'I don't want to get fat,' Sophia answered. Celia almost argued with her but remembered why she was there.

'Caroline. Have you seen George yet this morning?' she asked.

'No, Mrs Bridgeman,' she answered. 'Not yet. I thought maybe he'd already had his breakfast.'

'He's hardly going to get it himself,' Sophia unhelpfully added.

'Don't be rude, Sophia,' Celia silenced her.

'Maybe he's not feeling very well,' Caroline suggested. 'D'you want me to go and check on him?'

'No,' Celia snapped, a sudden unexplained feeling of anxiety creeping through her like a grass fire. George had been late before – many times – quietly playing in his bedroom with his toys, unwilling to join the family rituals that his young mind knew would be being played out two floors below, but this felt different somehow. 'I'll go,' she said.

Her daughter and the nanny exchanged bemused looks as she turned her back on them and walked quickly to the stairs, climbing them two at a time, her slim body and athletic legs making her progress rapid, but the closer she got the slower she seemed to move, until she was only feet away from his bedroom door, the silence from within drowned out by the relentless beating of her heart, all thoughts of the gym and lunch gone from her head.

As she eased the door open she could see the curtains were still drawn and the blue night-lamp was still on – not unusual for George, but it meant no one else had been in to see him that morning. 'George?' she softly called into the

12

room as the door opened wider, as if she didn't want to startle him if he was still sleeping, especially if he was unwell – another fever perhaps. 'George?' She moved into the room, the sickness in her stomach growing as she approached his bed, the thick duvet and plump pillows making it difficult to tell whether he was there or not, but as she closed the distance the realization dawned on her that the bed was empty, making her sprint the last few steps to where her son should have been. Pointlessly, desperately, she patted the bedclothes, pulling the duvet back and tossing it on the floor, even looking under the pillows, feeling increasingly dizzy. Quickly she pulled the heavy blackout curtains open, almost pulling them from their rail, flooding the room with bright orange light, the late autumn sun still low in the sky, barely clearing the adjacent houses.

She stood in the centre of the room, her eyes desperately searching for signs of life – a slight movement or a giggle coming from a hiding place. For a second she laughed at herself, realizing she must be in a game, a game to find a hiding boy. She dropped to her knees and peered under the bed, about to say the boy's name when she'd discovered him, but the words never came out and her smile was vanquished as she stared into the empty space, the panic returning – stronger now.

'Where the hell are you, George?' she asked the emptiness, pushing herself back to her feet and pacing the room, opening the wardrobe and searching places that in her heart she knew he couldn't be: his drawers and toy boxes, even under the mattress, until she had to admit he couldn't be in the room. For a moment she felt her throat swell and close, as if she was about to start crying, before she convinced herself it was only a matter of time before she found him.

She walked quickly from room to room, searching every wardrobe and cupboard, behind every curtain and under every table, checking every window was still locked from the inside, constantly calling the boy's name – threatening and encouraging him to reveal himself. But something in her soul told her the rooms were empty: the way the silence felt so still and lifeless. In the middle of her desperate search she suddenly stopped for a second, the memory of how the very atmosphere of a space would change when the boy was in it and the sudden fear she would never feel it again making her so nauseous and light-headed that she had to lean against the wall and try and control her breathing, swallowing gulps of air until the floor she was looking down at came back into focus. As quickly as she dared, Celia walked downstairs, her outstretched hand sliding along the wall for support until she reached the kitchen, her softly tanned skin pale now and her lips a little blue. The nanny saw her first. 'Are you all right, Mrs Bridgeman?'

Celia spoke without answering the question, her eyes growing ever wilder with thoughts and fears she'd never once in her life imagined having. 'Have you seen Mr Bridgeman this morning?'

'No,' the nanny answered, confusion spreading across her face. 'I thought he was away on business last night?'

'He was,' Sophia answered for her mother.

'Be quiet, Sophia,' Celia snapped. 'Are you sure he didn't come back very early this morning? Maybe he . . .?' Celia suddenly didn't know how to say what she wanted to say.

'He wasn't here when I arrived,' the nanny told her, 'and his car wasn't here either. Is something wrong?'

'The front door,' Celia asked, 'was it locked when you arrived?'

'Yes,' the nanny answered.

'All the locks?'

'Yes, Mrs Bridgeman. Is there something wrong?' the nanny asked again.

Celia's voice almost failed her as she tried to speak, the words weak and wavering. 'I can't find George,' she finally managed to tell them. 'He's gone. Someone's taken him.'

'That's not possible,' the nanny told her, her smile hiding her own rising fears. 'He must be hiding somewhere.'

'No,' she answered, her voice growing ever weaker as she slumped to her knees on the floor. 'He's gone. He's been taken. I can feel it.'

The nanny came to her side and bent over her, trying to encourage her to stand. 'Let's look again – together. I know we'll find him.'

'No,' Celia almost shouted, summoning the last of her strength, the tears rolling freely down her face now. 'Listen to me – he's gone. He's been taken. We've wasted enough time. I need to phone the police.'

'I'll phone Mr Bridgeman,' the nanny offered.

'No,' Celia spat, grabbing the phone. 'I'll do it.'

Sean looked from his office into the main office outside and decided that enough of the team had gathered for the meeting to begin. He exhaled, took a deep breath and walked the few steps next door, suddenly aware of the relentless noise; the laughter and loud chatter mixing with the seemingly constant ringing of land and mobile phones. He caught Donnelly's eye, but his other stalwart detective sergeant, Sally Jones, seemed to be holding a girls-only meeting with the other female detectives in the far corner next to the coffee- and tea-making facilities: a limescale-clogged old kettle and a fridge that smelled like something had died in it.

Donnelly knew his job. 'All right, all right,' he boomed across the office in his Glaswegian-tinged-with-London accent. 'This office meeting is officially open, so park your bums and listen up.' He seemed to make eye contact with everyone in the room while he waited for total silence, not speaking again until he had it, turning to Sean. 'Guv'nor – all yours.'

But before Sean could start, a dissenting voice spoke up.

'Guv'nor,' DC Alan Jesson asked in his Liverpudlian accent, 'when we gonna get a new case? I'm fucking skint. I need the overtime just to make ends meet here, you know.' The murmur of approval from the others told Sean they were all feeling pretty much the same way.

'Something will be coming our way soon enough,' Sean tried to assure them.

'How d'you know?' Sally asked. 'How can you be sure it'll be sooner rather than later?'

'Because the sea we fish in just got a whole lot bigger,' Sean answered in a voice almost too quiet to hear.

'I'm sorry,' Sally replied. 'I don't understand.'

'We're no longer a south-east London Murder Investigation Team, we're a London-wide Murder Investigation Team.' He watched the silent, blank faces trying to understand what he'd just told them.

'Excuse me?' Donnelly finally broke the stunned silence. 'We're a what?'

'We've just gone London-wide,' Sean explained. 'Express orders of Assistant Commissioner Addis. Featherstone told me earlier this morning – the Commissioner's agreed to it, so that's that. As of now, anything a bit special comes our way. Potential serial offenders, child murders by strangers, sexually motivated murders – all the good stuff's going to land on our desk. It won't be easy, but it will be interesting. Anybody not up for it needs to have the applications for a transfer on my desk by this time tomorrow. I'm sure HR can find you all suitable posts on division. You could even stay here at Peckham.'

'Stay?' Donnelly said. 'Then by inference if we decide to stay part of this team we'll be moving?'

'Yes,' Sean told him, beginning to enjoy the game.

'D'you mind telling us where to?'

'The Yard.'

Donnelly closed his eyes and groaned as he leaned back in his chair so much he risked over-balancing. 'Jesus. Not the fucking Yard. How am I supposed to get there from Swanley every day? And there's nowhere to park.'

'They've reserved us a few spaces in the underground car park.'

'Oh, that's all right then,' Donnelly said sarcastically.

'Sounds great to me,' Sally chipped in with a mischievous grin, keen to kick Donnelly while he was down.

'Aye,' Donnelly continued. 'It's all right for you, living in Putney. Putney to Victoria every day – lovely.

'Sorry, Dave,' Sally told him, her grin turning into a fully fledged smile.

'I'm all right, Jack, eh?'

'All right,' Sean broke it up, 'enough of the table tennis. Let's make this official – if you don't want to come with me, put your hand up.' He scanned the room, but saw no raised hands. 'I promise you there'll be no hard feelings. Many of you have wives, husbands, kids, so if the nature of the work or the travelling's too much I'll understand.' Still no raised hands. 'Dave?'

'Aye, fuck-it – why not? But there'd better be plenty overtime.'

'More than you could possibly spend.'

'Aye, there better be.'

'Right,' Sean snapped to attention, 'we're moving today.' The groans almost drowned him out. 'So let's get everything packed up and over to the Yard – Room 714, seventh floor in the North Tower. Take everything that's not screwed down and even stuff that is, if it's of any use. Take the computers, chairs, phones – everything we'll need to be up and running straight away.'

17

'Pickfords not moving us then, boss?' Jesson asked.

'Where d'you think you are, Alan – the City Police? This is the good old Met – remember? Pile everything into anything with four wheels that's been left in the yard with keys in and let's get out of this toilet.' He still felt eyes upon him. 'Well come on, then. What you waiting for?'

As the detectives burst into action, Sean slipped quietly into his office, summoning Donnelly and Sally with a nod of his head. Within a few seconds they were all gathered together.

'Problem?' Sally asked.

'Not yet,' he told her as Donnelly caught up with them.

'Not yet what?' he asked.

'A problem,' Sally filled him in.

'There's a first!' Donnelly replied.

'Yeah, well,' Sean continued, 'I've got a feeling we won't have to wait too much longer before something comes our way, and when it does it's clearly not going to be anything straightforward and not something we'll be able to quietly get on with. The Yard's full of senior officers with not enough to do who'll be more than keen to stick their noses where they're not wanted – and that means our business.'

'So?' Sally asked.

'So we need to be ready for anything,' Sean warned them. 'Which is why I need you two to keep a fire burning under everyone's arses until we're up and running at the Yard. Understand?'

'Yes, guv,' Sally answered.

'Whatever,' Donnelly agreed unhappily.

'I'm going to pack up some essentials and head over there ASAP – check out the lay of the land before anyone else gets there.'

'Looking for anything in particular?' Donnelly asked suspiciously.

'No,' Sean answered, too quickly. 'But let's just say I'd rather we used the phones we're taking with us than the ones that will have been left for us.'

'That's a bit paranoid isn't it, guv'nor?' Sally asked.

'It's the Yard,' Sean reminded her. 'Being a little paranoid can go a long way to keeping you out of the brown sticky stuff.'

'I've always avoided the place,' Donnelly added. 'Things can get very . . . *political* there very quickly. That's why I always stuck with the Flying Squad – squirrelled away in Tower Bridge, out of sight, out of mind – beautiful.'

'However,' Sean interrupted Donnelly's reminiscing, 'the Yard it is, so just be mindful and be ready,' he warned them. 'I've got a feeling something really nasty's heading our way, and heading our way very, very soon.'

2

Sean staggered along the seventh-floor corridor carrying a brown cardboard box that was heavy enough to make him sweat. The heating at the Yard was turned up high to please the ageing computers housed within. He checked the doors as he passed them – store rooms, empty rooms; occasionally a room with no sign, just a number and a few wary-looking people inside, silently raising their heads from their desks as he passed, disturbing their expectations of another day without change. He didn't bother to introduce himself but just kept walking down the unpleasantly narrow corridor that was no different to all the other corridors at New Scotland Yard, with the same polystyrene ceiling tiles and walls no thicker than plasterboard, all painted a shade of light brown that blended into the worn, slightly darker brown carpet. 'At least the floors don't squeak,' he whispered to himself, remembering the awful rubber floors back at Peckham as he arrived at Room 714 and its closed door.

He half-expected the door to be locked in a final gesture of defiance from the now disbanded Arts and Antiques Squad – a show of two fingers to Assistant Commissioner Addis, who Sean ironically always pictured living in a house surrounded by arts and antiques. Maybe one day Addis would get burgled and have to hastily re-form the squad in an effort to recover his own stolen treasures.

Sean balanced the heavy box on his raised thigh and tried the door handle, which to his surprise turned and opened, the door itself swinging aside in response to a good kick, allowing him to enter his new home from home.

Sean peered inside as best he could before stepping over the threshold. 'Jesus Christ,' he exclaimed as he walked deeper into the office, which was about half the size of the one they'd just left and looked like a hand-grenade had gone off in it. Clearly the Arts and Antiques boys and girls had been moved out in a hurry, leaving very little but rubbish and broken computers behind. He congratulated himself on the decision to tell his own team to ransack the Peckham office as part of the move. He dumped the box on an abandoned desk and crossed the office to the still-closed blinds – cheap, grey plastic venetians. He tugged the string, expecting the blind to neatly, if noisily, roll up to the ceiling, but the entire thing came crashing to the floor, the reverberating sound appearing to go on for ever as it bounced back and forth off the empty walls. Sean stood frozen, his face a grimace, long after the sound had faded. He turned back towards the door, anticipating a flurry of concerned people coming to investigate, but no one came, although he thought he heard laughter from further down the hallway. He moved along the line of blinds and gingerly pulled the strings until all were open and he was able to look down on the streets of St James's Park below, the traffic little more than a distant murmur.

Turning his back on the windows, he surveyed the office in the daylight and didn't like what he saw any better than before. It was going to be a real squeeze and arguments would abound as to who was entitled to a desk of their own, but at least there were two offices at one end of the main room, partitioned off with the usual polystyrene boards and sheets of Perspex, all held together by strips of aluminium. He made his way to the larger office and stepped inside, deciding it was about as big as his last one. He decided he'd give it to Sally and Donnelly to share while he took the smaller one. At the very least it might placate the unhappy Donnelly.

Leaving the office, he retrieved the heavy cardboard box that contained his most precious policing tools and entered the smaller office, dumping the box on the standard-sized desk that would soon be covered in keyboards, computer screens, phones and files. Under the desk he found the usual cheap three-drawer cabinet and miraculously the previous owner had left the keys in the top lock. Only someone leaving the force for good would abandon such a prized possession. Sean felt a twang of jealousy as he imagined the previous owner skipping out of the office after their last day at work, knowing they would never be returning. He shook the thought away and looked around for a chair, finding a swivel one pushed into the corner of the room, foam peeking from the rip in the seat cover. Never mind – it would have to do.

Before sitting he began to unpack the contents of the box – the few personal things first, placed on top of everything else where they were least likely to be damaged: a photograph of his wife, Kate, and of his smiling daughters, Mandy and Louise, and finally a small silver cross on a thin silver chain, given to him by his mother when he was just a boy. She'd told him it would protect him. It hadn't, but still he'd kept it without knowing why. He hung it over the corner of the frame that held Kate's picture and remembered being dragged to church as a child, never to return as an adult, despite his mother's frequent encouragement.

He continued to unpack his things: his *Detective's Training*

Course Manual – otherwise known as The Bible, a copy of *Butterworths Criminal Law* and the Police and Criminal Evidence Act, old files kept for reference, stationery and even the landline phone he'd commandeered from his old office back at Peckham. Every so often he glanced up from arranging his new desk to look exactly like his old one and stared into the empty main office – imagining, almost seeing how it would soon look – the characters who he so strongly associated with Peckham transported to this strange new environment, working away at computers, phones clamped between ears and shoulders as they hurriedly scribbled notes, the constant chatter and noise bringing the place to life. He blinked the imaginary detectives away, returning the office to its eerie emptiness and leaving him feeling strangely lonely. It wasn't something he felt often, not since his childhood when being alone generally meant being safe. He shook his head and continued to empty the box, but a voice close by broke the silence and made him jump a little, leaving him surprised that he hadn't felt the other person approaching as he usually would have.

'Settling in all right I trust, Inspector?' Assistant Commissioner Addis asked from the doorway.

'More moving in than settling in,' Sean answered.

'Indeed,' Addis agreed, a thin, unpleasant grin fixed on his face, his eyes sparkling with cunning and intelligence. 'The office is on the small side, I know, but I'm sure it will serve its purpose.'

'It'll be fine,' Sean told him without enthusiasm, returning to the task of unpacking.

'Good,' Addis said, walking deeper into the room. 'It's fortunate you've arrived early,' he added, making Sean look up.

'Really?' Sean asked, already concerned about what was coming next. 'How so?'

'Gives us time to chat – in private.' Addis looked around at the emptiness as if to make the point.

'About what?' Sean asked without trying to veil the suspicion in his voice.

'Your new position, of course – here at the Yard. I'm assuming Superintendent Featherstone briefed you?'

'He did – more or less.'

'You should thank me,' Addis told him without a hint of irony. 'You're free now. Free of all those tedious investigations a trained chimp could solve: husband strangles wife to death; drug dealer shoots other drug dealer; teenage gang member stabs other teenage gang member. I think we can leave the mundane to the less gifted to solve, don't you?'

Sean shrugged his shoulders. 'I suppose so.'

'Suppose so?' Addis asked. 'You know so I think. Yes?' Sean said nothing. 'You know one of the things we do really badly in the police, Sean? We waste talent. But I don't waste talent when I see it, Sean – I use it, in whatever way I think best.'

'And that's why I'm here?' Sean asked. 'To be used?'

Addis gave a short, shallow laugh before pulling a thin manilla file from under his armpit that Sean hadn't registered he was carrying until now. Addis flopped it on the desk, some of the documents inside spilling out, including a photograph of a radiant, beautiful child. 'Your first case,' Addis told him without emotion. 'A four-year-old child has gone missing in suspicious circumstances from his home in Hampstead.'

'Hampstead?' Sean asked, remembering the area or at least several of its pubs that were frequently used by detectives attending residential courses at the Metropolitan Police Training Centre in nearby Hendon.

'The boy apparently went missing overnight while his mother and sister were asleep. No signs of forced entry anywhere in the house, so it appears the boy has vanished into thin air. Quite the mystery. Right up your street – don't you think?'

'And the father?' Sean asked.

'Away on business, I believe. The local CID are at the address with the family eagerly awaiting your arrival.'

'Has the house been searched yet?' Sean enquired. 'Sounds like the kid's probably still in there somewhere, hiding.'

'The house's been searched by the mother, the local uniform officers and the local CID. No trace of the boy, which is why I've decided to assign the investigation to you.'

'I see,' Sean said, realizing that nothing he could say would deter Addis.

'If you find the boy hiding somewhere the others failed to look then all well and good,' Addis told him. 'But if you don't . . .' He let it hang for a while before speaking again. 'I understand you had some success a few years ago working undercover to infiltrate a paedophile ring known as the Network?'

'I did,' Sean admitted, slightly fazed that Addis had taken the time to research him so thoroughly.

'Then you'll have good understanding of how these people work.'

'And you think a paedophile is involved here?'

'That would be my guess,' Addis answered. 'And these people aren't council estate scum, Sean – before you start accusing the parents of being involved.'

'I was only thinking it's a little too soon to make any assumptions. If the family are wealthy there may be a ransom demand.'

'Well,' Addis said, allowing Sean his moment of contradiction, 'I'll leave that for you to discover. All the details I have are in the file.' Addis's eyes indicated the folder on the desk. 'Oh, and while I have you, I've decided your team needs a new name – to help you stand out from the crowd. As of now you will be known as the Special Investigations Unit. Should keep your troops happy: there's nothing detectives seem to like more than a bit of elitism – or at least that's what I've always found. Predominantly you'll still be investigating murders, but every now and then something else may come along.' Sean didn't reply, his eyes never leaving Addis. 'I'll leave you to get on with it. A quick result would be much appreciated: we could do with some positive press. If you need anything just pop in and see me – I'm never far away, just a few floors above. Report to me when you find anything, or Superintendent Featherstone if I'm not around. Until later, then.' Addis turned to leave.

'Mr Addis,' Sean called after him, making the Assistant Commissioner stop and turn, his face slightly perplexed, as if having his progress interrupted was a novel and unwelcome experience.

'Something wrong, Inspector?'

'No. It's just that I was brought up on a council estate,' Sean told him. 'I thought you should know.'

Addis grinned and nodded, impossible to read as he turned his back on Sean and headed for the exit, almost colliding with Sally as she barrelled into the room, unable to see where she was going due to the size of the box she was carrying. Addis jumped out of the way and cleared his throat to make her aware of his presence.

Sally peeped over the top of her box at the sullen-faced Assistant Commissioner and groaned inwardly. 'Shit,' she spurted, immediately realizing her mistake and hurrying to correct it: 'I mean, fuck . . . Sorry, sir . . . sorry.'

Addis glared at her and exited quickly into the corridor, leaving the bemused Sally scanning the room for Sean, eventually spotting him still standing in his new office. She dumped her box on the nearest desk and made for Sean who was already heading towards her, the file on the missing boy in his hand.

'Pompous twat,' she offered, with a jerk of the head towards the door Addis had just departed through. Registering that Sean was advancing in that direction, she added, 'Going somewhere, guv'nor?'

'Yes,' Sean told her. 'And so are you.'

Donnelly sat in the passenger seat while DC Paulo Zukov drove them through the increasingly dense traffic around Parliament Square, Donnelly shaking his head at the thought of having to use public transport to beat the traffic. 'The Yard,' he moaned out loud. 'Why did it have to be the Yard? They're selling the damn thing as soon as they can find a buyer. We'll no sooner get sorted than they'll have us on the move again. Bloody waste of time. Where to next, for Christ's sake – Belgravia?'

'Look on the bright side,' Zukov told him, 'we can tell everyone we're detectives from New Scotland Yard now. Better than saying you're from Peckham. And the traffic's not that bad – considering. You've just got to get used to it.'

Donnelly looked him up and down with unveiled contempt. 'Why don't you just drive the car, son. Let me do the talking and the thinking, eh. "You've just got to get used to it" – sometimes I wonder how you ever got into the CID. Let anyone in these days, I suppose. I'll tell you this for nothing – after a few weeks at the Yard you'll be wishing you were back at Peckham. Where do you live – Purley, isn't it? How you gonna get in from there every day?'

'Train,' Zukov answered precisely, too suspicious of Donnelly's reason for asking to say more.

'Oh well, let me know how that works out for you – hanging around on a freezing platform before being squeezed into a carriage with standing-room only, rubbing shoulders with the great unwashed every morning and evening. And how you gonna get home when we don't finish until three in the morning? There's no local uniform units to bum a lift from at the Yard.'

'I'll take a job car.'

'Oh aye. You and everyone else. Only one problem – we have a lot more people than we have cars. Better get used to sleeping on the floor, son.'

'I'll figure something out,' Zukov replied, promising himself he wouldn't speak again.

'You will, will you?' Donnelly condescended. 'Well, I'll look forward to seeing that. And while we're about it, remember to watch your back at all times. You make the same sort of mistake you made on the Gibran case and I won't be able to cover your arse, not at the Yard. Everything's changed for us now: senior management have got us right where they want us – under their noses. And I'm pretty sure why.'

The ensuing silence and air of mystery was too much for Zukov. 'Why?' he asked. 'Why do they want us right under their noses?'

'That, son, is for me to know and for you not to find out,' Donnelly told him. 'Now get us out of this traffic and to the Yard. I'm bursting for a piss.'

Sean and Sally pulled up outside 7 Courthope Road on the edges of Hampstead Heath and headed for the smart four-storey Georgian house that four-year-old George Bridgeman had apparently gone missing from, although Sean would assume nothing until he proved it was so. The house reminded him of other houses he'd visited, other investigations. Other victims whose faces flashed through his mind like images from a rapid-fire projector. He forced the distraction away, needing to concentrate on the job in front of him, his mind already clouded with thoughts of moving the office and all the admin and logistical headaches that would bring, as well as recurring day-and-night dreams about Thomas Keller and the women he'd killed. If he was to think the way he needed to think he had to clear his mind.

He paused at the foot of the steps just as Sally was about to ring the doorbell, making her hesitate while he looked up and down the street. He watched the last of the leaves falling from the trees and floating to the ground, some briefly resting on the two lines of cars parked on either side of the road before the bitter breeze blew them away, all the time waiting to see something in his mind's eye. But nothing came – no hint of what had happened, no feeling about what sort of person might have taken the boy, if anyone even had. He cursed Addis for putting thoughts of paedophiles and the Network in his mind – pre-wiring his train of thought before he had a chance to look around the scene. He gazed up and down the road once more, but still he saw nothing.

'Something wrong?' Sally asked. Sean didn't answer. She repeated the question a little louder.

'What? No,' he replied. 'I was just thinking it must have been freezing outside last night.'

'So?'

'Nothing,' he answered, moving next to her, stretching then crouching as he examined the four locks on the front door, all of which appeared high quality and well fitted. 'The report said all four locks were still on when the nanny arrived in the morning and that the mother checked all the windows on the house and the back door – again, all locked and secure. So how the hell did someone get in, grab the boy and get out, leaving the place all locked up, without being heard or seen?'

'He didn't,' Sally explained. 'That's not possible. The boy

must be hiding in the house somewhere, too afraid to come out now his joke's gone too far. We'll have a good look around, find him, talk his parents into not killing him and then get back to our unpacking.'

'But he's only four,' Sean argued.

'So?'

'When my kids were four they wouldn't have stayed hidden this long. They might now, but not back then. It's too long.'

'So you do think someone has taken him?'

Sean stepped back from the door, looking the house up and down before once again peering in both directions along the affluent, leafy road. 'I don't know,' he eventually confessed, 'but I've got a bad feeling about this.'

'Don't tell me that,' Sally almost begged him, rolling her eyes back into her skull. 'Every time you say that we end up in it up to our necks. We haven't even got the office up and running – the last thing we need now is a child abduction – *or worse*. A few days from now we'll be ready and willing, but not yet.'

'Too late,' Sean told her. 'For better or worse, this one's ours.' He flicked his eyes towards the doorbell.

With a shake of her head, Sally pressed the button, stepping back to be at Sean's side – a united front for when the door was opened, warrant cards open in their hands.

They heard the rattle of the central lock before the door was opened by a plain woman in her mid-thirties, brown hair tied back in a ponytail like Sally's, her inexpensive grey suit and white blouse the virtual uniform for female detectives. Neither Sean nor Sally had to ask whether she was the mother or the local CID's representative and she in turn knew what they were and why they were there, but they showed her their warrant cards and introduced themselves anyway.

'Morning. DI Sean Corrigan and this is DS Sally Jones – Special Investigations Unit,' Sean told her, drawing a sideways glance from Sally, who was hearing their new name for the first time.

'Special Investigations Unit?' the detective asked. 'That's a new one on me.'

'Me too,' Sally added, making the other detective narrow her eyes.

'We're based at the Yard,' Sean explained. 'It's a new thing that's being trialled – rapid response to potentially high-profile crimes – that sort of thing.'

The detective nodded suspiciously before responding. 'DC Kimberly Robinson, Hampstead CID.'

'Can we see the parents?' Sean asked.

'Of course,' Robinson answered, but instead of opening the door for them to enter she stepped outside and shut the door to behind her, leaving it slightly ajar. 'But before you do there's one thing bothering me,' she told them in a near whisper. 'Why has this case been handed over to you? Why has this case been handed over to anyone? Something like this would usually stay with the local CID until we get a ransom demand or . . .' she checked the door behind her before continuing '. . . until a body turns up. So why are you here so soon?'

'You know how it is,' Sean explained. 'Your boss gets to hear about something a little different and he tells his boss who tells his boss who tells my boss, whose interest is piqued and before you know it the case lands on my desk and here we are.'

Robinson studied him for a while before answering. 'Fine,' she eventually said, easing the door open and stepping inside. 'You're welcome to it. Parents are in the kitchen.'

'D'you have any background on the parents yet?' Sean asked quietly.

'He's thirty-eight, works in the City – a broker for Britbank, apparently,' she said in a lowered voice, before lowering it even further. 'She's a few years younger, a full-time mum, although round here that isn't exactly what it sounds like, if you know what I mean.'

Sally and Sean glanced at each other before following Robinson through the hallway, Sally closing the door behind them. She quickly and discreetly swept slightly envious eyes over the hall's contents: large, original oil paintings, Tiffany lampshades and polished oak floorboards. Sean also noticed a control panel for an intruder alarm attached to the wall.

As soon as they entered the large contemporary kitchen Sean was making mental notes of what he saw: Mrs Bridgeman pacing around the work area, her husband leaning on the kitchen island watching her but not speaking, while the nanny sat with their young daughter, trying to keep the crying child distracted with small talk and a drink.

'Mr and Mrs Bridgeman,' Robinson said, 'these officers are from the Special Investigations Unit, Scotland Yard. I believe they'll be taking over the investigation now.'

'Why?' Celia Bridgeman asked before Sean or Sally could speak, panic lighting her eyes. 'Has something happened? Have you found him?'

Sally could tell she was about to lose it completely. 'No, Mrs Bridgeman. Nothing's changed. We're just here to try and help find George as quickly as we can. Everything's going to be fine, but we'll have to ask you both some questions if we're going to do that.'

'More questions?' Stuart Bridgeman interrupted. 'We've already answered all the questions. Now you need to get out there and find our son.'

'Almost every officer in the borough is out there searching for George,' Robinson tried to reassure him, 'including dogs. Even the police helicopter's up and looking.'

Sean eyed Bridgeman for a while before considering his response. He felt an instant dislike for the man – his carefully groomed hair, golden tan and athletic build, and above all his arrogance, which more than matched his wealth. 'I can understand your frustration.' He managed to sound businesslike. 'But we really do need to ask you some more questions.

'Of course,' Celia took over, 'anything.' She wiped the tears away from her eyes with the back of her hand.

'I believe you were the one who discovered George was apparently missing, Mrs Bridgeman?' Sean asked.

'Not apparently,' Stuart Bridgeman interrupted again, '*is* missing. Who did you say you were?'

'I'm Detective Inspector Corrigan and this is Detective Sergeant Jones from the Special Investigations Unit.'

'Special Investigations?' Bridgeman asked, distaste etched into his face. 'What the hell does that mean?'

'Stuart,' his wife stopped him. 'You're wasting time.'

Bridgeman grudgingly backed down. 'Ask your questions, Inspector.'

'When you couldn't find George, what did you do?'

'I looked everywhere,' she told him, shaking as she spoke, involuntarily closing her eyes as she remembered the panic and fear, the feeling of sickness overtaking her body, 'but I couldn't find him.'

'Then what?'

'I checked the windows and doors.'

'And?'

'They were all closed and locked – all of them.'

'Even the front door?'

'Yes, and the front door.'

'All four locks?'

'No. Just the top lock.'

'How come?'

33

'Because Caroline had already arrived for work before I discovered George was missing.'

'Caroline being yourself,' he said looking over at the nodding nanny.

'I always put the top lock on,' she told him, 'so that the kids can't get out through the front door. It's the only lock they can't reach.'

'And that's how you found it?' he asked, turning back to look at Celia Bridgeman.

'Yes,' she replied.

Sean considered the nanny for a moment. Had she forgotten to put the top lock on when she'd arrived, fastening it later once she'd realized her mistake? Was it already too late by then – George had slipped out into the street and wandered off, or been taken away? The nanny looked relaxed and calm enough under the circumstances – he sensed no guilt or fear in her, even if it was the most logical explanation. But he was picking up on something else – a presentiment of foul play that made him consider the entire family for a second. It was impossible to look at them and not be struck by their wealth and privilege and even more so by their beauty. All of them beautiful, including both children. Had that been the flame that had drawn the moth to them?

Stuart Bridgeman's voice cut through his thoughts.

'This is all we need – a wannabe Sherlock bloody Holmes on the case. These stupid questions are a waste of time. You need to stop hiding in the warm and get out on those streets and find our son.'

Ignoring Bridgeman's rant, Sean directed the next question at him. 'You weren't here last night, Mr Bridgeman, is that right?'

'I was away on business. You know – earning money for my family. I work in the private sector. I have to earn my money, unlike some.'

Again Sean let it pass. 'So, where were you last night?'

'Why? Am I a suspect in my own son's disappearance?'

'No. I just need to know where you were.'

'Fine. I was in Oxford.'

'You got back quickly,' Sean prodded.

'I came straight back as soon as I heard. Wouldn't you – if your child had gone missing?'

'What time did you hear?'

'I don't remember . . . some time before nine.'

'And when did you get back here?'

'A little while ago – why?'

'It was ten thirty,' Robinson told Sean. 'It's in the crime-scene log.'

'That was fast,' Sean accused him, 'through rush-hour traffic.'

'So I broke a few speed limits – what the fuck do I care?'

'Stuart, please,' Celia appealed to him. 'You're not helping.'

'Here we go,' Stuart Bridgeman said, shaking his head. 'I wondered how long it would be before this all became my fault.'

Sean didn't have time to referee a domestic. 'Where did you stay? In Oxford – where did you stay?'

Bridgeman took several calming breaths before answering. 'The Old Parsonage Hotel – just outside the city centre. They'll be able to confirm I was there last night.'

Sean studied him, in no hurry to fill the uncomfortable silence. Bridgeman could have comfortably booked into his hotel but then come back in the night and taken the boy before returning to Oxford to await his wife's distressed phone call. But why would he want to abduct his own son? He decided not to push that line of questioning – not yet.

'I'm sure we won't be needing to check with the hotel, Mr Bridgeman,' he lied. 'But one thing's bothering me.'

'And what would that be?' Bridgeman asked, not attempting to disguise his frustration.

'I saw an alarm panel as I came through the hallway. I assume it's for an intruder alarm.'

'So?' Bridgeman asked.

'So, if someone did manage to break into the house, why didn't the alarm go off? Wasn't it set last night?'

'No,' Bridgeman told him, 'nor any other night since we've been here.'

'Why not?'

'Because it's the old alarm left here by the previous owners. They cancelled their subscription to the alarm company when we bought the house and I haven't got round to having it reactivated yet.'

'So the house wasn't alarmed?' Sean clarified.

'No,' Bridgeman admitted. 'But there's an alarm box on the front of the house. You would think that would deter most people from trying to break in.'

'So you haven't been here long then?' Sally asked.

'No,' Celia Bridgeman answered, never taking her accusing eyes off her husband. 'A little less than three weeks.'

'Where did you move from?' Sally continued.

'Primrose Hill.'

'Any reason for the move?' Sean asked.

'Camden seemed to be getting closer and closer,' Bridgeman explained, 'and Primrose Hill's full of very dull Russian bankers.'

'Did you change the locks when you moved in?' Sean questioned.

'No,' Bridgeman replied. 'Who changes the locks when they move into a new house? This is Hampstead, not Peckham.' Sean and Sally looked at each other, Sally failing to stop a small grin forming on her lips. 'The people we bought it off were decent people. In fact, the husband works not far from me in the City. They're hardly likely to come back and burgle us, are they?'

'But there are keys out there you can't account for?' Sean asked. 'In all likelihood there'll be keys for this house in the hands of others?'

'I suppose so,' Bridgeman agreed.

'Then we'll need a list of anyone who might have keys to the house: the estate agent you used, the previous owners, the removal company you hired – anyone who has access to the house.'

'Fine,' Bridgeman reluctantly agreed, 'but that'll take time. What are you going to do to find our son *now*?'

Sean nodded his head slightly, looking around at the faces watching him expectantly. 'I need to see the boy's bedroom. I need to see it alone.'

'It's upstairs,' Celia Bridgeman told him without hesitation, her pale lips trembling. 'On the second floor. Along the hallway on the right.'

'Thank you,' Sean replied and headed for the exit. 'I'll be back in a few minutes,' he told them, although he was mainly talking to Sally. The relief of being on his own, away from the parents' torment, guilt and anger felt immediately liberating as he headed for the stairs, stopping for a while to look around him, his eyes drifting towards the front door the nanny had sworn she'd locked. He believed her, but the front door somehow wouldn't let him look away, as if it held answers to the questions firing inside his head. But the answers wouldn't come. His mind was awhirl with distractions: the office move, Assistant Commissioner Addis, Thomas Keller still awaiting sentencing . . . The mental clutter was robbing him of the very thing that set him apart.

Work through the evidence, he told himself, looking at the windows he could see and noting they were all in good condition with security locks fitted and in place. *The door*, he told himself. *Someone came in through that door, in through it in the middle of the night and took the boy away. But how, who and why?* Still nothing particular stirred in his subconscious, no early ideas of who or what he could be about to hunt. He felt a rising panic at the thought of no longer being able to see or feel what the people he had to find and stop had seen or felt.

There was an alarm, but it wasn't working – did you know that? A man lives in the house, but he was away – did you know that? Have you been watching the family – and if so, for how long? He waited for answers or ideas, some coldness in the pit of his stomach that would tell him the darkness within him was beginning to stir – the malevolence that could lead him straight to the front door of whoever took the little boy. *You don't even know for sure he's been taken yet,* he reminded himself as he began to climb the stairs, careful not to touch the mahogany bannister that clearly hadn't been polished for a day or so. *Did you touch this bannister? In your excitement to reach the boy, did you forget yourself and touch the bannister? Did you leave me your finger-prints here, hiding amongst the prints of the family, the nanny, the cleaner? What did it feel like to be inside this warm house with its comforting sounds and smells – so different from the cold, empty street outside?*

'Shit,' he whispered as still nothing happened – no flash of inspiration or horror of realization, just blackness. 'If you're hiding somewhere, George,' he said, a little louder than a whisper, 'now would be a really good time to show yourself.'

As he stepped on to the first floor landing his eyes again swept over his surroundings: more oil paintings and Tiffany lamps, good quality carpet under his feet deadening the sound of his footsteps, stretching out in front of him and seemingly spreading into three of the four rooms he could see, the fourth of which he assumed would be a bathroom, the carpet giving way to floor tiles. He began to walk along the landing towards the staircase that continued its way upwards at the other end, but the scent of the mother leaking from the first room he passed made him stop and look around, checking he was still alone. *Did the carpet feel good under your feet – silencing your footsteps? Did it reassure you?* He moved to the bedroom where he knew the mother slept and moved slowly inside, breathing her in as he studied the room – her clothes tossed on the chaise longue for someone else to tidy and the bed only slept in on one side. Stuart Bridgeman had been away the previous night, but Sean felt only a fading presence of the father in the room, as if he'd stopped sleeping here days or weeks ago. Maybe he never had, just using it to store his clothes for appearances' sake – to keep the sad truth from the children? *Did you come in here? Did you stand where I am now and watch her while she slept – watching her chest rise and fall – hypnotized by her beauty? But you didn't come for her, did you?* Again the answers evaded him. He scratched his forehead and left the room, passing what was indeed a bathroom, a room used as an office and another made up as a spare bedroom, but almost overly tidy and sterile. Was this where Stuart Bridgeman spent his nights – making the bed immaculately every morning before the children, nanny or cleaner could discover it had been used – quickly moving his used clothes into the master bedroom to complete the illusion? Probably, Sean decided, but what did it mean? What, if anything, did it have to do with George's disappearance?

He left the room behind and climbed to the second floor and the children's bedrooms, his foot finding a loose floorboard and making it creak loudly. *Did you step on the creaking stair? Did it make you freeze with panic or fear? Or did you know it was there and avoid it? But how could you know it was there?* He could feel the ideas, even possible answers straining to break free, but the weeds of his everyday responsibilities and life kept strangling his newly flowering strands of thought. Finally he lifted his foot, the returning floorboard making the same loud creaking that would have been magnified ten-fold in the dead of the night. *No one came in here in the middle of the night and stole the boy*, he almost chastised himself as he strode up the final few stairs and along the hallway. *I'm letting things from the past fuck with my head. There's no mystery here – just a little boy whose joke's gone too far. The doors and windows are locked. No one came in here and the boy couldn't have left, so he's here – somewhere inside this house.* He reached George's room and unceremoniously pushed the door wide open, the sense of excitement that they would soon find the boy hiding instantly replaced by a deep sense of coldness. He felt as if he was stepping into a murder scene where the shattered soul of the victim still lingered, only there was no body, just an awful feeling of emptiness, as if the boy had never been there in the first place and the room was little more than a mock-up of a child's room: the silhouettes of clouds printed on the powder-blue wallpaper, the train mobile above the bed with its matching bedclothes. The duvet remained on the floor where the mother had thrown it, along with a dozen or so teddy bears and other soft toys. More toys were neatly stacked on the shelving units and play table. But none of it seemed real any more – it felt surreal, just like so many other crime scenes he'd seen. And although the answers to his questions failed to come, the sickness in his stomach told him something had happened to the little boy. But what?

He crouched down and picked up a small brown bear similar to one his youngest daughter Mandy kept in her bed and tried not to think of how he'd feel if anything ever happened to either of his daughters. Sadness and rage swelled inside him at the mere possibility, but a sudden feeling of another presence in the room made him spin around and forget his fearful imaginings. Celia Bridgeman stood in the doorway, both hands clasped over her heart, her eyes red and her skin pale as her lips opened and closed as if she was trying to speak but couldn't. 'You all right?' Sean asked and regretted it.

'No,' she answered faintly. 'I don't feel very well.' She staggered a little into the room, Sean catching her by the elbow and forearm as he led her to the bed to sit, cringing at the possible forensic evidence he may be complicit in destroying. He watched her trying to catch her breath, breathing in and out a little erratically, but it was enough to put a little colour back into her lips and face. He gave her some time and space. 'It's like a dream,' she told him, 'or I should say a nightmare – like it's not really happening. It can't be happening, can it? He must be here somewhere,' she continued, panic sweeping over her again as she tried to get to her feet.

Sean placed a hand on her shoulder, preventing her from standing. 'I need to look for him,' she pleaded, her red eyes swelling with fear and tears. 'I have to keep looking.'

'We'll all look for him,' Sean promised, 'but you need to help me help you.'

'I feel sick,' she told him, jumping to her feet and rushing from the room. A few seconds later he heard the sound of her retching in a nearby bathroom, retching that seemed to go on for a long time, before he heard the sound of a toilet lid closing and the flushing of water. She returned to the bedroom looking like a ghost, walking past him and sitting on the bed without speaking, lifting a floppy-eared rabbit from the floor and holding it tight to her chest while she stared at the wall opposite.

'Feel a little better?' Sean asked, keen to get her talking before she went catatonic on him.

'Not really,' she responded.

'I have some difficult questions that need answers,' he warned her. 'They're best asked when your husband's not here.'

'Stuart?' she asked in a conciliatory tone. 'Don't worry about Stuart – he's just scared and angry. He always reacts like that when he feels something is beyond his control.'

'I understand,' Sean assured her.

'You said you had questions.'

'Keys,' he began. 'Is there anyone no one's mentioned who could have keys to the house?'

'Not that I know of,' she answered.

'Anyone who shouldn't have keys to the house but does?'

'I don't understand.'

'I need to know if both your children are yours *and* your husband's – genetically?'

'Yes,' she answered, confusion etched into her face. 'Why?'

'Most children who are abducted are abducted by their estranged fathers,' he told her. 'If there was one and he had keys to the house, then . . .'

'There isn't,' she stopped him. 'How could you even think that? I'm his mother and Stuart's his father,' she insisted, but Sean sensed some doubt in her voice – and her eyes.

'Any problems with your marriage?' he asked.

'No,' she muttered, her eyes avoiding his.

'Could Stuart be seeing anyone else?'

'God no.'

'And you?' Sean ambushed her.

'No,' she swore, 'nothing like that. I wouldn't do that. I wouldn't do that to my children.'

'My children?' Sean questioned. 'Not our children, but my children?'

'Stuart's not around much,' she explained. 'He works hard for us – that's all I meant.'

Sean watched her silently for a moment as she continued to hug the toy rabbit – watching her eyes and hands, her feet that stayed flat and still on the carpeted floor – judging her. He believed most of what she was saying, but there were doubts and untruths hiding in her grief.

The longer he stood in the boy's room, the more sure he was that George had been taken. But why and by whom? His mind searched back for memories – going back more than ten years to when he was still a detective sergeant, deployed by SO10 on an undercover operation to infiltrate the Network, a paedophile gang who'd been grooming children during the early days of the Internet and then sexually abusing them, filming their exploits and circulating them to other paedophiles. He forced the face of the gang's leader, John Conway, into his mind, remembering the way he talked and moved, recalling his mindset – what excited him and motivated him. But Conway and his cronies groomed older children and always met the children a safe distance from their houses and schools, whereas whoever had taken George had risked coming into the house in the dead of night. And George was only four, too young to be groomed from a distance. *From a distance, but what about by someone close?* Conway's face melted into that of Sean's own father. But there had never been anything subtle about the abuse he'd suffered at the hands of his father. The face faded away, replaced by the things that continued to plague his mind: *There's an alarm, but you knew it wasn't working. A man lives in the house, but you knew he wasn't there. The floorboard creaks, but you didn't step on it. You knew all this because you know this house. You have to know this house – but how? Who are you and what do you want?* John Conway's face flashed back into his mind. *Slow down*, he warned himself. *You're making assumptions. You don't know he knew about the alarm, the husband being away, the damn floorboard. All you know for sure is that the boy is gone. Someone came to the house, entered without breaking in, took the boy and left, locking the house after them. Was Addis right? Could it have been a paedophile, acting alone or with others, going to the next level that the Network never reached – taking children from their own homes, the danger of the game making the moment of triumph all the sweeter.*

'You will find him, won't you?' Celia Bridgeman asked, making his attempt to build a mental picture of what could have happened tumble like a house of cards. He gave his mind a few seconds to recall and understand what she had asked before answering.

'Of course,' he answered, telling her the only thing he could. 'Cases like this can come together pretty quickly,' he added truthfully, although he already had his doubts this one would. 'You should all move out, just while we have the house searched by a dog team. And our forensic people always appreciate an empty scene. We need to do everything possible to give us the best chance of finding your son quickly.'

'Where should we go?' she asked, her voice forlorn and sad, as if moving out was giving up on the boy.

'Family, friends,' Sean suggested. 'Just for a couple of days while we do what we need to do with the house. In the meantime, try not to touch anything. We'll need a set of fingerprints from everyone who's been in the house since you moved in. Are you OK with that?'

'Yes,' she answered, 'if it'll help.'

'Good,' Sean told her, taking a last look around the room. 'I have to go now. Do you need some help getting downstairs?'

'No,' she replied. 'I'd like to stay here for a while – if that's all right?'

'Of course.' Sean slowly headed to the door, almost unable to take his eyes off the mother, her sadness and longing dragging at him like a magnet as he managed to pull himself from the room and into the hallway where he rested with his back to the wall for a few seconds before walking quietly to the staircase.

'All right?' Sally asked as he joined the others in the kitchen. Sean nodded.

'Mr Bridgeman,' he turned to the father, 'I was just telling your wife you'll need to move out for a couple of days' – Bridgeman tried to interrupt, but Sean talked over him – 'and I'll need those names: the estate agent, the removal firm, anyone who's been in the house since you've been here.' He took something from his warrant-card wallet and dropped it on the kitchen island. 'That's my card – ignore the landline number, it's old, but the mobile and email address are good. Call me if you think of anything.' He quickly turned to Robinson. 'I need you to wait here until my own Family Liaison Officer gets here. They won't be long.' Robinson just shrugged. He understood her keenness to escape. 'I have to go back and brief my team, Mr Bridgeman. You may not see me for a while, but rest assured I'll be working full-time to find your son.'

Sean headed for the door with Sally trailing in his wake, the crystal-clear air hitting him like a plunge into freezing water as soon as he opened the door, temporarily taking his breath away. He skipped down the stairs and headed for their car, then sat on the bonnet, breathing in as deeply as he could before blowing out great plumes of breath, trying to settle his spinning mind. But still he was left with only questions – questions to which he had no answers, just too many broken, ragged theories.

'Family Liaison Officer?' Sally asked. 'Why are we wasting our time doing all that? Let's stick a dog unit in there and find this kid.'

'He's not there,' Sean answered. 'If he was, the mother would have found him – I would have.'

'So he's got a secret hiding place nobody knows about. He can't hide from a dog.'

'I'm telling you, he's gone,' Sean insisted, the unintentional aggression in his voice silencing Sally.

She was silent for a moment, considering her next move.

'Listen,' she opened, 'maybe the Keller case is messing with your head a bit? Believe me, when it comes to having your head messed with, I'm an expert.'

'Meaning?' Sean asked, prepared to consider anything.

'Keller took his victims from their homes before he killed them,' she explained. 'Maybe that's stuck in your head, making you see similarities here that don't actually exist.'

'The boy's gone,' Sean insisted, his voice sad and resigned. 'But get a dog to check it over anyway. It might find *something*.'

Sally studied him for a moment, searching for things in him that not so long ago she'd seen in herself. 'OK,' she relented, 'so the boy's gone. Someone came in the middle of the night, somehow got in, took the boy and left, all without being seen, heard or leaving any signs of entry.'

'Either they had a key,' Sean told her, 'or they picked the locks.'

'Christ, Sean,' she reminded him. 'Lock-picking's bloody rare.'

'Good, then that helps us. But why lock the door after they'd left? Why would they do that?'

'Because they're insane.'

'Or because they cared about the people they left in the house – didn't want to leave them at risk. Exposed.'

'You mean the father?' Sally asked.

'Possibly.'

'Why would the father want to abduct his own son?'

'Why do some fathers slaughter their entire family at the first sign their wives might leave them?'

'I don't know,' Sally admitted. 'You tell me, Sean. Why do some men do that?'

'Better to destroy something you love rather than lose it.'

'That doesn't make any sense.'

'No. No it doesn't,' he agreed. 'Much like this case.'

'So what you want to do?'

'Keep an open mind.'

'Easier for some than others,' she mumbled.

'What was that?'

'Nothing,' she lied. 'How's your shoulder, by the way?'

'Sore. And you?'

'Better and better,' she told him.

'Is there something you want to ask me, Sally?'

'No,' she lied again. This was not the right moment.

'Then we're wasting time,' he told her. 'Time we don't have.'

Detective Chief Superintendent Featherstone sat in his office at Shooter's Hill Police Station looking at pictures of sailing yachts in the magazine he subscribed to and kept hidden inside a pink cardboard file marked *Confidential*. Owning a nice thirty-two-footer had long been his retirement dream, but constant pay-cuts, pay-freezes, allowance-scrapping and now attacks on the police pension were turning his dream into a fantasy. If he could make it to the rank of commander before he retired, the dream might still be alive – just. His mind drifted to Sean and the sort of results he seemed able to pull out of a hat. At the end of the day, he was Sean's supervising officer and therefore in a position to bask warmly in the reflected glory of Sean's successes – successes that might just get him over the line and promoted to commander before deadline-day struck. But only if things kept working out and Corrigan didn't fuck up. He liked the man and watched his back better and with more fervour than most senior officers ever would, but he wasn't about to put his head on the chopping block for anyone.

His daydreaming was interrupted by the shrill ring of the phone on his desk. He answered it slowly and without enthusiasm. 'Hello, Detective Superintendent Featherstone speaking.'

'Alan. Assistant Commissioner Addis here.'

Featherstone felt his heart drop and his bowels loosen slightly. 'Sir.'

'I've assigned that case we discussed to Inspector Corrigan,' Addis told him.

'That was fast,' Featherstone replied.

'I thought the sooner he got on with it the better. The quicker we act the more chance we have of finding the missing boy.'

'If there's been foul play, Corrigan's the best man to lead the investigation. He won't let anyone down.'

'I hope not,' Addis told him, making it sound like a threat. 'Let's hope your confidence in him isn't misplaced.'

'Like I told you in the beginning, sir, Corrigan has special qualities. In the field, he's one of the best I've ever seen – and I've seen some good ones.'

'Good,' Addis replied. 'Then once it's confirmed the boy is actually missing I suggest we get the media in and tell them how confident we are of bringing the investigation to a swift conclusion. Some good publicity for the Metropolitan Police would be very useful right now.'

'Publicity?' Featherstone asked, his voice riddled with concern. 'Don't you think it's too soon for publicity? Maybe we should give Corrigan and his team a little breathing space for—'

'Breathing space?' Addis asked mockingly. 'That's a luxury we don't have in the Metropolitan Police. Not any more. This is a results-orientated business, and Corrigan has been brought here to deliver those results. He has until tomorrow, then I'm briefing the press.'

Featherstone heard the line go dead, leaving the echo of Addis's words sinking into his consciousness. *A results-orientated business*. Is that what they were now – a business? He looked down at his magazine, open at a page showing a sleek thirty-two-footer, and his dreams of retirement and yachts faded as abruptly as his conversation with Addis had concluded.

'For God's sake, Sean,' he muttered under his breath, 'don't fuck this one up or Addis will have both our heads mounted on his office wall – and it's not like we'll be the first either.' Shaking the unpleasant thought from his head, he went back to reading his magazine.

Sally and Sean arrived back at Room 714 to the chaotic scene of a dozen or more detectives unpacking cardboard boxes containing everything from personal belongings to keyboards and phones they'd commandeered from their old office back at Peckham. The chaos they created was matched by the noise levels as they universally moaned and groaned about being moved, the size of their new office and the lack of power-points. At the centre of the discontent was Donnelly, conducting the orchestra of rebellion, his voice easily heard above the din as he searched for the strategically best placed desk. He wasted no time speaking his mind as soon as he saw Sally and Sean enter. 'This place is worse than Peckham,' he called to them. 'You couldn't swing a cat in here, and have you seen the size of the queue in the canteen? All I wanted was a cup of tea.'

'Not out here,' Sean told him, his eyes resting on the box Donnelly was holding. 'You share the larger side office with Sally. The smaller one is mine.'

'Excuse me?' he asked. 'I need to be out here, keeping

an eye on this lot. You may be the circus ringmaster, guv'nor, but I'm the lion tamer round here.'

'You said it yourself,' Sean reminded him. 'There's not enough room out here for everyone – so you get to share with Sally.' Donnelly was about to continue the argument when Sean silenced him and everyone else in the shambolic room. 'Listen up,' he shouted. His voice seem to freeze everyone where they stood, the sound of the guv'nor shouting rare enough to draw their immediate attention. 'I know this isn't ideal and we'd all like a few days to get sorted and settled, but that's not going to be the case, I'm afraid.'

'Meaning what?' Donnelly asked.

'Meaning we've just been given a new case.'

'You must be joking!' Donnelly said above the rising murmurs of disbelief. 'We can't take on a new case – we're in it up to our necks with this bloody move. There's not even a single computer up and running. We can't deal with a new murder investigation yet.'

'It's not a murder,' Sean told them, 'it's a missing person.'

'Not again,' Donnelly complained.

'It didn't take long for our last missing person case to turn into a murder investigation, remember? We have a four-year-old boy disappeared overnight from his home in Hampstead. His mother discovered he was missing earlier this morning. No signs of forced entry, but he's definitely gone.'

'Has the house been checked by a Special Search Team yet?' Donnelly asked.

'No,' Sean admitted.

'Well then, the boy's not gone anywhere. He's got himself a secret hiding place, that's all. Special Search Team will find him soon enough.'

'I don't think so.' Sean locked eyes with him. 'However,

you're right – the house needs to be searched properly. We have to be absolutely sure.' He looked across to DC Ashley Goodwin, a tall, fit, black detective in his late twenties. 'Ashley, sort out a search team and a dog unit and get the house checked. If the boy's alive and hiding, great. If his body's been hidden in the house then I want it found.'

'No problem,' Goodwin answered, plugging in the phone he was holding and immediately starting to make calls.

'Dave,' Sean turned to Donnelly, 'take Paulo and whoever else you need and get started on the door-to-door, but keep it local and as quiet as you can – we don't want to start a parental panic across North London.' Donnelly didn't reply; resigned to his fate, he simply reached for his jacket and indicated for Paulo to do the same. 'Alan, find out which Forensic Support Team cover Hampstead for Major Inquiries and get them to examine the house.' DC Alan Jesson, tall and slim, nodded as he scribbled notes. 'Maggie, I need you to go Family Liaison on this one.'

'Not again, guv'nor,' DC Maggie O'Neil pleaded in her Birmingham accent.

'Sorry, but I need someone with experience to keep an eye on the family and report anything out of the ordinary.'

Donnelly's ears pricked up. 'Are the family suspects?'

'Too early to say yes – too early to say no,' Sean answered, 'but if it turns out they aren't involved then someone came to their house, got in and took the boy all without breaking a single door or window. And what's more, they locked up behind themselves.'

'Then they must have had keys,' Goodwin deduced.

'Possibly.' Sean frowned, picturing the front door and its four locks. 'But if they didn't, then they must have somehow come through the locked door and secured it behind them when they left.'

51

'Why not a window?' DC Fiona Cahill asked.

'Because I checked the windows,' Sean answered. 'There's no way they can be shut properly and locked from the outside, leaving only the front door as a possibility.'

'What about the back door – if there is one?' Cahill continued, undaunted.

'There is,' Sean explained, 'but it was secured with old-fashioned bolts, top and bottom. You can't do those up from outside.'

The office felt silent as the detectives pondered the puzzle.

'So what does this mean?' Donnelly finally asked. 'What are we looking for?'

'We discount nothing yet,' Sean warned them, 'but if he was taken by a stranger then it's safe to assume he could have been taken by a known sex offender or someone who's gravitating towards it.'

'Then why not just snatch a child off the street?' O'Neil asked.

'I don't know,' Sean admitted. 'Perhaps because they thought it was too dangerous.'

'More dangerous than breaking into someone's house in the middle of the night?' Zukov queried, disbelief evident in his voice.

'We're just exploring possibilities here,' Sean reminded them, 'but if someone did go through the front door then it's possible they picked the locks.'

'Picked the locks?' Donnelly asked disbelievingly. 'Criminals smart enough to pick locks are about as rare as hen's teeth.'

'And that's exactly what I'm banking on,' Sean told him. 'That's our advantage. Sally, have the surrounding stations search their intelligence records for anyone with previous for using lock-picking to commit residential burglaries. If by some miracle you get more than a few, look for those who also have previous for sexual assault – ideally on children, but any type of sexual assault makes them a suspect. If you get no joy then check the local Sex Offenders Registers and see if anything takes your fancy.'

'No problem,' Sally assured him.

'OK, good,' Sean told his assembled team. 'Now you all know what you need to be getting on with, so let's get this show on the road. Dave—'

'Aye, guv'nor?'

'Get HOLMES up and running ASAP – make it a priority. We're gonna have a lot of names and information coming our way soon. Without the database we can't cross-reference a damn thing, and that's when we'll miss things – important things.'

'It will be done,' Donnelly promised.

'As soon as anyone has anything, let me know – I'll be in my office for the next few hours making the usual endless phone calls and God knows what else, so dust off the cobwebs, people, and let's get on with it. Remember, a four-year-old boy is apparently missing and if we don't find him – no one will.'

3

George Bridgeman sat on the bed in the room where he'd woken up cuddling his teddy – a floppy grey and pink elephant he called Ellie that had been his constant companion since the day he was born. He looked around the strange room the man had brought him to in the middle of the night, his wonderment at the myriad of toys that surrounded him only matched by his fear at being seemingly alone in an unfamiliar house. On the opposite side of the room he could see another child's bed, but the covers remained unruffled and pristine, the stuffed toys untouched.

George dropped his bare feet carefully over the side of the bed, fearful of what might be hiding underneath, and padded towards the empty bed, still clad in the pyjamas his mother had dressed him in only the night before. As he drew closer to the tempting toys, he was distracted by sounds coming from somewhere deeper in the house – voices, a man and a woman talking – deep, muffled voices he couldn't understand. Instinctively he looked for a window, but the only source of natural light came from the two skylights high in the ceiling, impossible to reach even if he wanted to, and escape wasn't yet on his mind. Why would he want to escape from the things the man had promised?

He moved towards the door to better hear the sounds coming from the other side: gentle music leaking through the wooden panels, mixing with the unfamiliar voices, making him swallow hard as his tiny hand reached for the door handle and began to turn it, first one way and then the other. But the door wouldn't open – he was locked in. He pressed his ear to the door and listened harder, trying to focus on the voices. The sudden scream of a distant child made him recoil from the door, his eyes wide and pupils dilated with sudden, unexpected terror. The woman's voice was raised now as the man's faded to nothing, then silence for a few seconds before they started talking again, quieter than before, barely audible. The sound of what he believed was a door closing heavily made him run back to the bed and jump under the covers, waiting – waiting for the voices to start coming upstairs towards him, ready – ready to scream like he'd heard the other child scream, his frail little body beginning to shake. He pulled Ellie close to his chest and cuddled her tightly – tighter than he'd ever held anything in his short life.

Sean sat in his office alone, his ear warm and sore from having the phone pressed to it too long and too hard, his eyes aching from staring at his newly connected computer screen. One minute he'd be thinking about the missing boy, his house and family, and the next he'd be on the phone to the stores trying to beg, steal or borrow the basics for the office and his team: paper, pens, more chairs and the forms of all kinds they needed for daily policework and to run an investigation. A loud double knock at his open door made him jump and look up as a smiling Featherstone entered without being asked and sat heavily in the one spare chair in the office. 'How's it going?' he asked.

'What?' Sean replied. 'The investigation or the move?'

'The investigation,' Featherstone clarified. 'You found the missing kid yet?'

'No,' Sean told him.

'Shame,' Featherstone continued. 'Would have made life a lot easier if you had.'

'Why are you here, sir? You're a long way from Shooter's Hill.'

'ACC wants an update,' he admitted. 'Wants to know how you're getting on.'

'We've only just started looking.'

'I appreciate that, Sean, but you know what assistant commissioners can be like – updates, updates, updates.'

'Then why didn't he just come down here and ask me himself?'

'Mr Addis likes a chain of command, when it suits him. A buffer-zone, if you know what I mean. It would appear I am that buffer-zone – so try not to drop me in it.'

'I'll do my best,' Sean assured him without conviction just as Sally hurried from her office and into Sean's, her body language making him sit bolt upright in anticipation. 'What you got?'

'Mark McKenzie,' Sally began without ceremony, 'male, IC1, twenty-three years old, last known address in Kentish Town where he's also a fully paid-up member of their Sex Offenders Register. He has previous for residential burglary, some of which he committed at night while the occupants were inside sleeping. And if that wasn't enough, he also has previous for sexual assault on minors.'

Sean felt his heart rate suddenly increasing as a picture of McKenzie began to form in his mind – climbing the stairs to little George's bedroom, moving silently past the room where his mother peacefully slept. 'And . . .?' he hurried Sally.

'And,' she continued, 'he's previously used lock-picking as a method of entry.'

'Jesus,' Sean said. 'How far's Kentish Town from Hampstead?'

'Not my neck of the woods,' Sally answered, 'but I think it's close.'

'It is,' Featherstone joined in. 'No more than a couple of miles.'

'Bloody hell,' Sean said. 'Does he come gift-wrapped as well?'

'Think he's your man?' Featherstone asked.

'He couldn't fit the profile more if he tried,' Sean answered.

'*If* the boy has been taken,' Sally warned them. 'Taken by a stranger.'

'You're right,' Sean admitted. 'You're right. We should keep an open mind, but he looks good – he looks really good. Has he been keeping his appointments to sign the Sex Offender Register?'

'As far as I know,' Sally answered.

'That doesn't mean he's not your man,' Featherstone cautioned.

'No,' Sean agreed, 'it does not. No amount of reporting to police stations could stop him entering a house in the middle of the night.'

'Then I can tell the Assistant Commissioner you're close to getting your man?'

Sean had seen Featherstone acting impulsively and impatiently before, but never to this degree. Clearly something or someone had given him an added sense of urgency. 'I wouldn't tell the Assistant Commissioner anything just yet,' he warned Featherstone. 'If he asks, just give him the generic bullshit and tell him we're following a few lines of inquiry.'

'But this McKenzie character looks good and Addis has

been explicit about wanting a quick result. He doesn't strike me as being a good man to fuck with.'

'I'll do the best I can, but you need to keep him at arm's length – even if it's just for a few days.'

'A few days – I don't know about that. Twenty-four hours maybe, but a few days—'

'Fine,' Sean told him. 'I'll take it, but I'll need surveillance on McKenzie up and running within a couple of hours. I want to know where he's going, what he's doing, who's he seeing—'

'Surveillance?' Featherstone stopped him. 'No chance.'

'Why?' Sean snapped. 'I need this bastard followed.'

'Sorry, Sean,' Featherstone explained, 'but there've been too many cases in the media lately of the police acting too slowly – following people around while the suspect remains at large and the victims remain missing, only to turn up dead a few days later in the places we should have just charged into and searched from the off. So let's not fuck about here. If you have a viable suspect – and you do – let's get in there and nick the bastard, spin his gaff and anywhere else he's known to have been. Our priority is to get the boy back – alive, preferably.'

'But if we can follow him for a while, I'll know,' Sean argued. 'I'll know for sure before we even make a move.'

'There's nothing to be gained from surveillance,' Featherstone reiterated. 'Act decisively – that's the way forward here. Now, you get on with what you've got to do while I go and see the Assistant Commissioner and spin him along for a bit. Hopefully the next time I see him I'll be able to give him the good news, yes?'

'Maybe,' Sean answered sullenly.

'Fine. Until then—' Featherstone was already springing out of his chair and striding from the office. No one spoke until he disappeared into the corridor.

'What's got him so rattled?' Sally asked.

'Eighteen months from retirement with Assistant Commissioner Addis all over his back – you'd be rattled too,' Sean told her. 'Now, get hold of Stan and Tony and let's pay McKenzie a visit.'

A few drops of sweat formed on Mark McKenzie's forehead as he searched his newly acquired, second-hand laptop for pornography that suited his particular taste. Hard-core child pornography was hard to find on the Internet unless you'd had a tip-off from a like-minded friend, but his well-practised fingers danced across the keyboard entering the words that experience had taught him were the quickest way to find what he was after. He wiped the sweat away with the back of his hand and considered turning the heating down in the small, squalid flat he rented above a fried chicken takeaway franchise. But once he found what he was looking for it would be better to be warm for what he had in mind. He felt the old familiar excitement beginning to spread through his body as his testicles coiled and swelled, constant licking making his thin lips appear red and full, as if stained by wine. He lit another cigarette and tried not to let thoughts of the police and what would happen to him if he was caught downloading child pornography spoil his magical moment as he drew ever nearer to his prize.

The very thought of the police, the entire criminal justice system, made him almost laugh out loud as he blew plumes of thick grey smoke at the computer's screen. They thought themselves so clever, but so long as he kept signing their pathetic register on time and turning up for their pointless interviews they'd leave him alone – alone to do whatever he wanted. Thoughts of the police faded to nothing as he finally found what he was looking for and amateur pictures of young, naked bodies began to fill his screen. This one even had half-decent sound. He took one last, hurried drag on his cigarette before stubbing it out and loosening the belt around his grubby trousers.

Just as he was about to take hold of his penis, the flimsy door to his flat exploded inwards, sending splinters of wood flying almost the full length of the living room. He jumped off his chair in shock, taking temporary refuge under the flimsy table. As soon as he saw the people in raincoats and suits bursting through the hole where the door used to be, he knew they were police and not the local vigilantes – even before they started calling into the flat, 'Police! Police! Stay where you are and stand still.' In a millisecond he remembered the laptop sitting on the table above his head and the damning evidence it contained. The fear of it being discovered turned his legs to springs as he rolled from under the table, stood and reached for the computer – but before his fingers could touch a single key one of the bastard policemen had crossed the room and knocked him back to the floor with a two-handed push to the chest. By the time he recovered his breath and his senses, the cop was standing over him, holding a warrant card in his face.

'DI Corrigan, you little prick. Consider yourself under arrest.'

McKenzie coughed violently before speaking, to the point where he almost vomited. 'I haven't done anything,' he pleaded, almost out of habit.

'Really,' Sean snarled. 'Then what the fuck is this?' He grabbed McKenzie by the back of his head and pushed his face close to the screen.

'I don't know how that got there,' McKenzie stammered, feigning amazement. 'Swear to God.'

'Don't lie to me, you miserable little shit. You lie to me, it'll only get worse for you.'

'I'm telling the truth,' McKenzie lied again. 'It's a

second-hand computer – the download was already on it – I just found it when I was clearing its memory.'

'Liar,' Sean told him, his voice threatening as his hand slipped behind McKenzie's neck and began to squeeze hard, the pain opening his mouth and making him whimper in pain. 'You're off to a bad start, McKenzie. Now it's time to start telling the truth.'

The sweat on his brow made the thin, brown hair of his long fringe stick to his forehead as his thin fingers tried to prise Sean's iron grip from the back of his neck, his dirty, broken fingernails scratching and drawing lines of blood on the back of Sean's hand. 'I'm not saying anything until I speak to a solicitor,' he managed to say between deep swallows. 'I know my rights.'

'Fuck your rights,' Sean hissed. 'The children you were convicted of assaulting – where were their rights when you were abusing them?' He thrust McKenzie's face closer to the laptop's screen. 'Where are *their* rights?'

'Maybe you should take it a little easy, guv'nor?' Keeping her voice low, Sally laid a hand on Sean's arm. This was no game of good cop, bad cop – she'd seen Sean like this before and knew it could mean trouble – trouble for them all.

'Anyone wants to leave, they can leave,' Sean told Sally and the other two detectives. 'Mark and I wouldn't mind being left alone, would we, Mark? We could have a private chat – get a few things straightened out.'

Sally sighed inwardly, but said nothing.

'I've got nothing to say to you,' McKenzie sneered through his pain, the fear leaving him as his mind began to spin with the possibilities of his situation.

'Wrong,' Sean shouted in his ear. 'Time to talk, McKenzie. Now, where's the boy? Where are you keeping him?'

McKenzie shook his head, trying to assess the situation and play it to his own advantage – to turn the tables on the police at last, especially the one who held him by the neck as if he was nothing more than an unruly dog. He couldn't stand any police, but this one was especially easy to hate. 'I don't know what you're talking about,' he answered. A sickening smirk twisted across his face as he fed off Sean's dark anger, sensing that he was the one in control, no matter how hard Sean squeezed his neck; no matter how much he might beat him or try to humiliate him. He held the power – for now.

'The boy?' Sean repeated. 'You snatched him from his bedroom in Hampstead last night, but where is he now? What have you done with him? For your sake, Mark, I hope he's all right.'

'I've got nothing to say to you – whoever you are.'

'I already told you who I am, Mark. You need to pay a little more attention and you need to answer my questions and you need to answer them now. Do you know what happens to child murderers inside, Mark? Look at you – you wouldn't last a week before someone stuck a sharpened screwdriver into your liver. You already know all about living Rule 43 inside, don't you, Mark – but a child murderer? How long before the screws *accidentally* leave your cell unlocked, eh?'

'You finished yet?' McKenzie asked, his smirk turning to a full-blown smile.

'Fuck you, am I finished!' Sean told him as he pushed his face into the computer screen, releasing him at the same time and stepping back before he did something he knew he'd regret. 'I'm just getting started, you disgusting piece of shit. Trust me, McKenzie, when I'm finished you'll know.'

Donnelly sat alone, surveying the interior of the café he'd found off Hampstead High Street, sipping the coffee he'd just bought, the price of which had made his eyes water. He regretted not opting for one of the many big-chain coffee shops and saving himself a few pounds, even though he couldn't stand the places. It had been a few years since he'd attended any training courses at the nearby Peel Centre Police College, but even in that time many of the independent cafés and restaurants had disappeared, overtaken by the ever-spreading international franchises. He sighed as he took a bite from his extortionate bacon sandwich and sipped the coffee that cost as much as a pint of bitter in his favourite pub. As his mind drifted back to the case in hand and his appointed task of organizing the door-to-door inquiries, he couldn't suppress a snort of disgust at the way his talents were being wasted. Not that he had any intention of actually knocking on endless doors himself, speaking to the disinterested and the over-keen alike – though he had reserved a couple of addresses for his special attention: the immediate neighbours of the Bridgemans.

He had quickly come to the conclusion that they were looking for some spectre who didn't actually exist. During his long service he'd seen a lot of strange things, but when a child went missing and there was no sign of a forced entry there was no need to look further than the parents. The boy was almost certainly dead already and probably still hidden somewhere in the house – a suitcase or holdall. Once the search team or dog unit found the body, they could crack on with the murder investigation, by which time he planned to be one or two steps ahead. Interviewing the neighbours would be the first of those steps.

Donnelly hadn't even met the missing boy's parents yet, but just sitting in this café in the middle of Hampstead told him the sort of people they would be: smug and self-important. God, he loved putting the squeeze on types like that. They always thought they were so clever – so much cleverer than a dumb copper. Which was just how he liked it, because they invariably thought they were smart enough to talk their way out of any situation. In reality, they always ended up digging themselves great big holes to neatly fall headfirst into. If they really were as clever as they thought, they'd say nothing – just like the everyday feral criminal from any housing estate in London would. *How I love hubris*, he told himself with a smile, the image of tearing their alibis to pieces across an interview table cheering him considerably. The cold, hard truth was that all he had to do was bide his time and wait for the body to turn up.

Kentish Town Police Station sat on the corner of Kentish Town Road and Holmes Road, blending in perfectly with its bleak surroundings, its Victorian architecture oppressive and forbidding, a relic from the past that seemed to hold the entire area back, despite its proximity to some of the wealthiest and most sought-after areas of London. From outside the building almost no signs of life could be seen within, just as the Victorians had wanted: small windows with thick, dimpled glass kept the secrets of its business from the public outside. That suited Sean just fine as he and Sally sat in the small office they'd borrowed from the resident DI, preparing to interview Mark McKenzie – who was currently languishing in the dingy, threatening cells that lay in the bowels of the building.

'So, how much d'you like McKenzie for our yet-to-be-established abduction?' Sally asked, breaking minutes of silence. Sean looked up from McKenzie's intelligence file, his expression telling her he hadn't heard her question.

'What?'

'McKenzie? D'you think he could be our man – if it's confirmed the boy has actually been taken?'

'The boy's been taken,' he assured her, 'and yes, he could be our man. His previous is perfect – especially his record of night-time residential burglaries while the families were at home, sleeping. He's a creeper, and that makes him a dangerous individual. You and I both know that. People don't do night-time burglaries while the residents are at home for profit alone – it gives them something else – a buzz, some perverted satisfaction. It makes them feel powerful and in control, even if half of them do end up fouling themselves with fear.'

'But not McKenzie,' Sally added. 'There's nothing in his records to say he ever defecated at the scenes of his burglaries.'

'Which means either he wasn't afraid or he's learned to control his fear, both of which make him all the more dangerous. Add to that the fact he has previous for sexual assaults on children, and has used lock-picking as a way of gaining entry . . . yes, I like him for this – a lot. But I could do with something a bit more concrete before we interview him. Which reminds me . . .' He grabbed his mobile from the desk and searched its memory for one of the newest members of his team, then hit speed-dial and waited.

'Guv'nor,' Goodwin answered.

'How you getting on with that search team and dog unit?'

'I'm gonna meet them at the house in a couple of hours, guv.'

'What's the hold-up?' Sean asked impatiently.

'Anti-Terrorist, guv. They've had them all tied up for days now. I had to be a little economical with the truth to pull them away for a few hours, so if you get an irate call from any brass, I'm afraid that'll be down to me.'

'If I do, I'll deal with it,' Sean assured him. 'You got a team and that's all that matters. Anyone gives you a hard time, you tell them I made the call on that one – understand?'

'Thanks, guv.'

'As soon as you get a result, let me know,' Sean told him and hung up.

'Problem?' Sally asked.

'The house hasn't been searched yet,' Sean told her, 'and won't be for a few hours.'

'Shall we delay the interview?'

'No. We'll do it anyway. We've got a missing four-year-old, we can't afford to wait around.'

'So,' Sally began, her eyebrows raised in exaggerated concern, 'we'll be interviewing a possible suspect who we have no evidence against about a crime we can't even prove has happened. This'll be interesting.'

'The crime's happened,' Sean almost snapped at her, 'and McKenzie's a good suspect. We go with what we've got. If the search teams or Forensics come up with anything else, we can always re-interview him.'

'If you think he fits the bill, that's good enough for me,' Sally told him.

Sean closed his eyes for a couple of seconds, allowing the images of McKenzie crouched by the front door of the Bridgemans' house to flow into his mind, the dark figure quickly and smoothly working the locks as his breath condensed in the cold night air, before slipping inside the house and moving silently towards the stairs that would lead him to the boy he knew was sleeping upstairs. *How did you know?* He spoke aloud without knowing it.

'Know what?' Sally asked, making him open his eyes.

'It's nothing,' he assured her, 'or at least nothing that's going to take us forward. Christ, my head's so full of crap at the moment I can barely think.'

'Then use your experience instead,' Sally encouraged him. 'You've dealt with paedophiles before. What about that undercover case you were on?'

'That was years ago.'

'These particular leopards never change their spots.'

'No,' he agreed. 'No, they don't.'

'So what was the job?'

'To infiltrate a paedophile ring calling itself the Network.'

'Sounds like fun,' Sally sniffed sarcastically.

'The Internet was just beginning to spread and typically the baddies were on to it before we were – grooming kids online before getting them to . . . to perform – sometimes with each other, sometimes with the men who'd groomed then. They'd film the abuse and post it on the Internet.'

'Why?' Sally asked.

'Because they were proud of what they did.'

'Sick,' Sally judged.

'Maybe, or maybe that was just the way nature intended them. Anyway, I infiltrated their top man in prison first, then on the outside we continued our relationship until eventually he let me into the heart of their organization, something they called the Sanctum, made up of the members who actually did the abusing and oversaw distribution of the pictures.'

'And you took them out?' Sally asked.

'We did. But the whole time I was with them, the head of the snake knew I was a cop – from the very first time he met me.'

'He was bullshitting you.'

'No,' Sean said without hesitation. 'He knew. John Conway knew.'

'Then why did he take you in?'

'Because he thought he could turn me,' Sean admitted.

'Thought he could turn you into a paedophile?' Sally asked, confused.

'What else?' he answered, the question lingering unanswered between them. He steered the conversation back to the present. 'But the Network groomed their victims, luring them to places where they could safely meet them. And the victims were older – all between nine and thirteen. Not like this one. Our guy goes into the house and takes them – and he takes them when they're still very young.'

'*Them?*' Sally asked. 'He's only taken one, if that.'

'Slip of the tongue,' Sean lied. 'Anyway, there's a damn good chance we have our man banged up downstairs. So, if you're ready . . .' He stood, gathering up the piles of reports he'd been reading in preparation for the interview.

'Ready when you are, Mr McKenzie,' Sally said. 'Ready when you are.'

DC Maggie O'Neil looked out of the fifteenth-floor hotel-room window at the view of Swiss Cottage and Maida Vale, the streets below twinkling and sparkling in the headlights, the crowded pavements bathed in the yellow light that leaked from the shop-fronts. The traffic was in gridlock, the sounds of which drifted up to the fifteenth floor and through the double-glazing. She'd offered the Bridgemans the use of a police safe house but they had unceremoniously turned her offer down, instead opting to find and pay for their own temporary accommodation, hence the three-bedroom apartment in the hotel in Swiss Cottage. Mr and Mrs Bridgeman took the largest room, while the nanny and Sophia shared the twin room. Maggie could use the small single room if she felt it was necessary for her to spend the night with the family, and so far she did.

She drew the curtains on the city below and turned to study the family, wishing she was tucked up at home in her small flat in Beckenham with her partner, who worked on the Mounted Division out of Wandsworth. She'd recently turned thirty and still hadn't told her parents and family back in Birmingham she was gay, although she suspected her older sister had worked it out by now – the lack of boyfriends, no marriage talk, no baby talk. But for the rest, their conservative Irish background seemed to mean they'd rather not know the truth than have to deal with it. Besides, her brothers and sisters had already produced four grand-children with the promise of plenty more to come, so it wasn't as if she was leaving her parents with no little brats to bounce on their knees at Christmas.

She watched the nanny chasing six-year-old Sophia around the living area, her excitement at staying in a London hotel on a school night making her even more difficult to deal with – all thoughts of her missing brother seemingly forgotten. How cruel and selfish young children can be, she thought to herself as Sophia's noisy protests against bedtime drowned out the urgent whispers from the small kitchen next door where Mr and Mrs Bridgeman had retreated in search of privacy.

'Do you need any help there, Caroline?' she asked the nanny, who continued to chase the six-year-old.

'No thanks,' she replied, 'I'm used to it. Come on, Sophia – it's time for bed.'

'You can't tell me what to do,' Sophia unhelpfully answered. 'You're not my mother.'

'Don't talk yourself into trouble, Sophia,' Caroline warned, prompting the six-year-old to turn her back on them and reluctantly head towards the bathroom, calling back without looking:

'Whatever.'

Caroline rolled her eyes in Maggie's direction before whispering, 'Proper little madam, that one.'

'What about her brother?' Maggie asked quietly. 'What's George like?'

'Not like this one. He's a really sweet boy,' Caroline managed to answer before her voice failed and her eyes unexpectedly filled with tears. 'I'm sorry,' she stuttered. 'I wasn't expecting to have to speak about him.'

'It's all right,' Maggie reassured her. 'In situations like this our emotions can sometimes ambush us. One second you think you're fine, then the next . . .'

'Poor George. Dear God, poor George. What's happened to him?'

'Don't worry,' Maggie told her. 'We'll find him.'

'How do you know that?' Caroline asked. 'I mean, how do you know that for sure?'

It was a question Maggie knew she had to avoid answering. 'How's Mrs Bridgeman coping?'

'She's doing a decent job of hiding it, but I can tell she's scared – really scared. This is killing her inside.' The sound of Mr Bridgeman's raised voice in the kitchen made them both freeze for a second, their eyes locked, neither speaking until the sounds from the kitchen returned to faint murmuring.

'And Mr Bridgeman,' Maggie asked, her voice hushed, 'how's he doing?'

Caroline suddenly looked uncomfortable, like a child being asked to divulge a playground secret to a parent. 'I don't know,' she answered. 'It's difficult to say. Sometimes men hide their fear behind anger – especially men like Mr Bridgeman.'

'Like Mr Bridgeman?'

'You know – powerful men – men who are used to being in control.'

'So who's he angry with?'

'With . . . I didn't say he was angry with anyone in particular, just that he was angry at what's happened. He's upset, you know.'

Maggie ignored her explanation, sensing there was more for her to find. 'Mrs Bridgeman? Is he angry with her? Or maybe he's angry with George about something.'

'Listen,' Caroline tried to backtrack, 'I don't really know

what's going on. I'm just the nanny. I look after the children – that's all.' She walked from the room in search of Sophia, leaving Maggie alone with her thoughts and doubts. She'd been Family Liaison Officer on plenty of cases in the past. Until a body was found, family members would never wander too far from the phone or each other, but after the body was found and confirmed as their missing loved one, family members would frequently seek solitude for their grief. She'd seen murders destroy families more often than she'd seen them bring them together – the parents of victims often divorcing in the aftermath of murder – but she'd never seen or felt a reaction quite like she was seeing in the Bridgemans: a devastated mother and an angry father who seemed to be doing everything they could to avoid being in the same room as her. The usual non-stop flow of questions from the terrified parents was absent; instead she could hear the constant murmur of their hushed, urgent voices coming from the kitchen. She reminded herself that she'd never dealt with victims like the Bridgemans before – wealthy and privileged. The families she'd worked with had all been comfortable at best, poor beyond most people's understanding at worst. Maybe this was simply how rich people dealt with things – she just didn't know. But something in her still-developing detective's instinct told her all was not as it should be, as if they resented her presence. It wasn't the first time she had encountered hostility as a Family Liaison Officer, but that had been from criminal families whose hatred of the police wouldn't be softened by the mere death of a family member. That wasn't the case with the Bridgemans – so what was wrong?

The loud buzzing noise filled the small interview room where Sean and Sally sat opposite Mark McKenzie and his state-appointed duty solicitor. Sarah Jackson was a fifty-six-year-old veteran of North London's police stations. Her plain, loose-fitting clothes covered a bulky five-foot-two frame and her round face was surrounded by short, curly hair. Ancient spectacles finished her look. Within minutes of meeting and talking to her prior to introducing her to McKenzie, Sean could tell she knew her business and would not be walked over, although he also sensed she was a straight player and wasn't here to do McKenzie any special favours. If he admitted to her he'd taken the boy then Sean would back Jackson to get him to admit it to them – for his own sake and the boy's. Sean's eyes never left McKenzie, who squirmed in his rickety chair and waited for the buzzing to fall silent. When it did Sean spoke first.

'The time is approximately eight fifteen p.m. This interview is being conducted in an interview room at Kentish Town Police Station. I am Detective Inspector Sean Corrigan and the other officer present is . . .'

'Detective Sergeant Sally Jones,' she introduced herself without needing to be prompted.

'I am interviewing – could you state your name clearly for the tape, please?'

'Mark McKenzie,' he answered curtly with a thin smile.

Sean continued to speak without having to think about the words, his mind already considering the questions he would ask – the small, ball-hammer taps he would keep making, attacking the veneer until finally McKenzie's protective shell shattered.

'And the other person present is . . .?'

Jackson answered without looking up from the notes she was busy scribbling. 'Sarah Jackson, solicitor here to represent Mr McKenzie.'

Sean was glad to note the lack of a self-important speech about rights, hypothetical questions and fairness. She'd stated her business and it was enough.

'Mark,' Sean continued, 'you are still under caution, which means you don't have to say anything unless you wish to do so, but if you fail to mention when questioned something that you later rely on in court it may harm your defence. Do you understand?' McKenzie just shrugged.

'I've explained all this to Mr McKenzie,' said his solicitor, keen to move on.

'And anything you do say can be used in evidence,' Sean finished. McKenzie said nothing. 'I'll assume that's also been explained.'

Jackson briefly looked up and over the top of her spectacles. 'It has,' she told him, leaving Sean a little unsure who she disliked most – him or McKenzie. Had she already done his job for him and browbeaten McKenzie into making a confession? He decided there wasn't enough excitement in the room for that.

'Mark, you've been arrested on suspicion of having abducted a four-year-old boy, George Bridgeman, from his home in Hampstead last night. Is there anything you want to tell me about that?'

'No comment,' McKenzie answered, looking Sean square in the face while his solicitor seemed to raise her eyebrows as she stared down at her increasing notes. *Was McKenzie going against her advice? And if so why?*

'Anything at all?'

'No comment,' McKenzie continued, already beginning to sound irritated.

'I'm sorry,' Sean quickly changed tack, 'are my questions annoying you in some way?' Jackson gave him a warning glance.

'No comment.'

'You live in Kentish Town – right?'

'What's that got to do with anything?'

'Pretty close to Hampstead, isn't it?'

73

'So what?'

'The boy went missing from Hampstead, from Courthope Road. Have you ever been to Courthope Road, Mark?'

'No comment.'

'Did you go there last night?'

'No comment.'

'Did you go there because you knew the boy would be there?'

'No comment.'

'Did you take the boy, Mark – a simple yes or no?'

'No comment.'

Sean leaned back silently for a few seconds before continuing, trying to read the man in front of him – trying to crawl inside his mind and see what he saw, feel what he felt – but nothing came to him. *Keep asking the questions – keep asking until the light begins to spill through a chink in his armour.* 'Funny how you answer some questions no problem, but then when it's about the missing boy you answer no comment.'

'That's his right, Inspector,' Jackson was obliged to interrupt.

'Of course,' Sean insincerely apologized, 'just an observation – that was all. So you've never been to Courthope Road in Hampstead?'

'I didn't say that,' McKenzie corrected him.

'So you have been there before?'

'I didn't say that either.'

'Then what are you saying?'

'Perhaps it would be better if you stuck to answering no comment,' Jackson advised him.

'And I'll ask you again,' Sean kept up, 'have you ever been to Courthope Road or not?'

'Like my solicitor says, no comment.'

'Mark, we're investigating the disappearance of a very

young boy. If you're involved in it then you really need to start answering my questions.'

'Disappeared? Sure of that, are you?'

'What d'you mean?' Sean asked, caught slightly off guard by McKenzie's question.

'I mean, have you searched the house properly yet? I know how you police do things – slow and steady, step by step, always afraid of missing something.'

'It's being done as we speak,' Sean told him bluntly. 'But I'm sure the boy is missing.'

'Then maybe his parents did him in and got rid of the body before they called you lot, knowing you'd come after someone like me to blame for it.'

'Is that how you see yourself – as a victim?'

McKenzie ignored him and shrugged his shoulders, the thin smile still fixed on his face. 'Or you're right. Someone went into the house and took him – took him away right under your nose.'

'Right under my nose?' Sean asked.

'You're a policeman, aren't you? You're supposed to stop things like this from happening.'

Was that McKenzie's motivation – some kind of twisted intellectual vanity? A misguided sense of needing revenge on the police and justice system for all that had happened to him? Take the boy to prove he could get away with murder? 'I suppose so,' Sean played along, 'but whoever took the boy was obviously extremely smart. They got in and out without leaving a single piece of evidence.' McKenzie's smile grew a little wider as his eyes grew narrower. 'Is that why someone took the boy – to show us how clever they are?'

'Maybe.'

'And is that someone you?'

'Ha,' McKenzie laughed, 'you'll have to do better than that.'

'This is not a game, Mark. Do you know what your life will be like if anything happens to the boy? Nowhere will be safe for you ever again.'

'Is that a threat?' McKenzie pushed back, making his solicitor look up like a teacher surveying a class of trouble-makers.

'No,' Sean answered. 'It's a warning.'

'Don't patronize me. I know what it's like to survive behind bars once they call you a sex offender. You bastards have put me away before, remember? But I survived all right, and I will again if I have to.'

'But this time it'll be child-abduction,' Sean warned him. 'You'll be the scalp everyone's looking to take.'

'Only if you can prove it,' McKenzie mocked, stopping Sean dead for a while.

'OK,' Sean continued after a few seconds, 'let's move on to something I can prove, and maybe we'll come back to the missing boy. Earlier today when you were arrested in your flat there was something on your laptop – care to tell me what it was?'

'You know what it was. But I told you – I just bought it second-hand. The stuff you saw was already on it.'

'Come on, Mark,' Sean gently encouraged, 'we've already had a look at it and it's clear the obscene images – the obscene images of children, Mark – were only downloaded seconds before we entered your flat. And seeing as how you were the only person there, it kind of means you had to be the one who downloaded them – doesn't it?'

'Must have been a glitch, or maybe someone downloaded it remotely from somewhere else.'

'On to your laptop?'

'It's possible.'

'Not with your previous it's not,' Sean told him. 'Are you aware of Bad Character Evidence? Have you discussed it with your solicitor?' McKenzie shrugged while Jackson briefly looked up to shake her head. 'It means if you rely on a story like that then we can tell the jury all about your previous convictions for downloading other, similar pornography, not to mention your convictions for sexually assaulting children. I really don't think that's going to help your cause.'

'You can't prove anything.'

'By the time the specialists at our computer laboratory have examined that laptop, I'll be able to prove plenty.'

'If you say so.'

'You're going back inside, Mark.'

'I don't think so.'

McKenzie's misplaced confidence was beginning to irritate him. 'Well at least we've established one thing – that you're a liar. A liar who, even when faced with the truth, still can't be honest.' McKenzie squirmed a little in his chair. 'Everybody in this room knows you downloaded the child pornography yourself and everybody here knows you took the boy.' Sally and Jackson now also shuffled uncomfortably in their chairs.

'Like I said,' McKenzie goaded him, 'you can't prove anything and you can't save the boy. You're too late.'

'What do you mean?' Sean asked, as calmly as he could. 'What do you mean, I'm too late?'

'That's for me to know and you to find out.'

'If you know something, you need to tell me.'

McKenzie's foot tapped fast and repeatedly as his excitement grew. 'I don't have to tell you anything.'

Sean's heart burnt with anger at McKenzie and fear for the missing boy, but he wouldn't play McKenzie's game any more – it was too easy for him to come up with sound-bite answers that might mean something or nothing. 'Did it feel good?' he began, 'being alone in the street in the middle of the night? Quiet and cold, nothing but the sound of the leaves in the wind.' McKenzie stopped tapping his foot and looked Sean in the eyes for almost the first time. 'You're good with locks, but it still must have taken a while to get the door open – were you scared someone would hear or see you, kneeling outside by the front door? It must have been difficult, working with gloves on, using those fine, small tools, but you had to wear them, because it was cold that night and you needed to stop your fingers from going numb, didn't you?' McKenzie squinted and frowned, his thin smile all but gone. 'And when you finally stepped inside the house, the warmth hitting you in the face, the smell of the family must have been almost more than you could bear – did it make you feel dizzy, like you were having a dream?'

'I don't know what you're talking about,' McKenzie interrupted.

'What did it feel like, Mark, climbing those stairs towards the boy's room – walking past his mother's bedroom while she slept – knowing you were going to take her baby?' Jackson glanced at him, her face betraying that she had children herself, no matter how grown-up they may be now – her mother's instinct stopping her from intervening even when she should. 'Did it make you feel special, Mark? Special like you never feel in everyday life? Did it make you feel powerful?'

'Guessing, guessing, guessing,' McKenzie hissed. 'All you're doing is guessing.'

'But why didn't you touch the mother? Is it because you're a coward? Because you were afraid of her – afraid to rape a grown woman in case she fought back?'

'This is going too far, Inspector,' Jackson finally interjected.

'Which is why it has to be children for you, doesn't it?' Sean ignored her, his voice louder than before. 'But why not the little girl? Is it only little boys that do it for you, Mark?'

'I think that's enough, Inspector,' Jackson insisted, her voice matching his until McKenzie spoke over the top of both of them.

'You think you're so clever – the police,' he spat at them. 'Fuck the police. I have the power here – no one else. I say what happens. We play by my rules – no one else's.'

'You have the power, Mark? Your rules? You seem to be forgetting something.'

'Yeah? And what would that be?

'That we've already caught you.'

McKenzie looked shocked for a moment, but then his blank expression began to grow into a smile and the smile into a barely audible laugh. His laughter grew until it was as loud as it was mocking and all the time he stared into Sean's eyes.

Sean was close to leaping across the interview table when his vibrating phone distracted him. 'Fuck,' he swore too loudly before remembering his every word was being recorded. He snatched the phone from his belt and examined the caller ID. 'Sorry, but I need to take this. For the recording, DI Corrigan is leaving the room for a short while.' He made sure the door was shut behind him before he answered. 'Ashley, what you got?'

'The Special Search Team and the dog have both been through the house,' DC Goodwin told him.

'And?' Sean asked impatiently.

'Nothing. The boy's definitely not still in the house.'

'They absolutely sure?'

'Sorry, guv, but the boy's gone, no doubt about it.'

'Christ,' Sean blasphemed. For all that he'd been convinced the boy had been taken, it was still a deeply disturbing jolt to have it confirmed. 'What about a scent? Did the dog pick up on any scent?'

'Sorry,' Goodwin explained. 'Too many people have been

through the house too many times, including the boy. The dog followed his scent to the front door, but once in the street it didn't know which way to turn.'

'OK, Ash – and thanks. You might as well get the forensic team in now – see what they can find.' He hung up, returned to the interview room and sat down heavily. 'DI Corrigan re-entering the interview room.'

'Everything all right?' Sally asked.

'Fine,' Sean lied. 'I'd just like to clear a few things up before we take a break.'

'Such as?' McKenzie asked, suspicious of Sean's surprise exit and re-entry. He'd been interviewed enough times to know the police weren't above an underhand trick or two to get a confession – especially from a convicted paedophile.

'The house George Bridgeman was reported missing from has now been thoroughly searched.' He paused for a second to give himself time to read McKenzie's face. 'There's no sign of him.' McKenzie's foot immediately started tapping uncontrollably again. 'A full forensic search of the house will be starting almost immediately – looking for any tiny traces of whoever went to the boy's room and took him. We've taken your clothes and body samples already: how long before we put you at the scene, Mark? How long?'

'Too long,' McKenzie grinned. 'Too long to save the boy.'

'We'll see,' Sean answered.

'You're too late,' McKenzie almost sang. 'You're too late. You're too late,' over and over again.

'This interview is concluded,' Sean told him, pushing the stop button that made a heavy click followed by a slight whirring sound, the noise reverberating around the room as Sean gathered his sparse interview notes and headed for the door as quickly as he could before McKenzie's mocking chants pushed him beyond control. Sally followed him out of the room, leaving McKenzie alone with his solicitor. They walked a few steps away from the door before speaking in hushed, conspiratorial tones.

'What d'you think?' Sally asked.

'He couldn't look more like our man if he tried,' Sean answered.

'Well, we know the boy's definitely missing now – so it's McKenzie or the parents.'

'In all likelihood,' Sean agreed. 'But what game is he playing? He neither denies taking the boy nor admits it. He seems to want to float somewhere in the middle. But why? If I could just get inside—'

'Inside what?' Sally jumped on him. 'Inside his head? Last time you did that, it didn't work out too well, did it?'

'We got our man,' Sean argued, 'and probably saved at least one life.'

'Yeah, and Keller almost took yours – remember? Maybe this time we can just do things normally. You know, follow the evidence, wait for back-up – that sort of thing.'

'Is that what you think George Bridgeman wants us to do – sit around waiting for the evidence to come to us? Is that what his parents want?'

'I guess that depends on whether they were involved or not. I'm beginning to think you're not even considering them as suspects.'

'I'm considering everything. Right now, I'm considering everything.'

'But you like McKenzie for it more than the other options?'

'Don't you? His previous. His lock-picking skills. The way he's behaving in interview. I have to like him for it.'

'Fair enough,' Sally agreed. 'So what do we do now?'

'Lock him up till the morning and then interview him again. Perhaps by that time we'll have something from Forensics to rattle his cage with.'

'And if we don't?'

'I don't know. I'll think of something . . . something to knock him out of his stride, with or without more evidence. He'll talk – eventually.'

'Why would he do that?' Sally asked.

'Because he wants to,' Sean explained. 'They all want to – that's half the reason they do what they do. He just needs a few more shoves in the right direction. I'm going to pop back to the Yard and see what's happening. Get hold of the local superintendent and have them meet you here in the morning to sort out an extension of detention for McKenzie. I'll meet you back here later tomorrow morning to interview him again. Once you've got it sorted, go home and get some rest while you can.'

'And you?' Sally asked, trying to sound matter-of-fact to hide her concerns.

'I'll get home later,' he promised as he headed for the exit. 'I'll see you in the morning,' he called over his shoulder and was gone.

'Here we go again,' Sally told no one. 'Here we go again.'

Donnelly stood on the doorstep of 9 Courthope Road, warrant card in hand, and waited for the door to be opened. He'd already visited the Bridgemans' neighbours on the other side in number five. The Beiersdorfs – Simon and Emily – had given him more than a few interesting tit-bits about the Bridgemans, even if they hadn't realized they were doing so: how they had no intention of moving their children from their current school some distance from home rather than send them to the excellent local private school. How they never really spoke to anyone or tried to socialize, keeping themselves very much to themselves and seemingly avoiding their new neighbours. And then there had been the occasional sound of heated voices raised in argument, the children being shouted at. They had been at pains to explain that they understood all couples and families argued from time to time, but the Bridgemans' arguments happened a little too often and were a little too disturbing.

Everything was turning out just how he thought it would.

The door was finally opened by yet another attractive woman, although she was slightly older than the norm for the street – she must have been in her early fifties. Nevertheless she had the same physical characteristics as the other women wealthy enough to live in this part of Hampstead: tall, slim, perfect skin and expertly dyed silver-blonde hair in a ponytail. She spoke in the same accent as everyone else too, almost a non-accent, but with just a hint of the aristocratic as she peered through the small gap the security chain allowed. 'Yes. Can I help you?'

'Mrs Howells?' Donnelly asked, flipping his warrant card open for her to examine. 'Detective Sergeant Donnelly from . . .' he struggled to remember the name of his new team for a second . . . 'Special Investigations Unit, New Scotland Yard.'

'How do you know my name?' she asked, still scrutinizing his warrant card, her first reaction one of suspicion.

'I've just been speaking with the Beiersdorfs from number 5. I took the liberty of asking them your name. I hope you don't mind.'

'No,' she lied. 'I assume this is about the little boy from next door?'

'You heard then?'

'Couldn't help hearing with all the police walking up and down the street. Have you found him yet?'

'No,' Donnelly answered. 'Sadly not.'

'His poor mother,' Mrs Howells said without feeling, 'she must be besides herself with worry.'

'She's holding up. Sorry I didn't catch your first name.'

'Philippa,' she told him.

'Well, Philippa, I was wondering if I could come inside and speak with you a minute?'

'It's very late. I was expecting someone from the police to call here earlier. Perhaps you could come back tomorrow?'

'Better to get it out of the way now,' Donnelly quickly told her, sensing she was about to close the door. 'Anything that might help us find the little boy – right?'

'Very well,' she relented, flicking the chain off the hook and swinging the door open for him. 'You'd better come inside.'

'That's very kind of you,' Donnelly said as he skipped up the stairs. 'Is Mr Howells also at home by any chance?' he asked.

'No,' she answered curtly while closing the door, 'he's away on business.'

'Pity,' he told her. 'Ideally I would have liked to speak to both of you.'

'I don't suppose my husband would know any more than I do,' she explained, leading him through the house to the large kitchen diner – a common feature in the houses of the street. 'We hardly know them – they only moved in a few weeks ago. But I suppose you already know that. Please, take a seat,' she told him, indicating a stool at the breakfast bar.

'And you popped round to introduce yourself?' Donnelly asked, keen to speed things along.

'Of course. This is a friendly street. We had a street party for the Jubilee and every Christmas we have a big party for all the kids at the local tennis club, that sort of thing.'

'But the Bridgemans didn't want to know?'

'You could say that. She seemed keener than her husband, but not exactly over-friendly.'

'So the husband seemed to be the one wanting them to keep their distance – is that fair?'

'I suppose so,' she answered. 'I assumed they were just shy and preferred to keep themselves to themselves.'

'Fair enough,' Donnelly encouraged.

'Exactly, but they'd only been here a few days when . . . well, quite frankly, the arguments started. Believe me, the walls of these houses are pretty solid, but you could still hear them – or rather *him*.'

'So it was Mr Bridgeman doing the shouting?'

'She joined in, but yes, mainly him.'

'Could you hear what they were arguing about?'

'Not really, although I did hear him calling her a lying bitch one time. I think at that point my husband and I vowed to have as little to do with them as possible and that's the way it's been.'

'What about the kids? How did they seem?'

'All right, considering.'

'And the children's behaviour?'

'Fine. The little girl . . .'

'Sophia.'

'Yes, Sophia, seemed to have a lot to say for herself, but the little boy . . .'

'George.'

'Yes, sorry, George was a very quiet boy, from what I could tell. But like I said, we don't really know them.'

'But on the occasions you did see them,' Donnelly pressed, 'maybe in the back garden or out the front there, how did the parents seem towards the children?' Donnelly's chirping mobile broke the flow of questions and answers, making him curse under his breath. The caller ID told him it was Sean. He answered without excusing himself. 'Guv'nor.'

'Where are you?' Sean asked.

'Door-to-door, as assigned. Speaking to the Bridgemans' neighbours, who are being very helpful,' he added for the benefit of the listening Mrs Howells.

'Good,' Sean told him. 'While you're doing that you should bear in mind the house has now been searched properly and the boy hasn't been found.'

Donnelly cursed inwardly twice: once for not being right about the boy's body being found in the house and again for not making sure DC Goodwin tipped him off about the search before he told Sean. The news must have come through while he was in with the Beiersdorfs. Damn it. Not to worry. His theory still held water. After killing the boy the Bridgemans could have easily moved the body from the house – perhaps to a secure place while they waited for the heat to die down before getting rid of it permanently. Or maybe they had already disposed of it. 'Is that so,' he finally answered.

'Yes, and the one we have in custody is shaping up nicely,' Sean continued.

'Has he admitted it yet?' Donnelly asked, disappointment at the prospect of being proved wrong mingling with satisfaction that the person responsible was in custody. He had no problem swallowing his pride for the sake of getting a conviction on some sick bastard kiddie-fiddler.

'No,' Sean told him. 'But he hasn't denied it either, and you have to ask yourself why he wouldn't deny it if he wasn't involved.'

'Because he's insane?' Donnelly offered.

'Not this one,' Sean explained. 'He's wired wrong, but he's not insane. Seems to want to play games too.'

'With us?'

'Apparently. Finish up where you are and try and get some sleep. Tomorrow's going to be an early start and a late finish, as is every day until we find George – one way or the other.' Donnelly heard the connection go dead.

'Sorry about that. Where were we?' Donnelly asked Mrs Howells.

'The Bridgeman children,' she reminded him.

'Aye, indeed. From what you could see, how did the parents behave towards their children?'

'OK,' she answered. 'Although . . .'

'Although what?' Donnelly seized on it.

'From the bits and pieces I've seen, they were fine towards Sophia, but . . .'

'But . . .?' he pushed her.

'Not Celia, but Mr Bridgeman always seemed a little . . . well, a little cold towards George.'

'Any idea why?'

'As I said, I barely know them. I'm just telling you what struck me from the little I've observed.'

'That's very interesting,' Donnelly told her. 'But he's fine towards Sophia?'

'Kisses and cuddles on the doorstep when he comes home – plays with her in the garden at the weekends.'

'Nothing unusual about a daddy's girl. I have a few kids of my own and my ten-year-old only has eyes for her old dad – much to the annoyance of her mother.'

'It's getting very late now,' Mrs Howells said with a polite smile Donnelly had seen a thousand times before. 'I really ought to check on the children.'

'Have you ever seen him, maybe, hit the boy?' Donnelly ignored her hints.

'No. No. Of course not.'

'Ever see him touch George in an inappropriate way?'

'I really don't think I should say any more.'

'Anything you tell me will be treated as confidential, Mrs Howells.'

'I've told you all I know. I never saw him abuse George in any way. It's just . . . he was . . .'

'Cold towards him,' Donnelly reminded her.

'Yes,' she admitted.

'And your mother's instinct told you something was wrong?' Donnelly tried to seduce her with praise.

'Yes – I mean no. I'm not sure, really I'm not. It's late, detective. I must . . .'

Donnelly tapped the top of the breakfast bar before standing and fastening his overcoat against the cold that waited for him outside. 'Of course,' he told her. 'You've been a great help.'

'I just hope I haven't misled you,' she told him.

'Oh, I don't think you've done that, Mrs Howells. I don't think you've done that at all.'

Sean cursed his nine-to-five neighbours as he searched and failed to find a parking spot anywhere close to the front door of his modest three-bedroom terraced house in East Dulwich, bought just before the wealth spread into the area from Dulwich Village and Blackheath. Maybe Kate was right – they should cash in while it was worth as much as it was and flee to New Zealand; perhaps then he would be able to afford somewhere with off-street parking instead of going through this nightly ritual of imagining his neighbours smugly tucked up in their beds while they thought of him having to park a couple of streets away. At least it wasn't raining. Finally he parked up and trudged back towards his house, passing cars that he knew would still be parked in the same places as he headed back to his own the next morning. Last home and first to leave – same as usual.

His head was still buzzing with the day's events: the office move, the new case, meeting the missing boy's parents, and most of all the interview with McKenzie and all the questions he'd thought of on the way home that he'd forgotten to ask during the interview. He had only a few hours before it would be time to head back to work and pick up where he left off, and experience told him that if he was to get any rest at all he needed to unwind; sit alone and watch something on the TV unrelated to any type of policework while he consumed as much bourbon as he dared to slow his racing mind without leaving him groggy in the morning. To his disappointment, as he entered the house he sensed Kate was still up, a sinking feeling in his belly making him feel guilty for seeking solitude. He eased the door shut behind him and headed for the kitchen where he knew she would be waiting.

'You're late,' she said, unconfrontationally. 'Or at least, later than you've been for a while.'

'They finally gave us a new case,' he told her, trying not to show his excitement and relief at once again being gainfully employed, once again leading the hunt.

'Oh,' she responded, not hiding her disappointment.

'They weren't going to leave me alone for ever.' He gave an apologetic shrug.

'No,' she agreed. 'I realize that. It's just, I was getting used to having you around a bit more than usual, and so were the girls.'

'We've had a good run, perhaps we should just be grateful for that.'

'Grateful!' Kate snapped, then immediately softened her tone: 'You were shot, Sean. I think you earned some time off.'

'Maybe,' he answered, desperately wishing he could just be alone as he pulled a glass and a bottle of bourbon from a cupboard the kids couldn't reach and poured two fingers before emptying his pockets on the kitchen table and slumping into a chair on the other side to his wife.

'Haven't seen you do that in a while,' she told him, her eyes accusing the drink in his hand.

'I need to sleep tonight and this'll help.'

'If I didn't know better, I'd say you look pretty pleased with yourself,' she told him.

'What's that supposed to mean?'

'Sitting there, drink in hand, hardly speaking, holier-than-thou look on your face.' He couldn't help but grin a little. Maybe she was right. Maybe he was enjoying being back in the same old shit. 'Yeah, that smile says it all.'

'Don't be so pissed off,' he told her. 'I'm a detective. They pay me to solve cases, catch the bad guys, save the day, remember?'

'I'm pissed off because I was worried, Sean. I called you, several times, and left messages, but you didn't call back – not even a text.'

He lifted his mobile from the table and checked for missed calls. Sure enough she'd called him several times. 'Sorry,' he told her. 'I must have been in the middle of an interview.'

'I don't know, Sean – it feels like we're heading back to the bad old days: me here alone with the kids while you run around trying to get yourself . . . We can do better than this, can't we?'

'It's only been one night,' he reminded her.

'You said it's a new case, so we all know what that means.' Sean didn't respond as a silence fell between them that only increased his yearning to be alone. 'So what is it?'

'What's what?' he asked unnecessarily.

'The new case.'

'A four-year-old boy gone missing from his home in Hampstead,' he answered, immediately regretting mentioning Hampstead.

'Hampstead?' Kate seized on it. 'Why are you investigating something that happened in Hampstead?'

He took a gulp of the bourbon before answering. 'They've moved us to the Yard.'

'Why would they do that?' she asked, her voice heavy with suspicion.

He swallowed the liquid he'd been holding in his mouth and waited for the burning in his throat to cease before answering. 'They've changed my brief,' he told her. 'We're to investigate murders and crimes of special interest across the whole of London, not just the south-east.'

'Have they centralized all the Murder Teams?' she asked, her voice tightening with concern.

'No. Just mine.'

Kate took a few seconds to comprehend what it could mean. 'So now they can dump anything from anywhere on you? That's just fucking great, Sean. I mean that's really just fucking great.'

'What d'you want me to do?' he asked. 'I had no choice.'

'Don't be so damn weak,' she chastised him. 'You could have said no.'

'That's not how it works – you know that.'

'Sean, it doesn't work at all. God, it was bad enough before and now it's going to be even worse, if that's at all possible. Everything we've planned for the next few weeks I might as well just scrap – just chuck it in the bin?'

The frustration at not being alone finally snapped him. 'I'm sorry if I'm fucking up your social calendar. I thought it was a bit more important to find this four-year-old boy before some paedophile bastard rapes and murders him. I'll tell his parents I can't help them any more because my wife's made dinner reservations – will that make you happy?'

'Fuck you, Sean, and your self-important, arrogant bullshit. I'm going to bed.' She sprang to her feet, almost knocking the chair over, then looked across the table accusingly. 'I don't suppose there's much point in asking when you'll next be home at a reasonable time?'

'That's not really up to me, is it? That's up to whoever took—'

'I've had enough of this crap,' she told him and turned her back on him as she headed for the stairs. He considered calling after her, trying to make the peace before it was too late, but that would mean more sitting and talking, lessening any chance he'd have of calming his mind enough to think as he needed, to think about who could have taken George Bridgeman. But the damage had already been done and the fight with Kate had only added more turmoil to the mix. Now he wouldn't be able to think or sleep.

'Fuck it,' he swore at the room and drained his glass. 'Why do I always have to be such a prick?'

4

The only window in the prison cell was made of heavy, opaque, square glass bricks through which the rising sunlight outside struggled to penetrate, but it was enough to stir Mark McKenzie from his shallow sleep. He'd grown used to sleeping in prison cells, at police stations or more permanent institutions. Although he slept better than most, he was still frequently disturbed by the comings and goings of prisoners elsewhere in the custody area – drunken fights and the screams of the mentally ill, locked up until the system decided what to do with them.

He pulled the regulation blue prisoners' blanket off and padded barefoot on the cold stone floor to the stainless-steel toilet which had been bolted to the wall in a purpose-built alcove of the small room to afford the user some degree of privacy if the cell was being shared. Mercifully he was on his own – the white paper forensic suit ensuring he would not be expected to share this Victorian hole with anyone else. But the suit also marked him out to police and villains alike as something special, and the other criminals had a dog-sense born of the need to survive that told them at a glance that he was no armed robber to be respected and revered; no suspected gangland assassin to be avoided or sucked-up to. No, they knew what he was – a sex case – a rapist or kiddie-fiddler. Either way, he wouldn't be sharing his accommodation with anyone – just in case. He didn't fear too much for his safety while he was banged up with the Old Bill – he knew they wouldn't let the other prisoners near him, and thanks to the advent of CCTV inside custody areas the risk of a visit from a uniformed Neanderthal administering summary justice was unlikely. But if he ended up going back to prison things would be different, even on Rule 43, segregated from the main prison population. He would be constantly living on his nerves, always aware that a vindictive prison officer – or, more likely, a bribed one – might leave a door unlocked just at the right time.

He tried not to dwell on the subject as he finished emptying his bladder and returned to his bed – a flat, blue, plastic mattress on a completely solid wooden bench affixed to the wall on three sides. He pulled the blue blanket back over himself to keep out the morning chill. Clearly some police bastard had turned the heating off in his cell knowing he only had a paper suit and thin blanket to keep out the cold.

As he lay on his back staring at the off-green ceiling his mind wandered back to his life as a young teenager living with his drunken stepfather who beat him for light enter-tainment and a mother who was too busy with much younger children from her new husband and too in need of the income he provided to do anything about it. And then the stepfather had started making accusations – whis-pering evil things in his mother's ear about how he seemed a bit too keen to help bathe the younger children – how he'd caught him sneaking out of their bedrooms in the middle of the night. Even though they couldn't prove anything, when he was only sixteen years old they had pushed him out of the door with a suitcase and two hundred pounds cash, given to him only once he'd promised never to come back. His pleas to his mother had fallen on deaf ears, but alone in the world he'd survived, living off a pittance of unemployment benefit in godforsaken bedsits until finally he'd been forced to take a job as an apprentice locksmith as part of his Job Seeker programme. After a few months he realized he was actually enjoying the job. Getting up every day knowing he had a purpose. Everybody in the small family business treated him with respect – treated him indeed as if he was part of their family as he watched and learned from the more experienced locksmiths. Soon he could fit almost any type of lock to almost any type of door and had even begun to learn the finer art of picking the locks open – a company speciality that had saved many a customer the expense of fitting new locks to doors that had unexpectedly swung shut on them. It started innocently enough as far as he was concerned – just a bit of harmless thrill-seeking – crouching in the dark at the doors of shops closed for the night, working his fine tools until the locks popped open, pushing the doors inwards until the burglar alarms were activated, then watching from a safe distance as the attending police berated the shopkeeper who they'd dragged out in the middle of the night to turn off the terrible noise, warning them that police would stop responding to their alarms if they couldn't even be bothered to make sure they'd shut their doors properly. His night-time games were amusing as well as giving him the opportunity to hone his new-found skills, but soon their appeal began to wear thin. He needed more.

The first few years of his life had been happy enough, – as far as he could remember – living with his mother and real father as an only child, but the admiring looks his mother drew from other men drove his father insane with jealousy – an insanity he tried to drown in drink, until finally his alcoholism chased him from the family home never to be seen again. He'd died a few years later and was buried in a pauper's grave somewhere in the Midlands. After that it had been a succession of strange men he was told to call uncle until such time as they became more permanent in his mother's life. Some had been decent enough, but most saw him at best as an inconvenience, while a few had treated him as something to be used and abused. All the while he'd had to watch the children of other families being loved and cherished by their parents – knowing that, while he was unwelcome in his own home, they would be sleeping soundly in warm, comfortable beds. If only he could *share* some of their life.

Finally he could wait no longer and at last he perfected the method of becoming part of another family without anyone ever knowing. He slipped into their houses through silently opened windows and doors, his lock-picking skills improving with each adventure, standing in the kitchens and living rooms of the families as they slept upstairs, knowing that if he was caught he would be accused of terrible things. But all he wanted was to be alone with them, safe and accepted – part of a *real* family.

For a long time he was too afraid to venture upstairs and stand in the same rooms as the sleeping children. Instead he'd settled for taking things to remind him of his innocent visits; not things of value, just little keepsakes no one would miss. But eventually that was no longer enough, and his fear of walking up the long, creaking staircases was overwhelmed by his need to see the sleeping children. So he took his first terrifying walk up the stairs, struggling to control his bladder and bowels as he slid past the parents' room and entered the room of a little girl bathed in her blue night-light.

It had been everything he'd dreamed it would be – standing, watching her little chest rise and fall under the covers, her long curly hair draped over her face like a beautiful veil. Her room was warm and pretty, with princesses and rainbows on her wallpaper, toys and dolls on every surface as she slept in her soft, comfortable bed, wrapped in a floral-patterned duvet that smelled of fresh orchids on a spring day. So this was how the other children had lived – cared for and adored, as far from his own childhood as it was possible to imagine. Tears had rolled down his face as he'd stood watching her – tears of happiness for her and sadness for his own lost childhood. After what seemed an age he left her room and slipped away as quietly as he'd arrived, taking one of her dolls from the shelf as he did so – being sure to lock the window behind him, leaving it just as he found it.

Time and again he paid his visits to the sleeping, always taking something small and personal from the child's room – just another toy lost or misplaced, soon forgotten by both parents and child alike. His collection of soft toys and dolls was squeezed into a suitcase stored under his bed for when he needed their help to relive his innocent little visits.

But his wage as an apprentice remained small and while he was in the houses he saw many things of value: watches, jewellery, cash in purses and wallets. Small things at first, but as he became bolder the things he took grew larger: laptops, iPads, Blu-ray players. He knew just the landlord in just the pub to sell them to – no questions asked, cash over the counter. Finally his luck ran out as he let himself out of the back door of a semi-detached in Tufnell Park, straight into the arms of a waiting uniform police constable who was quietly investigating a call from a concerned neighbour who thought they'd heard something suspicious in next-door's garden. Obviously he'd been unable to explain the laptop and iPhone they'd found in his bag and once it was established he was not the lawful occupier of the semi-detached he was arrested for residential burglary and handed over to the local CID for further investigation.

He could still clearly remember the abject terror he'd felt when the detectives had handcuffed him and said they were going to take him back to his bedsit to search it for further stolen goods – his mind suddenly unable to think of anything other than the suitcase under the bed and the damning evidence it contained. Trying not to sound too desperate, he told the police he'd happily admit to the burglary and that therefore there was really no need to search his home. But his pleas had been ignored.

Thirty minutes later he could only stand and watch in horror as the younger of the two detectives pulled the suitcase from under the bed and flicked open the latches, throwing open the lid to reveal the toys inside. 'From my childhood,' he'd lied before the detective could speak. 'My parents were going to throw them away so I brought them here. I was going to try and sell them – some of them might be worth something.' Before the detective could question him his colleague distracted both of them as he began to pull watches, credit cards, mobile phones and jewellery from a drawer in a chest.

'Hello there,' he mocked as he let the items he'd found fall through his fingers like pirates' gold. 'Looks like you've been a very busy boy, Mark.' McKenzie's eyes had never left the suitcase until to his astonishment and relief the younger detective closed it and slid it back under the bed before moving quickly to his colleague's side to examine the items that seemed far more interesting than a suitcase of old toys, and certainly easier to trace and prove as stolen. 'You're fucked,' the detective added for good measure, 'properly fucked.'

It was all he could do to suppress the smile he felt warming his insides as he continued to thank God that the burglary he'd been arrested for had been one of the rare occasions when he hadn't taken a toy from the child's room as a trophy. If he had, the suitcase under the bed would have meant so much more to the young detective, but now it had simply been forgotten. He admitted to eight different residential burglaries, listening carefully as the police listed the property taken from the homes, always fearful the toys he'd taken would be on the list, but they never were. Perhaps the parents of the children had never noticed them missing in the first place. Or maybe they had, but not until days after the burglaries, by which time their minds, their imaginations had failed to make the connection.

Four months later, as a first-time offender, he was sentenced to nine months imprisonment and was out in five, jobless and homeless until the Probation Service found him another shithole of a bedsit. With so much time on his hands and bitterness in his heart old, dark, disturbing longings soon began to stir in the pit of his soul and he knew that merely standing by the sides of their beds wouldn't be enough any more. Besides, if the police were looking at him, they'd be looking at him during the night, as they would any night-time offender.

And so it was that he found himself stalking playgrounds during the day, always waiting for his opportunity, waiting for the watching mothers to look away at the wrong moment, for the young child to wander too close to where he hid. Which was exactly what the little boy had done that fateful Wednesday afternoon. He led him away through the woods, touching him and making him do things as he listened to the cries and screams coming from the playground, as the mother and the other hens frantic-ally searched for the little boy. He'd finally panicked and

99

run deeper into the woods leaving the boy alone, sobbing. But he soon became lost and disorientated, voices seemingly closing in on him from all sides, so he decided to hide in the hollow of an old tree, covering himself with dead leaves as the sound of a barking dog joined the chorus of shouts and screams. Eventually the hound came so close that he could hear its sniffling and scratching and he made a last desperate run for it, only for the huge, terrifying beast to bring him down hard within a few paces. A uniformed dog handler arrived, but was clearly in no hurry to call the beast to bay, and in that moment he knew he'd been labelled forever – labelled as a child-molester, hated by all but his own kind. As a residential burglar he'd already been treated by the police as something ugly and suspicious, but that was nothing compared to the treatment he'd received after his arrest for the sexual assault of the child. It seemed everywhere he turned someone would be singing in a whisper: *Sex case. Sex case. Hang him, hang him, hang him.*

His first week in prison had been a living hell, but somehow he'd survived in the open prison population until he was eventually moved to a segregated wing on Rule 43 with all the other sex offenders. His two-year sentence had given him plenty of time to think about the bastard police and their revelling at his expense and now he had this new bastard cop all over him – Detective Inspector Corrigan. Soon they would learn that it was he who held the power in this particular game – he who would lead them by the nose. And when the time was right it would be he who humiliated them all – all the bastard police, but especially Detective Inspector Sean Corrigan.

Sean swung into the new Inquiry Office at Scotland Yard shortly after eight a.m. and was immediately confronted by a scene of chaos as his team continued to unpack cardboard boxes and rearrange the furniture, crawling under desks to search for power-points and telephone sockets. Donnelly stood in the middle of the maelstrom, conducting affairs without offering to help, while Sally took refuge in her office, her head buried in reports. She gave a start when Sean rattled on the side of her open door.

'Bloody hell,' she told him, pressing her hand to the scars hidden under her white blouse, smiling as she spoke. 'You scared me.'

'Sorry,' he apologized, his eyes inadvertently falling on the hand covering her chest. 'I wasn't trying to sneak up on you.'

'I know,' she assured him, her hand slipping down to her lap. 'Can't hear anyone approaching above that din out there.'

Sean stepped inside her office and closed the door. 'Did you get the extension of detention OK?'

'Yeah, the local superintendent was most obliging. But it still only gives us a few hours before we either release him, charge him or try our luck with the magistrates to get a further extension.'

'Hopefully it won't come to that. We'll get back to Kentish as soon as we can and re-interview him – see if we can't put the frighteners on him a bit and get him to talk.'

'Any ideas how we're going to do that?'

'I don't know. Maybe tell him that the papers and TV are on to him – digging up his past. Let him know we can't protect him if he doesn't confess, that he'll have to take his chances out on the streets alone – with everybody knowing who he is and what he's accused of.'

'Bit below the belt.'

'We've got a missing boy, Sally, and a convicted sex-offender and residential burglar with a history of using lock-picking to gain entry. He's a more than viable suspect, which means I'm within my rights to tell the media his name – in an effort to trace his movements the night the boy went missing. If that puts him in danger at the hands of the public then there's not much I can do about it.'

'You seem to be forgetting we have a duty of care to look after anyone we know or suspect is in clear and immediate danger.'

'Care that we will offer and McKenzie will refuse.'

'It doesn't matter whether he accepts it or not – we have to provide it.'

A devilish grin spread across Sean's face. 'Which is exactly why Featherstone and the Assistant Commissioner will have to give me a surveillance team to follow McKenzie in the event we have to release him.'

'Oh, that's sneaky,' Sally told him with an appreciative grin of her own.

'Just want to make sure I've got all the bases covered. Now get next door and see if you can't bring some order to that rabble – we need an office meeting. I doubt half of them have a clue what's going on. I'll join you in a couple of minutes.'

Sally immediately bounced into the main office, shouting and cajoling the mess of detectives into something approaching order. Sean took a few deep breaths before following her, but was frozen by the photograph Sally had attached to the whiteboard in her office – the photograph of a smiling George Bridgeman dressed in his nursery school uniform – the type taken by a professional photographer visiting the school. He realized it was the first time he'd stopped to look at any pictures of the missing boy properly – his beauty and innocence he'd noticed the first time he saw a photograph of the child suddenly seemed even more striking. His thoughts travelled back to the boy's family, and

102

once again he found himself asking whether it was their very beauty that had attracted the monster in the first place. *Was McKenzie visually driven – irresistibly drawn by the physical beauty of the family?* Sally's voice brought him back to the here and now.

'Ready when you are,' she told him. Sean nodded and walked into the main office, all eyes immediately falling on him as the image of George Bridgeman continued to burn itself into his conscience.

'For those of you who spent all of yesterday back at Peckham, I understand you're probably not yet up to running speed on our new case.'

'Another MISPER, isn't it?' DC Tony Summers asked in his husky Manchester accent.

'It is,' Sean confirmed.

'Not again,' moaned DC Tony Summers whose size and thick blond hair had earned him the nickname Thor amongst his colleagues.

'The last case we had started as a MISPER,' Sean warned them, 'and we all know how that one ended. This time, for those of you who don't already know, the missing person is a four-year-old boy called George Bridgeman. We have limited time to find him before everyone's going to start assuming the worst and before the media are either informed or find out about it themselves. When that happens, we need to stay focused and separate from the inevitable circus – let Press Bureau do their job and we'll get on with ours. Understand?' His team nodded that they did. 'We've had night-duty teams searching the streets around the family house, but nothing so far. Now we've got daylight, further teams will continue the search and expand it on to Hampstead Heath. We'll be using dogs and India 99 will be searching from above if the weather stays fine. OK – updates. Dave, anything from Forensics yet?'

Donnelly remained seated, pausing to clear his throat before speaking. 'They worked through the night at the family home of the missing boy and have lifted multiple prints, including some shoe prints, and fibres. They've seized a few items the suspect may have touched to get to the boy and will be submitting them to the lab this morning for a DNA sweep, but there's been a ton of people through the house – not just the family, but their cleaner, nanny, the removal men, the estate agent and any one they showed around the house when they were trying to sell it. And no doubt there'll still be traces of the previous family all over the place too. Basically we're looking at dozens of sets of prints, and the same for DNA. Other than that – no traces of blood or signs of a break-in.'

'So we know our suspect entered, took the boy and left without leaving any obvious trace, other than possibly prints and/or DNA.'

Cahill winced. 'If the media get hold of that they're going to start making him into some sort of urban bogeyman.'

'They don't need the details of the break-in,' Sean assured her.

'What break-in?' Donnelly reminded him.

'You know what I mean,' Sean answered. 'Tell Forensics not to waste their time trying to compare the prints to the family, etc. Just get them all up to Fingerprints and have them run against sets already in their database. Maybe we'll strike lucky and get a hit against someone with previous convictions.'

'Fair enough,' Donnelly agreed, seeing the sense in Sean's suggestion.

'Which leads me to the suspect we already have in custody: Mark McKenzie, white, twenty-three years old, and he already has convictions for residential burglary and the sexual assault of a young child. He's known to have used lock-picks to enter houses at night in the past and he lives only a couple of miles from where the boy was taken.'

'Fuck me,' DC Jesson added in his Scouse accent. 'What are we waiting for? Let's just charge him now.'

'I agree,' Sean told the baying room, 'he's an outstanding suspect, but we need to investigate this properly and thoroughly. The boy's still missing and McKenzie isn't talking.'

'Doesn't sound like we need him to talk to prove he's guilty,' Jesson continued. 'We've probably got enough to do him on method alone.'

'Perhaps,' Sean told them, 'but I need him to talk if we're to find the boy quickly. So far he hasn't admitted taking the boy, but he hasn't denied it either.'

'What does that mean?' Cahill asked.

'Means he likes playing games,' Sean answered. 'Maybe this is his play at being famous. You can never tell with someone like McKenzie.'

'Or maybe it's not him at all?' Donnelly dropped a fly in the ointment, silencing the room.

'Got something you want to share?' Sean asked, barely hiding his irritation.

'Had an interesting chat with the Bridgemans' neighbours last night,' he explained. 'The Beiersdorfs at number five and Philippa Howells at number nine.'

'Go on,' Sean encouraged, trying to get Donnelly's sideshow over as quickly as he could.

'Both say the same thing: the Bridgemans have kept themselves to themselves since moving in and don't appear to want to socialize. Also, both sets of neighbours have heard plenty of raised voices coming from the Bridgemans' house. My pal Philippa told me it was Mr Bridgeman who seemed to do most of the shouting. She also noticed that although he rarely scolded his daughter, he seemed cold towards the boy.'

'But not Mrs Bridgeman?' Jesson asked.

'According to Philippa, she was fine towards the boy.'

'So there's something going on between the boy and the father?' Cahill joined in.

'The boy's only four,' Sean reminded them. 'I know as well as anyone that four-year-olds can be a pain in the backside, but you don't start hating your own children because of it.' DC Maggie O'Neil tentatively raised her arm. 'What is it, Maggie?'

'I was going to raise it in private with you, guv'nor, but seems the cat's out the bag.'

'Go on.'

'Last night, when I was with the family, I picked up on the hostility between George's parents. A lot of whispered conversations they certainly didn't want me to hear.'

'It's early days,' Sean warned them. 'It may turn out their marriage was on the slippery slope even before George was taken. You don't need me to remind you that families don't always stick together in adversity.'

'True,' Maggie agreed, 'but when I spoke to the nanny she said that Mrs Bridgeman was devastated by George's disappearance, but that Mr Bridgeman was just angry.'

'Did she say who with?' Sean asked, unable to so easily dismiss the Bridgemans as suspects in his own mind now, no matter how much he wanted McKenzie to be guilty.

'No,' Maggie answered. 'Just that he was angry.'

'Hidey-fucking-hi,' Donnelly interrupted. 'Let's get 'em in, both of them, Mr and Mrs.'

'We haven't got enough to arrest them yet,' Sean warned him off. 'So Mr Bridgeman's a bad-tempered bastard – so what?'

'Not arrest them,' Donnelly suggested. 'Get them in as primary witnesses, but interview them on tape separately under caution – shit them up a bit. Divide and conquer them before they pull together for self-preservation and concoct a pack of well-ordered lies.'

'Not yet,' Sean insisted. 'This isn't the time to go in like a bull in a china shop. If we do that and it turns out you're wrong, we'll be slaughtered. Let's not show them our hand just yet. Besides, we need to concentrate on McKenzie first. It won't look good if we're treating the parents as suspects while we're still interrogating McKenzie. Let's get him sorted first, one way or the other, then we can think about the Bridgemans.'

'By then it might be too late,' Donnelly told him.

'It might already be too late,' Sean countered, and regretted it. 'Listen, we have two very different but promising lines of inquiry. McKenzie remains our prime suspect until I say different. As for the Bridgemans, find out whatever you can, but do it subtly and without dragging them in for interview, understand?'

'Fair enough,' Donnelly agreed, taking what Sean said as a green light to go after the parents.

'Sally and I will be re-interviewing McKenzie again soon and will make a further decision after that, but for now do the jobs you're given – and for Christ's sake, try and get this bloody office sorted.'

Detective Chief Superintendent Featherstone was just about to devour a large cooked breakfast he'd carried down to his office from the canteen when his desk phone rang, drawing a string of obscenities from his still empty mouth. He answered the phone as he continued to watch his egg yolks solidify.

'Alan – Assistant Commissioner Addis here.' Featherstone's appetite faded quickly. 'I was wondering whether you had any updates for me on the Bridgeman case? I would have popped down and spoken to DI Corrigan myself, but I'm away from the Yard this morning promoting the new Safer Neighbourhoods Scheme in Lambeth, of all places.'

'I understand things are progressing well enough,' Featherstone tried to buy some time and space. 'No stone's being left unturned.'

'What about this suspect you told me about? He sounded very promising.'

'Somebody McKenzie,' Featherstone recalled. 'He's still in custody over at Kentish Town.'

'Has he been interviewed yet?'

'I'm not entirely sure, sir. I'll be getting an update this morning,' Featherstone answered, making it up as he went along.

'I need you closer to this, Alan,' Addis warned him. 'We can't afford any more bad press. We need the boy found as a matter of urgency. If he's already dead then we need someone charged with his murder without delay or we'll have a panic on our hands. A child murderer at large does not read well.'

'Then perhaps we should keep the press out of it for a while longer,' Featherstone tried to stall him, 'until we have a positive result lined up?'

'No, we can't afford to do that. If they get wind of it from another source before we inform them there'll be hell to pay and I'll never get them back on side. I've made my decision – arrange a press conference for this evening. It's time to get the media and public involved. I'll do the briefing myself. Let me know when you've sorted it out,' Addis ordered and hung up, leaving Featherstone holding an empty phone still pressed to his ear as he stared at his congealing breakfast.

Finally he hung up and pushed the plate as far away as he could across his desk, his already significant regrets at allowing himself to become involved with Assistant Commissioner Addis growing by the second.

* * *

108

'The time is approximately ten a.m.,' Sean announced for the tape, 'and this is a continuation of the first interview of Mark McKenzie who's being questioned regarding the disappearance of a four-year-old boy – George Bridgeman. Do you understand why you're here?' Sean asked.

'No comment.'

'I'm just trying to clarify that you understand why you're here, Mark.'

'I said no comment.'

'Fine. That's your right. Can you tell me where you were Monday night to Tuesday morning of this week?'

'No comment.'

'The boy having been taken from his home sometime during that time.'

'No comment.'

'If you have an alibi that can place you somewhere else then now's a good time to tell me and save a lot of people a lot of trouble and time – including yourself.'

'No comment,' McKenzie continued with a smirk, the involuntary tapping of his foot returning.

'Then you don't have an alibi,' Sean tried to bait him.

'That's not what my client said,' Jackson got involved. 'He merely declined to answer your question.'

'My apologies,' Sean told her. 'Speaking of declined, yesterday you declined to deny that you had taken the boy. I'll give you the chance to do so again, Mark. Are you telling me that you had nothing to do with the boy going missing? A simple yes or no will do.'

'No comment.'

'Tell me you had nothing to do with it, Mark, and you never know, I might even start to believe you.'

'You expect me to make your job easy for you,' McKenzie answered, unable to resist any longer. His hatred of the police drove him to torment Sean as the police had tormented him on so many occasions, knowing he was defenceless. He couldn't go running to the media with tales of torture and evidence-planting – as far as everyone else was concerned he was a sex-offender and had got what he deserved. Now it was his turn to be the tormentor 'You're the police, you're the detectives, yet you can't even find one missing boy?'

'We'll find him, don't worry about that,' Sean told him.

'Really?' McKenzie mocked. 'And how you going to do that?'

'As we speak there are specialist search teams combing North London with dogs and helicopters. How long d'you think it's going to be before we find him? And when we do, we'll find the evidence that will hang you.'

'Is that what you'd like to do to me, Inspector – hang me? Isn't that what they sing to people like me in prison – *Sex case. Sex case. Hang him. Hang him. Hang him*?'

'It doesn't have to be like that,' Sean changed tack. 'If you help us find the boy, if you tell us where he is, then I can help you.'

The smirk fell from McKenzie's face as he began to chew his bottom lip. 'It's too late anyway,' he told them, looking and sounding suddenly solemn. 'It's too late.'

'It's not,' Sean kept going, sensing a breakthrough. 'No matter what's happened, it's not too late. Tell us where the boy is, alive or otherwise, and we can talk about it – we can talk about anything you want.'

'No.' McKenzie immediately clammed up again. 'You can't prove anything. I'm saying nothing.'

'Damn it, Mark,' Sean continued, frustration beginning to show as he sensed McKenzie slipping away, 'how long d'you think it'll be before we can prove you were in the house? We've just sent dozens of fingerprints and forensic exhibits to Fingerprint Bureau and the lab – how long before we find out some of them belong to you? How long, Mark?'

McKenzie looked worried again – deeply worried. 'No. If you could prove anything you would have charged me by now or . . .'

'Or what?' Sean seized on McKenzie's hesitation. 'Or what, Mark?'

'Nothing,' he answered, leaning back in his chair, away from Sean.

'Listen,' Sean told him, 'pretty soon my Assistant Commissioner is going to go on television and tell the world that a young boy was snatched from his own bed while he slept. The reporters are going to ask him if we have any suspects and you know what he's going to tell them, Mark? He's going to tell them your name and he's going to show everyone a picture of you.'

'He can't do that,' McKenzie protested.

'Yes he can, Mark, because you're a credible suspect and we're well within our rights to ask the public for their help in tracing your movements during the last couple of days. For Christ's sake, a four-year-old boy is missing. We can do pretty much whatever we like to help find him. Your name and photograph, Mark, all over the TV and papers – the Internet. If you don't start talking, if you don't admit your involvement then, yes, you're right – I can't charge you. Which means I'll have to release you – back out there with all those people just waiting for you – all those angry people, Mark. What d'you think they'll want to do to you?'

'That's not entirely true, Mark,' his solicitor advised him. 'If the police believe you could be in danger then they have a duty of care.' McKenzie looked blank. 'They have to protect you – no matter what.'

'I don't want their protection,' McKenzie barked. 'I don't trust them. I'll take care of myself.'

111

'Mark,' Sally jumped in, 'George has been missing for almost thirty-six hours now. He's only four years old and therefore incapable of surviving for long on his own, especially with these freezing nights.'

'So?' McKenzie asked, his eyes narrow with suspicion.

'So, it won't be long before we have to assume he's no longer alive, whether we find a body or not,' Sally explained. 'When that happens, you'll no longer be a suspect for abduction, you'll be a suspect for the murder of a child. You'll be the most hated man in Britain, and not everybody will be as fussy about proof as we are.'

'Don't lie to me. I already am a murder suspect.'

'That's not true,' Sally argued.

'Yes it is,' McKenzie insisted. 'You think I killed the boy – I know you do. So why don't you just charge me with murder? Do it!' He banged his fist on the table. 'I want you to, so just do it.'

'Admit to it and we will charge you,' Sean told him.

'So long as you can convince us you're telling the truth,' Sally qualified.

'I'm not going to admit to anything,' McKenzie told them, his face tight with desperation. 'I'm not going to help you. If you're so sure I'm guilty, then charge me and we'll see each other in court. And when the boy's body is found it won't be me the media comes after – they'll soon forget about me. It'll be you they hunt down.'

'I don't think so,' Sean replied.

'Then charge me and let's find out.'

'I'll decide when to charge you, and then I will see you in court and you will be found guilty and you will go to prison – for the rest of your life,' Sean warned him.

'Then do it,' McKenzie challenged him, his voice raised as he smiled through gritted teeth. 'Do it and let's get this over with.'

'No,' Sean told him, stretching to turn off the tape recorder. 'This interview is terminated.'

'You can't do that,' McKenzie insisted.

'Then tell me what happened,' Sean demanded.

'No,' McKenzie answered, slumping in his chair. 'No. I won't tell you anything.'

'In that case, this interview is over,' Sean told him and pressed the off button with a loud click.

'What now?' the solicitor asked.

'No doubt you'll want a further consultation with your client, and we also need some time to consider what action we'll be taking.'

'Don't take too long, Inspector,' Jackson warned. 'You're running out of detention time and I don't see any further lines of inquiry that could justify an application at the Magistrates Court for a further extension.'

'You'll find magistrates can be very obliging when it concerns a missing child,' Sally told her. 'We'll keep you informed.'

Both she and Sean left the interview room and closed the door behind them, walking a few steps away from it before feeling safe to talk.

'Well?' Sally asked. 'What now?'

'We stick to the plan,' Sean answered. 'Once he's released, he'll be in danger from the public, therefore we have a duty to protect him.'

'You mean follow him?'

Sean shrugged innocently. 'All I know is this means Featherstone and Addis have to give us a surveillance team – R versus Brindle – remember? And whilst they're looking after him they might as well report his movements to me. Nothing wrong with killing two birds with one stone.'

'You'll be popular with the brass.'

'Fuck 'em. We don't have enough to charge him so we have to let him go, and if we have to let him go I want him

113

followed. Who knows – he may panic and lead us straight to George Bridgeman.'

'Or he may go to ground and stay there?' Sally suggested.

'He could.'

'Then perhaps we should keep him in custody a while longer and see what Forensics and Fingerprints come up with? The magistrates will give us an extension – what choice do they have?'

'No,' Sean insisted. 'He's too confident he's left nothing. Besides, if we get a match we'll just re-arrest him. With a surveillance team up his arse at least we'll know where he is if we need to bring him back in. I'll call Featherstone and as soon as we have the surveillance scrambled we'll bail him straight into their hands.'

'He's going to suspect he's being followed,' Sally pointed out.

'No matter,' Sean argued. 'It might make him nervous, then he'll be all the more likely to make a mistake. We'll brief the surveillance team to make it look like he's lost them if he starts giving them the run-around and then we'll find out what he doesn't want us to see.'

'If you say so,' Sally reluctantly agreed.

'Good,' Sean told her.

'So long as you still think he's our man.'

'He has to be.'

'Then why was he so desperate for us to charge him?'

'I don't know,' Sean admitted. 'Maybe he wants the notoriety?'

'So why not admit it?'

'Because he's not ready to burn all his bridges yet . . . who knows with his type? Ian Brady still won't tell anyone where some of his victims are buried. Maybe McKenzie needs to feel he has sole possession of George.'

'Weird and disturbing,' Sally told him.

'A troubled soul,' Sean said, more to himself than Sally.

'Another one?' He didn't answer the question.

'Do me a favour and hang around here until I get the surveillance sorted out. When it's done, we'll get back to the Yard.'

'No problem.'

'Don't worry about McKenzie. He can play his fucked-up games as long as he wants, but he'll screw up soon enough. Like I say: they always do.'

Mrs Bridgeman led Donnelly along the corridor and into the kitchen of her house in Hampstead. He hadn't told her he was coming. 'I was expecting DC O'Neil,' she told him. 'No one else – not unless . . .'

'DC O'Neil will be along very shortly,' he explained, 'but I thought I should call round and make sure you're settling back in OK after your night away.'

Celia Bridgeman looked exhausted and soulless. 'You haven't found him though, have you?'

'No,' Donnelly answered, 'but we will.' An awkward silence filled the room.

'Would you like a drink or anything?' Mrs Bridgeman managed to ask.

'Aye,' Donnelly replied cheerfully, 'cuppa tea would be grand.'

She looked at the nanny and lifted her chin. The nanny filled the kettle and started preparing the mugs.

'How do you like it?' Caroline asked.

'Builders' tea for me, please – plenty milk and two sugars.' Caroline returned his smile while Mrs Bridgeman remained lost in her own painful thoughts, almost oblivious to their presence. 'Actually,' Donnelly continued, 'I need to check something for the forensic boys in George's bedroom – perhaps, Caroline, you could show me the way?'

She looked a little cautious for a second before realizing she'd been given a gilt-edged chance to escape from Mrs Bridgeman's despair, even if it was just for a few minutes. 'Will that be all right, Mrs Bridgeman?' she asked.

'What?' Mrs Bridgeman replied. 'I'm sorry, I didn't hear what you said.'

'Will it be all right if I show the detective George's room?'

Donnelly saw her shrink at the mere mention of her son's name, the horror and terror of what she must have been going through not lost on him, despite his outward appearance.

'Yes. Yes. Of course,' she answered, before returning to staring at the floor.

'This way,' Caroline told Donnelly, leading the way out of the kitchen and to the staircase.

Donnelly followed close behind her as he observed the interior structure of the house, which mirrored those on either side. He waited till they'd cleared the first flight of stairs before speaking again.

'Sophia not at home today?' he asked.

'No,' Caroline answered. 'I was happy to look after her, but Mr Bridgeman thought it best if she returned to school and got back into her normal routine as soon as possible. "Normalize things," he said. I don't know – he might be right, I suppose.'

'And Mr Bridgeman?'

'Went back to work, although he said he won't be late.'

'To *normalize* things?'

Caroline stopped for a second and looked over her shoulder at Donnelly, who was two stairs lower. 'You'd have to ask Mr Bridgeman about that.'

They carried on walking until they reached George's room, Caroline standing aside to allow him to enter, seemingly reluctant to go inside herself. 'I'll leave you to it then,' she told him and made to leave.

'Actually . . .' he raised a hand to stop her. 'I did have a couple of questions I thought you could help me with. I'd ask Mrs Bridgeman, but frankly she doesn't look capable of answering them just yet.'

'Questions about what?'

'Questions that could help us find George. That's what we all want – isn't it?'

'Of course.'

'Good. How long have you worked as the Bridgemans' nanny?'

'A couple of years now. What's this got to do with George? I thought your questions were going to be meant for Mrs Bridgeman?'

'They would have been,' he told her.

'Then you're checking on me?'

'Caroline,' Donnelly admitted, 'we're going to check on everyone. Don't take it personally.'

'Hard not to.'

'Do your best. Now, did the Bridgemans find you through an agency?'

'Yes, the Help 4 Mums Agency. They cover Hampstead, Highgate, Primrose Hill – a few more areas.'

'All the rough areas, eh?' Donnelly joked, trying to get her to relax her guard. Caroline said and did nothing. 'But Sophia is six and George is four. Did Mrs Bridgeman cope on her own before you, or was there another nanny?'

'Mrs Bridgeman?' Caroline laughed sarcastically. 'Cope on her own with two kids? I don't think so – cramp her style a little too much, don't you think? The likes of Mrs Bridgeman weren't brought up to look after children.'

'So she had help before you started here?'

'Yes, another nanny from the same agency – a friend of mine, actually.'

'And who would that be?'

'Tessa – Tessa Daniels.'

'How long did she work for the Bridgemans?'

'She started a few weeks before Sophia was born and stayed on until George was about two.'

'Which is when you started?'

'Yes.'

'Were there problems between Mrs Bridgeman and Tessa?'

'No. None that I know of.'

'Then why change her?'

'That's what these people do.'

'Why?' Donnelly asked, genuinely confused.

'To stop you getting over-familiar with the children, or sometimes the husband. The likes of Mrs Bridgeman won't tolerate competition – real or imagined. Anyway, like I said, they all do it.'

'And was she?' Donnelly asked, sniffing a route in.

'Was who what?' Caroline frowned, impatient.

'Was Tessa getting over-familiar with the children – with Mr Bridgeman?'

'No,' she told him. 'Tessa knew better than to get mixed up in anything like that, and Mr Bridgeman's hardly the sleeping-with-the-nanny type.'

'There's a type?'

'Yes, and he's not it.'

Donnelly reluctantly gave up the line of questioning. 'But there seems to be a lot of tension between them, don't you think? Perhaps it's just the situation.'

'No,' Caroline let her guard slip, 'that was there even before poor little George went missing.'

'But there's no suggestion Mr Bridgeman was having an affair with anyone?'

'No,' Caroline answered less confidentially, as if Donnelly was wrong, but getting closer to the truth. Donnelly seized on it immediately.

'So Mr Bridgeman wasn't playing away from home, but what about . . . what about Mrs Bridgeman?'

'All I know is that, since I've been here, Mrs Bridgeman hasn't been seeing anyone else,' she told him, holding both hands out towards him, palms turned upwards.

'How do you know?'

'Trust me,' she told him, 'I'd know.'

'Aye,' Donnelly agreed. 'I'm sure you would. But then why all the hostility between them, and why the coldness towards George from Mr Bridgeman?'

'Listen,' she whispered conspiratorially, 'you didn't hear this from me, and if anyone finds out I told you I'll lose my job – but if it helps find George then I suppose you need to know.'

'Need to know what?' he asked, managing to hide his rising excitement.

'Tessa told me that while she was working for the Bridgemans there was a suspicion that Mrs Bridgeman was seeing another man. Apparently Mr Bridgeman found out about it and they've never been the same towards each other since.'

'If it spoiled things between them so irreversibly then why didn't they get divorced?'

'I don't know – you'd have to ask them that. Maybe they did it for the children – maybe they did it for appearances' sake. These people aren't like the rest of us.'

'So when was this supposed affair?'

'Before George was born,' she answered, but something in her demeanour told Donnelly she wanted him to ask her more.

'How long before?'

'Shall we say about . . . nine months.'

Donnelly paused to take in the implication. 'I see,' he eventually told her. 'That can't have been easy for Mr Bridgeman – these last few years?'

'No,' she agreed. 'I don't suppose it has.'

'I think I need to speak with Mrs Bridgeman,' he told her. 'Alone.'

'You won't tell her I said anything, will you?' Caroline pleaded.

'You can be sure of my confidentiality . . .' Donnelly put on his most reassuring tone, inwardly adding the proviso, . . . *until we use the information to bury the Bridgemans, that is*. 'I'll be very discreet. Best you stay out of the way until I've had a chance to speak with her.'

'Fine,' she agreed, already regretting letting Donnelly into the dark little family secret.

'And thanks for your help,' he added as he squeezed past her and headed back down to the kitchen where Mrs Bridgeman stood in the same spot he'd left her, still staring at the floor, lost in her own excruciating nightmare.

'How you doing?' Donnelly asked, to get her attention more than out of genuine concern.

She looked up slowly, staring at him in a state of confusion, as if she could hear him, but not see him. After a few seconds she shook her head quickly and answered. 'I'm fine.'

'I doubt you're that,' he told her.

'I meant under the circumstances.'

'Of course. Would you like to sit down?'

'No. I'd rather stand.'

'Can I fix you a cup of tea or anything?'

'No,' she snapped, then added in a softer tone, 'I said I'm fine.'

'No problem,' he backed up before beginning to lay his groundwork. 'Kids – little sods, eh? Drive you mad when you're with them, then you miss them like hell when they're not around.' She didn't respond. 'I've got five, myself.' She looked up, an almost puzzled expression on

120

her face. 'Ten-year-old twins,' he told her, 'a couple of teenagers and a wee nipper who's only four.'

'That's a lot of children,' she finally joined in.

'Aye. A real handful. The wife's a saint though – keeps them all on the straight and narrow and somehow juggles the accounts to keep the bills paid, or at least most of them.'

'Can't be easy.'

'You mean on a cop's wage?'

'That's not what I meant. I just meant with five of them.'

'It's OK – you're right – it is bloody difficult on a cop's wage, but the overtime helps. No such worries for you though, eh?' he asked, looking around the state-of-the-art kitchen his wife could only dream about.'

'Money isn't everything,' she said as she watched him.

'Oh, I agree. In fact I'm always telling the wife the exact same thing: money isn't everything. The most important thing is to stick together when times are tough – just like you and your husband are now.' She momentarily glared at him, just as he'd wanted her to, her eyes answering questions her lips would never respond to. 'Although in situations as stressful as this, sometimes the parents can take out their frustrations on each other – it's neither unusual nor unreasonable. My advice would be, don't be too hard on yourselves if you have the odd cross word.'

'Thank you,' she told him, her eyes still burning with mistrust.

'Still, I'm a wee bit surprised he's gone to work today. Would he not rather be here with you – in case we find something?'

'He had to go to work. He had no choice.'

'There's always a choice,' Donnelly gently tried to provoke her into saying more. 'Still, if you want a house like this, in a bit of London like this, private school, nanny, top-of-the-range kitchen then I suppose work has to come first, eh?'

'Appearances can be deceptive,' she couldn't help telling him, regretting it as soon as she had.

'Indeed they can.' He bided his time. 'Are you sure I can't make you that cup of tea?'

'I'm fine, thank you.'

'Not much a cup of tea can't fix.'

'Will it help find George?' she demanded.

'No, Mrs Bridgeman, alas it can't do that.'

'Then perhaps you'd have a better chance of finding him if you were elsewhere?'

'Everything's covered,' he assured her, pretending to misunderstand the inference. 'We've got every man, woman and dog looking for him. Right now I'll best serve George by being here – with you.'

'How so?'

'Oh, you know – the more we chat the more I may discover.'

'How can talking about me help you find George?'

'Not just about you, but about George as well . . . and your husband. You may remember some little thing that could turn out to be important.'

'Such as?'

'Something from your past, maybe? Something you haven't told us yet. Something you may have forgotten.'

'Like what?' she asked, folding her arms across her chest.

'Like, are either of your children from another marriage, either yours or your husband's?'

'No.'

'If not a marriage – perhaps a previous relationship?'

'No. This is ridiculous.'

'Then perhaps an affair?'

She smiled in disbelief and looked through the ceiling at

122

the nanny who remained two floors above them. 'Has someone been talking out of school, Sergeant?'

'Call it my detective's instinct,' he lied.

'And what does your instinct tell you?'

'Oh, I don't know – that George is your son, but not Mr Bridgeman's.'

'Well then your instinct would be wrong.'

'And your husband's instinct – is that wrong too?'

'I don't know what you mean.'

'Has he ever asked for a paternity test?'

'No. He'd never do that.'

'But you thought that he might – one day?'

'He'd never do that – he's too proud.' Too late she realized she'd said too much.

'So he has his doubts about George being his son?'

'You'd have to ask him about that. But I can assure you George is *our* son, and right now all I want is to get him back. Can't you understand that?' Tears exploded from her eyes and ran heavy and fast down her cheeks, dripping off her. 'I just want my son back. Please, help me find my son.'

Donnelly moved forward, quickly and nimbly taking hold of her by her shoulders, sure she could take no more cross-examining for now. 'Don't worry,' he comforted her, switching from interrogator to Samaritan. 'We'll get your boy back or we'll die trying. You can be sure of that.'

Featherstone drove through heavy south-east London traffic heading towards Bexley Police Station where another one of the Murder Investigation Teams he oversaw had picked up a new case – a straightforward enough domestic murder, no kids involved. By all accounts the husband wasn't denying caving his wife's head in with a claw hammer and the detective inspector leading the investigation expected to have him charged with her murder by dinnertime. Featherstone was as pleased about the impending quick and tidy result as he was about the fact both victim and suspect were white. Since the Stephen Lawrence Inquiry, whenever a detective superintendent heard of a new murder on their patch the first question was always, *What's the colour of the victim?* If they were black the next would always be, *What's the colour of the suspects?* Many a superintendent had sighed with relief when the answer had confirmed the crime had no possible racial overtones.

The ringing of his hands-free system snapped him out of his happy little world. Caller ID told him it was Sean.

'Sean – got some good news for me?' he asked.

'Still working on it.'

'Then what you after?'

'I haven't got enough to charge McKenzie – our prime suspect.'

'So let him go.'

'I intend to, but I'm still convinced he could be our man. When the ACC does his press briefing I need him to name McKenzie and show a photograph of him, asking the public to help trace his movements over the last couple of days.'

'Bloody hell, Sean. Why don't we just take him to London Zoo and chuck him to the lions?'

'He'll survive, but we'll need a surveillance team on him just in case – for his own protection, as required by R versus Brindle.'

'Hold on a minute . . .' Featherstone smiled to himself. 'If I didn't know better, I'd say this situation had been manufactured.'

'Maybe, but can you sell it to the Assistant Commissioner?'

'I'll sell it,' Featherstone confidently told him. 'He's doing the press briefing this evening. I'll make sure he has the stuff about McKenzie.'

'This evening?' Sean asked, concerned Addis was moving too quickly without checking with him first. 'He's not hanging around.'

'You'll find Assistant Commissioner Addis is not a patient man,' Featherstone warned him. 'He's doing his briefing this evening, but I can tell you now he wants to be back on Sky News within twenty-four hours with something *positive* to tell them. There's a student union march through the West End next week and TSG are bound to kick someone's head in, so the powers that be are desperate for a good news story before the inevitable happens.'

'I can't promise anything,' Sean answered, 'but with a surveillance team on McKenzie my chances will be better.'

'I understand, but Addis won't. I'll get you the surveillance team anyway.'

'Thanks,' Sean prepared to sign off. 'You never know – one day the brass at the Yard might realize it doesn't matter what we do – the media's always gonna beat us with whatever stick's available. Why fight a war you can't win? Wasting everybody's time.'

'They're an optimistic bunch, the powers that be. For them, there's no such thing as a lost cause.'

'Call that optimism?' Sean asked bitterly. 'More like blind ignorance.'

'Ours is not to wonder why . . .' Featherstone reminded him. 'You'll have your surveillance team within a couple of hours. Where d'you want them?'

'Kentish Town nick – they can pick McKenzie up when we bail him.'

'Will he be looking for them?'

'Probably.'

'I'll call you once it's sorted,' Featherstone told Sean and hung up. 'R v Brindle my arse,' he said aloud. *You're a sly one, Corrigan, I'll give you that, but so is that snake-in-the-grass*

Addis. If we don't get this one solved soon, he'll have us both skinned and stuffed as a warning to others.

George Bridgeman sat on the floor of the room that had seemed strange and unfamiliar not so very long ago, but was now already beginning to feel like his home from home. He played with the toys that had been left in the room, presumably for him; strange toys that he wasn't used to – not like the toys he had at home. At first, in his confusion he had pushed them to one side, but gradually they had begun to intrigue him, and unlike most of the toys he had at home he didn't grow tired of them within a few minutes. As he played, his thoughts drifted from his home and family – at least for a time, but soon the rumbling of his empty stomach reminded him he hadn't been fed yet today. All he'd had was a beaker of water from the night before to relieve his dry mouth and quell the emptiness in his belly for a little while. It was the first time in his young life that he'd ever felt real hunger or thirst.

As his blood sugar dropped to an uncomfortable level his concentration waned and he pushed the wooden puzzle he'd been working on to one side and thought about his family, how much he missed his mother, her soft, comforting words and the embrace that instantly made any situation better – any pain only fleeting. He thought of his sister, who teased him nearly all the time, but who could also be so kind and caring towards him, particularly when their parents weren't watching – sharing her sweets with him and letting him join in her games. Anyone who was mean to him while she was about had better watch out.

And then there was his father, who none of them seemed to see much of, but especially him. He often tried to think of what he might have done that made Daddy so cross with him, but he just couldn't think of anything – at least nothing he thought was terribly naughty. Every time Daddy shouted at him, his mummy would always tell him not to worry and say he'd done nothing wrong, although she'd always wait until Daddy had gone first. Sometimes he was so scared of making Daddy angry that he hardly dared move for fear of spilling a drink or dropping something on the floor. Yet when his sister did the same, Daddy said nothing. He always tried to be a good boy.

Sudden noises from the other side of the door pulled him away from his thoughts – more voices like the ones he'd heard before, of men and women talking. And children's voices too, both excited and upset. But they only ever lasted a few minutes at most before they fell away, the sound of a door closing punctuating the silence that followed, until the next time the voices came. While most of the voices constantly seemed to change, as muffled as they were, there was always one voice that remained – monotone and constant – a man's voice that he was sure he recognized.

Sean and Sally walked along the ground-floor corridor at Scotland Yard passing rank-less people in suits and the occasional uniformed senior officer with shoulders covered in what all other cops referred to as scrambled egg. Sean couldn't help but wonder where they were heading and what they did, but was wholly unable to think of anything that they could be doing that could possibly be of use to him, with the exception of fronting the occasional press conference or giving the necessary level of authority to covert operations. Other than that he did his job in spite of them, not because of them. He answered his ringing, vibrating phone without breaking stride.

'DI Corrigan.'

'Guv'nor, it's DS Handy here.'

'Colin,' Sean knew the DS, who ran one of the Central Surveillance Teams. 'By virtue of the fact we're speaking to each other, I'm assuming you got the McKenzie follow?'

'We did indeed. I heard you were involved and thought it'd make a change from following suspected terrorists around Ealing all week.'

'I can imagine. Where are you now?'

'All plotted up outside Kentish Town nick, waiting for your man to show.'

'I'll let the custody sergeant there know to bail him. He should be out a few minutes after that. Did Featherstone get you a picture of my man?'

'I'm looking at it as we speak.'

'Good. Let me know if anything happens. Happy hunting.'

'Thanks,' Handy answered and hung up just as the lift arrived to carry Sean and Sally to the seventh floor.

'Everything all right?' Sally asked as the doors slid shut on them.

'Yeah, fine. Surveillance is up and running.'

'That's something, I suppose.'

Her response drew a displeased look from Sean, who was about to challenge her when the lift jerked to a stop and the doors hissed open, allowing two mid-ranked uniforms to step inside. By the time they reached the seventh floor and stepped from the lift he'd forgotten what she'd said and was back on his mobile.

'Custody Suite, Kentish Town,' announced the curt voice on the other end.

'DI Corrigan speaking, Special Investigations Unit. You have someone in custody for me I need bailing – a Mark McKenzie.'

'Yeah, I know the one,' the voice answered. 'What's the reason for bailing him, and when and where d'you want him bailed to?'

'For further inquiries,' Sean told the voice. 'You can bail him back to Kentish Town a month from today. Anything else?'

'No,' the voice assured him. 'That'll be done, no problem. Have a nice day.'

The line went dead just as he and Sally entered their new main office. They walked straight through the mayhem and into the side office Sally shared with Donnelly, who was at his desk talking to Zukov. Sally's narrow-eyed stare lifted Zukov to his feet behind her desk. Donnelly nodded towards the open door and Zukov took the hint.

'I'll leave you to it then,' he told them as he squeezed past Sally in the doorway and melted into the main office beyond the Perspex.

'Just back from Kentish Town?' Donnelly asked.

'Yeah,' Sean answered.

'Just back from Hampstead myself. Been having an interesting little chat with Caroline, the nanny, not to mention Mrs Bridgeman.'

'Really?' Sean asked, his tone making him sound less interested than he was. 'And what did they have to say for themselves?'

'Which one?'

'Why don't we start with the nanny?'

'Aye, Caroline Reiss. She was most helpful. Let me into a little family secret.'

'Which is . . .?' Sean asked impatiently.

'Which is that rumour has it in the dim and distant past Mrs Bridgeman had an affair. The previous nanny who worked for them at the time happens to be pals with Caroline, which is how she found out.'

'How is any of this relevant to George being taken?' Sally asked. 'Mrs Bridgeman had an affair – big deal – they seem to have survived it.'

'Ah, but you haven't heard the best bit yet,' Donnelly teased them.

'Which is?' Sean asked again.

'The affair apparently occurred about nine months before wee George was born,' Donnelly told them casually.

'Ooops,' Sally finally said to break the silence. 'That changes things.'

'Who did she have the affair with?' Sean asked.

'I don't know,' Donnelly replied.

'How come?'

'Because I didn't ask.'

'Why the hell not?'

'Because she'd had enough.'

'Fuck's sake, Dave,' Sean continued, 'when did you get all sentimental? Her kid's missing and if there's an estranged father in the picture we need to know who the fuck he is.'

'Slow down, guv'nor. She hasn't actually admitted to having an affair yet, and she's adamant wee George is her husband's child.'

'Which means nothing,' Sean reminded him.

'I know,' Donnelly agreed, 'but let's give her a day or so to think about what all this could mean, then I'll take another crack at her.'

'We don't have that sort of time,' Sean insisted.

'This could also mean Mr Bridgeman might be involved in George's disappearance,' Sally interrupted. 'From what we've heard so far, he's pretty cold towards the boy.'

'Aye,' Donnelly agreed, 'and the nanny told me pretty much the same as she told Maggie: he's always been almost resentful of the boy. Maybe now we know why.'

'So what are we saying?' Sean asked. 'That we may have a long-lost lover who could have taken the boy, or an embittered husband who may have killed the boy and got rid of the body?'

Sally shrugged her shoulders, leaving Donnelly to answer. 'That's about the size of it.'

'OK, fine.' Sean accepted the possibilities. 'Keep digging and see what you can find. If Mr Bridgeman took the body away to get rid of it then he probably used his own car, or his wife's. Have the cars seized and hand them over to Forensics. Make up some bullshit to get them to volunteer handing them over, but if they give you any shit, arrest Mr Bridgeman and seize them anyway. I'd rather you didn't nick him, but if you have to . . . I'll get Featherstone to expand the search teams out to a three-mile radius from the home. I don't want a single abandoned building left unsearched. I don't care if it's a warehouse or a shed. I'll get Addis to authorize roadblocks and we need to spread the door-to-door further afield. The media appeal Addis is doing later today should make people aware of what we're up to, so people might start talking to us.'

'Does this mean we're concentrating everything on this being somehow linked to Mr Bridgeman or a blast from the past coming back to haunt Mrs Bridgeman?' Donnelly asked.

'No,' Sean answered. 'We still have McKenzie.'

'Who we've got nothing on,' Donnelly argued.

'Not entirely true,' Sean told him. 'His modus operandi for previous offences is so close to this one that we could almost charge him on method alone. If I just had a bit more—'

'But we don't,' Donnelly stopped him. 'We don't have enough to charge him on method alone, so what do we have?'

'He just feels right,' Sean tried to explain.

'Meaning?'

'Meaning he reminds me of someone from the past who also liked to play dangerous games.' John Conway's face drifted through his mind like a ghost.

'Oh aye, and who would that be?' Donnelly asked.

'No one you know. He was the leader of a paedophile ring I investigated once.'

'And McKenzie reminds you of this guy?' Donnelly continued.

'Kind of.'

'Can you be a bit more specific?' Donnelly pushed.

'No,' Sean admitted. 'I wish I could, but for some reason the penny's not dropping. Mckenzie's motivation – I don't know – I can feel it, but I just can't tie it down.'

'There's no need to complicate this with paedophile witch-hunts,' Donnelly insisted. 'The chances that the boy was snatched in the night by some bogeyman paedophile are a million to one – a million to one,' he repeated for emphasis. 'As we all sadly know, the vast majority of child murders are committed by a member of the child's family. Paedophiles who murder are a very rare breed – you know that. Let's get on with what's more likely and concentrate on the family.'

'Paedophile murderers may be uncommon, but no one's saying the boy's been murdered,' Sean argued.

'Why else would anyone take him?'

'That's what I'm trying to work out.'

'Boss, I reckon you're wasting your time,' Donnelly told him, his voice resigned to Sean's will.

'Maybe I am, but we stay on McKenzie until he's either charged or eliminated from the investigation. You keep the pressure up on the family, but try not to be too obvious. And find the previous nanny, see if she can't give you the name of Mrs Bridgeman's supposed ex-lover. If she can't, try and persuade Mrs Bridgeman to spill the beans. Mr Bridgeman works in the City, right?'

'Aye,' Donnelly answered.

'Then get his car number plate over to them and have them run it on their VRM Recognition System. Let's see if he's been coming and going from work as he should've been. Meantime I'll keep digging on McKenzie – see what I can't turn up. Have Zukov drop the door-to-door proformas in my office ASAP. Maybe a neighbour's seen someone matching his description in the area prior to the boy being taken.'

'Fair enough,' Donnelly surrendered.

'I'll be in my office if anyone needs me,' Sean told them and walked out the door, around the aluminium stand-post and into his own goldfish-bowl of an office where he pulled out his tatty chair and slumped heavily into it, immediately standing again to empty his uncomfortably full pockets. As he tossed his phone on to the desk it began to ring. He grabbed it and sat in the same movement, examining the caller ID. It was Kate. He puffed out his cheeks and tried to force his thumb to accept the call, but it wouldn't move, until finally the ringing stopped and his wife was gone. He grabbed the nearest pile of reports he could find and pulled them across the desk, picked up the first one and began to read.

He could feel the hateful eyes burning into his back as he stood in front of the custody sergeant who never once looked him in the face as he prepared his bail forms. But it wasn't just police eyes that poured their scorn upon his soul – it was the eyes of the other prisoners too. Not only did his ill-fitting, desperately old and unfashionable clothes mark him out as someone who'd had his own clothes seized for forensic examination, but the cell-to-cell grapevine had been working constantly during the night, ensuring that by morning all the burglars, drug dealers and muggers knew there was a sex-case in the cells. Not just a sex-case, but a paedophile too. If they could reach him they'd beat him to death and he knew it. But standing in front of the custody sergeant waiting for his bail notice he didn't fear them – he felt strong and powerful, in control for the first time in a long while. The police wouldn't dare let anything happen to him – not while the boy was still missing. If they found the boy then things would be very different, but until that time he held all the cards. He just needed to work out how to best play his hand – to his advantage and to Corrigan's maximum humiliation.

DI Corrigan, the personification of everything the police meant to him: snarling, arrogant and self-obsessed, convinced of their own superiority and righteousness, like they were some sort of super-humans preordained to rule over everybody else. They destroyed lives like his without a second thought or moment of compassion, then headed to the pub for a celebratory drink as he was led away to prison hell, never once trying to understand him or truly discover why he had to do what he did. No matter what they thought, they were no better than the vile, tattooed thugs who waited for him in prison – career criminals who heaped misery on people, but who for some reason considered themselves his master. Soon he'd have his revenge on the police – leading Corrigan like a pig to the slaughter. But it would all be for nothing if they found the boy first.

'This is yours,' the custody sergeant told him, handing him a copy of the bail notice and jolting him out of his dreaming. 'Be back here in a month's time or you'll be liable to arrest, do you understand?' McKenzie nodded that he did. 'Don't fucking nod your head at me,' the sergeant snapped. 'Answer the question properly.'

'I understand,' McKenzie answered calmly, thoughts of revenge keeping him strong and confident. He took the bail notice from him. 'Time for me to leave, I think. Mustn't keep your colleagues waiting.'

'I've no fucking idea what you're talking about,' the sergeant answered truthfully.

'No,' McKenzie told him as he neatly folded his bail papers and slipped them in his pocket. 'I don't suppose you do.'

Sean's eyes and shoulders ached in equal measure as he piled the latest of dozens of reports he'd read on to the growing mountain marked *complete* and leaned back in his chair, stretching his arms above his head and yawning widely before allowing them to fall heavily back on to his desk. None of the reports had contained anything of even the slightest interest – no potential witness saying they could have seen someone matching McKenzie's description in the relevant location at the material time; no grainy snap shot from the tube station's CCTV that could be him; no stop-and-search forms filled out by a local uniform cop that could be him. Nothing. Sean rubbed his already closed eyes, the image of McKenzie immediately filling the blackness, before melting into the face of someone else – John Conway, the ghost from Sean's past – before that too warped and shifted until it became the face of his own father, causing him to snap his eyes open as if a loud noise had disturbed him while he slept.

The image left him feeling numb for a while, until he was able to force his mind to move on, to think solely of George Bridgeman and what could have happened to him. 'Where are you George?' he asked the room. 'What the fuck's happened to you? Who took you from your bedroom while you slept, feeling safe and warm?' But the questions had no answers – no snapshots of the man he hunted flashed in his mind. For almost the first time in his entire career he sensed nothing. 'Come on, George,' he pleaded, 'help me help you. Help me find you.' But still nothing.

His mind was so cluttered with everyday concerns and chores he was beginning to feel like an everyday, average cop relying on nothing more than tangible evidence, gathered by methods that had been tried and tested for over a hundred years combined with the advances in forensic science. But he'd relied on his vivid imagination and insights for so long he now felt lost and impotent without them. The fear of no longer being able to think like his quarry, to stay one step ahead of them and the other cops overpowered the fear he had of seeing his father in his mind's eye. He forced his eyes to close and breathed in slowly and deeply, over and over, until he could feel his body begin to relax, the stresses and strains of moving office, of having Addis looming over him, the fight with Kate, all slipping away into the abyss as he concentrated solely on little George. The boy's face took shape behind his closed eyelids, burning into Sean's mind, the face becoming the child's entire body, curled under his duvet as he peacefully slept – the picture of the sleeping boy growing smaller, disappearing into the distance as his imaginings left the room, always looking back where he'd come from, through the doorway and along the corridor, down the stairs, past the mother's room and then more stairs, passing through the closed front door like a ghost where he immediately saw the figure again, still crouching, working away at the locks.

He hardly dared breathe as the picture grew clearer in his mind: the calm, unhurried image of the man jiggling the tools that penetrated the middle lock until it finally clicked open, the man carefully packing his fine tools away before standing and easing the door open, stepping inside from the bitter cold to the warm, inviting scent of the house. 'How did it feel,' Sean asked the faceless man in his mind, 'entering the house of the family in the middle of the night? Did you go straight to the boy, or did you stand for a while, breathing them in, becoming whatever it is you dream of becoming?' He superimposed the face of McKenzie on to the face of the man now moving towards the stairs and liked the fit. 'Is this how it felt in those early days – those special early days when you first started breaking into other people's homes? Did it feel so good because they gave you something you'd never had? And what was that – was it love and acceptance? Had your own family rejected you? Were your tastes too much for them to stomach? So they threw you out, but here, in the houses of others you were finally part of a family again, even if they didn't know you were there.'

The more he thought, the more he imagined, the more McKenzie's face fitted the man he watched slowly climbing the stairs in the Bridgemans' house. 'But taking trophies isn't enough any more, is it? You need more.' Sean opened his eyes, the seeds of an idea floating in his mind like so many pieces of a broken mirror until they all came together to form an answer that was another question. 'You took things belonging to the children, didn't you? Before you started taking things to sell, you just took things belonging to the children. Only we never found out. Or we did, but we missed the relevance – we didn't understand its importance. And now that's not enough. Now the only trophy that helps you relive your fantasies is the children themselves, isn't it? The children are your trophies. Only . . .'

The phone ringing on his desk crushed his hypnotic concentration, an iron curtain crashing down in his mind, derailing his train of thought at the most critical time. 'Fuck it,' he shouted, loud enough to be heard in the adjoining main office. He snatched the phone, furious at yet another pointless interruption. 'What the hell is it now?' he almost screamed into the mouthpiece.

'Happy New Year to you too,' Featherstone replied, unfazed by Sean's telephone manner. 'Just thought I'd let you know the Assistant Commissioner is about to start briefing the media down in the conference room, in case you wanted to join him.'

'No thanks,' Sean answered, calmer now, but unapologetic.

'Any last-minute updates you want me to get through to him – any sign of an imminent breakthrough?'

'Isn't the arrest of McKenzie a *breakthrough*?'

'Only if you're close to charging him.'

'I don't have enough to charge him yet, hence the surveillance.'

'I know, but are you close?'

'That's hard to say. You know how these things are – one minute you have nothing and the next everything falls into place,' Sean explained.

'So what does your gut tell you?'

Sean took a breath before answering. 'It tells me I'm close,' he lied, knowing that in truth he had little or nothing on McKenzie. But he needed to use the press briefing to his advantage, to pile the pressure on McKenzie and try and panic him into making a mistake that would lead to George Bridgeman – dead or alive. It had happened before; the killer had successfully disposed of the body in an effective hiding place where it would rot away for all eternity, only to then panic and move it to another, less considered, less remote location. With the surveillance team following McKenzie, Sean knew now was the time to try to make him panic into returning to the boy or his body. 'You can tell the Assistant Commissioner I'm very close. You can tell him we have very reliable information on the boy's whereabouts that we're looking into as a matter of priority.'

'I can tell Addis that?'

'It's important he gets it in time for the briefing.'

Featherstone sighed loudly into the phone. 'Are you sure this is how you want to roll the dice?'

'I have no choice,' Sean answered and waited nervously for Featherstone's answer.

'OK. I'll tell him, but a word to the wise, Sean – if you tell him it is so, then it had better be so.'

'I understand,' Sean told him, his belly tight with anticipation and anxiety.

'Try and watch the briefing if you can,' Featherstone told him. 'Addis will expect it.'

Sean listened as the phone went dead, his mind once more cluttered with the barriers – barriers that stopped him thinking how he needed to. Barriers that stood in the way of ever finding George Bridgeman alive.

Heavy raindrops bounced off the windscreen, the wipers failing to cope with the downpour on the outside while the heaters failed to prevent it misting on the inside. Sally leaned forward, the seatbelt pressing uncomfortably against her chest, which still ached when anything dug into her, and wiped the obscured windscreen with her gloved hand. Light spilled down on her from the street lights above, refracting and intensifying as it travelled through the raindrops, each ray turning into hundreds that dazzled her eyes and made the road little more than a blur of coloured lights.

To her relief she found a space just big enough to park her car not too far from the front door of the converted Victorian house that contained her top-floor flat. The flat's poor state when she'd bought it had made it just about affordable despite its location in Putney, south-west London. Of all the properties she'd viewed after abandoning the flat where she'd been attacked, it seemed comfortably to be the worst. But many of its supposed drawbacks were the very things that drew her to it. It was small, having been constructed in the loft, with many of its ceilings sloping so low half the room was unusable, and the windows were small, too small for a person to slip through, most of the natural light being provided by heavy framed skylights that she kept shut and locked; it was accessed by three steep flights of stairs; and the neighbours were easily heard through the thin partition walls. These were all the attributes she'd hunted for – the things that comforted her after the attack, that helped make her feel safe in her own home. Once she'd checked the outside of the building to make sure there were no drainpipes running anywhere near any of the windows she made an offer at the full asking price straight away. The estate agent didn't argue and the deal was done.

After checking the road in front and behind, she jumped from her car, checked twice she'd secured it properly and jogged along the pavement with her thin raincoat over her head and her mid-height heels clicking against the soaked pavement until she was safely under the cover of the front porch. She searched in her small, uncluttered handbag, another of the many deliberate changes she'd made since Sebastian Gibran entered her life, and pulled her keys from the internal zip-pocket, smoothly and quickly opening the front door. She searched the road for signs of danger before pushing the door open just wide enough to slide through the gap, closing it firmly behind her and standing in the darkness inside. She waited, listening for any sounds that shouldn't be there, but also to prove to herself that she could – that she could stand in the greyness without fear overtaking her. To her relief, her breathing and heart rate remained reasonably calm and steady. After a few moments more she pushed the light timer switch and gave herself about thirty seconds of light to reach the next landing. She heaved herself away from the front door and climbed the stairs one at a time, the sounds of her neighbours still awake and living their normal lives comforting her all the way to the first-floor landing where she found the next light switch and continued her ascent until she reached her own front door, the keys for which she already held in her hand. As she slid the first key into the lock she paused for a second or two, looking back down the staircase, listening hard, just in case. Satisfied, she unlocked the three locks and pushed the door open, the light from inside flooding into the hallway just as the timer plunged it back into darkness.

Sally stepped inside her sanctuary, closing the door behind her without locking it and moving deeper into the front room, glad she had left the light on all day so she wouldn't have to step into a dark flat, but disappointed that she still felt it necessary. At least she'd made it to the point where she could bear to leave the rest of the flat in semi-darkness, though it had taken her months to get there.

She moved quickly, going from room to room turning the lights on – but only lamps, not the overhead ones. Another step forward in her *recovery*. For months, the mere act of touching a lamp had filled her with so much anxiety it would almost instantly bring on a panic attack as the memories flooded back: turning the lamp on *that night*, the red light flooding her flat and the sense of *him* standing right behind her. The lamp had been the last thing she'd touched before . . . Sally shook her head to stop herself thinking too much about the attack and continued switching on a lamp in every room, searching every dark corner – just in case. Having confirmed that she was alone, she returned to the living room and secured the front door.

Next she turned the television on for company, kicked her shoes off and padded across the floor to her small, neat kitchen where she grabbed a wine glass from the cupboard and cursed the fact she no longer smoked. She made her way to the freezer and yanked open the door. The bottle of vodka lying seductively on its side appeared to be almost calling to her, begging her for attention. It took all her strength to slam the door shut and reach for the already open bottle of chardonnay in the adjacent fridge instead, from which she poured herself a modest glass and sat at the small kitchen table. She searched her compact handbag and quickly found the tramadol. She popped two from the packet and threw them into her mouth, washing them down with a good swig of her wine and waited for their soothing effects to wash over her. *No vodka and no tears*, she thought to herself. Dr Anna Ravenni-Ceron would be very pleased with her.

5

Mid-morning and Sean had already been back behind his desk in his new office for several hours, enjoying the early peace before the main office grew crowded and noisy. His claustrophobic, uncomfortable office in New Scotland Yard was already beginning to feel like home, thoughts of Peckham now more like distant memories than recent events. His desk had been exactly as he'd left it the night before, right down to the half-read report about another paedophile local to the scene of George Bridgeman's disappearance. The possible suspect had previous for snatching children, but Sean had already largely discounted him – he'd never committed a residential burglary and he'd never shown any lock-picking skills. He'd skimmed through the rest of the report and tossed it into the tray marked *complete*. Twisting the stiffness out of his neck, he closed his eyes for a second to consider McKenzie. God, he prayed he was stupid enough or scared enough to make a fatal mistake while he had the surveillance team up his arse. It had taken two hideous murders and three abductions before he'd been able to find and stop Thomas Keller – he couldn't bear the same thing happening here. *No*, he reassured himself, he had his man, now all he needed was the evidence to prove it. For all McKenzie's slyness and criminal cunning, he was still impulsive – Sean was sure of it. He saw the boy and the family and acted on an immediate, uncontrollable desire, leaving behind him the signature of his method that pointed to him as the guilty party just as surely as if he'd left his fingerprints all over the scene. McKenzie was caught and he knew it. Now all he could do was what so many other killers before him had done – face the police and the media and try and front it all out: portray himself as either a witness or an innocent man falsely accused. But the charade could never last long. All McKenzie's provocation and snarling half denials would be nothing more than his twisted moment in the sun, his one chance to revel in his own infamy before being buried in the prison system, denied access to the trashy paperbacks that would no doubt be written about him. Sean ground his teeth in anticipation of the day when McKenzie's tower of lies tumbled down.

A picture of Kate on his desk pulled him away from thoughts of McKenzie's downfall and instantly saddened his heart. Much to his relief, she'd been asleep when he arrived home the previous night and remained so when he rose so early that outside it was still pitch-black and not a single bird was singing in the new day. He'd showered and dressed in the semi-darkness, using only the light from the night-lamp that burned all night for the sake of their children, leaving the bathroom door open just enough to let the light in. He'd tiptoed down the stairs and out of the house, breathing an audible sigh of relief as he cleared the front door and walked along the cold, still road just as some of the neighbouring houses began to flicker into life. He'd comfortably beaten the worst of the traffic as he'd driven north through south-east London and over

Lambeth Bridge, around Parliament Square and along Victoria Street before swinging right into Broadway and disappearing into the Yard's underground car park. But he needed to break the chill with Kate sooner rather than later, before it turned into an Ice Age.

Donnelly striding into the main office caught his attention and he summoned him with a look. The sergeant changed direction like a bird in flight and sauntered into Sean's office, where he remained standing to let Sean know he had no intention of staying long. 'Problem?' he asked.

'No,' Sean answered, 'just checking how you got on with the Bridgemans' cars.'

'They agreed to hand them over for forensic examination,' Donnelly told him. 'No problems.'

'How did you swing that?'

'Told them suspects sometimes liked to play games with us – leaving clues in unlikely places just to see how smart we are.'

'And they went for it?'

'A few grunts and growls from Mr Bridgeman, but they handed over the car keys – eventually. Both motors are under cover at Lambeth as we speak.'

'Good. Make sure you keep the heat under the Forensic boys and girls. I want all things forensic to do with this case treated as a matter of priority. Understand?'

'Perfectly,' Donnelly replied. The phone ringing on Sean's desk ended their conversation, but Donnelly stayed put.

'Sean Corrigan,' Sean spoke into the mouthpiece.

'Morning,' Featherstone answered without introducing himself.

'Sir.'

'Just phoning to see if you caught Addis's media release last night?'

'No,' Sean admitted. 'I was too busy here.'

'Well, if he asks, you tell him that you did see it, OK?'

'Fine. Why?'

'Because that's what he'd expect you to do.'

'If you think it's necessary.'

'I do,' Featherstone warned him. 'As far as he's concerned, he did it for you and your case – even added the little extras you wanted about being close to a breakthrough. He'll have the right hump if he thinks you couldn't even be bothered to watch it. Anyway, the genie's out of the bottle now and the world is watching. A child taken from an upmarket family living in their upmarket house in their upmarket London enclave – the news boys are gonna be like a pit-bull with a dead cat on this one, at least until we can give them someone to feed on.'

'You mean a suspect?' Sean asked.

'No,' Featherstone corrected him. 'We've already given them a suspect – your man McKenzie, remember? What they really want is an *accused*.'

'I'm working on it.'

'Then work fast,' Featherstone advised him. 'You as good as promised Addis a quick result, so you had better deliver. Don't expect him to take any flak to save your skin. They don't call him the Bramshill Assassin for nothing,' he added, referring to the Senior Police Officer Training College that had a long and established reputation for back-stabbing and one-upmanship.

'We're doing our best,' Sean protested.

'Then let's hope your best is good enough. Call me if anything changes.'

Sean listened to the line go dead and slowly replaced the receiver, his cheeks puffed out in exasperation. 'Problem?' Donnelly asked.

'Always,' he answered.

'Powers that be after a quick result, eh?' Sean just

shrugged. 'Then why don't we give them one and drag the parents in? Like I said, interview them under caution plus three – separately, before they start working as a team and concoct something plausible and difficult to prove a lie.'

'Not yet,' Sean argued. 'Maybe if Forensics turn something up that implicates them, but not until then.'

'Why not?'

'Because it'll undermine McKenzie as a suspect. Think of the disclosure down the line,' Sean pointed out. 'Hardly looks as though we truly believe he's our prime suspect if we're interviewing the Bridgemans at the same time we're following him.'

'Disclosure's irrelevant until we have someone charged, and apparently we're a long way from that.'

Sean's mobile rang, halting their discussion again. Sean raised his hand to silence Donnelly.

'Morning, guv'nor, DS Handy here. Thought you'd want a morning update on the surveillance.'

'I'm listening.'

'After he got bailed he went straight home and stayed indoors for a couple of hours before changing his clothes and showing himself again. He headed to a local takeaway – kebab, chips, side of hummus and a can of Coke, if you're interested – then home and indoors for the rest of the night. First show today was just after eight thirty a.m.; made his way to a local café this time – egg, bacon, chips, toast and tea – took his time over it too, then jumped on a bus to the Archway Road.'

'Archway?' Sean queried. 'Did he go anywhere specific?'

'Only a hardware shop, Asian-owned: Archway DIY—'

'Imaginative,' Sean chipped in.

'Does what is says on the tin. Full address is 173 Archway Road. He was in there for a good fifteen minutes. I put one of my people in the shop with him, but they couldn't hang around that long without showing out – it's not exactly Homebase in there.'

'Did they see what he bought?'

'Sorry. Couldn't get close enough and couldn't stay long enough.'

'Bollocks,' Sean snarled. 'Where is he now?'

'Got back on the bus and headed home. Been there ever since, which isn't long. Problem?'

'No. No problem. Was he carrying anything he could have bought in the shop?'

'When he came out he tucked something into his jacket pocket, but we don't know what. Do you want me to send one of my team into the shop to ask what, if anything, he bought?'

'No,' Sean replied. 'I don't want to burn any of your team. You stay with the target and I'll check the shop out.'

'Understood.'

'Something up?' Donnelly asked as Sean put the phone down.

'Could be.' Sean was on his feet, reaching for his jacket. 'Grab your coat – you're coming with me.'

'Oh aye. Where to?'

'Archway Road, to visit a hardware shop.'

'Why?'

'Because I need a new screwdriver,' Sean quipped.

'What?' Donnelly screwed his face up in disapproval.

'Never mind,' Sean told him. 'I'll explain on the way.'

Stuart Bridgeman sat alone in his office in the family home in Hampstead with the door closed and his modern jazz music playing just loudly enough to drown out any sounds of life coming from the rest of the house. Nothing he tried seemed capable of distracting his racing mind from the situation he was trying not to face. Having to see his wife was bad enough, but having the female cop hanging around the house all hours was pushing him closer and closer to the edge of he didn't know what. His wife, the cop, even the nanny must think he was a fool if they imagined he hadn't noticed the endless whispered conversations. He knew exactly what – who – they were talking about. The more they conspired against him, the more isolated and bitter he felt towards all of them. Had he not continued to provide for them all, given them everything they could ask for – despite the rumours and betrayal? He'd always done what was necessary for the family, even taking care of George, despite knowing the truth, despite feeling no love towards the boy – despite being reminded of his wife's betrayal every time he had to look at him. Could anyone really blame him for losing his temper, even if he was honest and admitted the boy himself had done no wrong? When a new male lion takes over a pride from the old patriarch, the first thing they do is kill the lion cubs that aren't genetically theirs – not out of cruelty, but out of an overpowering urge to ensure their own genes will dominate and survive. And now George was gone and he didn't know how he felt about that. All he knew was that the eyes of suspicion had fallen upon him. At least, no matter what happened, he'd always have Sophia. Regardless what truths bubbled to the surface.

A gentle, nervous knock at the door chased away the thoughts that he knew would be back again and again. He considered telling whoever it was to go away, but remembered the cop lurking in his home. 'Come in,' he called out, like a headmaster summoning a naughty child. The door opened slowly and only enough to allow his wife to slip into the room. She closed the door softly before speaking.

'I was going to make something to eat – do you want anything?' she asked.

'No,' he told her, his eyes falling away from her and back to the dossier on his desk he'd been pretending to read.

'You should eat,' she persisted. 'You don't want to make yourself ill. We could do without that right now.'

'I said no,' he scolded, staring without raising his head making his eyes appear demonic. She backed off for a few seconds until his eyes returned to the dossier.

'Stuart,' she tried once more to reach him. 'We need to stick together on this. No matter what happened in the past – we need to stick together now.'

'Or what?' he growled. 'Worried what people might start to say about us? About you? You never seemed to care about that before.'

'Do we have to talk about that now?'

'I don't want to talk about it at all.'

'Damn it, Stuart, this isn't about us! This is about George. This is about my son.'

'*Your* son,' he seized on her slip. 'That about says it all, doesn't it? *Your* son – not our son, but your son.'

'That's not what I meant,' she tried to recover.

'Then what did you mean?'

'I just want my boy back,' she told him, her voice weak now as the tears glazed over her eyes. 'Dear God, what's happened to him? Where's my son?'

'Why don't you ask that cop out there what's happened to *your son*? They're supposed to have all the answers, aren't they? And while you're asking her, why don't you ask her why the police took our cars?'

'But they told us why they needed our cars, why would I—'

'You stupid bitch! Did you really believe all that bollocks about suspects leaving clues hidden around the place? They took our cars because they think *I* took George. Don't you understand? Maybe they even think we killed him.'

'That's absurd,' she argued. 'Why would they think that?'

'Why? Because they know your dirty little secret.'

'How could they?'

'Oh, come on. Haven't they already been asking you about it? Insinuating?' The puzzled look of recognition on her face told him what he already knew in his heart. 'Of course they have. It's only a matter of time before they arrest me, but it won't help them find George. It won't help them get you your little boy back.'

'Why are you being so cruel?' she demanded. 'He's your son too, damn you. Why did you say that?'

'Why did I say what?' he asked, a look of disgust on his face.

'That I won't get George back. Why would you say a thing like that?'

'I'm just telling you what the police think,' he insisted, only less confident now – less sure of himself and not so confrontational.

'God help me,' she hissed, moving a few steps closer, pointing at him accusingly, 'if I ever find out that you've done anything to hurt George, I swear I'll kill you myself.'

Stuart Bridgeman went pale as he struggled to find an answer, but he was spared by another gentle rat-a-tat-tat at the door.

'Everything all right in there?' DC Maggie O'Neil asked.

'Yes,' Celia Bridgeman lied through the door. 'Everything's absolutely fine.'

They abandoned their unmarked car by the side of the road on double yellow lines with the vehicle's log-book tossed unceremoniously on the dashboard to identify it as a CID car to any passing traffic wardens – not that the ones from the local council would take any notice. Sean led the way as they strode across the pavement, already tugging his warrant card free from his inside jacket pocket. Donnelly was close behind, but nowhere near as enthusiastic. As they entered, a loud, electronic buzzing noise filled the hardware shop, replacing what would once upon a time have been a bell. The Indian shopkeeper, somewhere in his sixties, short and slim with an immaculate grey beard and complete with turban, appeared from behind the counter where he'd been crouched while rearranging the fine display of nuts and bolts. 'Can I help you, sir?' he immediately asked in his thick Indian accent.

'Police,' Sean told him unceremoniously, holding his warrant card out in front of him. 'I'm Detective Inspector Corrigan and this is my colleague, Detective Sergeant Donnelly. I need to ask you a few questions about a customer who came to your shop earlier this morning.'

'Of course. No problem,' the shopkeeper answered without any nervousness or hesitation. 'I was a police officer myself many years ago,' he added, 'so please, anything that you want, just ask.'

'Was that back in India?' Donnelly asked.

'It was, sir. In Bombay. My father was also a police officer and so was my grandfather, but it was easier to be a police officer there than here I think. Trust me, everyone I ever questioned soon admitted their guilt. Not so many rules back then.'

Sean was already tired of the police-club chat. 'I'm sure,' he interrupted. 'Sorry, I didn't catch your name . . .?'

'My name is Mr Nashua. I moved to this country with my family—'

Sean cut him short. 'Mr Nashua, a man came into your shop earlier . . .' He rummaged in his jacket pocket for the photograph of McKenzie. 'This man,' he said, carefully placing it on the counter. 'I need to know what he wanted.'

'Yes, yes,' Nashua acknowledged, 'I remember him. He was here not long ago.'

'Yes, but what did he want?' Sean hurried him. 'Did he buy anything?'

'He looked around for a bit. I was a bit suspicious at first – he seemed to be looking out the window, checking outside, as if he was waiting for someone to join him in my shop. I can always spot a thief who has only come to steal from me, but this one seemed more interested in what was going on outside the shop rather than the things inside.'

'Mr Nashua, please,' Sean appealed. 'Did he buy anything?'

'Oh yes – eventually. He seemed to know exactly what he wanted.'

'And what was that?' Sean persisted.

'He bought an MLPX,' Nashua told them. 'A very good one too. It cost almost one hundred pounds.'

'A what?' Donnelly asked.

'An MLPX,' Nashua repeated. 'A master lock-picking kit. In the right hands, a set like that could open pretty much any standard lock in the world – and this man who bought it seemed very much to know his business. He asked me about the quality and size of the picks, hooks, wrenches, diamonds – everything. I thought this man must be a qualified locksmith – yes?'

'You could say that,' Sean answered, still looking at Donnelly. 'What say we pay our locksmith friend a surprise visit?'

'I don't see we have any choice,' Donnelly agreed. 'Only . . .'

'Only what?' Sean pressed.

'I don't recall anyone mentioning we'd seized any lock-picking tools when he was first arrested.'

'That's because we didn't.'

'So why does he need a new set?' Donnelly asked.

'Because tools leave distinctive marks. Once the lab open up the locks from the Bridgemans' house they should find

153

tool marks – some may match the tools he used to open them, the rest will fit with the keys normally used to unlock them.'

'You had Forensics take the locks from the front door?'

'Of course.'

'That's a hell of a long shot.'

'It is, but McKenzie probably knows it's possible.'

'So he ditched the tools he used at the Bridgemans?'

'Looks like it.'

'Then we need to find them,' said Donnelly.

'Would be useful,' Sean agreed. 'Have Zukov make sure all the search teams are aware we're looking for tools used for lock-picking. He may have dumped them not too far from the scene. Tell him to download some pictures from the Internet so people can see what he's talking about or it'll mean nothing to most of them.'

'No problem,' Donnelly assured him. 'It will be done.'

'Is there a problem?' Mr Nashua asked, aware that the detectives had forgotten he was there.

'No,' Sean told him with a wry smile. 'No problem at all.'

A smile of self-satisfaction fixed itself to his face as he looked out of his first-floor window at the people of all creeds and colours scurrying along Kentish Town Road below. Every few minutes the sight of a child electrified his body with an excitement he couldn't control and tightened his belly and groin as he licked his dry lips and waited – waited for the inevitable.

As soon as the car came into view crawling along in the rest of the traffic some criminal instinct told him it was them, but he felt no panic or fear – no need to scramble around his tiny, sparse flat to find and destroy any incriminating evidence before they found it. He felt calm and in control, as if everything he'd been planning was coming together better than he could have expected. Corrigan had been a gift – a gift that must have been sent from a greater power – the conduit of all his planned revenge. They had thought him beaten and humiliated. Now it would be him who would teach them the true meaning of defeat and public humiliation.

He drew the stained net curtains to better conceal himself while still keeping watch on the approaching car. It stopped and squeezed itself into the tightest of parking spaces, holding up the traffic and provoking a cacophony of horn blasts. He knew the occupants wouldn't give a damn about the inconvenience they caused, such was their all-consuming arrogance and ignorance. As he watched them climb from the car he realized he was grinding his teeth in anticipation and hatred, eager to continue the game he knew he couldn't lose. They crossed the pavement and became impossible to see once they were directly below him – at the communal entrance that ultimately led to his front door.

Slowly he moved away from the window and sat shaking a little at the only table in the flat, wishing he still had a laptop to log on to so that he could download incriminating items to tantalize Detective Inspector Corrigan with – sending him on yet more wild-goose chases, leading him further and further away from the boy and himself closer and closer to final victory.

He listened for the sound of splintering wood – the sound of Corrigan's career beginning to shatter, but was disappointed to hear instead one of his neighbours' intercoms buzzing. He immediately knew what Corrigan was up to – threatening or cajoling one of the other occupants of the filth-infested flats to open the communal door so they could sneak up the stairs like sewer rats.

Quickly he gathered the items he had laid out on the

table in front him: an *A to Z of London* with the missing boy's street circled in red pen, other houses also circled in red, along with a few local schools and – his crowning glory – areas of nearby woodland. He'd enjoyed himself that morning, chuckling to himself as he marked the map and scribbled the apparent ramblings of a dangerous madman across the pages of a notebook that he now placed on top of the *A to Z*. He sat back, trying not to grin as he heard the footsteps climbing the stairs – neither running nor tiptoeing, just steadily walking – not as he'd expected them to come. The departure from how he'd expected things to happen caused a rare moment of panic, a fluttering in his chest like a hummingbird's wings.

Again he waited for the splintering of wood and the yells of the police commanding him not to move or suffer the consequences. He stared at the door, muttering quietly to himself. 'Come on, come on,' he muttered under his breath, willing them to smash open the flimsy, scarred door; the hastily replaced lock from their last visit would be no match for a well-placed kick from a policeman's boot. But the fireworks never came – only a firm knock. 'Shit,' he hissed, frozen to his chair, unable to answer the knocking that came again when he didn't answer. 'Who is it?' he asked, his voice hoarse and quiet. He cleared it with a cough before repeating himself. 'Who is it and what do you want?'

'You know who it is and what we want,' Corrigan told him, his tone overconfident and belittling – the conqueror coming to conquer. 'I need to speak with you, Mark. Open the door.'

'What about?' he asked, still sitting in his chair staring at the thin door, imagining the smiling, self-congratulating cops on the other side, so sure they had the evidence to prove he took the boy.

'You know what about.' Corrigan's tone didn't waver. 'This is not the sort of conversation you want to have in public.'

'In public?' he asked, momentarily confused, suspicious Corrigan had plans to try and conduct his investigation in the glare of the media spotlight, ensuring that anybody who listened knew the police had decided he was their prime suspect.

'Your neighbours, Mark,' the voice explained. 'Walls have ears and all that.'

'I see,' he answered, weighing up his options, still hopeful they might grow impatient and kick the door open – more evidence of heavy-handed police intimidation. But the thought of his irate landlord having to provide yet more new locks forced him to a decision. The stinking flat wasn't much, but it was a roof over his head – a roof he'd need for some time to come, no matter how things worked out. 'Just give me a minute,' he told them as he stood, gathering the maps and notebooks and quickly hiding them under the bed, slipping them through a slit he'd made in its underside before moving purposefully to the door and turning the single Yale lock. He peeped through the gap at the two detectives standing like terracotta soldiers with their arms by their sides – Corrigan and another one he didn't recognize, thick-set with a prominent moustache, strong-looking. 'I see,' he told them. 'You again. What d'you want now?'

'Mark McKenzie,' Sean began, pulling his warrant card from his coat pocket, holding it low at his side, showing it inconspicuously to him. 'I'm Detective Inspector Sean Corrigan and this is Detective Sergeant Dave Donnelly.'

'I know who you are,' he snapped, his glare turning to Donnelly, 'or at least I know what you are.'

'Mark, I'm arresting you on suspicion of the abduction of George Bridgeman.'

'This is ridiculous,' he argued. 'I was only released last night.' A sudden wave of nausea strangled his confidence as the fear and realization they may have discovered something that could undermine all his plans flashed in his mind before shrinking away again like a retreating wave on the beach. No. If they were rearresting him this quickly, everything was exactly as he wanted it.

'As of now, you're under caution – you do remember the caution, don't you, Mark?' Sean asked.

'I remember it.'

Sean and Donnelly pushed their way into the small flat, carrying McKenzie back inside with the tide of their bodies and closing the door on the outside world. 'Under Section 18 of the Police and Criminal Evidence Act we have the power to search your flat for any evidence relating to the offence for which you've been arrested, and for evidence of any similar offences you may have committed – but I guess you already knew that too,' Sean told him.

'I did,' McKenzie agreed. 'I also know I that should have my solicitor here before you start searching.'

'You can call your solicitor if you like, but we don't have to wait for them to get here before searching.' Sean began to circle the flat like a wolf circling a flock of sheep.

'Why d'you need your solicitor here for a search?' Donnelly asked. 'Got something to hide, Mr McKenzie?'

'No,' he answered. 'Let's just say I've had bad experiences with the police in the past.'

'I can't think what you mean,' Donnelly smirked, casually opening drawers and rifling through their contents.

'Oh, you know,' McKenzie told him. 'Things found in my home that hadn't been there before the police started searching.'

'That's a pretty serious allegation,' Donnelly played with him. 'Did you make a complaint?'

'No,' McKenzie admitted.

'Aye, well, not much we can do about that now then, is there?'

'Perhaps if you tell me what you're looking for I could save you the bother of searching,' McKenzie offered, ignoring Donnelly's comment.

'You know what we're looking for,' Sean accused him.

'I have no idea.'

'We'll rip this place apart to find it if we have to,' Sean threatened.

'And that bothers me how?' McKenzie asked, looking around his own home with distaste printed across his face, allowing his eyes to linger a little too long on the single bed pushed into a corner of the bedsit. He resisted the temptation to smile as he noticed Corrigan immediately seizing on his apparent mistake, striding across the room and unceremoniously pulling the soiled quilt back and tossing it on the floor.

Sean kicked the quilt and pillow around until he was satisfied they hid nothing, but still McKenzie's face told him he was looking in the right place, something McKenzie confirmed by licking his drying lips.

Sean flicked the entire mattress up on its side to search the space under it, its cheapness and lightness making it easy to lift, but there was nothing to be found. Briefly he looked back at McKenzie. 'I'll find it,' he warned him. 'No matter where it is, I'll find it.'

'I don't know what you're talking about,' he lied.

'Really?' Sean asked sarcastically. 'Well, I guess we'll see about that.'

McKenzie's eyes never left Sean as he dropped to his knees and peered under the bed before stretching an arm underneath and pulling out the items that lay hidden there: old newspapers and magazines, shoe-boxes full of photographs from a better time, postcards, letters and long irrelevant documents that provided a chronology of his life. None of it interested Sean, who pulled a small Maglite torch from his belt and clicked it on, shining it underneath the bed.

'Got something?' Donnelly asked.

'Just an old trick I used to use when I was undercover – if I had something I really didn't want anyone to stumble across.'

Donnelly and McKenzie watched in silence as Sean scanned the underside of the bed until he found what he was looking for: a six-inch slit in the nylon material. Sean checked the entrance to the slit for booby-traps before carefully sliding the torch into the darkness, using it to light the way and pull the opening wide apart, revealing the *A to Z* and the notebook. With his other hand he reached in and pinched the items between his fingers, pulling them free and carefully placing them on the bed-base above, mindful that he'd forgotten to wear gloves of any kind, something that he quickly remedied by snapping on a pair of forensic latex ones.

'Found what you're looking for?' Donnelly asked.

'No,' Sean answered, 'but I've found something.'

'So you and Mark here share the same secret hiding place. Interesting,' Donnelly added, drawing quick-fire glances from both Sean and McKenzie.

Sean opened the *A to Z* first and flicked through to the pages covering Hampstead and the surrounding area, the neat red circles leaping out at him like tracer bullets, his eyes frantically searching until he found the street the boy had been taken from – Courthope Road – ringed in red, just like numerous others. 'Jesus Christ,' he said, loudly enough for both Donnelly and McKenzie to hear, his gloved finger tracing the pages to the areas ringed in red, several of which marked remote areas on Hampstead Heath.

'Problem?' Donnelly asked.

'Yes,' Sean answered, 'but not for us – for him.' He turned and nodded once towards McKenzie, who stood silent and motionless, his eyes wide with anticipation and trepidation, afraid he wouldn't be able to control what he'd begun – wouldn't be able to control Corrigan.

Leaving the *A to Z* open on the damning page, Sean turned his attention to the accompanying notebook, immediately noticing that it appeared almost new and largely unscathed – something that niggled at him, his instincts warning him that the book should look well worn, as if McKenzie had hardly been able to bear not to have it in his hands for even a second. But the fact the boy had only been taken recently chased his doubt away. As soon as he opened the notebook, the same garish red ink stared up at him, obscene scribblings detailing extreme sexual acts and acts of excessive violence between people of all ages and sexes, along with sketches and rough diagrams illustrating the words. Crude drawings of what looked like Christ on the cross littered most pages, as did caricatures of the devil and demons, all frolicking with the naked, deformed, wounded and bleeding humans – the most grotesque creatures of hell paying the children special attention. Sean again glanced briefly over his shoulder at McKenzie. 'You're fucked, McKenzie,' he announced. 'Your throat cut by your own hand.'

Donnelly realized what was happening before even seeing the map and notebook, snatched the handcuffs off his belt and stepped towards McKenzie, spinning him around and snapping the cuffs on his wrists. 'Can't have you running off anywhere, can we?' he told the startled-looking man.

'I'm not saying anything until I see my solicitor,' McKenzie protested.

'You don't have to,' Sean told him, pointing at the damning evidence lying on the bed-base. 'These say it all for you.'

'You can't prove they're mine. And even if they are – so what?'

'Do me a favour,' Sean replied, walking towards him while Donnelly went the other way, eager to see what Sean had seen. 'But there's something else you have that I need.'

'I don't know what you're talking about.'

'Now is not the time to fuck with me,' Sean warned. 'Where are they?'

'Who?' McKenzie asked, trying to stall. 'Where are who?'

'Not who,' Sean told him, his voice growing louder. 'The items you bought from the hardware-shop – where are they?'

'You're mad,' he accused Sean. 'I haven't been to any hardware-shop. Why would I go to a hardware-shop?'

'Don't lie to me,' Sean warned. 'Where are they – the lock-picking tools you bought from the shop in Archway Road? I know you were there, Mark.'

'You had me followed?' he asked calmly, quietly enjoying the expression on Sean's face as he realized he'd shown his hand and burnt the surveillance team. 'You must have, otherwise how could you have known?'

'So you admit it?' Sean recovered.

'I'm not admitting anything.'

'This isn't a game, Mark, and I'm not playing. You're in deep shit. Now, where are the items you bought from the hardware shop?'

'I'll tell you what,' McKenzie sneered, 'you start searching this rat-hole you and your kind condemned me to live in and I'll tell you when you're getting warm.'

'I've got a better idea,' Sean replied, jabbing him in the crotch with a snap of his knee, folding McKenzie in half as he fell to the floor, his hands cupped around his private parts to ease the pain and protect them from further blows.

'You want to play games? OK – let's play a new game. This one's called, you tell me where the tools are or have more of the same.'

'You can't do this,' McKenzie groaned, spittle spraying from his thin, pale lips. He knew Corrigan was dangerous – he'd almost depended on it, but he hadn't planned on being tortured. His intense fear and dislike of physical pain of any type threatened to cause him to cave in and confess all. 'You can't do this to me.'

'Oh yeah, and who's going to stop me?' Sean asked, looking around the room as Donnelly deliberately kept his back to them.

'I won't tell you anything,' McKenzie insisted. Sean slapped him hard across the face, the sound of the blow reverberating around the flat, mixing with the pitiful little scream that escaped from McKenzie's mouth.

'That's probably not true, is it, Mark? You see, I think you're going to tell me everything I want you to.' Sean's voice was full of quiet malevolence and danger – as if torturing prisoners was an everyday occurrence, just another part of his job.

'Leave me alone,' McKenzie demanded. 'You won't get away with this.'

'The tools,' Sean hissed at him. 'Tell me where the tools you bought from the hardware shop are. And the others – the ones you used on the house you took the boy from – where did you dump them?'

'I've already told you: I don't know what you're talking about.'

Sean snapped the heel of his shoe into McKenzie's shin, just below the knee, causing a jolt of excruciating pain that brought tears to his eyes as he gripped the injured limb and rolled side to side to try and distract himself from his agony.

'We can keep doing this,' Sean told him, 'or you can tell me what I need to know.'

'You're insane,' he spat back. 'You're crazy.'

Sean reached out with both hands and gripped the collar of McKenzie's unbuttoned shirt, twisting it in on itself to make a tourniquet around his neck – cutting off his oxygen and damming the spent blood in his brain. McKenzie tried to break free, but Sean was too strong and his grip too tight. He held him without speaking until McKenzie's eyes began to bulge.

'Tell me,' Sean shouted in his face, watching as McKenzie turned his head, his eyes rolling the rest of the way and pointing accusingly towards a corner of the room.

'Maybe you should take it easy, guv'nor,' Donnelly warned, heading back towards the unevenly matched combatants, ready to peel Sean off his prey if he had to. But Sean had already loosened the shirt around McKenzie's neck and dropped him to the floor, where he lay panting for breath, one hand around his reddening neck and the other pointing shakily at Sean.

'I want to make a complaint,' he managed to mumble. 'I want him arrested,' he told Donnelly. 'You saw what he did – arrest him. He tried to kill me.'

'If he'd tried to kill you, you'd be dead by now,' Donnelly answered, 'so shut the fuck up. And next time, save yourself a bit of bother by answering our questions when we ask them.' He looked away from the still prostrate McKenzie towards Sean, who was already in the corner of the room McKenzie's bulging eyes had looked to. 'You got something?'

Sean was crouching to examine the floor. 'Carpet's loose over here,' he answered, 'like it's been pulled away more than once.'

'Hello, hello,' Donnelly said, looking at McKenzie. 'Another wee hiding place, Mr McKenzie?'

He didn't answer, his eyes once again wide with the infinite possibilities of the next few seconds – Corrigan's unpredictability only now fully revealing itself to him, increasing both the danger and the possible rewards.

Sean pushed the tips of his fingers between the skirting board and carpet edge, gripped the frayed ends and pulled – the carpet peeling back like the skin of an over-ripe fruit to reveal old floorboards, the shortest of which wobbled slightly when he rocked it with his hand. He pressed down on one side and the short board flipped on its side as it broke loose. 'One of the boards isn't nailed down,' he called over his shoulder, tossing the board to one side and retrieving his torch. He placed it in his mouth to free the arm that now snaked under the floor, his gloved fingers coiling around the plastic bag he'd seen in the torchlight. As he pulled it free, he looked inside like an excited child with a bag of treats, a satisfied grin spreading across his face. 'Jackpot,' he said quietly as he emptied the suede roll-up case from the bag, untying the loose knot and unrolling the holder to reveal an array of delicate metal tools within. Even from a distance Donnelly could see they were lock-picking tools.

'Game's up for you, Mark,' Donnelly told him. 'Now, where's the boy?'

'You're the police,' McKenzie answered. 'You're supposed to be the detectives, the ones with all the answers – so why don't you detect him yourself?'

Sean was up and across the room in a second, pushing past Donnelly, eyes on fire with a fury he couldn't control as he again grabbed McKenzie by the shirt collar and half pulled him off the floor, his face so close their breath became one. 'Tell me where the boy is,' Sean demanded. 'Tell me where the boy is or I swear you won't leave this room in one piece.'

'You can do what you like to me, but I won't tell you where he is – no matter what.'

'We'll soon see about that,' Sean told him, his wrists beginning to twist as he tightened the shirt around McKenzie's throat.

A heavy hand landed on Sean's shoulder, prompting him to back off.

'Careful, guv'nor,' Donnelly warned quietly. 'Don't give him a way out – know what I mean?'

Sean loosened his grip, but kept hold of McKenzie. There was more than one way to torture the truth out of him.

'When you broke into all those houses – when you convinced everyone you were just another housebreaker looking for things to steal, you were hiding the truth from them, weren't you?'

'I don't know what you're talking about.'

'You weren't there to steal, were you? Not in the beginning. You were there for the children, weren't you?'

'I needed the money, that's all.'

'You're lying,' Sean accused him. 'I can smell your lies. All the houses had children in them and you knew that before picking the locks in the middle of the night and letting yourself in, didn't you?' McKenzie shook his head, his mouth hanging open. 'Did you take things, Mark? Things belonging to the children – things special to them? Did taking their things allow you to relive being in their houses with them over and over and over again? Every time you felt the urges, the needs returning, you could get out the things you'd taken and look at them, couldn't you? Touch them, breathe in their scent, just as if they were the children themselves. Did you mark maps, Mark, ring the houses you'd been inside in red, just like you have with George Bridgeman's house? Did you need to do that to keep the connection even more alive – another reminder of your little visits in the night?'

166

'You can't prove I did any of that,' McKenzie finally spoke. 'You can't prove anything.'

'I can prove plenty,' Sean told him. 'I've got enough here to finish you, Mark, and with your previous you don't stand a chance. Tell me where the boy is, and I can promise things won't go as badly for you as you might think – but only if he's still alive.'

'And if he's not?' McKenzie asked, his eyes narrow and cunning.

'Then tell me where he is anyway,' Sean answered. 'Give the family some peace and the courts will have more sympathy for you.'

'Sympathy?' McKenzie snarled. 'That's what you think I want – sympathy? I don't want your fucking sympathy – I want justice. Justice for everything that's happened to me. You owe it to me.'

'Everything that ever happened to you, you brought on yourself,' Sean told him. 'As for justice – you'll get that, Mark. That much I promise.'

Sally settled into the large comfortable armchair in the spacious office in Swiss Cottage and immediately felt herself begin to relax totally, something she'd learned to do during her previous half-dozen or so meetings. She surveyed the now familiar room as she waited for the soothing voice that she knew would soon come. 'So, how have you been?' asked Dr Anna Ravenni-Ceron.

'Good,' she answered. 'Getting there – with your help.'

'And I'm glad to help,' Anna answered. 'It's good for me to get back to basics and help someone like you – to see the person you really are returning.'

'You must have thought I was a nightmare when you first met me,' Sally winced.

'Not to me you weren't, although you had every right

to be. What happened to you could destroy most people, especially a woman in the police, but you've been progressing better than I could have hoped for. Perhaps that in itself owes something to the fact you are a policewoman.'

'Maybe,' Sally answered, unconvinced.

'Even at the height of your difficulties, you were politer than most of your colleagues.'

'Outsiders make them nervous.'

'I noticed. How is DI Corrigan, by the way?'

'Sean? He's . . . Sean. Why do you ask?'

'I found him interesting,' Anna told her.

'Professionally or personally?' Sally asked, slightly defensively.

'My interest could only ever be professional. Why ask – has he said something about me?'

'No,' Sally replied, a little too quickly. 'Not that I know of. Has he called you at all or tried to contact you?'

'No,' Anna told her. 'Nothing.'

'I'll tell him you said hello,' Sally told her.

'Please do,' Anna answered, sensing it was time to move forward. 'Now – how have things been at work? Still unusually quiet?'

'They were, but we've picked up a new case – a four-year-old boy's gone missing from his home. We have a pretty decent suspect.'

'And how have you felt, being involved in a live investigation?'

'Fine. Glad to be busy again, although the break did me no harm – gave me a chance to move forward with my life without too many distractions getting in the way.'

'I agree,' Anna told her. 'It's easy to bury your head in work and pretend everything's all right, but ultimately it means you're never addressing things that need to be addressed.'

'Well, I feel much better now.'

'And the drinking?'

'Better.'

'In what way?'

'In that I'm drinking less. I'm off the vodka completely.'

'Excellent. Are you drinking less now than after the attack or less now than before it?'

'Less than even before it, and I'm still off the smokes too. If I keep going, I'll be completely vice-less.'

'You say that as if it's a bad thing.' Anna smiled.

'Not bad, just boring.'

'No harm in the occasional glass of wine, just remember to keep track of what you're drinking.'

'Sounds like the office Christmas party's off limits, then?'

'Go, just don't drink.'

'Jesus!' Sally laughed. 'If I do that everyone'll think I'm pregnant. I'd rather they thought I was mad.'

'Clinically depressed is the term I think you meant to use.'

'Yes. Sorry. Of course.'

'And the drugs – the painkillers?'

'Under control: ibuprofen and the occasional tramadol.'

'Do you really need them any more? Have you seen your doctor about taking them?'

'I can still feel the pain in my chest from time to time.'

'Do you think the pain is possibly more psychological – in your mind?'

'Well, when I feel it, it's in my chest and it bloody hurts.'

Anna backed off. 'Perhaps you could try dropping the tramadol and just using ibuprofen?'

'I like the tramadol,' Sally admitted. 'It helps me sleep.'

'You still have trouble sleeping?'

'A bit. I struggle to get to sleep and then things wake me up and I need the tramadol to get me back to sleep.'

'You mean your nightmares wake you up. Nightmares about the night you were attacked.'

'Yes,' Sally answered abruptly, as if lingering on the subject would induce the nightmares she still feared more than anything.

'Tell me about them,' Anna encouraged.

'I've already told you.'

'Tell me again. The more we talk about them, the better chance we have of stopping them.'

Sally breathed deeply and closed her eyes, reluctantly allowing the vivid memories to rush to the front of her mind, her hands suddenly tensing as her fingers curled and gripped the arms of her chair. 'They're always the same,' she began, 'always exactly the same.'

'Go on,' Anna softly encouraged. 'Nothing can hurt you here.'

'I'm in a strange place – a house – a big house, but there's nothing in it – no furniture or anything, but everywhere is lit by a red light. Everywhere is red. I start walking from room to room – I think I'm trying to find a way out, but I can't be sure. Each room just leads to another and another and I can't find a way outside, there are no doors or windows, just doorways that lead to the next room and the next and . . .' Sally stalled, her lips pale and dry, a slight sheen of sweat forming across her forehead and above her lip.

'Keep going,' Anna tried to help her.

'I'm scared and I start to panic – I run from room to room, crashing into walls and tripping over things I can't see and then I hear something, someone close behind me and I look over my shoulder but keep running and then I feel it . . .'

'Feel what?'

'The pain, the unbelievable pain in my chest . . .'

'What do you do next?'

'I look down at my chest and see it . . .'

'What?'

'The knife – the handle of a knife buried to the hilt in

170

my chest. I'm not wearing any clothes and can see where the blade's . . . I'm sorry I can't . . .'

'Try to go a little deeper, Sally. We have to get through this to get better. The dreams are your mind's way of trying to deal with what happened, to help you be able to talk about what *actually* happened.'

Sally breathed deeply again before speaking. 'I can see the blood running from my split skin and when I look up from the wound I see him, standing smiling in front of me, the red light making his teeth and eyes look blood red.'

'Who do you see, Sally?'

'It's him – Sebastian Gibran, always him. And then he stretches out his hand and takes hold of the knife handle and . . . and he slowly pulls it out of me . . . and I just stand there and let him. I can't feel any pain any more, just a feeling of uselessness. Once the knife's out, he licks the blood off it and he says . . . he says – *It's time to kill the little pet.* And then he puts the point of the blade on my chest, directly in line with my heart, and slowly pushes it through my skin and I feel it scraping past my ribs and piercing my heart and then . . . and then I wake up. My sheets are soaked. The pain and fear gradually fade, until I'm sure it was just a dream, and I take some drugs. It only ever comes once a night, so usually I can get back to sleep and be OK for work in the morning, more or less.'

'OK, Sally, you did really well,' Anna stopped her. 'I think we should leave it there for the day and pick up where we left off next week if you can make it.'

'Sure.' Sally took a deep breath and opened her eyes for the first time since she started reliving the night when Gibran tried to kill her. 'There's just one thing.'

'What's that?'

'Why did he say, *It's time to kill the little pet*? What does that mean?'

'I don't really know,' Anna lied. She knew exactly what Gibran had meant – that he considered her to be nothing more than Sean's pet. It would do Sally's recovery no good to know it – not yet. 'It's probably just something he said during one of his interviews that subconsciously you remembered.'

'Oh,' Sally sounded confused. 'It's just I never listened to his interviews. I never wanted to.'

'Something else then,' Anna suggested.

'Of course,' Sally pretended to agree. 'Probably nothing. Probably nothing at all.'

As Sean and Donnelly strode across the main office at New Scotland Yard, Sean noticed Sally was nowhere to be seen. He grabbed DC McGowan as they crossed paths. 'Stan – you seen Sally?'

'Not for a couple of hours,' McGowan told him.

'Does she know McKenzie's been re-arrested?'

'Yeah,' McGowan answered. 'As does everyone else.'

'OK, thanks.' Sean made for his office with Donnelly in tow. No sooner had they entered and sat without removing their outdoor coats, peeling the lids off their takeaway coffees, than the main office was plunged into deathly silence by the arrival of Assistant Commissioner Addis. The decorative symbols of his senior rank twinkled from his epaulettes and he smiled like a politician as he paused at the desks of detectives he didn't know to peer over their shoulders at their tasks, nodding sagely as if he understood what each of them was doing. Meanwhile he inched ever closer to Sean's office.

'Heads up,' Donnelly whispered. 'Scrambled egg heading our way.'

'This is all I need,' Sean muttered in reply as they resumed their silent vigil until Addis finally reached the office and entered without asking. He looked around for a spare seat and found none – neither Sean nor Donnelly showed any sign of offering to give up theirs.

'I hear your prime suspect is back in custody,' he told them.

'You've been told already?' Sean asked.

'Good news travels fast,' Addis answered.

'Bad news travels even faster,' Donnelly chipped in, showing his usual disregard for senior uniformed officers of all types. They couldn't sack him for being disrespectful and his total lack of desire to go any further than the rank of detective sergeant gave him all the protection he needed. Addis ignored him and directed his questions towards Sean.

'You must be very confident he's our man to have arrested him again so soon after releasing him – not to mention after the press conference I did.'

'I am,' Sean told him.

'Then I'm confused as to why you're here instead of at Kentish Town, interviewing him.'

'We booked him in and called his brief, but she can't get to him for a couple of hours. Then she'll want a lengthy consultation, by which time it'll be getting too late to interview him. Besides, this way we give Forensics a few more hours to try and find something to bury him with.'

'It doesn't matter how late it gets,' Addis argued, 'we still have a missing four-year-old boy. We can interview him in the middle of the night if we need to.'

'I understand that,' Sean answered, 'but he's not talking. Trust me, if he was going to spill the whereabouts of the Bridgeman boy he would have done it at his flat – when he was alone and scared.'

'You questioned him away from a police station and without legal representation?' Addis demanded.

'Like you said, sir, we still have a missing boy. I was within my rights to try and get him to tell us where the boy is.'

'But he didn't tell you?'

'No, he didn't.'

'Then there's no need to make any note of the conversation,' Addis told them. 'No point handing his defence team a stick to beat us with if it was a waste of time anyway.'

'Fair enough,' Sean agreed without telling him he had no intention of *officially* mentioning the questioning of McKenzie in his own flat.

'And I was told he had tools to break into houses and maps – including one showing the location of George Bridgeman's home,' Addis went on. 'Sounds like pretty damning evidence. Do you really need forensics as well?'

'Maybe not,' Sean answered, 'but if I can get it, I will. It's worth delaying the interview for. If I can hit him in the interview with something definitive from Forensics then he might start talking. He might tell us where George is.'

'Do you have enough PACE time left to play it this way?' Addis asked. 'He was in custody for quite a while last time you had him in.'

'He was rearrested on new evidence,' Sean explained. 'The clock starts again.'

'I see,' Addis acknowledged. He may never have done a day's honest coppering in his life, but he had an encyclopaedic knowledge of the law and police procedure, born of endless exams and courses at Bramshill Senior Police College. 'Still, I don't want this dragged out any longer than necessary,' Addis warned them. 'It may not seem like it to you, but this investigation is coming under the intense glare of our friends in the media. I can see them salivating at the thought of a child murderer on the loose amongst the rich and privileged of North London – something to fill their papers and evening news slots with – so let's get this wrapped up as soon as possible, one way or the other. If you're happy you've got your man, then get on and charge him. I shall expect some good news tomorrow. Until then, I'll leave you in peace. I have to attend a dinner with the Mayor this evening, but I am contactable if something notable happens. Gentlemen.' He dismissed them with a nod and glided from the office.

'I have a very bad feeling about that man,' Donnelly declared.

'Best keep him close,' Sean told him, 'where I can control him.'

'Fine, but he's no Featherstone,' Donnelly warned. 'He's an altogether more dangerous animal.' Sean merely grunted and got to his feet, searching his desk drawer for his house keys. 'Going somewhere?'

'Yeah – home. I, like our Assistant Commissioner, am contactable if anything changes. Everybody knows what they're doing and I need some head-space. I can't think here – not at the moment. I need to get away from all this admin crap and try to work out how I'm going to break down McKenzie in this interview. I like him for this one, but there's something not quite right about it – something he's hiding, aside from the boy's whereabouts.'

'Such as?' Donnelly asked.

'I don't know,' Sean admitted. 'It might be nothing, but I can't help feeling he *wants* us to come after him – wants us to pin this one on him.'

'Maybe he does,' Donnelly agreed. 'He wouldn't be the first wanting his fifteen minutes of fame.'

'I know, but that's not it. Something else is going on. I don't know. Fuck it. Tomorrow we'll interview him and he'll probably spill his guts. Probably can't wait to relive the experience in an interview – making sure we get all the nasty little details. God, I hope the boy is still alive.'

'And d'you think he is?'

'Truthfully – no. But that stays between us,' Sean told him.

'Fair enough.'

'Right, I'm going home for a row. I'll meet you back here first thing. We can go over to Kentish Town together. Until then, let's just pray for George Bridgeman. Let's just pray that I'm wrong.'

After a consultation with his solicitor lasting more than two hours, McKenzie was finally returned to his cell. He'd been suitably vague when answering her questions, treating her like she was another cop instead of his legal representative, much to her frustration and annoyance. Not that he cared – fuck her. Fuck them all. This was his game and his rules. It ended only when he said it ended, and he wasn't ready to call time – not yet.

The thought of Corrigan brought a satisfied smile to his face. He had him running around just the way he wanted him – like a rat gorging itself on poisonous bait. The image of Corrigan twitching and convulsing in the throes of death only broadened his smile. For a moment he regretted not provoking him further when they were alone in his flat – just him, Corrigan and the fat one. If he'd pushed him hard enough, he was sure Corrigan would have given him a beating – a beating that would have left him bruised and cut, all of which would have only added to his ultimate cause. But then again, pain was never something he could tolerate. If Corrigan had inflicted too much, he might well have confessed too early and ruined everything. No, better to play it just as he had.

He could barely wait for the day when he finally brought Corrigan's world crashing down – when the arrogant detective would be forced to stand in court and apologize for his incompetence. He only hoped he would be close enough to look into his eyes as he realized he'd been outmanoeuvred and out-thought by the man he'd treated like so much shit on the bottom of his shoe. Suddenly he felt a chill run along his spine as he remembered those startlingly blue eyes. Not the eyes of a cop – something else. Something much more dangerous – like the eyes he'd seen on a select few men he'd crossed during his prison time – men the other prisoners respected and feared. The sort of men who others knew would kill with only the slightest provocation and with no qualms. But how could a cop have such eyes? It didn't make any sense. Feeling suddenly cold, he pulled the useless blue blanket over himself to try and stave off the chill, real or imagined.

He tried to improve his mood by thinking of the boy – the boy they were so desperate to find – picturing him locked in a room, shivering and terrified, waiting for his keeper to return. Ugly images of things being done to the boy played in his mind, producing the old familiar feelings in his body as his hand crept under the pathetic blanket and he gripped himself, his movements soon becoming frantic as the images of the boy grew increasingly vivid, until he felt the warm stickiness seeping into his hand and through his fingers. He closed his eyes in ecstasy, stifling his groans of pleasure as he waited for his body to relax, his taut muscles becoming less and less rigid until he could breathe normally again, listening for sounds outside his cell. But he heard nothing. His indulgence had gone unnoticed.

When he opened his eyes, he thought of Corrigan again and smiled. Soon he'd pay them back for ruining his life and branding him an outcast. Soon it would be Corrigan who was the outcast – an outcast from his own kind as they looked to distance themselves from his failure and humiliation. Now all he needed was a sign. A signal from the boy's keeper that it was time.

*   *   *

As his freezing breath swirled away into the darkness outside, escaping from the light that spilled through the glass in the front door, Sean couldn't help but look carefully at the keys in his hand before turning his attention to the locks at the entrance to his own home. They were adequate enough for everyday security, but no more so than those at the Bridgemans' house. He unlocked the last one and pushed the door open, the sound of music playing softly in the kitchen telling him Kate was still awake and working instead of watching television and relaxing – all signs that did not bode well. He locked the door behind him and headed for the music and light without stopping to take off his coat and jacket.

'You're home early,' Kate said without sarcasm, despite the fact it was almost nine p.m.

'Hardly early,' Sean answered.

'It is for you.'

'I suppose so. Thought I'd come home and see my wife before things go completely crazy. I'm sorry about the other night.'

'I am too,' she replied without looking or sounding as if she meant it.

'You could be a little bit more forgiving.'

'Sean,' she answered, exasperated, 'I've been at work all day, then I came home to look after the kids, and since they've been in bed I've been catching up on the paperwork I didn't have time to do because the A and E department was a bloody madhouse today. And I've still got bonfire night in south-east London to look forward to, so I'm sorry if I can't be a doting wife right now.'

'Fair enough,' Sean didn't argue, keen to avoid more harsh words, trying to think of something to say to end the silence. 'Bonfire night sounds like fun.'

'Sure. Endless flow of idiots who've set themselves on

fire.' Sean failed to stifle a little laugh. 'It's not so funny when they're children,' Kate reprimanded him.

'No,' Sean agreed, instantly serious.

'Speaking of children,' she continued, 'how's your case going?'

'All right – I think.'

'You think? That's not like you.'

'I have a suspect in custody who looks good for it.'

'And the boy?'

'Still missing. Haven't you been watching the news?' Kate rolled her eyes at him. 'I guess not then,' Sean finished.

'Won't he tell you where the boy is?' she asked.

'Not yet.'

'Why?'

'Because I'm not asking the right questions.'

'Why not?'

'Because my mind's fucked,' he told her. 'This move to the Yard, senior officers sticking their noses into my business twenty-four hours a day – I can't breathe, let alone think. Never thought I'd see the day I missed Peckham.'

'So that's the reason you're home before the early hours,' Kate suddenly accused him, but without venom. 'To try and get your head straight before you interview whoever it is you've got locked up. Your body's here, but your mind's still at work, yes?'

'I've got to get this one solved quickly,' he appealed to her. 'If I don't, then you and the girls won't be seeing me at all. And to solve it I need a confession or . . .'

'Or what?' Kate encouraged him.

'Or a body,' he answered.

'Jesus, Sean,' she told him. 'That's a bit cold.'

'It's the truth. Bodies provide evidence and evidence solves cases and convicts bad people.'

'Well, on that cheery note,' Kate declared, closing the

lid of her laptop, 'I'll bid you goodnight. You're not the only one around here with an early start and a long day ahead of them.'

'No, I don't suppose I am,' Sean acknowledged, trying to sound sympathetic, but in truth he was just disinterested, too absorbed by his own obsessions to care.

'Are you coming?' Kate asked as she stood.

'Not just yet,' he answered.

'Sorry. I forgot you need a little time to *get your head together*.'

'Yes,' he told her bluntly. 'Yes I do.'

'I'll see you later.' Her voice sounded resigned as she allowed her hand to trail across his shoulders as she passed him on her way to the stairs and bed.

He sat still and silent while he waited for the house to settle, the music swallowed by the closing of the laptop. Once he was satisfied he wouldn't be disturbed, he closed his eyes and waited for images and thoughts to race into his mind, but the first thing to enter his consciousness was Anna Ravenni-Ceron, her long curly black hair allowed to escape from the unruly bunch it was usually kept in on top of her head – strands hanging in front of her face and obscuring one of her deep brown eyes as she smiled at him. He imagined her slender neck and naked shoulders, although he'd never actually seen her that way. He had no idea why she danced in front of his mind's eye, just that he liked it. He allowed the image to grow, revealing more of her nakedness as she turned her back on him, looking over her shoulder and smiling seductively – teasing him. But her image was suddenly chased away with a jolt – her twirling beauty replaced by the face of George Bridgeman, pale and lifeless. Sean's physical desires faded to nothing as George Bridgeman stared at him accusingly with his startling green eyes, demanding to know why Sean hadn't saved him. Why he'd forsaken him?

The sudden sense of panic almost made him grab his coat and jacket and head straight back to the Yard or even to Kentish Town to drag McKenzie from his cell and do whatever he had to do to get the truth from him. But if he hadn't talked in his flat, then he wouldn't talk now – not without some new leverage to prise the truth from him.

Sean eased himself back into his chair and considered his next move. The first thing that came to mind was putting in a call to Dr Canning, the pathologist he preferred to use for murder investigations, warning him to expect a body sooner rather than later – the body of a child, probably at an outside scene, somewhere secluded. He was about to reach for his phone when he remembered the last time he'd called Canning and warned him to expect a body. When his hunch had proved correct, it had left him feeling somehow complicit in the murder of the woman whose body they found the very next day, as if by acting on the premonition he had made it come to pass. His hand moved away from the phone lying on the table, unwilling to damn George Bridgeman to the same fate.

He tried to shake the haunting images out of his mind – to bring back the dancing Anna, but the boy's pleading face wouldn't go away. Desperate to break the spell, he jumped from his chair and headed for the cupboard where his bourbon and solitary glass tumbler lived. He poured a decent-sized shot and swallowed it in two gulps before refilling it and heading back to his chair, enjoying the abrasive feel of the thick liquid as it slid towards his stomach. His eyes flickered shut and he allowed the images of the boy and McKenzie to completely flood his mind, but try as he might he couldn't bring the two together – he couldn't see McKenzie's face on the silhouette climbing the stairs towards the boy. He thumped the table in frustration and disappointment; robbed of a sense he had come to rely on, he felt like a hunter who'd forgotten how to track its prey, impotent and useless. 'It'll all make sense soon,' he promised himself. 'I just hope it won't be too late.'

6

The quiet Victorian Street that gently snaked between Highgate Hill and Archway Road was at its widest halfway along where a wide triangular clearing at the junction with Winchester Place gave it the appearance of being a cul-de-sac. The sky was almost completely hidden by a thick canopy of trees whose golden leaves made the gentle breeze sound more like a storm, and the street lamps were spread too far apart to provide much light.

The man pulled the collar of his thick jacket up around his neck to keep out the bitter cold of the night and crouched down in the porch of the tall red-brick, three-storey house, unconcerned by the pale light of the doorway shining above him. He could have gone next door where other children slept, where there was no porch light, but he wouldn't. This was the only house he was interested in. Without a hint of panic or fear he knelt next to the bag he'd placed on the ground and unzipped it – the sound drowned out by the soughing of the wind in the leaves as he removed the head-torch from inside, turning it on and slipping it over his head, adjusting it until he was satisfied it was fit for purpose, its cylindrical beam of white light moving in the semi-darkness as if it was a part of him. Next he rubbed his hands vigorously and blew his hot breath into them for warmth, making sure they were flexible and full of feeling before sliding them into thin, warm gloves, holding them up in front of his face and examining them, like a surgeon before operating. Next he took the rolled-up suede case from the bag and unfurled it as carefully as if it contained diamonds.

The heads of the delicate, shiny tools poking from their pockets stared back at him, his head-torch making them sparkle like jewels as he scanned the contents before selecting one that looked like a long, thin, metal toothpick. He dropped gently on to his knees and bent towards the bottom deadlock, the effort pushing the breath from his lungs so that it swirled around his head like a mist before disappearing. He inserted the tool into the lock, ever so gently manoeuvring it until it seemed to have been gripped by some unseen force inside. Satisfied, he returned the beam of light to the suede case and selected two further tools – the first with a small hook on one end and the other with a tiny diamond-shaped head. He placed the hook into the lock upside down, as if he was trying to prise open its jaws, while he slid the diamond-headed tool smoothly into the waiting keyhole, moving it forwards and backwards with almost no grip, the entire action making only a tiny scratching noise – inaudible to anyone outside or inside, unless they were incredibly close to the source of the sound, which he knew at this time of night they would not be.

After no more than thirty seconds he felt the lock open, the soft click lost in the wind. He felt no sense of euphoria, no excitement or anticipation, just satisfaction. Reclaiming his tools, he stood to reach the top deadlock, relieved to stretch the stiffness from his knees before repeating the procedure with the same effect. He took a minute or so to look about the street, watching the fallen leaves racing along the gutters, tumbling over each other before forming piles, trapped in corners, held captive by turbulence.

He took another moment to consider his actions. He had been told to come. He had been told to take the child away. His instructions had been clear. He must draw strength from the fact he was not alone, for who was he to question the cause for which he had been ordained? He must *save* the children. His doubts quickly faded into the night like his breath as he returned to his tool kit, exchanging the diamond-head and toothpick instruments for what looked like a miniature knife welded on to a long metal handle. He inserted the hooked tool into the central Yale lock, its opening little more than a jagged slit, impenetrable to all but the most skilled hand. But his were such hands and within seconds he again felt the lock click open. Now all that stood between him and the inside of the house was a turn of the handle.

Wasting no time, he quickly and carefully packed his tools and torch in the sports bag and eased the front door open, the warmth and smell from inside rushing out at him, overwhelming his senses, momentarily making it impossible to swim against the tide and push himself into the house. But push himself he did, slowly and painstakingly closing the door behind him, aware that this was the most dangerous time – the time when it was most likely that someone inside would sense the change in the atmosphere his entrance had caused.

His thick jacket made him feel instantly too warm as the house's central heating wrapped around him. Soon he would feel the sweat running down his spine. But he didn't have time to take it off, and besides he would soon need its protection again when he left the house with the chosen child.

He didn't dwell on the comforting normality and order of the house – didn't search through the downstairs rooms for things of value or trophies to fuel the fantasies he didn't have. No: he was here for one purpose and one purpose only – to save the child with the vulgar name, given to her by vulgar parents who knew no better and deserved even less. How could they have been blessed with a child when he and his love had been deprived of such a gift from God?

He walked along the downstairs hallway, lit only with the faint glow coming from the kitchen, no doubt left on to guide any thirsty night-time wanderers and now guiding him to the foot of the staircase. A gloved hand rested on the bannister as he began to climb, slowly and without a sound, grateful for the thick, new carpet he once again felt underfoot, nevertheless careful to avoid the stairs that he knew would creak and betray his presence. He arrived at the first floor where the parents slept in the darkness of their room, but with the door open in case their two-year-old needed them in the middle of the night. The only illumination was the pale blue light from the floors above where the other children slept. He floated past the bedrooms and continued his ascent to the summit of the house where he knew the little girl slept. But first he had to pass the bedroom on the second floor occupied by her older sister. She would have learned enough of the world to be frightened of it and would not be as easily and quickly placated as her younger sibling. She might scream and raise the alarm.

With the utmost care he tiptoed past the older child's bedroom and began the final climb towards the one he had come for – the one he'd been guided to take.

By now the sweat was running down his back and a light sheen coated his face, but he was oblivious to it as he stepped on to the landing of the top floor. There was only one room

186

up here, converted from the old attic – a strange place for a young child to sleep when there were other bedrooms closer to her family she could have used. Another sign of her parents' neglect and lack of love, he decided. Clearly his actions were justified.

Before entering the bedroom he placed his bag carefully on the floor and searched inside for the special thing he'd brought with him – the thing that would instantly buy her trust and her silent cooperation. He pulled it free from the bag, the sight of it in the dim light making him almost smile as he imagined the little girl's face when she saw what he had brought for her.

Leaving his bag on the landing, he slowly pushed the door to her room open, the faint illumination emanating from her night-lamp enough for him to see her lying in her bed underneath a blue-and-white patchwork quilt, her face slightly obscured by her shoulder-length blonde hair. Her breathing was heavy enough to be audible as she stirred slightly, reacting to the presence in her room, but not waking fully as her toys and dolls looked on – dozens of silent witnesses with unseeing eyes, unable to testify to what was happening in the room with slanted ceilings and walls decorated with pictures of ponies.

He began to cross the room towards her, stepping as softly as he could until he reached her bedside, dropping to his knees and trying to speak, holding the precious thing close to his own face so it would be the first thing she saw when her eyes flickered open. But his voice deserted him, the words lost in his sudden confusion and fear. Taking children from their homes in the middle of the night – how could this be right? Soon enough, though, he remembered who had told him he must and why, fortifying his belief and giving him courage. He swallowed painfully and licked his lips before they parted.

'Bailey . . .' he whispered her name through trembling lips and waited. She stirred under her quilt, but still didn't wake. 'Bailey,' he repeated, forcing himself to utter the name so distasteful it made him recoil from his own words. 'It's time to wake up now, Bailey.'

The little girl's pupils moved under her still-closed eyelids, as if she was having a bad dream, until at last they began to slowly open, before closing again. As her mind processed the glimpse of information, her eyes suddenly opened wide in delighted surprise, her hands reaching out for the precious thing, the presence of the man almost unnoticed, so deep was her joy and excitement. He saw her chest fill with air as she prepared to call out the name, and quickly put his finger to his lips and released a long, quiet 'Sssssssh.' Finally Bailey registered that she and the precious thing were not alone her bedroom and her expression became more concerned. He smiled a friendly, warm smile, his eyes glinting with kindness. 'It's time to go now, Bailey,' he whispered, 'to a special, magical place where only the best children are allowed. Would you like to come?'

'Are you a friend of my mummy?' Bailey asked, imitating his whispering.

'No,' he answered, his face becoming instantly more serious, 'not a friend of your mummy. I'm someone who loves you. Someone who loves you more than your mummy ever will.'

Sean entered the office a little after seven a.m. feeling even more tired than he had the night before. The coldness between him and Kate and his feelings for Anna only added to the confusion of his cluttered mind as he tried to prepare mentally for the interview with McKenzie later that morning. He decided to wait until at least eight before he hassled the forensic team for some information he could use. His usual lab liaison sergeant, DS Roddis, might be a bit of a cold fish, but he was one of the best in the business and he tolerated Sean's constant meddling and harassment for updates. On this case, however, he'd be dealing with the team covering north-west London; so far as Sean was concerned they were an unknown quantity, which meant he'd have to be more restrained in his dealings with them. He made a note to speak to Addis about having Roddis and his crew attached to the Special Investigations Unit on a permanent basis. The Assistant Commissioner was bound to refuse, but he might then offer a compromise and hand Roddis over, perhaps even allow him to put together a small team for Sean's exclusive use.

No sooner had Sean hung up his coat and jacket than he saw Sally entering the office looking a lot more sprightly than he felt, carrying a tray of coffees and a brown paper bag that was beginning to show grease marks. He watched her drop off a couple of takeaway cups to some of the other early arrivers before heading his way. She entered his office just as he sat down.

'Morning, guv'nor,' she announced cheerfully, holding up the greasy bag. 'Breakfast.'

'No,' he answered, 'but if that's coffee you can pass one over here.'

'Naturally,' she told him, placing a cardboard cup in front of him. 'Black, no sugar.'

'Thanks,' he said, tossing the plastic lid into the metal bin that lived by the side of his new desk.

'Pain-au-chocolat?' she asked, waving the greasy bag in the air.

'Christ, no.' He grimaced, leaning away from the offending article. 'God save me from pain-au-chocolat. Anyway, what you so happy about?'

'Better than being miserable,' she told him. He didn't

answer. 'I hear you're interviewing McKenzie this morning
– again.'

'I am.'

'Need someone to sit in on it with you?'

'I think Dave has that honour, although if he doesn't show
up soon you're more than welcome to join me.'

'Any idea what you're going to ask him?'

'Not really.'

'And the boy – do you think he could still be alive?'

Before he could answer, Addis burst into the main office
and marched across to them, a manilla file clutched in his
hand. He took one step into Sean's office and came to a halt
as they stared at him, waiting for him to speak, years of
dealing with senior officers telling them he had something
he very much wanted to say.

'So,' he began, 'this suspect of yours, Mark McKenzie, tell
me again how sure you are he's responsible for the abduction of George Bridgeman.'

Sean and Sally looked at each other, sensing a trap, before
Sean answered: 'As sure as I can be at this time, but I haven't
ruled out other possibilities.'

'As sure as you can be?' Addis repeated. 'Then perhaps
you can explain this?' He stepped forward and dropped the
folder on to Sean's desk. Again Sean and Sally exchanged
glances before Sean leaned forward and picked up the folder,
slowly opening it as if it could be booby-trapped. As soon
as the cover fell open he saw the Missing Person Report
inside and felt his spirits sink and his gut tighten.

Addis spoke again. 'Bailey Fellowes – IC1, five years old,
disappeared in the middle of the night from her home in
Highgate – which, if you're not already aware, is not exactly
a million miles away from bloody Hampstead.'

'A coincidence,' Sean faintly offered.

'A coincidence?' Addis echoed, stifling his rising voice at

the expense of going bright red in the face. 'Read the bloody report, Inspector: no signs of a break-in. A wealthy family living in an exclusive area of North London. Child seemingly vanishes in the night. Christ, what an embarrassment! Just yesterday I was on the bloody television telling the world we were close to solving this damn case. You even had me name McKenzie. You've made me look a fool, Inspector.'

'How did you get the report before me?' Sean changed the direction of the argument. 'Any suspicious missing persons cases involving children are supposed to come to me first.'

'I countermanded that order,' Addis told him. 'We have a chain of command here at the Yard. You would be wise to remember that. Now get the hell over to Highgate. The local CID are waiting for you to take over. And get McKenzie out of custody, for God's sake – this whole fiasco is embarrassing enough without us wrongfully imprisoning somebody. I want this matter solved as soon as possible before it drags the whole Service down with it. I don't care how you do it – just get it done. We need a result.'

'What d'you want us to do?' Sean fought back. 'Pick someone at random and make them fit the crime? Make the crime fit them?'

Addis rounded on him in an instant. 'Don't take that tone with me, Inspector. I don't employ people without knowing a lot about them first. I'm fully aware of the types of under-cover work you've done in the past, and how you got results then. And I know a lot more about the Sebastian Gibran investigation and how you made sure he'd never walk free than you imagine.'

Sean considered him in silence for a while, trying to decide whether Addis was just guessing or whether he really did know something, and if he did – how? 'I wasn't aware you were in any way involved in the Gibran case.'

'There's a great many things you're not aware of,' Addis reminded him. 'I make it my business to know what's going on everywhere within the Metropolitan Police. It's my job to protect the force's reputation and the reputation of the people who belong to it. I won't let anyone drag it down – you need to remember that. Now, get over to Highgate and get this matter resolved. A full report – on my desk – by lunchtime.' Addis scowled at them one last time before spinning on his heels and marching from the room.

Sally broke the silence. 'For a second there he reminded me of him,' she told Sean.

'Of who?'

'Gibran. He said the same things about his job – about how it was up to him to protect his company. Protect its reputation and people. I wonder if he knows what he sounds like?'

'I don't suppose so,' Sean answered. 'He doesn't know anything about Gibran or that case. He's just trying to make us think he does.'

'Why?' Sally asked. 'And what did he mean about he knows more about how you put him away for good? Did you do something you shouldn't have?'

Sean had never told her how he'd taken her bloodstained warrant card from her bedside cabinet in the Intensive Care Unit. How he'd given it to Donnelly, telling him to make sure it was found during the search of Gibran's house. But he didn't believe he'd done anything that he shouldn't have; rather, he'd done what absolutely needed to be done. Gibran hadn't played by the rules and the only way they were going to take him down was to put the rule book to one side – temporarily.

'No,' he told Sally. 'I did exactly what I had to do. Don't worry about Addis – he knows nothing.'

192

'Why do I get the feeling you're not telling me everything?' Sally replied.

'You're just getting jumpy. Let it go.' He opened up the Missing Person Report and began to scan the pages. 'We've got bigger problems than Addis.'

'Same offender?' Sally asked, happy to leave Gibran in the past.

'Yes. Whoever took George Bridgeman's taken this one too. But who and why?'

'Well, whoever it is, it isn't McKenzie,' Sally reminded him. 'Unless he's Harry Houdini.'

'Damn it,' Sean said, shaking his head. 'How could I be so wrong about him? I thought we had our man. I thought he was just biding time until we could bury him. Two missing children. Jesus Christ – this is going to be the biggest thing since Fred West.'

'Not if we get the children back alive,' Sally told him. 'Then everyone will forget about it within a couple of weeks – including Addis. No deaths – no news.'

'You're right. But what the hell are we supposed to do now? Where do we go from here?'

'To Highgate,' Sally told him. 'We look for the things we missed and we start again. What else can we do?'

'We start again,' Sean repeated her words. 'Only now we have two missing children and not a bloody clue what's happened to them.'

'Do you want me to arrange for McKenzie to be released?'

'No,' Sean snapped. 'That fucker can stay locked up for a few more hours.'

'Why?' Sally asked.

'Because he may not have been playing the game I thought he was, but he's playing a game nonetheless. First time we interviewed him I knew there was something not right – the way he would neither admit nor deny anything I put to him. I knew the little bastard was up to something.'

'You didn't say anything.' Sally's tone was accusing.

'I was going to – once I'd worked it out. Now I need to know why and I need to know for sure he's not involved.'

'How could he be? He was locked up in Kentish Town nick all night.'

'Maybe he's not working alone,' Sean suggested. 'People like McKenzie find strength in the group. He takes one child, then to make him look innocent someone else takes the next while he's in custody. He goes nowhere until I'm sure.'

'Fair enough,' Sally agreed, already standing and pulling her coat back on. 'I'll drive – you think,' she told him.

'Think?' Sean replied quietly. 'There's something I haven't done in a while.'

'Sorry?' Sally asked.

'Nothing,' he assured her. 'Just . . . nothing.'

Forty minutes later they arrived at the address in Highgate. It was situated in a beautiful, broad street with a dense canopy of brown and gold that swayed in the breeze, each movement releasing hundreds of leaves at a time to float gently to the ground. Even in the mid-morning the noise from above was intense – if anyone cared to pay it any notice. Sean did – looking up at the branches above his head as he stepped from the car – imagining how loud the noise must have seemed in the middle of the night – comforting and camouflaging to the man who stalked the street looking for the house he'd already selected. For this was no random act: he'd come for the child – the child he'd already ordained as his next victim.

As they approached the house the little girl had been taken from, Sean was struck by the similarity between this street and Courthope Road in Hampstead. Not so much the physical similarities, of which there were few other than the height and quantity of the trees, but more by the *feel* of both streets – quiet sanctuaries close to the heart of the metropolis, almost eerie and a little unnerving, as if the houses and trees had borne witness to some terrible act that had changed and stained the atmosphere there forever. He felt a chill that made him shiver and turn his coat collar up against the cold.

'You all right?' Sally asked.

Sean ignored the question. 'Do you see any similarities between this street and the one in Hampstead?' he asked.

'They're both affluent, quiet and residential,' Sally answered, 'but nothing startling. The houses are different and the road shape's different. Why – have you seen something?'

'Not really,' he answered, then added: 'Just a feeling.'

'What sort of feeling?'

'This place makes me feel displaced – like déjà-vu, or like I can't clear my head, as if I was under water or in a dream.'

'Come on,' Sally encouraged him. She understood him better than almost anyone else and had since stopped aban-doned any scepticism where his insights were concerned. 'Let's go see the parents.'

Sean looked her in the eye for an unnaturally long time before nodding and walking the last few steps to the porch of the house, stopping when he reached the short flight of steps, his arm stretched out to the side to ensure Sally didn't go further. He stared at the front door, his imagination turning day to night as the figure of a man slowly formed behind his eyes, crouched by the front door, calmly and carefully working his fine tools to unpick the locks. Sean looked up at the porch light that had been left on in the morning panic, its weak glow almost unnoticeable in the daylight and insufficient for the intruder's purposes at night.

'He used a torch,' he suddenly said out loud. 'He needs

195

light to work the locks. To do it as quietly as he needs to, he needs light.'

'Makes sense,' Sally agreed, aware that the fact alone was of little importance, but for Sean to be able to build the picture he needed to see every detail. These were his foundations.

'But it would have to be small, like a miniature Maglite – something he could hold in his mouth for at least a few minutes while his hands were full.' Sean paused for a second, feeling the cold of autumn wrapping around him, imagining the freezing, harsh metal of a torch in his mouth, the discomfort distracting him from the vital work his hands needed to perform. 'No,' he contradicted himself, 'no he wouldn't put it in his mouth. Something else.'

'A head-torch,' Sally suggested, 'like a miner's hat type thing, only not on a hat, on a headband like those things you see cyclists wearing.'

'Yeah,' Sean agreed, as he continued to stare at the invisible figure. 'Something like that.' But although he could see the man, he couldn't feel him – couldn't even begin to understand him. Why did he have to break into the houses to take the children? Why did he want the children? Why these particular children?

'Anything else?' Sally asked after a long while.

'No.' Sean admitted defeat, wondering why there was no police tape cordoning off the porch area as he began to climb the few stairs until he was close enough to see the telltale signs of aluminium dust on the door, handle and locks. 'They've already checked for prints,' he told Sally.

'I noticed,' she replied. 'Someone's in a hurry.'

'Addis,' Sean muttered. 'I can smell his interference already.'

'Then best we get on with it,' Sally sighed, and rang the doorbell hard, in the way only cops and postmen do. They waited silently for it to be answered – listening as heavy, purposeful steps beat their way towards them, giving cruel, practical thoughts just time enough to invade Sean's mind. He prayed the children were still alive, but if they were not, or if one was not, then he prayed they would find the body soon. With the body would come nightmares, but also evidence. Evidence of the man he sought, his state of mind and motivation. If the body showed signs of violence and sexual abuse, he could limit his suspect searches to violent paedophiles, motivated by their twisted desires and anger bred by their own stolen childhoods. But if the body was relatively untouched, with no signs of abuse, then he would be hunting a different animal altogether – a tortured, guilt-ridden beast, motivated by some insanity that neither psychiatrists or pharmaceuticals had been able to touch or cure. Either way, it would give him a route into his quarry's mind, a way to build a picture that would enable him to think like him and therefore predict him. Once he had that he could build the path that would lead to the door of the man who'd taken the children.

The door was swung open by a short, stocky man in his fifties with a crown of unkempt, curly, hazel hair that fitted his poorly fitting, cheap blue suit perfectly. He adjusted the ancient glasses that balanced on the end of his nose and spoke in a thick Welsh accent, despite having spent most of his adult life in London. 'Can I help you?' he asked, although he knew what they were.

'DI Sean Corrigan,' Sean told him quietly, discreetly showing him his warrant card. 'My colleague, DS Sally Jones, from the Special Investigations Unit.'

'How you doing?' the stocky little man replied, holding out a hand that Sean accepted. 'DI Ross Adams, from the local CID. I've been expecting you. My sergeant, DS Tony

Wright, is inside looking after the family. Special Investigations Unit, you say? I don't think I've heard of you before.'

'No,' Sean answered. 'It's a new thing.'

'Is it now?' Ross grinned. 'Sounds very important.'

'Perhaps you can tell me why this porch hasn't been sealed off for Forensics?' Sean asked, keen to change the subject. 'This is a crime scene, isn't it?'

'Mr Addis . . . Assistant Commissioner Addis, he thought discretion was the order of the day. We had the door and its furniture examined when the street was nice and quiet like. Don't want to draw unwanted attention by stringing police tape all over the house like bloody party streamers, do we now?'

'Addis?' Sean asked. 'Addis told you to do it?'

'He did indeed. Now, if you're finished, you'd better come inside and have a look around.' He pushed the door wide open and walked back into the darkness inside. Sean and Sally looked at each other for a second before they followed him, Sally carefully closing the door behind them while Sean spotted what he was looking for: the control panel of an alarm system. 'I take it you've read the Missing Person Report?' Adams called over his shoulder.

'We have,' Sean answered.

'Then you know about as much as we do. Little girl seems to have just disappeared,' he told them, his voice lowered as they approached the kitchen and the family. 'Mum put her to bed about eight p.m. and checked on her about eleven. Everything was fine and normal. The au pair went to get her up for school about seven thirty this morning and she was gone – nowhere to be found. The parents and au pair have searched the house and so have we, and the uniforms who came here first. They recognized similarities between what they were being told and your case: one of them had seen a news article about it or something. Anyway, they thought they'd better tell us and here we are.'

'How did Addis find out about it?' Sean asked, Addis's involvement still troubling him.

'Not from me,' Adams told him. 'Must have had someone at the Yard monitoring Missing Person Reports as they were going on to the PNC. Here we are then,' Adams almost cheerfully declared as they reached the kitchen. Always the kitchen, Sean thought, where families gather in good times and desperate times. Nathan and Jessica Fellowes sat close to each other at the table – a heavy block of mahogany that he guessed had been artificially aged to look antique. He was immediately struck by the similarity in general appearance of Mrs Fellowes to Mrs Bridgeman: the same toned, athletic body, luminous skin and immaculately faked ash blonde hair. But Jessica Fellowes' facial structure was slightly different, as if she wasn't from quite the same stock as Celia Bridgeman. Mr Fellowes also had a physique honed over many hours in an expensive health club with a personal trainer, tanned skin and pushed back, dark brown, wavy hair, the product of an upmarket stylist rather than a side-street barber. But his appearance somehow lacked the self-assurance of Stuart Bridgeman, his jet-black eyes betraying a crueller upbringing, as if he had only recently joined the ranks of the rich and privileged. DS Tony Wright, tall and muscular, his angular face and shaved head adding to his athletic appearance, despite his advancing years, stood leaning against the window frame with the expression of a man who really didn't want to be there. Sean noticed Mrs Fellowes clutched a white-backed piece of paper to her stomach that he instinctively knew would be a picture of the missing girl.

'Mr Fellowes – Mrs Fellowes, this is DI Corrigan, from

the Special Investigations Unit – come to take over the investigation and get your little girl back for you.'

Adams' over-the-top introduction earned him a glare from Sean.

'Special Investigations?' Mrs Fellowes asked, her gravelly voice and London accent catching Sean by surprise. 'You think she's been taken by the same animal who took that little boy, don't you?' Sean looked at Adams who looked at his feet.

'How much has DI Adams told you, Mrs Fellowes?' Sean asked. He had no intention of trying to gild the lily – it was way too late for that.

'He told me you couldn't be sure – that maybe, somehow she just got out of the house on her own.'

'And what do you think?' he continued.

'I think someone took her,' Jessica answered. 'I think whoever took that little boy has taken my Bailey.'

'So do I,' Sean admitted.

'Jesus Christ,' Nathan Fellowes managed to say before allowing his face to sink into his hands.

'You haven't found that little boy either, have you?' Jessica asked.

'No,' Sean told her, 'we haven't.'

'So why should I believe you're gonna find my Bailey?'

'Because I'm your only hope,' Sean told her straight.

She stared silently at the only man who could return her child – the child she'd carried in her belly for nine months and held to her swollen breasts to feed for another eighteen. For a moment she thought she could still feel her suckling, but told herself it was simply more recent memories of breast-feeding Bailey's two-year-old brother.

'It's an unusual name,' Sally spoke to break the silence, 'Bailey?'

'It's what I'd drunk too much of when I conceived her,' Jessica admitted, head held high on her stretched neck in

200

defiance at being judged. 'We thought it would be . . . fun. We regret it now, but you can't just change a kid's name.'

Sean examined her as she spoke, wondering whether she was as hardnosed and tough on the inside as she tried to look on the outside. Her strained, red eyes told him she wasn't. 'I like it,' he lied. 'It's a bit more interesting than most other names.' Jessica said nothing. 'Anyway,' he moved on, 'time is crucial so I won't waste it. I need to ask you a lot of questions, some of which you won't like and some of which you may have already been asked. Firstly, I noticed the house appears to be alarmed. Was it set last night?'

'No,' Nathan Fellowes answered through his despair, sliding his hands away from his face. 'We've only been here a couple of weeks. There's an alarm control panel in the hallway, but it's from the old alarm the previous owners had. We haven't had it changed over yet. They were supposed to come and install the new one today.' He shared the same somewhat heavy London accent as his wife.

'So it wasn't active?' Sally asked.

'No,' Nathan replied.

'And you've only been in the house a couple of weeks?' Sean added.

'Yeah. So what?' Nathan asked, looking from Sean to Sally as they turned to look at each other. *Who would know that?* Sean asked himself. *Who could know both families had only recently moved in and had no alarm systems?*

'OK,' Sean cleared his head, 'I'm going to need the name of the alarm company you were going to use and the names of the removal company you used and the estate agents too. I'll also need the names of all tradesmen that have been in the house since you moved in and the name of the family that were here before you.'

'That might take some time,' Nathan argued, overwhelmed by Sean's demands, but desperate to help.

'Make it your number one priority,' Sean told him without sympathy, sure the shared facts of both families had to mean something crucial – had to be the route to whoever had taken the children. 'Do you have any other children?' he continued before anyone else could speak.

'Yes,' Jessica answered. 'Two: Trisha and Jacob.'

'How old are they?'

'Trisha's eight and Jake's only two.'

'Do you have a nanny or have you ever had a nanny?'

'I've had help with the children,' Jessica told him defensively, as if it was a sign of some maternal failing. 'We have an au pair working for us now. She's looking after Trish and Jake while this—'

'I'll need her name and that of anyone else you've used in the past – particularly since you had Bailey.'

'OK,' Jessica agreed. 'I'll get the names together for you as soon as I can.'

'You think someone who worked for us – who we trusted to look after our kids – might have taken Bailey?' Nathan Fellowes asked. 'Why would they do that?'

'I'm just considering every possibility at this moment, Mr Fellowes. We don't know anything for sure yet.'

'Then what do you know for sure?' Nathan angrily demanded. Sean had seen it many times before – projected anger borne of frustration and fear. But that didn't make it any less dangerous or tolerable.

'I know I need you to get me those names,' Sean told him, 'right now, please.'

Nathan pushed himself away and up from the table, his red eyes glaring at the four detectives standing in his kitchen. Sean knew what he was thinking: should he launch himself at the police and force them to subdue him and take him away – away from this living hell? He wouldn't have been the first to use violence as an escape.

'Fine,' Nathan finally agreed and strode out of the kitchen.

Sean turned to Jessica. 'I need to ask you something. Something personal and unpleasant, but I need to know.'

'Go on,' she agreed guardedly.

'Are any of your children from a previous . . . or another relationship either of you may have had?'

'What?'

'It's not unusual,' Sean explained, 'not today, but I need to know if there's an estranged father or perhaps mother out there who may feel they have a right to take Bailey.'

'No,' she answered without hesitation. 'All our children are all ours.'

'Fine,' Sean believed her. 'I had to ask.' Again she didn't reply. 'I need to see Bailey's bedroom.'

Jessica filled her lungs to capacity to steady herself before speaking. 'I'll show you,' she agreed, half desperate to be back in the room that made her feel closer to her missing child and half terrified to stand in that room, looking at the empty, unmade bed – the scent of her baby heavy in the air.

'No,' Sean insisted. 'I need to see it alone.'

She looked at him silently for a long time, occasionally glancing at Sally for unspoken clues as to Sean's true intentions. Sally remained stone-faced. 'You do what you gotta do,' she finally told him. 'It's the room in the loft space. It's the only one up there.'

'Unusual for a five-year-old to want to . . . isolate themselves like that,' Sean accidentally voiced what he was thinking.

'Her choice,' Jessica told him. 'She thought it would be special – like it was her princess's tower.' Her fingers curled tightly around the photograph she was still clutching.

'I see,' Sean replied. 'I won't be long,' he added and walked from the kitchen, aware of the eyes that followed him through the doorway, exhaling as quietly as he could through pursed lips once he'd escaped into the quiet, dimly lit hallway.

He took a few seconds to look around as he cleared his mind. Almost everything was tastefully and expensively decorated or arranged – *almost everything*. But the house was a reflection of its occupants: the occasional overly showy statue or figurine, painting or Persian rug, betraying their origins. Sean tried to think if it could somehow be relevant to Bailey's disappearance, but nothing stirred in his instinct, although it was becoming increasingly difficult to trust that – the tool he had relied on for so long suddenly so blunt, unfit for purpose.

He began to climb the wide, carpeted staircase, thinking of his own house and how tiny it now seemed compared to a *real* family home – thoughts that made him stop halfway towards the first floor. *Think*, he told himself. *Think. Forget home. Forget Addis and the others. Think – think like him.* He began to climb again, the new carpet soft under his leather-soled shoes, completely masking the sound of his footsteps as he kept to the side of the stairs to avoid any invisible footprints the stealer of children might have left, even though he knew they'd probably already been trampled by frantic parents. *You knew there was thick carpet on the staircase – you knew your footsteps wouldn't be heard as you climbed these stairs, but how? How did you know that? And you knew there was an alarm, but that it wasn't working yet. How did you know? Did you know it was due to be fixed today – is that why you came last night, because you had to, before the house was alarmed?*

He thought about the possibility of the suspect being an alarm fitter and how perfect that cover could be, with access to everything he would need to know about the family, the inside of the house and the alarm system itself. The terrifying simplicity of it made him shudder. If they got a hit on the alarm company, if it was the same company for both houses, the same engineer, then he'd have his man. *Look for the cross-overs*, he reminded himself. *Look for the thing that connects the two families – there has to be one and it has to be the answer, somehow.*

He continued to climb the stairs, quickly peering into each room on each floor, increasingly convinced the man who stole Bailey away had not been into any of the rooms, not even looked inside – because he didn't have to. *You knew exactly which room was the girl's – you came in and you went straight to her room, but how did you know? How could you know that unless you've been in this house before? Just as you'd been in the other house before you took the boy. So you know these families, you sick, twisted bastard – you know these families. But what are you? Some passing tradesman they hardly even noticed, even though you were watching them, learning everything you needed to know before shattering their lives? Or had the families taken you into the bosom of their homes, only for you to commit the ultimate betrayal of trust? Which one are you, damn it? I will find out and I will find you.*

Before he knew it he was standing outside Bailey's bedroom, the climb through the house something he couldn't even remember. *What did it feel like standing here? What did it feel like standing in the warm house, knowing the object of your every desire was sleeping on the other side of this open door? – dreaming of you coming for her, wanting you, but why do you want them? What are you taking them for?* Again he considered the fact that no bodies had been found, his mind swimming with possibilities as to what that could mean, remembering that as a virtual rule the only killers who tried to ensure their victims were never found were those who have a strong connection to them – something so strong it would lead the police straight to their door: a husband who kills his wife, a business partner who wants it all, an organized criminal getting rid of a turf rival, a parent killing their own child. Strangers rarely went to the trouble of concealing their victims well enough to never be found – even those who were highly organized and motivated.

Images of all the victims he'd seen flashed through his mind, a series of macabre stills fast-forwarding through his memory: some mutilated, others apparently with barely a mark. Bodies in wheelie bins, next to train tracks, left in the street, abandoned in the woods, tossed into running water, and those left in shallow, pointless graves, gnawed and bitten by foxes and rats. *So either you know these children personally*, he told the unseen monster, *or they're . . . they're not dead. You've taken them, but you haven't killed them, and you haven't killed them because . . .* he suddenly felt so close to a breakthrough into the mind and motivation of the taker that his head began to pound as if he was suffering a severe migraine *. . . because you don't have to . . . because . . . because . . .* The answer came like light pouring into a black hole *. . . you haven't hurt them. You haven't touched them. You take them, but don't lay a finger on them. You love them!* He allowed his mind to stop thinking, to grow calm. *But if, when, they don't return your love, what will you do?* Once again the face of Thomas Keller burnt itself into his consciousness. *Will you turn on them like Keller turned on the women he'd taken? Will you leave them in a dark wood for me to find?*

He waited for the answers, but none came. 'Damn it. I'm guessing – nothing more than guessing. Christ,' he swore quietly as he once more tried to concentrate, to think like the man whose footsteps he now walked in, raising his hand to the partially open door, resting no more than a fingertip on the yet-to-be-examined wooden surface and pushing it fully open – slowly waiting for it to swing fully aside. *Did you stand here and watch her sleeping? Watch her chest rise and fall – listen to her breathing? Did her scent almost drive you mad with desire, make you want to rush into the room and do the things you'd dreamed about doing to her while her parents, brother and sister slept soundly below? Maybe you wanted to, but you didn't. How did you control those needs that burn in the pit of your stomach?*

He sighed without knowing it and walked into the room, not stopping until he was exactly in the centre where he stood completely still, staring at the empty, unmade bed, biting down hard on his bottom lip, the pain preventing any unplanned thoughts from ambushing him while he tried to clear his mind and create the blank canvas he needed to paint the picture of what had happened here last night. The girl had been taken, but that was only a small part of it. What coming together of circumstances and opportunities had led to the cataclysmic event that could result in the violent end to a young, innocent life?

Toys from all corners of the room watched him as he looked around – their glass eyes as lifeless as the eyes of the victims that had haunted him as he'd climbed the stairs. And like so many of the dead, they looked as if they might come to life at any moment – sealed plastic lips of dolls unable to tell him what they saw. Sean felt their eyes as he moved towards Bailey's abandoned bed and knelt by its side, eyes wide and nostrils flared as he instinctively searched for anything that didn't belong: the faint scent of cigarettes or alcohol, chloroform or ether; a tiny drop of blood or a small patch of discoloured, flaky material made that way by semen or saliva. But he saw and smelt nothing out of place. *How*, he asked the ghost, *how did you come into this room in the dead of night and take this girl – take this girl without a sound or even the slightest sign of a struggle?*

'What do you want them for?' he demanded under his breath, his lips thin and pale with anger and frustration, that soon gave way to an overwhelming sadness. 'Please don't hurt them,' he whispered. 'Don't hurt them and I won't hurt you. As God is my witness, I'll do everything I can for you, just don't hurt them.'

He closed his eyes for a fraction too long, allowing the snarling, savage faces of the gang of paedophiles who called themselves the Network, to poison his thoughts, their faces morphing into the shapes and colours of the bizarre, hand-made animal masks they wore during the orgies of child abuse they called *chicken feasts*. His eyes jolted open to chase the images from hell away.

Sean searched in his coat pocket until he found a loose pair of surgical gloves that he painstakingly pulled over his hands, making a mental note to let Forensics know that if they found traces of talcum powder it would most likely have come from his gloves. Once his hands were covered he ran them over the surface of the blue-and-white patch-work quilt, partly to see if any foreign objects revealed themselves, but more significantly to try and connect with the little girl. If he couldn't think like the taker then perhaps he could try and see what she had seen – feel what she had felt. Perhaps that would bring the answers? 'Why didn't you fight?' he whispered. 'Why didn't you scream or call out? Weren't you frightened?'

He thought about his last question for a few seconds, looking around at the peaceful room, sensing no brutaliza-tion of the atmosphere, no lingering feeling that something violent or terrible had happened there. 'No. You weren't frightened, were you? But why not? Why weren't you afraid of this man who came into your room in the middle of the night? Did you know him, know him like he knew this house? Did you trust him – trust him like George Bridgeman trusted him? Did he make you feel safe – loved and safe?' Sean suddenly found himself rubbing his face with his glove covered hands, the smell and feel of the latex making him gag slightly as he lost his train of thought, feeling as far away from truly understanding what was happening as he'd ever been.

'Shit,' he swore and pushed himself back to a standing position, surveying the room with his hands on his hips, studying the faces of the silent dolls and teddy bears and the array of other soft toys that seemed to surround him. Slowly he began to move around the room, circling its borders where most of the lifeless creatures were gathered, his hand occasionally stretching out to touch one or move one slightly to see what was behind them. The room reminded him so much of not just George's, but of his own children's rooms, their infant sanctuaries, colourful and safe – places where the outside world didn't exist – where they were protected from all the evils of reality. He couldn't help but smile as he recognized some of the toys that he'd also seen in his daughters' rooms, until he found himself back by the bed, the far side of which was covered in dozens more dolls and toys. He scanned each and every one, looking for others he recognized from home, his need to connect with his own children suddenly overwhelming. Something caught his eye, hidden in amongst the other toys, a doll whose eyes seemed to burn into his own, as if she was desperately trying to tell him something, beckoning him. He leaned over the bed and gently pulled the doll free from the crowd, its incredibly blue eyes glittering in her porcelain face and contrasting with her long, curly, black hair. She was dressed in a long, handmade, lace dress that looked like a wedding dress from the 1930s, giving her the appearance of an antique rather than a toy. As he held the beautiful doll he was just beginning to feel a slight smile spread across his lips when the sense of someone behind him made him spin around to face the door.

Jessica Fellowes stared at him blankly, her eyes as glassy and lifeless as those of the doll he held. 'What are you doing?'

she asked, protective of her daughter's room, uncomfortable at having a strange man handling her things.

'Looking,' Sean answered.

'For what?'

'Anything. Anything out of place.'

Jessica's eyes fell on the doll he held. 'Like that doll?' she asked, her dead eyes flaring with anger. 'Like you shouldn't find a doll like that in a house owned by people like us? What is it – too *classy* for people like us?'

'No,' Sean protested, the doll suddenly heavy and awkward in his hands. 'I was just—'

'Nathan and I earned everything we have. We weren't born with silver spoons in our mouths like most of the people in this street who can hardly even bring themselves to speak to us. Nathan started as little more than the tea-boy – only sixteen he was, but he showed them – showed them how good he was – working in the City, surrounded by all them superior bastards, just because they went to the right schools and the right bloody universities. He proved he was better than them and this is our reward, so we'll spend our money how we bloody well like. But that doesn't mean we can't have taste. What did you expect – that I'd only ever let Bailey have Barbie dolls and crap?'

'No,' Sean explained. 'It's just that it reminded me of something my wife would want to buy for my girls, even if they didn't want it.'

She walked deeper into the room and gently took the doll from him, holding it in one hand as she smoothed its long hair with her other. 'I didn't want to buy it,' she admitted. 'Stupid thing cost a fortune, but Bailey insisted and I can be such a soft touch – you know how it is with kids.'

'Absolutely,' Sean confided, trying to remember the last time he'd been in a toyshop with his daughters.

'Anyway, she made a liar out of me. She plays with it all

the time.' She shook her head disapprovingly and smiled despite the quiet tears that had begun to trickle from the corners of her eyes. 'Look at all these toys,' she said. 'Didn't have toys like this when we were kids. Didn't have any money – not like now. Me and Nathan back then – both our families always pot-less, trying to survive on our council estate in Holloway, trying to find a way to escape.'

'Looks like you did.'

'Yeah, we did. All the way from Holloway to Highgate – you know we were brought up less than two miles from here, but it feels more like two hundred miles. Different world.'

'That's London,' Sean reminded her, thinking of his own home's proximity to some of the toughest council estates in south-east London.

'I suppose,' she agreed. 'But I tell you now, I'd give it all up in a second to have my Bailey back. They can take it all, just give me my daughter back.'

'I don't believe this is about any sort of ransom,' Sean explained.

'That's not what I meant,' she told him. 'I know she wasn't taken for money. I mean that if we don't get her back then this is all for nothing. Everything we've achieved will be for nothing. Our lives will never be the same again. They'll never be good again, not without Bailey.'

'Don't give up hope,' Sean encouraged.

'Haven't you?' she caught him cold. 'Do you really think she's all right?'

'I think there's a good chance of it, but I need to find her quickly, and to do that I need you to do everything I ask and do it as quickly as you can.'

'I'll do anything,' she told him, almost pleading. 'Just promise me you'll bring her back. You'll bring her home. I don't think I could go on if something's happened to her, if she's—'

'I promise,' Sean assured her, the weight of the oath heavy on his shoulders and conscience. 'I need to go now. I've got a lot to sort out. Are you coming downstairs?'

'No,' she answered. 'I'd like to sit here for a while.'

'Of course,' he agreed. 'I understand. I'll have a Family Liaison Officer assigned to you full time. If you think of anything that could help, anything at all, you need to tell them, or if you'd prefer you can call me – any time.' He slipped a business card from his pocket and handed it to her. She nodded that she understood and sat slowly on the unmade bed, staring down at the porcelain doll in her lap, still smoothing its hair. 'I'll be in touch soon,' he told her and walked from the bedroom, closing the door, giving Jessica privacy for her grief.

He headed down the stairs moving far quicker than he'd climbed them, snapping the latex gloves from his hands and being careful not to touch the no doubt already contaminated banister rail. The house that had seemed so large and spacious now felt claustrophobic and oppressive. He cleared the bottom two stairs in one bound and strode into the kitchen where the three detectives stood alone. 'Mr Fellowes?' he immediately asked.

'Not back yet,' Sally told him.

'Hopefully he's getting what we asked for,' Sean replied before turning to DI Adams. 'My people will be here soon to take this over. In the meantime, see if you can't get the family to move out so Forensics aren't tripping over them.'

'I'll do my best,' Adams assured him.

'Once you have the names of the removal people etc, email them directly to me,' Sean continued, pulling out another business card. 'My email address is on there. Phone me if you have to.'

'Going somewhere?' Adams asked.

'I've got a lot to get through. Can't do it standing around

here,' Sean answered, sensing Adams' annoyance. 'Listen, I know you're busy, but I need someone who knows what they're doing to babysit this one until I get things up and running. The eyes of the world are on us. Someone needs to watch over this family, just for a while.'

Adams looked at DS Wright, who still hadn't spoken, and then back to Sean. 'All right. I can give you a couple of hours, then you'd better have your people here to relieve us.'

'I will,' Sean promised. 'And thank you.' He summoned Sally with a nod of his head and made for the exit, calling back to Adams as they walked: 'Call me as soon as they come up with the names,' he reminded him, wasting no time in making for the front door and out into the street beyond, breathing in the fresh cold air like a man who'd escaped from a dungeon.

'You all right?' Sally asked, hands thrust into her coat pockets against the cold, wishing she still smoked.

'Yeah, I'm fine, or at least as fine as I'm going to be.'

'So where are we heading in such a hurry?'

'To see McKenzie.'

'McKenzie? Why we wasting our time with him?'

'Just because he was locked up last night doesn't mean he wasn't involved,' Sean explained.

'You think he could be working with somebody else – maybe numerous somebody elses?'

'We have to consider it, after everything he's told us, after everything we've found out about him.'

'D'you want me to call ahead and get his solicitor there for the interview?'

'No,' Sean snapped, running his fingers through his light brown hair. 'No brief. I need to see him up-close-and-personal – need to see his eyes when I ask him what I need to ask him.'

'And what's that?' Sally asked, suspicious and concerned.

'Why,' Sean told her. 'I need to ask him why.'

'Why what?'

'Why he'd want me to think he took George Bridgeman. Why would he do that? Why would anyone do that?'

'Well, I guess we'll find out,' Sally said. 'Soon enough.'

'Yes,' Sean told her. 'Yes we will.'

Thirty minutes later Sean and Sally were following the gaoler at Kentish Town Police Station along the old, stone corridor of the cell passage. The eyes of the inmates were pushed up against their spyholes in the hope of catching a glimpse of life beyond their stone and metal prisons. The abuse was punctuated by the occasional wolf-whistle that Sean assumed was for Sally's benefit.

'Your man's in here,' the gaoler told them, unclipping a huge bunch of keys from his belt. 'Been as quiet as a mouse. Wouldn't even know he was here if it wasn't for the need to feed him.'

'He'd hardly want to attract attention to himself,' Sally pointed out, 'given his alleged crime.'

'Oh, they already know he's here and why,' the gaoler said. 'The jungle drums have been in full swing. Which interview room d'you want to use?'

'Maybe none,' Sean answered. 'I just need a quick word with him in his cell – if that's all right?'

The gaoler looked him up and down, trying to judge if he had any malevolent intent before making his decision. 'Fair enough,' he finally conceded, 'but the custody sergeant has already made a note in McKenzie's custody record that you're here to interview him, just like you said you were. So if I was you I'd be quick and no funny business, you understand? No unexplained marks, please. I'll tell the custody sergeant it's just an intelligence interview you're after. Should keep him happy so long as you're not too long.'

'We won't be,' Sean promised, 'and thanks.'

'No need,' he answered, peering through the spyhole before pushing the large, grey key into the main lock. 'Fucking child molester. Should hang the fucking lot of them,' he declared and turned the lock that opened with a smooth, heavy clunk. 'Mr McKenzie,' he told the dozing prisoner, 'some detectives here to see you, so get your arse up and pay attention.' McKenzie stirred and sat up on the wooden bed. 'Remember what I said,' the gaoler reminded Sean and Sally. 'Just a few minutes. That's all you'll get away with for a cell visit.' With that he spun on his heels and marched from the cell, closing the door on his way out without locking it.

'What d'you want now?' McKenzie immediately asked, trying to straighten his scruffy hair with his fingers as he smiled, self-satisfied.

'What else?' Sean told him, sitting next to him, trying to be as menacing as he possibly could without saying or doing anything threatening. 'To talk.'

'I've said everything I'm going to say.'

'Ah, but that was before last night.'

'I don't understand,' he responded truthfully. 'Last night I was banged up in here.'

'You were,' Sean admitted. 'And while you were locked up nice and tight another child was taken.' Sean noticed that instantly, but only fleetingly, McKenzie looked disappointed.

'What did they look like?' McKenzie asked.

'Who?' Sean replied. 'The child?'

'Yes,' McKenzie answered. 'What did they look like?'

'Why do you want to know?' Sally asked, but Sean already knew the answer – McKenzie was trying to share the experience of taking the child, feel the thrill of entering the family's home in the dead of night to snatch their most precious thing away while they slept. McKenzie no doubt imagined things were being done to her as they spoke – things that made his groin tighten and his lips dry with excitement. Sean could see him becoming agitated at the thought of being privy to the details he craved. McKenzie's vile longings made him want to reach out and strangle him, but he needed to keep him talking – he needed to know.

'She's five years old,' he began.

'She,' McKenzie repeated, his eyes growing wide with anticipation. 'It's a girl.'

'She,' Sally interrupted spitefully. 'She's not an *it*.'

'Yes,' Sean silenced her, needing to keep McKenzie on the hook. 'I've seen her photograph – she's very pretty.'

'Her hair?' McKenzie asked, too excited to form a full question.

'Blonde,' Sean answered, 'with pale blue eyes.'

McKenzie eyed him with suspicion, unsure whether they were even telling him the truth about another child being taken. 'Do you have a photograph of her? Can I see it?'

'No fucking way,' Sally swore before Sean raised a hand to slow her down. 'You can't show him, Sean. You know what he's doing.'

'It's all right,' he told her, slipping his hand inside his jacket pocket where he had a small photograph of Bailey, knowing he was feeding McKenzie's fantasy, allowing him to put a face to the poisonous images forming in his mind, vicariously sharing in the abuse he imagined she was suffering. He took hold of McKenzie's hand and placed the photograph in its palm, feeling McKenzie's body relaxing into ecstasy as he stared down at the small picture, releasing an involuntary and lengthy sigh as he did so, his left leg beginning to tap uncontrollably.

'This is wrong,' Sally protested. Sean and McKenzie ignored her.

'Can you help us find her?' Sean asked.

'What?' McKenzie replied, so lost in his new world that he hadn't heard Sean properly.

'Can you help us find her?' Sean repeated. 'Do you know where she is?'

McKenzie's eyes narrowed as he considered Sean's questions, sensing a new opportunity. 'Can I see more photographs?' he asked. 'If I can see more photographs perhaps I can help you.'

'What do you need to see photographs of?' Sean asked, a little confused, but ready to assume McKenzie was just seeking more ways to flesh out his fantasy about the missing five-year-old.

'Her bedroom,' McKenzie told him, 'and her house.'

'That could be difficult,' Sean responded. 'Difficult to justify why we had to show you those things.'

'Then I won't be able to help you.'

'Surely you either know where she is or you don't.' Tiring of his own game, Sean couldn't keep the irritation from his voice. 'Same goes for George Bridgeman – you either know where he is or you don't.'

'Let me have the pictures and I'll help you.'

'No,' Sean insisted. 'You have to give me something first.'

'Such as?'

'Who are you working with?' Sean asked bluntly. 'Tell me who you're working with.'

'What d'you mean?'

'What was your role in this? Did they just use you to get the front doors open? Who's controlling things?' Sean demanded.

'Don't you know?' McKenzie asked with an ugly smile. 'Do you really still not understand?'

Sean sat back, rocked by what he believed he was being told by his still prime suspect. He snatched the photograph of Bailey from McKenzie's hand and grabbed him by the hood of his forensic paper suit, twisting it in his hands to make an instant tourniquet around McKenzie's swelling neck. 'No more fucking games. Where are they?' He loosened his grip enough to let McKenzie speak through his still grinning teeth.

'I couldn't have put it better myself,' he spat.

'What do you mean? What do you mean?' Sean demanded, resisting the temptation to once more tighten his grip.

'Like you said,' McKenzie sneered: 'games, games, games, games. That's all this was: a game. I don't know anything about these missing children – I never did.'

'You're lying,' Sean insisted.

'No – no, I'm not and you know it. You needed a suspect and you picked on me – an easy target – hated by everyone. I knew you were going to try and make the evidence fit me no matter what, at least until the evidence itself proved it couldn't be me, no matter how much you wanted it to be.'

'I don't know what you're talking about.'

'So I decided to play my own game – never denying it nor admitting to anything, leading your surveillance to the hardware shop and buying the lock-picking tools. I knew you'd have me followed – you made it so easy for me. I knew it could only last until *he* took another child, but that was long enough.'

Sean released his grip and pushed McKenzie away from him. 'Jesus Christ, that's why you looked so worried when we talked about forensic evidence during that first interview – not because you thought it would implicate you, but because it might implicate somebody else and then we'd begin to suspect you weren't involved. But why?' Sean asked. 'Why would you want us to think you'd taken the boy?'

'To show everybody what a fool you are,' McKenzie said. 'An ignorant fool, just like all your kind. You think you can be police, prosecution, judge and jury. Well, I showed you. I proved to everyone you can get it wrong and that you treat people like me as if we were nothing but filthy animals – animals without even the most basic of human rights – to live in freedom and without fear.'

'This is bullshit,' Sean insisted. 'What's the real reason you wanted me to come after you? Tell me,' he almost shouted into McKenzie's still smiling face, looking up at him, breathing hard as he began to cackle like a witch.

'I met a lot of interesting people when I was locked in that stinking prison,' McKenzie explained. 'A lot of people who told me how to play the game, told me I was missing out, missing out on something every time I was wrongly arrested and held prisoner by the police.'

'What are you talking about?' Sean asked, the dark anger inside him boiling up from deep, hidden places, images of McKenzie's smashed and broken face seeping into his mind, his teeth cracked and bleeding, his nose shattered and gushing.

'Five thousand pounds for a wrongful arrest, they told me,' McKenzie continued. 'Two hundred pounds for every hour you spend locked up, not to mention my very public defamation of character. Should all add up to a tidy little sum, don't you think?'

Sean felt his fists clenching as he stared into McKenzie's small yellow and brown teeth, knowing he could knock most of the front ones straight down his throat with one well-placed punch. 'Money?' he spat into his face. 'All this was for money? You deliberately misled an investigation to find a missing four-year-old boy to make some money?'

'No,' McKenzie corrected him. '*You* misled the investigation – *I* just played along. So I had a lock-picking set – so what?

It used to be my job. And a few scribbles on a map – it could be anything. And now I'll see you in court, only I won't be the defendant this time, *you* will be, and I'll be the innocent victim.'

'You ignorant fool,' Sean told him. 'You've admitted to deliberately misleading my investigation and you think you're just going to walk away from that?'

'Admitted what?' McKenzie taunted him. 'Admitted it where? Here, in this cell, with no solicitor present and no recording? What I've told you here means *nothing. Nothing.*'

Sally saw the muscles and sinews tighten in Sean's neck and face, his fingers curling into ever tighter fists. 'Sean,' she warned him. 'Sean – it's not worth it. He's not worth it.' The muscles in the side of his face rippled as he fought to control the nearing storm, until finally his jaw unclamped and his blurred vision returned to normal.

'You'd better just pray they're both still alive,' he warned McKenzie, standing and stepping away from him before the rage could return.

'They're not alive,' McKenzie taunted him. 'They're already dead and you know it – you can feel it. If someone like me took them then they're already dead.'

Sean froze, as if McKenzie had unwittingly planted a seed of thought in his mind that now needed to be nurtured, fed and watered so it could germinate and flower into something important he didn't yet fully understand.

'You're telling me that if you had taken them they'd already be dead? Is that what you're telling me?'

'Yes,' McKenzie continued, the smile falling from his now deadly serious face, eyes wild and dilated.

'Why?' Sean asked. 'Why would you kill them?'

'Abduction and child rape means life in prison – why risk leaving a live witness? Once you've crossed that line, there's no turning back – not for anyone.'

'You'd kill them just to get rid of a witness?'

'Why not?' McKenzie answered coldly. 'It wouldn't make anything any worse.'

'So the killing would mean nothing?'

'No. Nothing more than a necessary evil.'

'And their bodies?'

'What?'

'What would you do with their bodies?'

'Get rid of them.'

'How?'

'Does it matter?'

'It matters to me. How?'

'I don't know,' McKenzie told him, sounding confused for the first time, as if the *game* was slipping into new, unplanned territory and he didn't like it.

'How?' Sean barked at him.

'Maybe we should get an interview room,' Sally interrupted, 'get this on tape?'

'How?' Sean ignored her. 'How would you get rid of the bodies?'

'Just get rid of them,' McKenzie stumbled. 'Dump them somewhere – it wouldn't matter.'

'Would you bury them?' Sean asked. 'Conceal them – try to hide them?'

'No,' McKenzie argued. 'What would be the point? They'd be found sooner or later. Better to just dump them somewhere and do it quickly – reduce the chance of being seen.'

'And have you crossed that line, Mark?' Sally asked.

'No,' he answered. 'It hasn't come to that yet for me. I pray it never will.'

'Then they weren't taken by someone like you,' Sean talked over them.

Silence filled the room until McKenzie finally spoke again. 'How do you know?' he asked. 'How could you know?'

'Because we haven't found any bodies,' Sean told them sombrely. 'We haven't found any bodies.'

When they got back to New Scotland Yard, Donnelly was sitting alone in the office he shared with Sally. Sean made directly for him, pulling his coat off and chucking it over Sally's desk and sitting in her chair without thinking. Sally pulled up a spare chair without giving it a second thought and waited for someone to begin.

'Well?' Donnelly asked, arms spread open. 'What's going on? Is this second missing child I'm hearing about linked to ours?'

'Yes,' Sean confirmed. 'Whoever took George Bridgeman also took Bailey Fellowes.'

'Great,' Donnelly said, rolling his eyes in disbelief. 'Well, you weren't the only one to waste your time: DNA results are back from samples we had examined that belong to George Bridgeman. Stuart Bridgeman is his biological father.'

'Does he know yet?' Sally asked.

'He knows,' Donnelly replied.

'And his reaction?'

'Not that of a man who's just found out he killed his own son, if that's what you mean. More just relieved.'

'Then we can all but dispense with the idea of him being a suspect,' Sean told them. 'None of which helps us right now.'

'No,' Donnelly agreed, 'I don't suppose it does. But I would have put a lot of money on one of us being right: McKenzie and Bridgeman were both more than viable suspects. Jesus, what a waste of time.'

'McKenzie wasn't a waste of time,' Sean argued.

'Really?' Donnelly questioned. 'How so?'

'Because we learned from him. He told us who we should be looking for – or rather, who we shouldn't be looking for.'

'Go on,' Donnelly encouraged.

'McKenzie told us that if the children had been taken by someone like him their bodies would have been dumped without much care and easily found. If a paedophile had taken them we would have at least one body by now, I'm certain of it.'

'Assuming they're dead,' Sally pointed out.

'Again, if someone like McKenzie had taken them, then at the very least I believe the boy would have been killed by now. Otherwise, why take another child?'

'Maybe he's another Thomas Keller and wants a *collection*, only with this one it's children, not women?' Sally suggested.

'No.' Sean shook his head. 'This is no Thomas Keller and it's no Mark McKenzie. It's something completely different. I believe the children are still alive. Both of them.'

'Why?' Donnelly demanded. 'What makes you so sure? And if they're alive, who took them and why?'

'Who took them?' Sean repeated the question. 'I don't know. But whoever it was has a link to both families. They must have. We find the link, we find the suspect. Why they took them – I don't know yet. But it wasn't to abuse them and it wasn't to kill them.'

Sally and Donnelly looked blankly at each other until Sally spoke. 'Then why? Why were they taken?'

'I don't know,' Sean repeated, his neck and shoulders tense with irritation at the lack of ideas, 'but just because he doesn't appear to leave any forensic evidence behind, it doesn't mean he has to be some career paedophile who's evidentially aware.'

'I don't understand where you're coming from,' said Donnelly.

'He doesn't leave fingerprints because he wears gloves,' Sean explained.

'Agreed,' Donnelly encouraged.

'But maybe he just wears them to keep his hands warm – to keep his fingers nimble. It was freezing cold last night and the night George Bridgeman was taken.'

'But once he's inside, if he's not thinking about avoiding leaving evidence then surely he'd make a mistake – maybe even take his gloves off?' Donnelly suggested.

'Not necessarily. He enters, skilfully, climbs the stairs to where he knows the child is, grabs and leaves. He doesn't dwell in the house, doesn't relish the time spent there – just in and out. He doesn't waste time looking for trophies either. He's not interested in any of the normal things we'd expect, all of which greatly reduces the opportunities for mistakes to be made.'

'He doesn't need trophies,' Sally interrupted. 'He has the children. They are the trophies.'

There was a moment of silence as Sean and Donnelly stared at her and considered the implications of what she'd suggested.

'Just a theory,' Sean backtracked. 'Something we should consider – bear in mind.'

'Then why these particular two children?' Donnelly asked.

'I don't know,' Sean told them, the frustration at not being able to see the road ahead, not being able to make the leaps he'd so often made in the past, weaving the strands of tangible evidence together with his own instinctive insights to bridge the gaps in, was beginning to wear him down. 'I can't think straight with all this shit going on around me.' Again Sally and Donnelly glanced at each other. 'Listen,' Sean continued, rubbing his temples, 'call an office meeting with whoever's here and let's get everybody looking for whatever it is that links these families.'

'Right now?' Donnelly asked.

'Yes,' Sean snapped back. 'Right now.'

'What about McKenzie?' Sally asked. 'He's still in custody in Kentish Town.'

'Hand him over to the local CID,' Sean told her. 'They can take over the investigation into the child porn we found on his laptop. They won't like it, but they'll do it anyway. Anything else?' Donnelly and Sally shook their heads like scolded schoolchildren. 'Good, then let's get this meeting up and running.'

Sean watched as his two sergeants heaved themselves out of their chairs and made their way into the main office, Donnelly immediately shouting across the room, turning all heads whether they were on the phone, in conversation or otherwise. He waited until he felt the office was ready for him, pushed himself to his feet and joined his team next door, holding one arm aloft apologetically before speaking.

'All right, everyone – any rumours you may or may not have heard about a second child going missing are unfortunately true.' He waited for the slight murmur in the room to subside. 'Let me save you the bother of asking a load of unnecessary questions: Yes, the abductions are connected. How do we know this: because of the method of entry and type of house, family and geographical areas, as well as age of the children, albeit they're different sexes. So let's not waste time wondering whether they are connected, just take it from me that they are.' He noted the occasional shrugged shoulder and averting of eye contact. No detective liked being dictated to, no matter who by. 'What we need to concentrate on is finding what links these two children, George Bridgeman and Bailey Fellowes. What links these two families?'

'What about this McKenzie suspect you brought in?' DC Jesson asked. 'Sounds like a solid suspect.'

'He's no longer a viable suspect in this case,' Sean told him. 'No need to discuss him any more.'

'What about the father of the boy?' DC McGowan asked.

'No longer as strong a suspect as he was. He is the biological father and his reaction to finding that out hasn't been the reaction of a man who's just discovered he'd murdered his own son. It just doesn't feel right any more. We need to look for something else – some other link.'

'Like what?' Maggie asked.

'Anything,' Sean told her. 'A nanny, an au pair, a teacher, an estate agent or removal man. We have names from the families, so let's start checking them.'

'What pre-school does Bailey go to?' Maggie continued.

Sally flicked through her CID notebook, referring to notes she'd taken from DI Adams back at the house while Sean had been in Bailey's bedroom. 'Small Fry in Holly Lodge Gardens, which is apparently between Highgate and Hampstead.'

Maggie quickly checked her own notes and shook her head. 'No luck,' she told the room. 'George Bridgeman went to Little Unicorns in Southwood Lane, Highgate.'

'Just keep looking and checking,' Sean told them. 'There's a link and we will find it, but we need to find it fast. These abductions are not random – they're planned – meticulously planned. These children and these families have been chosen for a specific reason. We need to find out what that is. Within the next hour we should have all the names of the Fellowes' nannies, au pairs, removal men, the lot. As soon as they're in, we start cross-referencing to everything we have from the Bridgemans. This bastard's made his first mistake – he's taken another child and that means we can use cross-referencing to identify him, so let's get on with it.'

His message delivered, Sean turned towards his office, pulling Donnelly with him.

'Problem?' Donnelly asked.

'No,' Sean answered, 'but I need you to keep everyone at it while I'm not here, understand?'

'Oh aye. Where you going, if you don't mind me asking?'

'To see a man about a dog,' Sean told him, causing Donnelly's eyebrows to arch with intrigue. 'Look,' Sean explained pulling his coat on and filling his pockets, 'I just need some air and space to clear my head. Just watch the ship while I'm away.' He headed into the main office and towards the exit as Donnelly mumbled under his breath.

'Give her one for me, guv'nor. Give her one for me.'

7

Sean stood on the pavement outside an art deco building in Swiss Cottage, north-west London, close to the bizarrely styled nearby pub that lent its name to the entire area. Throngs of pedestrians marched past him as he searched through the dozens of name plates next to the building's entrance for the one he needed, their footsteps drowned out by the incessant din of the traffic, exhaust fumes making the air acrid and difficult to breathe. He eventually spotted the one he was looking for, but found himself hesitating before pressing the intercom, a voice in his head telling him to run away – run far away and never come back. He breathed in deeply, coughing slightly on the exhaust fumes as he pushed the doubt away and rang the buzzer. After a few seconds he heard a voice he didn't recognize.

'Dr Ravenni-Ceron's office.'

Dr Anna Ravenni-Ceron, the psychiatrist and criminologist who'd been attached, against Sean's wishes, to the last case he had investigated. At the time he'd been so intent on tracking down Thomas Keller and preventing him from abducting and murdering any more women that he'd not even noticed his feelings towards her changing, although he knew he'd come to at the very least respect her determination. But since he'd got out of hospital he'd thought of her more than he'd ever expected to, and now he was standing on the pavement outside her office.

He cleared his throat before answering. 'I'm here to see Anna.'

'Do you have an appointment?' the voice asked suspiciously.

'I don't need an appointment,' he said into the metal box hanging on the wall. 'Just tell Dr Ravenni-Ceron that Detective Inspector Sean Corrigan is here and needs to see her.'

'Can I ask what it's about?' the box replied.

'It's personal,' he answered, regretting it immediately, wishing instead he'd told the inquisitive voice it was confidential. He winced at his mistake and waited for a response.

'I see,' the voice eventually replied. 'I'll just see if she's available. Wait there a minute please.' He was about to argue, but the connection went dead.

'Shit,' he cursed, hopping from one foot to the other, trying to defend himself against the cold and his growing feeling of awkwardness, sure that he was as conspicuous as he felt standing in the doorway of the art deco monolith. Finally the intercom crackled back into life.

'Dr Ravenni-Ceron will see you now. We're on the third floor, room 323. You can take the lift or you can use the stairs.' The door clicked open and the line went dead. He paused for a second before opening the door and entering, sure his feet would take over and lead him away, but instead they took him inside and up the stairs to the third floor, doubts and anxiety giving way to excitement and anticipation.

When he reached room 323 he was relieved to discover

there was no intercom to negotiate, just an unlocked door and a secretary in her early thirties sitting behind a desk in the small, simple reception. She stood as he entered, speaking in a voice he recognized from the intercom, although it was warm and friendly now instead of cold and metallic.

'Detective Inspector Corrigan, I presume?' she asked with a smile.

'Yeah,' he answered, so eager to be alone with Anna that he almost overtook the secretary as she escorted him the few short steps to the office door.

'Dr Ravenni-Ceron's office,' she announced, stepping aside for him to enter.

'Thanks,' Sean managed to say before filling his lungs with air and stepping through the door, which closed softly behind him.

At first he almost didn't see Anna sitting behind her antique leather-topped desk. The design and style of the office was so close to how he'd imagined it that he felt as if he'd been here many times before, although this was his first visit. The multiple layers of shelves stacked with leather-bound books that he assumed were about psychology and other matters of the mind, art deco lamps and shades to match the building, and even a comfortable leather reclining chair. A deep-red Persian rug covered the oak floor. A voice he hadn't heard in many months broke his mental meandering.

'Hello, Sean,' Anna said, her voice relatively neutral, but with a hint of nervous excitement. 'Long time no see.'

'Too long,' he answered. 'My fault entirely.'

'Can I ask what brings you here?'

Sean cleared his throat before speaking again. 'A new case.'

'A new case?'

'Yes.'

'The one that's been on the TV and all over the papers – the child abducted from his own home? Sounds like the sort of thing they'd like to have you investigating.'

'But that happened in Hampstead,' he challenged her. 'I cover south-east London, not north-west.'

'Not any more, I hear,' she told him. 'Special Investigations Unit, isn't it? London-wide?'

He assumed Sally had been speaking out of school during her sessions, but his assumption was wrong.

'You hear right,' he admitted, 'and yes, I've got the investigation into the missing boy. Only now there's a missing girl as well.'

'Oh,' Anna replied, surprised and disturbed to hear of a second child being stolen from their family. 'I'm sorry to hear that.'

'So am I,' Sean told her sharply, a moment of silence falling between them.

'Please, take a seat.' Anna waved him to an armchair facing the desk. 'So how can I help?'

'I could do with a second opinion,' Sean confessed. 'I can't work out what's going on in the mind of whoever's taking them. Why they're doing it.'

'Go on,' Anna encouraged.

'We don't have a body yet, despite the fact he's now taken another child.'

'And what does that tell you?' she asked.

'It tells me that he hasn't killed – *yet*.'

'The news reports said he took the boy from his own home, but there was no mention of how he got in,' she prompted, even though she already knew the answer. She couldn't afford to let Sean know that she was already aware of details that hadn't been released to the public.

'He used expert lock-picking skills to enter. Then he took

the children from their beds in the middle of the night without making a sound or leaving a trace – no evidence of a struggle or drugs being used to subdue the victims. After he left, he locked things up behind him, as if—'

'As if he didn't want to leave the remainder of the family vulnerable,' she finished for him.

'It's a possibility,' Sean admitted, without telling her he'd already considered it and hadn't yet ruled it out.

'Uhhm,' Anna sighed. 'So when he's carrying out the abductions he's highly organized.'

'I believe so,' Sean agreed.

'And most highly organized killers are perversely disorganized when it comes to getting rid of the body.'

'That's normal,' he agreed again.

'So if the children had indeed been taken by a killer you would be right to expect to have found a body by now . . .' Anna continued to think out loud. 'But if he's taking them with the intention of abusing them, then perhaps he hasn't killed them yet.'

'He would have, by now.'

'Why?'

'To get rid of any witnesses,' Sean answered coldly.

'Possibly,' she considered.

'Definitely,' he insisted, McKenzie's face and words imprinted in his mind.

'Then there's a simple conclusion,' Anna told him. 'They were neither taken by a killer nor by an abuser. They were taken by a possessor.'

'A *possessor*?' Sean questioned. 'I don't understand,' he half-lied.

'Someone who means them no harm, but who wants to possess them, keep them as their own, perhaps?'

'Like who?'

'Like . . . like a woman.'

'A *woman*?'

'Yes, one who perhaps sees these children as needing her. She may see herself as their rescuer, not their abuser. Tell me, do the families have other children?'

'Yes,' he answered. 'Why?'

'Interesting. It could be a sign of her subconscious guilt – she takes a child, but leaves the family with other children, which also explains why she secures the houses when leaving and perhaps how she can get the children from the house without them being scared enough to raise the alarm. Children are inherently less afraid of women than they are men.'

'No,' Sean shook his head. 'A lot of what you're saying makes sense, but I can't see a woman picking the locks and entering those houses – I just can't.'

'We're capable of more than you think, Sean,' Anna told him. 'But I take your point: house-breaking would be a highly unusual crime for a woman.' They sat in silence for a while. 'So perhaps there are two people working together – a man and a woman. She selects the children, possibly at random, but more likely because she knows them somehow, and he takes them for her. A childless couple who have no hope of having their own, perhaps?'

'That's interesting,' Sean told her, but his unexcited eyes told her she wasn't offering him anything new.

'No, it's not,' she replied. 'You'd already considered it.'

'Maybe,' he admitted with a shrug.

'Then why don't you tell me why you're really here?'

Her question was met only with the piercing blue of his eyes.

'Can I get you a drink? Tea or coffee, perhaps?' she asked, needing some respite from Sean's intensity.

'No thanks,' he answered, watching her stand and straighten her charcoal grey pencil skirt, her small, heavy breasts moving slightly under her white blouse.

'I need a drink of water,' she told him, walking to the small water-cooler in the corner of her office, standing with her back to him as she took her time filling the plastic cup. She heard the creaking of his chair as he rose, felt the distance between them close as he came to her, standing too close behind her, making her tremble. She pushed herself back into him when she felt his arm curl around her waist, unable to control urges she'd long been pretending to herself she didn't have.

'Made you feel alive, didn't it?' he whispered into her ear. 'Being around me and the others – a real-life murder investigation – hardly ever sleeping or eating, your only thought to catch the bastard that took those women. Killed those women. Everything else in your life suddenly seemed trivial and futile.'

'Maybe,' she whispered back. 'It was . . . it was . . .'

'Thrilling,' he answered for her. 'It thrilled you. But now everything's back to normal, just like it used to be. Only it never can be, not for you. You need more now. You always will.'

'You're right,' she admitted. 'You're right. I need more.'

He pulled her closer so he could feel her chest rising and falling, the curves of her back pressing against his body as her buttocks fitted into his groin making his testicles curl and tense as his penis began to flush with blood – his arm tightening around her waist as the other slipped around her chest and cupped one breast releasing her sweet warm breath as she sighed and turned to face him. She gripped his face in her hands, pulling his mouth on to hers, biting softly on his lower lip while her right leg rose and curled around his thighs, locking them tighter together. His tongue entered her mouth and she imagined it exploring the place between her legs, imagined him inside her as they moved as one on the floor of her office or across her desk. But without warning her conscience betrayed her and defeated her desire. She untwined her leg and pushed against his chest with both hands, pulling her lips, swollen with passion, away from his searching mouth. 'No,' she told him. 'This is wrong. We can't do this.'

'Yes we can,' he argued, still searching for her warm breath.

'We're both married, Sean,' she reminded him. 'We can't do this. It's wrong.'

He detected the change in her voice – in her breathing – and knew the passion had passed. 'Christ,' he told her. 'Can't we just do something we want, instead of what people expect of us for once? Nobody needs to know.'

'We'll know,' she told him. 'We'll know, Sean.' She pushed him harder, increasing the distance between them until it was obvious their brief affair was already over, although their hands still rested gently on each other. 'I want to, but I won't,' she continued. 'We could do this and I'd be fine. I could go home tonight and I'd be fine. I'd wake up in the morning and I'd be fine. But you wouldn't be, Sean – you wouldn't be fine.'

'You don't know me as well as you think you do,' he argued.

'I know you well enough.'

'Is that your professional opinion or your personal one?'

'Both,' she told him, any trace of passion gone from her voice. 'If we were to do this it would destroy you, Sean, and everything you are.' He looked at her blankly. 'Don't you understand? It's your wife and family that anchor you. Without them you'd be lost, drifting without a purpose or belief. You betray them, you betray yourself and you'd never recover. Don't cross a line that you can never come back from.'

Finally he untangled himself and stepped away, her words mingling with something he remembered McKenzie saying: *Once you've crossed that line, there's no turning back – not for anybody. Don't cross a line that you can never come back from.* Thoughts of Kate and his daughters rushed into his aching mind – the family that was growing up without him, becoming little more than strangers to him. He felt dizzy and searched for a chair to sit in.

'Sean?' Anna asked. 'Are you all right?'

'Yes,' he managed to lie. 'I'll be fine.'

Anna studied him for a moment in silence before speaking. 'I don't think you really wanted this to happen, no matter how much I did.'

'Then you'd be wrong.'

'Would I? This isn't about me, Sean. We both know it. It's as if you're trying to be something you're not. Why?' He said nothing. 'Is it something to do with the new case? Trying to get the scent back by putting yourself on the edge, by risking everything that's important to you?' Still he didn't answer. 'It is, isn't it? That's why you're here.'

'I'm getting nowhere with this investigation,' he finally admitted. 'I can't work out his motivation. Can't get inside his head.'

'Sounds as if you already have,' she contradicted him. 'You could very well be right: maybe this one isn't doing it to torture and kill. Something else, perhaps?'

'Yeah, but what?'

'As we were discussing before . . .' They exchanged an awkward glance. 'The abductor could be working with someone – a male and female working together to take the children – to take them and keep them as their own. To love them.'

'I'd considered it,' Sean told her.

'But?'

'But how could they ever hope to get away with it – raising abducted children as their own?'

'You're assuming they're rational.'

'One delusional person acting alone I can consider, but two fantasists sharing the same obsession – an obsession as unusual as this? I don't think so.'

Anna considered him for a minute, surprised at how dulled his instincts appeared to be. 'I agree,' she told him, making him look her in the eye. 'But in a case like this I would expect to find one delusional and one rational person. The rational person no doubt knows exactly what they're doing and that ultimately it's doomed to failure, but they do it anyway out of a need to please or even appease the delusional one. A husband trying to satisfy a wife; a lover trying to please a more dominant partner . . . It could even be a dynamic between siblings or some other type of family relationship – a mother and son?'

'Maybe,' Sean half agreed, stretching and rubbing the back of his neck. 'But one thing I'm sure of is that our suspect knew both families. We'll keep cross-referencing names until we get a hit, and when we do I'll have my prime suspect. Then they can tell us *why* themselves.'

'Good luck,' Anna told him as he stood to leave.

'Thanks,' he answered. 'I've got a feeling I'm going to need it. And I'm sorry if I . . . if I did anything to make you feel . . . uncomfortable. I wouldn't want you to ever feel that way around me.'

'I never could,' she replied without smiling. 'Just don't cross that line. You'll lose yourself if you do.'

'I won't,' he promised, knowing that if he couldn't with her he wouldn't with anyone.

'Sean,' she stopped him as he headed for the door. 'If you ever need anything, just call me – OK?'

'I will,' he assured her. 'I'll keep you posted,' he promised and was gone, leaving her standing in front of her desk imagining what could have been – imagining them together, instead of watching him walking away.

* * *

237

Forty-five minutes later Sean had completed the tortuous journey across Central London that had taken him past Marble Arch and Hyde Park Corner and along the rear garden walls of Buckingham Palace before battling his way past Victoria station and finally into Victoria Street and down to Broadway and the Yard. He'd cursed being moved to Central London from Peckham more than once and was in a less than joyous mood as he swept into the main office, pictures of Anna swirling in his mind, the smell of her perfume still on his clothes and face, her taste still on his lips. He was unsure about why he'd really gone to see her – whether it he'd been driven by simple, natural desire or she'd been right and he'd merely gone to her to feel danger again – to risk losing everything just to put himself on some sort of edge that might kick-start his instincts. He caught sight of the photographs of the missing children staring at him from the whiteboards – innocent children snatched from their warm beds and safe homes by some nutjob. Whether whoever was responsible intentionally meant to harm the children or not, they were still insane as far as he was concerned. He wasn't in the mood to sympathize.

He ignored everyone he passed as he made his way to his office, slumping into the chair behind his desk. He stared back out into the office at the photographs, the children's eyes seeming to follow him, their smiling faces, immaculate hair and perfect school uniforms mocking his own miserable childhood. He spoke quietly to himself. 'Why didn't anyone come and take me? Why didn't you come and take me? I would have gone with you.' His own question made him sit bolt upright. 'Is that it? Were they being abused – is that why you took them away?' But the eyes in the photographs told him differently – Bailey's more than George's, but even the boy's were content enough. Not like the few pictures of himself as a child – haunted and defeated. And the parents too, none seemed like the type of animal he knew so well – like his father. He slumped back in his chair. *Something else then*. The vibrating phone in his pocket broke his daydreaming. He pulled it free and looked at the caller ID. His cheeks puffed before he answered.

'Sean – it's Superintendent Featherstone. Got any updates for me?'

'No. Not really.'

'What about this second missing kid?'

'Too early to say much,' Sean lied, unwilling to explain his early theories.

'Bad news, all the same,' Featherstone told him, 'another kid being taken. Are you sure they're connected?'

'They're connected. Same suspects.'

'Suspects?' Featherstone seized on Sean's tired mistake.

'I'm keeping an open mind,' Sean tried to deflect him.

'You think it could be a paedophile ring?'

'Like I said, I'm keeping an open mind.'

'Well that's fine by me,' Featherstone began. 'I understand the score, but Addis won't be so forgiving. He'll want something solid on the hurry-up, get my drift?'

'I'll do the best I can.'

'I know you will,' Featherstone told him. 'There's something else you need to know.'

'Such as?' Sean asked, sitting forward in his chair.

'Addis is going back on the telly tonight – to do another appeal for assistance.'

'Probably can't hurt.'

'Unfortunately he's going to publicly apologize as well.'

'For what?' Sean asked, sitting ever more upright.

'The *investigation*'s failings.'

'Failings?' Sean responded. 'The *investigation*'s failings? You mean *my* failings?'

'I'm sure you're doing all you can,' Featherstone weakly reassured him, but Sean wasn't listening.

'Why doesn't he take me off the case then – give it someone from SCG north-west – see if they fare any better?'

'Because he knows you're the best man, the best team, for the job – no matter what else he says. So let's just try not to piss him off too much and get this one solved. If it's too late to save the missing kids, we'll have to manage that as best we can, but at least if we have a suspect in custody who's going to stay there we can put a positive spin on things for the media and the public.'

'It's not too late,' Sean snapped back without thinking.

'Not too late for what?' Featherstone asked, confused.

'Nothing,' Sean tried to cover his slip.

'Whatever. Just remember, Sean, if push comes to shove, it won't be Addis who takes the fall – no chance of that. And just for the record, it won't be me either. Be careful, Sean.' The line went dead.

'Fuck,' he swore loudly enough to be heard in the main office. His phone began to chirp and vibrate again, the caller ID telling him it was Kate calling from her mobile. 'Jesus,' he muttered more quietly, deciding to let it ring out before changing his mind and answering, images of Anna tormenting him as he tried to sound normal, his betrayal and guilt burning in his chest.

'Hi. It's me,' Kate replied cheerfully. 'Where are you?'

'At work – where else? What about you?'

'Work too.'

'Busy?'

'Not really. Not at this time of day, unless we're really unlucky. How's it going?'

'Badly,' he told her.

'Something happened?'

240

'Another kid's gone missing, a little girl this time – taken by the same person.'

'Oh,' Kate answered, trying to hide the tell-tale sounds of selfish disappointment in her voice. 'I'm sorry,' she said. 'I mean, I'm sorry for the girl and her parents.'

'I know you are.' They listened to each other silently down the phone for a few seconds, his guilt and regret growing in the silence.

'I suppose that means we won't be seeing much of you – anything of you for a while?'

'What can I do?' he asked.

'We need to get away from this,' she told him, making him sink back in his chair. 'This is no way to live – to raise kids.'

'Not now,' he pleaded. 'Let's not do this now. Not right now.'

'OK,' she agreed, her voice soft and reconciliatory, 'but have you thought about New Zealand any more? It has to be better than this.'

'I've looked into it,' he reminded her. 'My shoulder's fucked – I'd never pass the medical, not without more surgery.'

'If you went to your physiotherapy sessions, that would help.'

'I'm too busy for physiotherapy,' he told her before realizing his mistake.

'Exactly.' She seized on it. 'You owe your job no loyalty,' she told him. 'You've given them everything and they've taken it all without giving a damn thing back. It's time to look after yourself . . . and your family.'

He considered her words for a second. 'OK. I promise to keep the physio appointments.'

'And?'

'And to check out New Zealand again, providing the shoulder improves.'

'Good,' she told him, the relief obvious in her voice. 'And try to get home at some point, even if it's just for a little while.'

'I will,' he promised.

'OK. I'll see you later. Be careful.'

'I miss you,' he suddenly found himself saying, 'and the kids – tell them I miss them too.'

'Then you know what to do,' she told him and hung up, leaving him with his mobile still pressed to his ear as he stared into space.

Donnelly entered without being asked, waving a fistful of thin files in the air.

'Busy?' he asked, looking at the phone against Sean's face.

'No,' sighed Sean, tossing it on to his desk. 'Got something for me?'

'Aye – the names of the families' nannies and au pairs and employment records for the teachers from both nurseries used by them. There's a few dozen names to go through there, but it's not too bad.'

'What about the removal companies, estate agents, etc?' Sean asked impatiently.

'Still working on them, but they're going to take a bit of time.'

'Time's something we haven't got,' Sean reminded him.

'Aye,' Donnelly agreed. 'D'you want me to load these names on to the system – put them on a spreadsheet?'

'Sure, but let me have a look at them first.' Sean beckoned him closer, holding out his hand for the files. 'I'll give you a shout when I'm done.' Donnelly left him to it.

Sean sighed and shuffled the files on his desk, opting for the one containing the names and details of nannies and au pairs. It only took a few minutes to discount them all: none had worked for both families. He pushed the file aside and pulled the two from the nurseries in front of

242

him, opening them together, laying them side by side so he could see the names on both lists at the same time. He looked at the first name on the list of employees from Small Fry Nursery and ran his finger down the list on the file from Little Unicorns Nursery until he was satisfied the name didn't appear on both before moving to the next name and repeating the process over and over until he was more than halfway through the list, his index finger searching for the name of Nicola Beecher. Suddenly he froze, adrenalin flooding his body – the name appeared on both lists. She'd worked at both nurseries. 'Well, well,' he whispered. 'Nicola, Nicola. I'd better take a look at you.' He resisted the temptation to flick straight to the more detailed employment records, disciplining himself to continue his search through the list of names. *There could be another.*

His index finger ran faster down the list of names now, impatient to complete the task, but as he searched for the penultimate name on the list of employees from Small Fry his hand froze again as he found the same name on the list from Little Unicorns – Hannah Richmond. 'Would you believe it?' he asked himself and immediately headed to Donnelly's office.

'Have you checked the names on the lists from the nurseries?' he asked in an almost accusatory tone.

'No,' Donnelly admitted. 'I was going to do it while I loaded them into the system. Why?'

'We have a hit – in fact we have two.'

Donnelly sensed the excitement in his voice. 'That's not too surprising,' he cautioned. 'Two nursery schools close to each other – I'm almost surprised you didn't get more.'

Refusing to be deflated, Sean sat at Sally's unused desk and began to read through the personnel files of Nicola Beecher and Hannah Richmond.

'Do the schools know we have these files?' he asked without looking up.

'Yeah, sure,' Donnelly answered. 'I told them we could get a Production Order if they wanted, but both said it wasn't necessary. Missing kids and all that – they were pretty keen to help. Wouldn't do their image much good if they were seen to be uncooperative.'

'No,' Sean agreed, flicking through Nicola Beecher's file, 'I don't suppose it would.' A quick check of her employment dates showed she would have come into contact with both George Bridgeman and Bailey Fellowes. 'She would have had access to both children,' he relayed the information to Donnelly, 'and working in the nursery means she has access to their personal details – addresses, parents, siblings.'

'Not exactly,' Donnelly threw another fly in the ointment. 'She's currently working at Little Unicorns, George Bridgeman's nursery.'

'So?'

'So she'd have access to George's current details, but not Bailey's. Remember, Bailey's family moved house only recently – she wouldn't know that.'

'Unless she'd watched them,' Sean told him, 'or had them watched. Or maybe she just asked around – asked some of her old friends from Little Unicorns.'

'Possible,' Donnelly agreed.

'It's more than possible,' Sean argued.

'OK,' Donnelly tried to slow him down. 'Say it's possible, even probable, but why? Why would a nursery teacher be snatching away wee kiddies she's come into contact with?'

'To get what she wants most, but can't have.'

'Children of her own,' Donnelly answered after a pause. 'It makes sense,' Sean tried to convince him. 'We have 'no bodies, no signs of violence, no ransom demand – it makes sense.'

'I can't see a bird picking locks and entering houses in the middle of the damn night.'

'Nor can I,' Sean agreed. 'That's why I think she'll be working with someone else – a man. Probably someone newish on the scene, someone she's been waiting for – someone she could talk into doing her dirty work – someone who's desperate to please her.'

'Get me the kiddies or there'll be no hanky-panky for you,' Donnelly offered.

'Something like that,' Sean despairingly agreed, still searching through the personnel records, his finger momentarily resting on the small passport photograph of an attractive woman with short auburn hair before moving to Nicola's background and family details. 'Fuck it. No good. She's married – three kids and in her mid-forties.'

'Husband's run off with the kids and a bit of crumpet half his age?' Donnelly unhelpfully suggested.

'No,' Sean dismissed him. 'She's no good for it.'

He tossed her now useless file aside and pulled Hannah Richmond's towards him, hurriedly searching for her personal details, dwelling for a second on the passport photograph of a slightly dumpy woman with long, light brown hair, before beginning to read silently to himself, praying for a miracle. *Hannah Richmond, thirty-six years old, home address 22a Agar Grove, Camden Town. Marital status: single, no children, next of kin: her mother.*

'This one,' Sean declared without a hint of triumph. 'Hannah Richmond, currently working at Small Fry Nursery as an assistant teacher, but also worked at Little Unicorns doing the same. This could be our woman.' Quickly he checked her employment dates, speaking to Donnelly as he did so. 'Her employment dates confirm it: she worked at

Little Unicorns at a time that would have given her access to George Bridgeman.' He at last looked up at Donnelly. 'Who's the Family Liaison Officer for the Fellowes?'

'I gave that particular unenviable task to young DC Goodwin,' Donnelly answered. 'Thought the experience would do him good – teach him it's not all cops and robbers.'

Sean quickly found Goodwin's mobile. He kept all his team's numbers in his contacts, past and present. He dialled, pacing the office as he waited for an answer.

'Ashley speaking.'

'Ash,' Sean began, 'are you with the family at the moment?'

'Of course, guv'nor.'

'Ask them if they know a teacher's assistant at Bailey's nursery called Hannah Richmond. I'll explain why later.'

'Hold on a second,' Goodwin told him, leaving Sean listening to muffled voices in the background until Goodwin's clear voice returned. 'I'm getting blank looks here, guv'nor.'

'She's white, mid-thirties, heavy to medium build, long brown hair. I've only got a passport photograph here – I can't tell you much more.' More muffled voices from the other end of his mobile.

'No. Sorry. No one here knows her. But Mrs Fellowes says their au pair usually takes the kids to and from school, so it's not surprising she doesn't recall a teacher's assistant.'

'Is the au pair there?' Sean asked.

'No. At the park with the kids.'

'Shit. All right, I'll get back to you,' Sean told him and hung up, turning to Donnelly. 'Is Maggie back with the Bridgemans?'

'Should be.'

He quickly found and called her number, which was answered almost immediately.

'Guv'nor?'

'You with the Bridgemans?'

'Yes,' Maggie answered. 'I was just explaining to them what happens next.'

'Never mind that,' Sean interrupted, 'ask them if they know a woman called Hannah Richmond. She used to work at Little Unicorns with George.'

'Hold on,' she told him as he endured more distant mumbles before Maggie spoke to him again. 'They're asking why you want to know.'

'Tell them . . .' Sean began, before realizing his voice was raised in frustration. 'Just tell them,' he repeated, more quietly, 'that I'll explain everything as soon as I can, but right now they need to answer the question.'

'OK. Give me a second.' Sean rubbed his forehead while he anxiously waited for Maggie to come back to him. 'Yeah, they know her.'

'Know her or remember her?' Sean asked, momentarily confused.

'They know her,' Maggie confirmed.

'She must have made quite an impression on them.'

'Not really,' Maggie explained. 'She wasn't just an assistant teacher at George's nursery, they used her for private child-minding when they were between nannies – which is strictly against school rules, hence they were a little reluctant to tell us at first.'

'Ask them what she was like.'

'OK,' Maggie answered with a resigned tone. 'Give me a minute.' He listened to more infuriating, unintelligible background chatter for what seemed like hours. 'They say she was very nice, completely obsessed with the kids, didn't appear to have a social or love life. I guess that's what made her such a good child-minder: she was reliable – always available.'

'Thanks, Maggie,' he told her before hanging up, caressing the growing stubble on his chin between his index finger and thumb as he stared down at the small, lifeless photograph of Hannah Richmond, her eyes like the dolls' eyes from Bailey's bedroom – looking, but not seeing. His hand drifted from his face to the photograph, his finger circling Hannah Richmond's plain face as he accidentally spoke out loud. 'They're beautiful, aren't they – these children you've taken? Flames to the moth.'

'Excuse me,' Donnelly interrupted, stopping him before he could say any more.

'What?' Sean asked, looking up, unaware of what he'd said.

'You said something.'

'It was nothing – just thinking out loud. We need to take a close look at this woman. We need to totally change our suspect outlook – change their profile.'

'You sure about this?' Donnelly questioned. 'Seems like hell of a risk. Wouldn't we be safer checking out more local paedophiles or even looking at some further afield?'

'No. This one has good local knowledge. These attacks aren't random – they're planned – planned meticulously. They even have knowledge of the inside of the houses: where the children sleep, the fact they're not alarmed – everything they need to know, they know.'

'But how could this . . . this Hannah Richmond know those things? There's no evidence or suggestion she's been in either home – in the Bridgemans' old home, sure, but not their new one.'

'But whoever's taking the children for her could have been inside. Maybe the new man in her life was one of the removal men, the alarm fitter, anything. Where are those damn names, anyway?'

'We're working on it,' Donnelly told him.

'Then we need to work faster. There'll be more connections here, I'm sure of it – more connections between the families and the houses. We need to find them before we have another missing child on our hands – or worse.'

'Worse?' Donnelly asked. 'I thought you said she was taking them because she wanted to keep them – to love them?'

'I did, but that doesn't mean she's not deranged. For all we know she could be schizophrenic and not taking her medication. Which means she's dangerous, whether she knows it or not.'

'I don't know, boss.' Donnelly shook his head. 'I'm still not convinced this isn't just some kiddie-fiddler nut-job. It could just blow up in our faces if we go down this route.'

'It's not a paedophile,' Sean insisted. 'I'm sure of it.'

'Why?' Donnelly asked. 'Why so sure?'

'Because of what McKenzie said: if they'd been taken by someone like him they'd already be dead by now and we would have at least one body.'

Donnelly's shoulders slumped. 'It's unusual, I admit, but I still feel like we're going out on a limb here, with this Hannah bird.'

'It's my call, so I'll be the only one out on a limb.'

'That's not what I meant.'

'I know,' Sean told him.

'Then what are we going to do?'

'Get the surveillance team back up and running and put them on Hannah Richmond,' he answered, already reaching for his desktop phone and punching in the extension number he knew off by heart. A few seconds later the other end was picked up.

'Detective Superintendent Featherstone speaking.'

'Boss, it's Sean. I need a favour.'

'I'm listening,' he answered, his tone neutral.

'I need the surveillance back.'

'I thought this McKenzie bloke was done and dusted as a suspect.'

'He is,' Sean agreed. 'I need them for someone else.'

'A new suspect?' Featherstone asked, interested now. 'Care to share?'

'I haven't got time to go into it right now. Can you trust me?'

'Sure,' Featherstone replied after a pause.

'Then I can have the surveillance?'

'You can have the surveillance,' Featherstone told him, 'but not until the day after tomorrow. They're all tied up on an Anti-Terrorist job until then. I'll never be able to pull them away. Sorry.'

'Don't worry about it,' Sean replied. 'The day after tomorrow will be fine.'

'You sure, given the nature of this case?' Featherstone seemed slightly surprised at Sean's calm reaction.

'Day after tomorrow will be fine,' Sean answered and quickly hung up.

'You've got that look again,' Donnelly told him. 'Like you're about to do something you shouldn't.'

'Surveillance can't cover until the day after tomorrow.'

'So I gathered.'

'So we'll cover it until then.'

'You didn't tell Featherstone that,' Donnelly quizzed.

'No,' Sean replied. 'There's no way he'd let me pull most of the team away from other inquiries to cover a suspect like Richmond. He'd be too scared it was slowing down the investigation.'

'And he might have a point.'

Sean ignored him. 'Take five people and three cars. Have whoever you want, but get the surveillance up and running. Cover Richmond until two a.m., then I'll take over with a relief team.' He glanced at his watch and looked across the main office at the darkness beyond the windows. 'It's too late to pick her up leaving work, so cover her home – address is in the file, somewhere in Camden.'

'I hope you're right about this,' Donnelly told him, shaking his head in concern.

'So do I,' Sean answered, 'because if I'm wrong, then I really haven't got a clue what's going on here. Not a single, damn clue.'

8

Hannah Richmond stared at herself in the large square mirror that hung in her kitchen, attacking her long dull hair with an old comb, desperately trying to make it look presentable. Finally she gave in and tossed the comb on to the table as she straightened her only suit and admired her image – not something she was used to doing, but these last few months had been different – life-changing. She'd met a man and he'd already told her he loved her and wanted to marry her – the sooner the better. She was the first to admit he wasn't exactly the man of her dreams, or probably anyone's, but he was good and decent, and he was keen to please her – to bow to her every whim. More than anything else she was happy now and hadn't even had to take her anti-depressants lately, despite warnings from her doctor about the possible side effects of dropping her medication so abruptly. 'Doctors,' she said to herself. 'What do they know?'

She should have been going to work today, but an opportunity too good to ignore had come up and she was going to take it – grab it with both hands, that's what her man had told her to do, so that's what she was going to do.

She was dressed in her best and almost ready to head out. She needed this and knew the children needed her. School would be expecting her into work later that morning, but she wouldn't be able to make it, not today. She'd wait a little while longer, then phone in and tell them she was sick with that stomach bug that was doing the rounds. More than a few children at the nursery had had it, so it shouldn't give rise to too much suspicion.

She thought of the nursery as she tried to apply a little make-up, something else she wasn't used to doing. But her man reckoned it suited her, so she'd taken to using it more often, although still only for special occasions, or when she needed to make an impression, like this morning. Small Fry was all right – the other teachers were pleasant enough, if a bit condescending at times, and most of the children were adorable too, although some took after their parents: arrogant and self-important, acting as if they were royalty, speaking in their clipped accents just to make sure everybody knew they belonged to *the right set*. They barely even looked at her, let alone spoke to her, unless they wanted something – child-minding usually, then they were all smiles and niceties, until they'd got what they wanted. I trust you to look after my children, but don't expect me to treat you like an equal, or even a person. 'Don't deserve children, most of them,' she told her image in the mirror. 'Can't see the point in having them if you don't want to be with them.' She'd buried her jealousy well all these years, that twisting feeling she got in her belly every time she saw or heard a parent treating their child with contempt and disdain, as if they were nothing more than a burden. And yet all this time, all these years, all she'd ever wanted were children of her own. But she could never meet the right man – any man – until now. And she was already in her thirties – it might be too late for her. She couldn't take that chance – she had to have children.

Hannah Richmond pulled on her thick winter coat, grabbed her old handbag and headed for the front door of the small ground-floor flat she'd bought off the local council years ago. It was in an ugly modern tenement block – something that looked as if it had been made out of giant pieces of black and white Lego. As she undid the various front-door locks the bathroom door behind her opened and her man stepped out, his badly receding hair still wet, a towel wrapped around his ample waist. He hadn't bothered to shave. 'You're out early,' he said in his thick London accent. 'Dressed to kill an' all. Something on at work?'

'I won't be going to work today,' she told him, her usually smiling face as serious as he'd seen it.

'Oh. How come?'

'I have to go and see a family,' she explained. 'The children need me. I'll see you later.' She opened the door and moved to step outside.

'Not even a kiss?' he called after her, stopping her in her tracks. Her lips broke into a faint smile as she waited for him to come to her and they quickly kissed before she stepped over the threshold and was gone.

Once she was outside she moved quickly away from her block, her chest fluttering with anxiety in case she was seen by a work colleague, her planned lie about being sick aborted before birth. The worrying thought intensified the morning chill, prompting her to pull her collar up around her neck and lower her face. Her new shoes clicked and clacked on the hard pavement as she headed towards Camden Town and beyond – to the address where she knew the children would be waiting for her.

*   *   *

His fitful sleep was punctuated by confusing, irrational dreams – images, memories and people from his past and present knitted together in a bizarre patchwork of events: the missing children for some reason in his own home, playing with his own children, but being cared for by his mother, not Kate – Anna waiting for him upstairs, in the bed that he shared with his wife. He watched himself climbing the stairs, his heart pounding as he avoided the creaky floorboards, just as the *taker* had. This was his own home, yet still he moved stealthily towards the bedroom and Anna, pushing the door slowly open and seeing him – seeing him on top of her, forcing himself on her. He walked as if walking through quicksand to the bed, Anna's pain and humiliation bringing tears to his own eyes as he reached out to the man on top of her, grabbing him by the back of the head and twisting his face away from Anna's and towards himself, the laughing, mocking face of his father staring into his own. He looked down at Anna, pleading with him to help her, her lips moving, but no words coming out as his father's laughter drowned out all sound. 'Help me,' her silent lips pleaded. 'Help me.' But he couldn't, and he ran from the room, fleeing back down the stairs to the children and his mother. Only she was gone and once more it was his father who waited for him, standing behind the four children who kneeled in front of him, laughter still pouring from his black mouth and blood-red lips. The children's eyes begged him to rescue them – their silent mouths mimed words almost identical to those Anna had mouthed: 'Help us. Help us.' But he couldn't move; no matter how much he struggled, he couldn't move. Suddenly his entire world began to shake as sounds from the real world penetrated his nightmare.

'Guv'nor,' the voice of DC Tony Summers tried to reach

him. 'Guv'nor.' His conscious mind began to stir as he eyes flickered open and reminded him where he was and what he was doing.

'Fuck,' he grumbled. He tried to work the stiffness out of his neck after sleeping sitting upright in the front of the unmarked car for several hours. 'Jesus. What time is it?'

'About quarter-past-seven, boss,' Summers answered, his voice quiet, despite their safe distance from the address they'd been watching since two a.m. 'The target's at her front door.'

Sean rubbed his eyes then blinked as he tried to focus on the front door of the ground-floor flat little more than fifty metres away. 'Looks like she's dressed for work,' Summers offered.

'Maybe,' Sean answered, less convinced. 'A bit early for nursery school though, don't you think?'

'They start early these days, boss. Pressures of the modern world and all that,' Summers explained in his Lancashire accent.

'Or she's going somewhere else.' Sean grabbed his radio before Summers could answer, speaking informally on the private channel: 'You seeing this?'

'Yes,' came the reply from Sally in one of the other two unmarked cars.

'Wait a second,' Sean stalled her as the shape of a man, naked but for a towel around his waist, came into view. He watched the couple briefly kiss before parting, the target turning her coat up against the cold. *Is that the new man in your life?* Sean thought to himself. *Is he the one you've been waiting for?* He pressed the radio to transmit. 'She's on foot. Doesn't look like she's going for a vehicle. Sally, Tessa and I will follow her on foot. Everyone else run parallels with the cars and try to stay close.'

'Received,' Sally's voice answered. 'Received,' DC Tessa Carlisle echoed.

'All foot units use mobiles to stay in touch. Leave the radios with the cars.'

'Received,' Sally and Carlisle both acknowledged.

Sean tossed the radio to Summers and slipped out of the car and on to the pavement, quietly pressing the door shut before following Hannah Richmond's footsteps, always staying at least fifty metres behind her and as far out of her eyeline as possible. He walked in line with any trees or bus-shelters so he could conceal himself with a quick swerve if she turned. Pulling his mobile from his coat pocket, he called Sally, speaking as quietly as he could as he tailed the target along the road that was deserted but for them.

'Sean?'

'Are you with me?'

'Yeah – about thirty metres back, on the other side of the road. I can see you, but not the target. Tess is about another twenty metres back on your side.'

'Good, but we need to get closer,' he told her. 'She'll be in central Camden in a couple of minutes. She could lose us easy.'

'Understood,' Sally agreed and hung up. Sean slipped his mobile into his outside coat pocket, leaving his hand resting on it in case a call caused it to vibrate, and quickened his pace, closing the distance on Hannah Richmond before she made it to central Camden.

As she approached the end of Agar Road he could see she was about to enter St Pancras Way, where the pedestrian traffic was already growing dense. He rushed to close the distance, but quickly had to move behind a thick oak tree when she suddenly slowed and looked back. After a few seconds he peeked around the trunk and saw she'd moved on. She seemed far more nervous than a normal person on their way to work. He continued his pursuit, calling Sally as he walked – just another businessman who couldn't wait until he reached his office before beginning the day's calls.

'Problem?' Sally asked.

'She's looking for something,' he warned her. 'She's done one check behind her already and keeps looking around.'

'Did she see you?'

'I don't think so. She's just crossed St Pancras Way into Camden Road and is heading towards the tube station.'

'Let me take the lead,' Sally told him, 'to be safe.'

'No,' he argued. 'There's no time. Just stay close.' He hung up and continued the chase, glad to be in a wide, busy street; mingling among so many other people in suits and coats was his best possible disguise. He'd closed the gap between them to ten metres, but still she periodically twisted her head from side to side, as if constantly checking for danger. She walked past Camden tube station and into Chalk Farm Road, where she stopped at a bus shelter, pulling her collar as far as she could over her face, standing behind the advertising boards, concealing herself from the view of the passing traffic. Sean had no choice – he stopped at the same bus stop, waiting to feel her eyes burning into the back of his head. He pulled his phone free again when he was as happy as he could be she was paying him no heed and quickly typed a text message:

@ bus shelter, west side, chalk farm rd. T is held. All bus routes north west – AWAY from her work. where going??

As soon as the message was sent he flicked the phone on to silent mode and slid it back into his pocket and waited for its vibrating to go through his hand like an electric shock. Seconds later he received Sally's reply:

Tess and I will join you at stop with T. OK?

He tapped in his reply:

Ok.

As he slipped the phone out of sight he saw Sally approaching the bus stop, halting a few feet short of the shelter, pulling her coat tight against the chill, moving from foot to foot, just another office worker trying to keep her feet from freezing. Next DC Carlisle appeared from behind a couple she had been using as cover, walking straight into the shelter without looking around, sitting on one of the unoccupied bench-bar seats and immediately pulling a worn paperback from her small handbag. All the time Hannah Richmond continued to glance about her, yet failed to notice the three cops.

Sean risked a sideways glance as he pretended to be looking for the bus, sensing the target's agitation as soon as he saw her in the corner of his eye. But whatever she was looking for – whatever she was *expecting* – it wasn't them. *What are you up to?* Sean asked himself. *Where are you going and what are you afraid of – us? The police? You look for us, but you don't see us. Is that what I'm doing with this case – looking but not seeing?* An approaching bus broke his thoughts, its front sign stating it was heading towards Hampstead High Street and then on to Golders Green, the wrong side of the heath for Small Fry Nursery. All three detectives held their ground, waiting for the target to make her move or not. If there had been more of them following a surveillance-aware target then maybe one or two would have got on the bus anyway, just to keep the target disorientated, but working in a team of three they couldn't do that even if they thought it necessary.

As soon as the doors of the bus were fully open, Hannah shuffled across the pavement and stepped on board, swiping her Oyster Card and heading up the stairs and to the back of the bus. Any lingering doubt that she might be headed for work was dispelled. The detectives waited until the other passengers from the stop boarded before quickly following them on to the bus, each giving the driver a flash of their warrant cards held concealed in the palms of their hands. The bemused driver was used to having the occasional cop on his bus, but three in a row made him look up and follow their progress on his onboard security cameras, watching them climb the stairs and fan out on the top deck – Sally taking the front near the stairs, Sean the middle section and Tessa the rear, sitting just one behind the target on the opposite side.

Sean allowed himself to relax for a while, happy the target was secure and well covered, feeling a sense of growing excitement as he considered Richmond's behaviour and direction of travel, her potential as a prime suspect growing with every passing minute. The niggling thought that this could simply be her day off prompted him to try and remember what her employment record had said, but he couldn't recall anything about her having days off in the middle of the week. He momentarily considered having Donnelly call the nursery and check, but decided against it – for now.

As the bus continued its journey Sean tried to imagine Hannah Richmond leading him straight to the missing children. Would she try to justify her actions, or would she turn out to be another delusional case, motivated by some twisted logic or ideology that could only ever make sense to herself? His thoughts projected forward to the inevitable search of her flat and no doubt the arrest of her partner and conspirator, each turning on the other in desperate attempts to save their own skins – love quickly replaced by betrayal. What types of drugs and medication would he find in her bathroom cabinet? Anti-depressants? Anti-anxiety drugs? Sleeping pills? He expected to find them all, the profile of the woman sitting only a few feet away forming and solidifying in his mind, and with it his plan of how to interview her – how to break her. His phone vibrated as it received a text and made him jump a little before he realized what it was. He looked down at the screen he'd been cradling in his hand and read the message from Tess:

She's getting off.

He felt a little flutter in his chest as he realized the chase would soon be back on. A few seconds later the target passed him in the aisle while he pretended to be looking out of the window, his eyes straining to catch her in his peripheral vision as she walked to the top of the stairs and disappeared down them, glancing back along the bus just before she did so. As the target descended, Carlisle quickly got to her feet and followed. Sean was behind her, but held at the top of the stairs where he was briefly met by Sally, who whispered, 'Short bus ride.'

'Where to now?' Sean wondered, waiting for a few other passengers to disembark before he and Sally skipped quietly down the stairs, through the folding doors as they were shutting and out on to the pavement and into the cold air. Carlisle was a clear twenty metres ahead of them, no more than ten metres behind the target, who was heading north along Haverstock Hill, approaching Belsize Park underground station. But before she reached it she turned left into Belsize Grove, a quiet residential street of small town-houses for the very well-heeled, shining four-wheel drives crammed into every available parking space. He was extremely glad she hadn't descended into the underground system, where she could have been too easily lost, but the peaceful quietness of the street made her difficult to follow without making themselves conspicuous. He and Sally had no choice but to hang back, leaving Carlisle on point, though if the target was looking for her she wouldn't be able to continue for much longer and not be spotted.

His phone vibrated in his hand. He pressed answer without checking the caller ID. 'I'm listening.'

'She's turned right into Primrose Gardens,' Carlisle's voice told him quietly. 'I need to go straight on or I'll show out,' she continued. 'Sorry, guv.'

'Do it,' Sean agreed. 'I'll take over.' He hung up and stuffed the phone in his pocket. 'Let's go,' he told Sally as he broke into a fast jog, Sally keeping up with him until they reached the junction with Primrose Gardens. 'I'll go,' Sean said. 'Hang well back and keep out of sight. If she makes it to the next junction I'll call you. You can pick her up from there, all right?'

'Fine,' Sally agreed. 'Good luck.'

Sean took off into Primrose Gardens, easily picking up the target in the empty street, but she was getting too far ahead. He had no choice but to increase his speed until it was unnaturally fast. He risked drawing attention, but he had to close the distance or lose her, especially if she ducked into one of the many houses lining the street. He used what street furniture he could to disguise his approach, noticing she was now on her mobile phone. Taking instructions? 'Come on,' he encouraged her with a whisper. 'Come on, Hannah. Take me to them. End this thing.'

Still she talked on her phone, although she seemed to be listening more than talking, looking increasingly agitated and uneasy, as if she was receiving troubling news. Finally she stopped dead, looking all about the street, clearly searching for something. Sean ducked into the recessed entrance to a house so he could continue to watch her without being seen, peeking around the corner and praying the occupant didn't appear and make a noisy scene. He tugged his warrant card from his inside jacket pocket so he'd have it ready just in case they did, but nobody appeared. Hannah finally ended her conversation and slowly replaced her mobile in her handbag, but still she looked unhappy and on edge, checking up and down the street before she started to cross the road, heading for a house directly in front of her.

'Come on, come on,' Sean almost begged, his heart pounding, his mind occupied by one thing and one thing only – find the children.

From his vantage point he saw her climb the few stairs leading to the front door of a townhouse that was as smart as all the others. She paused at the door, fumbling inside her handbag for something unseen – keys, he assumed. *This has to be it*, he told himself. *This has to be it.* He sprang from his hideout and moved fast and silently across the road and along the line of the railings in front of the buildings, the angle tight enough to keep him concealed from the target until he was almost upon her, his chest sore from breathing the freezing cold air, feeling the sort of excitement that few people doing normal jobs would ever feel. Excitement that could become an addictive need to be on the edge.

He closed the space between them quickly now, her back still turned to the street as she struggled with unfamiliar keys in unfamiliar locks. When he was still a few metres away he saw her body jolt forward as if she was falling through a suddenly open door. His mind was already made up: the only option was to act without delay – no sitting back, watching the address. Either it was her or it wasn't. Either the missing children were inside or they weren't. No amount of surveillance was going to change that now.

Before she could close the door, Sean was on her, grabbing her arm hard around the bicep and bundling her into the hallway of the townhouse, her eyes wide with terror, her mouth locked open in a silent scream as children appeared at the far end of the hallway, little more than silhouettes, except for their eyes – staring in fear and disbelief as Sean pushed Hannah Richmond against the wall, moving his hand from her arm to her chest, just below her neck. 'Don't move,' he told her, blinking as he looked along the hallway, trying to grow used to the dimness, trying to focus on the children who stood frozen, side by side, eventually realizing he was looking at three children, not two.

'Don't hurt me,' Richmond pleaded. 'Please, God, don't hurt the children. I'll do anything you want – just don't hurt the children.'

Sean heard her clearly enough, but her words didn't fit the scene – didn't fit her – the prime suspect. 'What?' he asked, staring into her terrified face.

'The children,' she repeated, calmer now, resigned to her fate. 'Please don't hurt the children.'

It took him a second before he realized she had no idea who he was. He felt the warrant card in his hand and quickly held it up for her to see, all the while keeping her pinned to the wall, the sounds of sniffling, crying children growing ever louder, disorientating him as the situation began to feel less and less like a rescue scenario. 'Police,' he told her loudly, just as Sally burst through the open door, her eyes wide and wild as she tried to assess the scene before her.

'You all right?' Sally asked him.

'I'm fine,' he reassured her. 'We need to secure the house.'

'I'm sorry,' Richmond suddenly blurted. 'I'm really sorry, but it's not my fault. I didn't know this was going to happen. This wasn't supposed to happen.'

'What are you talking about?' Sean snapped at her. 'What didn't you know was going to happen?'

'This is only the second time I've looked after them,' Richmond explained. 'The mother was supposed to wait for me, but she said she had to go to work.'

'What?' Sean asked, his eyes narrowed in confusion.

'I was only seconds away from getting here when she phoned me – said she'd already left and that the kids were alone waiting for me.' Sean released her and walked deeper into the house towards the cowering children, his eyes showing him the crushing truth – these weren't the children he was looking for. 'The mother shouldn't have left them alone,' Richmond continued. 'She shouldn't have done that, but Rachel's almost twelve and she's very grown-up. It was just a few minutes.'

Sean and Sally turned and looked at each other, his heart sinking as fast as Richmond's guilt was fading. 'You're their child-minder?' Sean asked disbelievingly.

'I can't afford to get into trouble with the police,' Richmond pleaded. 'I'll lose my job. I can't afford to lose my job.'

'You're supposed to be at work today,' Sean told her. 'Why didn't you go to work?'

'I needed the extra money. It won't happen again, I swear, but please don't tell the school about this. Please.'

'Who were you speaking to on the phone?' Sean demanded, desperate to hold on to her as a suspect, 'outside in the street – who were you talking to?'

'I told you,' she answered, 'the children's mother – Mrs Gardner. She just wanted to check I was close, you know, because the children were alone, but I didn't know she'd left them. I would never have taken the job if I'd known she was going to do anything like this. Please don't tell the nursery.'

'Christ,' Sean said, finally taking his hand away from her chest and stepping backwards, screaming inside as he fought the urge to run from the house and keep running until he was far away from this debacle. 'I'm not going to tell the nursery,' he told her, shaking his head. 'I'm not going to tell anybody.' He walked along the hallway without speaking, past Sally and into the light and cold outside, running his hands through his light brown hair as he allowed his eyes to close, feeling Sally's presence before he heard her.

'Where the hell are these children, Sean?' she asked. 'What's happened to them?'

He opened his eyes and turned to face her. 'I've no idea,' he told her, his voice sounding shaky and broken. 'No bloody idea at all.'

9

Douglas Allen moved quickly and nimbly around the small sparse kitchen on the first floor of his Edwardian terrace as he prepared lunch. Despite the meal preparation the kitchen was spotless, everything in its place, the old wooden table neatly laid for three – one adult and two children. Fading framed photographs from another era decorated the walls, mostly photographs of himself and his beloved wife – holidays in English seaside towns, the two of them together around the table set for dinner. But there were no pictures of children anywhere to be seen. An antique cuckoo-clock hung on one of the walls, ticking loudly as its brass pendulum swung gently back and forth. On another wall, a second clock, rescued from an old ship, lovingly restored and synchronized to keep beat with the cuckoo. The walls they hung on were painted in magnolia and regularly washed clean of any settling grease. The children's plates and cutlery were smaller than his own, but essentially the same. He felt it was important they learned to use a knife and fork as soon as possible and shuddered slightly at the memories of seeing children as old as seven and eight having their meals cut up for them by their parents, or more likely their nannies, on the odd occasions when he had ventured into local cafés.

His appearance reflected that of his kitchen: he was quite small, only about five foot eight inches, clean shaven with greying hair immaculately groomed and smoothed back over his head with some old-fashioned hair tonic. His fifty-eight years had taken their toll on his body and he now sported thin wire-framed spectacles and a slight potbelly. But he was as quick and light on his feet as he'd been back in the days when he and his wife were regular visitors to the local ballrooms, although those, like his wife, had gone now. He wore a starched apron to keep his shirt and tie clean while he finished preparing the meal. He carried the two smaller plates to the table and the waiting children who sat peacefully waiting for their lunch. 'There we are,' he told them, stepping back proudly, a pleasant smile on his face as he awaited their judgement before collecting his own plate and joining them at the table. 'You can have a drink after you've eaten.'

'I want a drink now,' Bailey Fellowes argued. 'I always have a drink with my food.'

Allen's smile shrank to a small grin. 'Not any more,' he explained. 'You shouldn't fill yourself up with drinks before you've eaten your meal. It's not good for you.'

'That's not what my mum says,' Bailey continued to argue as George Bridgeman looked on, his gaze flitting between them as they took turns to speak.

'No, I don't suppose she did,' Allen agreed.

'And I don't like this sort of food,' she persisted.

'It's good food,' Allen told her in his accent-less voice, deep and baritone, like voices from the past. 'You need to eat. You hardly touched your breakfast.'

'And I don't like these weird clothes. They smell funny.'

'But they're new and I've washed and pressed them,' he replied, his smile replaced by concern.

'But they don't smell like my clothes.'

'You're lucky to have them. They cost me a lot of money.'

Bailey pushed her plate away from in front of her, making Allen's already straight back stiffen even more. 'I'm not eating this.'

'But it's sausages,' Allen told her, confused by her ingratitude. 'All children like sausages, don't they?'

'I like sausages,' George joined in, something in his childhood instincts telling him not to push the man who had brought them here any further, memories of his father's quick temper never too far away.

'You're a good boy,' Allen told him, inducing a broad smile on the boy's face.

'I don't like mashed potatoes or vegetables,' Bailey pushed. 'I never have to eat them at home.'

'I know,' Allen told her. 'That's why it's better for you to be here.'

'No it's not,' Bailey argued, her voice rising as her eyes grew misty. 'I want to go home. I miss my mummy.'

'This is your home now,' he explained, 'at least until we can all move somewhere better – somewhere in the countryside – on a farm. You'd like that, wouldn't you?'

'You said you'd take me to a magic place – that's why I came with you. This isn't a magic place – this is a dump. You don't even have a television.'

'You're being rude now, Bailey. I won't have rude children in my house. Rude children need to be punished.'

'You can't punish me. You're not my dad. I don't know you. You're a bad man. My mummy told me about men like you. I shouldn't have gone with you.' Water pooled in the bottom of her eyes before spilling over into tears.

'Don't,' he raised his voice to her before he had a chance to quell his rising anger, swallowing it back down before he spoke again. 'Don't say those things. I'm not a bad man. I'm not like the men your mother warned you about. I'd never hurt you – either of you. I brought you here to protect you. To give you a better life.'

'I like it here,' George innocently claimed, having already learned in his short life how to defuse tension. Allen smiled at him and rested a hand on the boy's head.

'I know you do,' he replied. 'I know you do. What's not to like?' They sat in silence listening and waiting for Bailey's gentle sobbing to fade and die, the sound of the grandfather clock outside in the hallway chiming to warn them it was one o'clock. When the chimes fell silent, George broke the uneasy silence.

'Whose are the voices we can hear?' he asked. 'Downstairs? We can hear them from our bedroom sometimes – during the day.'

'There's nothing for you to worry about,' Allen tried to reassure him. 'They're just . . . *friends*.' There was more silence before George spoke again.

'And sometimes we can hear music too.'

'What type of music?' Allen asked, unconcerned.

'Children's music, I think,' George answered.

'All music is for children,' Allen told him. 'That's another thing your parents should have taught you.'

'Why aren't we allowed downstairs?' George continued.

'Because . . .' Allen stalled, 'there are things down there that could be dangerous to young children.'

'Like what?' George asked, intrigued and excited.

'Things,' Allen answered. 'Now let's not talk about it any more.'

'Why do we have to stay in the bedroom when you're not there?' Bailey asked, her voice still bitter. 'Even during the daytime?'

'What's the matter – don't you like your bedroom?'

'I do,' George answered quickly.

270

'At home I have my own bedroom,' Bailey told them.

'You don't need a room of your own,' Allen explained, managing to stay calm, 'but if you're good I might let you use the rest of the house when I'm downstairs. But you must never try to come all the way downstairs. Like I said, it could be dangerous for you.'

'Are there bad people down there?' George asked.

'No,' Allen told him. 'Just friends. Enough questions for now, please. It's time to eat. I have to go out later, but not until you've had your bath and are tucked up in bed. You'll be quite safe until I return. Now, let us say the Lord's Prayer before we eat.'

'My dad says there's no such thing as God,' Bailey mocked him through her glassy eyes.

'Then that's just one more thing I have to teach you about,' he gently scolded her. 'Now put your hands together and close your eyes: *Our Father which art in heaven, Hallowed be thy name. Thy kingdom come. Thy will be done in earth, as it is in heaven. Gives us this day our daily bread. And forgive us our debts, as we forgive our debtors. And lead us not into temptation, but deliver us from evil: For thine is the kingdom, and the power, and the glory for ever. Amen.* Now eat.'

'Where are you going?' George asked. 'After you put us to bed? Is it a secret?'

'No, George,' Allen told him. 'There are no secrets in this family.' He took a deep breath before continuing, as if the news he was about to impart was particularly important. 'I have to go and see someone,' he explained. 'Someone who needs us – someone who needs a proper family.' He smiled as he lifted his knife and fork. 'Now, eat your lunch.'

Sean sat in the waiting room outside Assistant Commissioner Addis's office, high up in the tower block that was New

271

Scotland Yard. Despite the ubiquitous grey plastic blinds and low ceilings with fluorescent light strips, the room was as plush as anything Sean had seen in the Police Service. The chair he was sitting on was in fact a low-slung sofa that could have done any office in the City proud, and the carpet underfoot seemed new and clean, even though it was thin and inexpensive. A flat-screen TV hung on the wall opposite, tuned to Sky News. He wondered whether Addis was waiting in his adjoining office until the investigation into the missing children came on the television – as if to emphasize the point he hadn't yet made.

The thought made him look away, and he began instead to study Addis's young, attractive secretary as she continually took pieces of paper from one pile, typed something into her computer, then placed the paper on top of a different pile before repeating the process, regularly stopping to answer the phone. She dealt with most of the calls without having to trouble Addis. Not once did she look up at Sean; she hadn't acknowledged his presence since she'd registered his attendance and asked him to take a seat and wait. He decided Addis must have plucked her out of some obscure post somewhere, no doubt considering her a suitable addition to the other decorations littered about the place: ceremonial silver truncheons, honorary badges from other forces around the world and, of course, Addis's many promotion and commendation certificates, earned on the backs of hard-working cops who risked their necks every day on the streets of the metropolis – something Addis had only ever done fleetingly, if at all.

The intercom on the secretary's desk made a loud buzzing sound and the hairs on the back of his neck stood up. He watched and listened as she pressed the transmit key and spoke. 'Yes, sir? Of course. I'll send him straight in.' Sean was on his feet before she even turned to speak to him.

'Assistant Commissioner Addis will see you now, Inspector.' He headed for the closed interconnecting door, pausing at her desk before entering Addis's office.

'Do I get a last request?' he asked her with a wry grin.

She tried not to smile, but couldn't resist; too young to be without joy.

'I don't know why he uses that thing,' she whispered, looking accusingly at the old-fashioned intercom. 'He could just use the phone and dial my extension.'

'Maybe he doesn't know how to,' Sean whispered, giving her a wink and making her cover her mouth to hide her broadening smile.

He took the few steps to the door and knocked, looking back at the young secretary as he did so, rolling his eyes when Addis answered. 'Come, come.' He pushed the door open and stepped inside, closing the door behind him and taking a seat opposite Addis's oversized desk without being asked, daring him to challenge him.

'You wanted to see me?'

'Of course I wanted to bloody see you,' Addis barked. 'So you could explain this latest fucking disaster. It's not bad enough you've already made one unlawful arrest, now you've damn near made another. What in God's name is going on?'

'McKenzie wasn't an unlawful arrest,' Sean reminded him, 'and nor would the second have been, although in the end it wasn't necessary.'

'Inspector, you almost arrested a bloody nursery teacher for nothing. Are you trying to make us look like fools?'

'She had a link to both families – it was worth checking out.'

'Was it, bollocks!' Addis told him. 'We can't afford to chase any more wild ideas. For God's sake, she was just moonlighting as a damn babysitter.'

273

'I didn't tell you that,' Sean said, his eyes narrowing with suspicion, trying to recall who he'd told, who could know about Hannah Richmond and who would have told Addis before he had a chance to manage the situation – Featherstone? Donnelly? Sally?

'No you didn't,' Addis agreed by way of warning, giving his words time to sink in before speaking again, deliberately calmer now. 'So what next?'

'We look for leads, we look for links between the families and we chase them down – that's all we can do.'

'We don't have time to just plod along,' Addis insisted. 'We need some ingenuity, some good old-fashioned gut-instinct.'

'What,' Sean asked, 'you think I'm going to suddenly see the offender's face in my mind, where he lives . . . works? I'm going to see him standing on a street corner and suddenly say *That's the guy we've been looking for?*' Addis stared at him without speaking, his expression telling Sean everything he needed to know. 'You do, don't you? You really think I'm going to simply pluck the man we're looking for out of thin air?'

'Isn't that what you *do*, Inspector? Isn't that how you solved the Keller case, the Gibran case and others before, by using your unique *insight*?'

'No, no it isn't,' Sean lied more than he knew he was. 'I looked at the evidence – I pursued leads. I just saw things in the evidence that other people missed. If they'd have looked properly they would have seen too.'

'And in this case, you don't *see* things in the evidence, or can't?'

'No,' Sean admitted. 'Not yet.'

'I see.' Addis leaned back into his comfortable black leather desk chair. 'Then what do you suggest we do, given that you appear to be well and truly stuck?'

'Like I said, we'll keep pulling in the evidence and cross-referencing until we find the link between the families.'

'And if another child goes missing in the meantime, while you're *cross-referencing*?'

'Then it'll be easier to establish any links,' Sean told him matter-of-factly. 'It was always possible that more than one person would be linked to two affluent families living comparatively close to each other, but to be linked to three – that would almost certainly identify them as the prime suspect.'

'But the only link between the two families was this Richmond person,' Addis pointed out, 'and you've already . . . eliminated her from your inquiries.'

'No,' Sean argued. 'She was the only link we've identified *so far*. That doesn't mean she's the only link. There has to be someone else. There has to be someone linking the families. These children were selected – carefully chosen.'

'Why?' Addis jumped him.

'I don't know,' Sean admitted, staring straight into Addis' eyes. Neither man spoke for an unnaturally long time.

'This isn't very encouraging, Sean,' Addis eventually broke the silence. 'In the absence of anything new, I suggest we do another media appeal – this time flanked by both sets of parents. Perhaps we can somehow touch this animal's sense of compassion – persuade him not to harm the children – if he hasn't already.'

'It's a good idea,' Sean told him and meant it, 'but the parents need to do most of the talking – more them and less us. And have the mothers do most of that: whoever's taken the children will be more likely to feel sympathy for the mothers than the fathers – even if the abductor is a woman herself.'

'I agree,' Addis replied, as if he'd had the same idea. 'And

I want you to be present at the appeal – sitting next to me, in between the parents.'

Sean went cold inside. The thought of sitting in between the parents, their sadness and pain leaking out and seeping into him while Addis bleated on as the cameras pointed straight at them, searching them for signs of weakness, filled him with fear. 'I wouldn't advise that,' he blurted out.

'Really?' Addis asked, nonplussed. 'Is there a problem?'

'I'm still on SO10's books,' Sean remembered, desperate for an excuse to avoid the media show, 'which means I'm still technically available for undercover deployment. They wouldn't be very happy if I was to stick my face all over the telly and papers.'

'You did a media appeal for the Gibran case,' Addis reminded him, making Sean swear inwardly. 'SO10 didn't seem to mind then. Besides, SO10 come under my umbrella, so you won't get any trouble from them. I can assure you of that.'

Sean kept thinking. 'I wouldn't recommend it for other reasons as well – reasons that relate to the offender's state of mind.'

'Such as?' Addis demanded.

'I believe they'll respond to an authority figure better than someone who's less visibly identifiable.'

'You mean they'd rather see a uniform than a man in a suit?' Addis took the bait.

'Exactly,' Sean answered, swimming in relief.

'The uniform of a high-ranking police officer,' Addis continued.

'Precisely,' Sean encouraged him. 'If he sees you alongside a *detective* then we might lose his trust. We don't want him to feel hunted.'

'Very well,' Addis relented, 'but I need you to prepare me

a full briefing of anything and everything you feel could be useful for the appeal – anything that might help us flush this bastard out – understand?'

'I understand,' Sean told him, already standing to leave, as happy as he could be with the outcome of the meeting. 'I'll have it for you before close of play.'

'And, Sean,' Addis stopped him. 'Let's make sure I don't have to do another media briefing – with another family. That could put you in a very difficult position. Do I make myself clear?'

'Perfectly,' he answered, never looking away from Addis's dead eyes, like the black eyes of a shark. 'I understand perfectly.'

'Good. Because it would be a shame if this privileged position you've been given was to prove too much for you.' Sean's mouth opened slightly to answer, but Addis cut him off. 'That will be all, Inspector. You may go.' He looked down at the reports on his desk as if Sean wasn't there – as if he'd never been there.

Early evening and the large, modernized pub close to New Scotland Yard was already growing busy with a mix of off-duty cops and workers from the surrounding offices, the two groups separated by the quality of their suits and the loudness of their voices. Any drinking establishment this close to Scotland Yard was automatically assumed to be police property by the cops who used it as their regular watering hole, but civilians were tolerated so long as they behaved and didn't get in the way of the bar – although attractive women were always given special licence to behave more freely. Sally weaved her way through a group of almost exclusively male detectives who paid her little attention, having already identified her as one of their own. She tried not to spill the two overflowing drinks as she carried them across to a nearby table where Donnelly waited for her, cursing the day the smoking ban had come into effect and praying for the onset of spring when he could again take his pint outside and enjoy a smoke. Sally slid him his drink and sat next to him, backs to the wall, facing the entrance. Cops liked to see everyone as they arrived – just in case.

'Cheers, Sal,' Donnelly thanked her.

'I don't think we'll be making this place our regular,' she answered. 'Costs an arm and a leg. Almost ten quid for a pint and a glass of house white.'

'For fuck's sake,' Donnelly moaned, 'I hate the bloody Yard and I hate paying West End prices for a pint when I'm in bloody Victoria. Look at this place,' he told her, surveying the modern, minimalist surroundings with an expression of distaste, 'what a dump. Give me the Bee Hive back in Peckham any day.'

'You mean give you back free drinking,' Sally teased.

Donnelly feigned indignity. 'I paid my way. Never asked the landlord of that fine establishment for anything per gratis and never expected anything either.'

'Doesn't mean you didn't accept the odd one,' Sally said with a grin.

'Careful, Sally,' he warned her. 'The walls of the pubs around here have ears. You never know when the rubber-soled brigade are listening,' he continued, using the police slang for Internal Affairs.

'I'd like to think they've got better things to worry about than your subsidized drinking,' Sally told him.

'Don't you believe it,' Donnelly scoffed before taking a long draw on his pint, licking the froth from his moustache before speaking again. 'Anyway, more importantly, how's the guv'nor doing? Shared any secrets with you lately?'

'Such as?'

'Such as who's taking these wee kiddies?'

'No,' Sally answered honestly. 'He thought Hannah Richmond was a real go, until it blew up.'

'As he did with Mark McKenzie,' Donnelly added. 'Also a . . . mistake.'

'Whereas you wanted to haul George Bridgeman's parents over the cobbles,' Sally reminded him.

'Ah well,' he replied with a shrug of his heavy shoulders. 'Nobody's perfect.'

'Indeed they're not,' Sally agreed in the tone of a strict school teacher before taking a sip of her wine.

'Well,' Donnelly continued with a shake of his head, pint held only inches from his lips, 'he's not the man he used to be – I'll tell you that for nothing.'

'What's that supposed to mean?' Sally demanded. She'd grown closer to Sean since she'd found him bleeding and helpless on Thomas Keller's filthy kitchen floor. She'd saved him then from a psychopathic killer and she'd save him now from his own kind if she thought she had to.

'Just that he seems a bit out of sorts,' Donnelly mused. 'Not quite the Sean of old.'

'What d'you expect?' she argued. 'First they mothball us for almost six months, then they drop this nice little mess into our laps and expect Sean to be able to magically solve it.'

'Sean, now is it?' Donnelly picked up on her slip. She'd never called him anything other than guv'nor or boss in front of the others before.

'All I'm saying is, he's bound to be a bit rusty – we all are. He just needs a little time, that's all. He needs to get the scent for it again.'

'Is that why he went after McKenzie and this Hannah bird – trying to get the feel for it?'

'Probably,' Sally admitted. 'At least he was doing

something, not just sitting in his office praying for a miracle, or sitting in a pub drowning his sorrows.'

'Aye, well perhaps he'd better start praying for a miracle now,' Donnelly told her, 'because if he doesn't crack this one soon he'll be in the brown smelly stuff – and us along with him. The eyes of the world are watching, Sally – the eyes of the world are watching.'

It had already been a long day and it wasn't over yet. Every inch of his body ached and throbbed after spending the best part of the night sitting in the front seat of an unmarked police car on what ultimately turned out to be a wasted endeavour. He looked up from the endless reports and loose bits of paper littering his cheap desk and peered into the adjoining office only to see that it was empty. A quick scan of the main office confirmed that neither Sally nor Donnelly was anywhere to be seen. He was pretty sure what sort of place they were probably in, even if he didn't know exactly where, and as they were the only ones who would be likely to enter his office without announcing themselves first, he knew he was unlikely to be disturbed.

Confident of solitude he unlocked his middle cabinet drawer and slid it open. It contained only one thing – his private journal, a visible record of his whirlpool of thoughts and ideas, captured before they escaped his consciousness and were lost for ever. He lifted the book, which was leather bound and about the size of a large photo-album only thinner, and placed it carefully on his desk, opening it at the very beginning and moving steadily through it, page by page, reading his own words, trying to decipher the dozens of small sketches and chaotic graphs – a multitude of names circled and linked to other circled names, each line in a different colour signifying something he'd long since forgotten. But they all related to other cases – old cases solved and consigned to the scrapheap of his memory. So many names: of paedophiles, murderers, witnesses, suspects, the dead. One name made him stop and linger longer than any other, his finger caressing the letters, circling the small cut-out from a surveillance photograph he'd glued on to the page. James Hellier, real name Stefan Korsakov – the man who could have killed him anytime he'd wanted to, but who in the end saved his life, although his motives for doing so were never entirely clear. Maybe he just couldn't stand the thought of someone else taking his life? 'Where are you now, my old friend?' Sean whispered to the small photograph. 'And what the hell are you up?' The cold shiver running up his back urged him to move on, flicking through page after page of disorganized notes and scribbles until he came to a nearly blank page halfway through the book. The only words were those written across the top: *George Bridgeman – Abduction* and a little further down: *Bailey Fellowes – Abduction*. The rest of the page was barren – the accusation obvious: he couldn't think any more, not the way he needed to.

He smoothed out the pages and lifted a red fine-tipped felt pen from an old mug he used as a penholder and flipped the top off, holding it above the notebook as if he expected it to magically lead his hand and start writing for him – solving the puzzle of the missing children without his help. He tried to force thoughts into his mind, but only the broad strokes, stuff he'd already covered with Sally and Donnelly – with Anna – would come. Nothing incisive, nothing that allowed him to cut through the rock and find the diamond. *The abductor knew the children, but how? They knew the families, but how? They knew the houses, but how? They even knew the alarms weren't working, but how did they know that? The alarm fitters checked out OK and were from different companies, so not that* . . . He knew he was asking the right questions, but he needed the answers and they wouldn't come.

He allowed the pen to fall from his fingers as he leaned back in his chair with a sigh of resignation, running his hands through his light-brown hair, the tiredness of the last few days suddenly creeping up on him and threatening to drag him into sleep. He quickly straightened in his chair and replaced the lid on the pen, blinking furiously to keep his eyes from sealing themselves closed, his hand scribbling thoughts that almost came from his subconscious, released by the extreme tiredness of a mind too exhausted to resist any more. He read the words as they took form on the pages, columns of facts on each side of the book, one list headed *GB* and the other *BF – Scene One* written under George's initials and *Scene Two* under Bailey's. The words he wrote under *Scene One* he then repeated under *Scene Two*, circles and lines linking the two across the divide on the page. *No signs of violence. No blood. No evidence of drugs being used. No evidence of restraint. No noise. No nothing. Conclusion: the victims went with the offender willingly.* 'They wanted to go with you. They had to have, but why? Why did they want to go with you?' He leaned back before immediately springing forward, tapping the pages with the pen. 'They went with you because they know you. But you're not a family member, you're not a teacher or child-minder and the families don't appear to share any friends or at least no one the children could know well enough to go with in the middle of the night. So how do they know you?'

He stood up, not moving, just standing, staring down at the new words in his old journal, allowing the questions he'd asked to whirl around the room, spin around his head, until at last the simplicity of the solution began to take shape. He sat down again and rested a hand on the book. 'Maybe then . . . maybe, you don't know the families – you don't know these children?' His eyes closed for a few seconds while he tried to understand his own conclusion. 'Or at least you don't know them like I thought you did. You have no historical link to them – you're not a trusted friend of the family – no one the children could have known well. But you're not a stranger, you can't be, because they went with you willingly and you know these houses – these homes.' He felt any answers slipping away as quickly as they'd started come, his imagination trying to stop them fading into the dark recesses of his subconscious. 'Damn you,' he hissed through clenched teeth. 'You know the children, you know the houses, you know everything you need to know, but you can't be closely connected to the families or I would have had you by now. So something else. Something I haven't thought of yet. Something so fucking obvious I can't see it for staring at it.' He exhaled heavily and slumped into his chair, his mind drifting Thoughts of the case were banished as images of his wife and children invaded – and of Anna. Extreme tiredness was making him lose control over his consciousness.

'All right,' he told himself, his voice still hushed. 'All right. We look further afield – someone who could have had access to both children, but something the parents wouldn't necessarily think to remember.' He began to scribble some notes between the two columns of information, anything he could think of that could possibly link the families – the children.

Do they share the same GP or practice? Have they visited them lately? Have there been any visits to the hospital? Do the parents remember any over-familiar doctors or nurses? Do the missing children belong to any of the same after-school or weekend clubs? Where did the families last go on holiday and did the children use any kids' clubs? Do they share a local favourite restaurant, playground,

283

sports club, holiday club . . . The list went on and on until he finally stopped, staring down in dismay at all the possibilities. 'Conventional. Conventional,' he found himself repeating over and over. 'Conventional and slow – too slow. Even if you selected the children this way, how could you know the inside of their houses?' He wrote the words in bold capital letters across the length and width of the page: *Too slow, too slow, too slow* underlining it to emphasize his frustration. The pen in his hand began to move again, writing the same word over and over, each time in a different style and size, covering every inch of the open pages: *Blind. Blind. Blind. Blind. Blind. Blind*.

The house was his, still and quiet, warm and comforting, the familiar sound of a grandfather clock's pendulum swaying in the hallway making him feel as if he belonged – as if he was meant to be here. Above him, the Hargraves slept soundly, oblivious to the intruder in their midst. He closed the door behind him and secured the Yale lock, moving deeper into the house, their home, aware of the sounds and odours of the interior, the dark patches where the street lights couldn't reach – where the shadows lived. He was acutely aware of all these things, all these things that were just as they were before, but he didn't relish them – didn't take time to become one with the house – with the family. He wasn't here for the family – just the boy.

Douglas Allen took a slow, deep breath before moving across the wooden hallway of the immaculate five-storey Georgian house in Primrose Hill – one of the capital's most exclusive ghettos for the rich and celebrated. He was relieved to feel the mint condition Persian rug under his feet, covering the wood, his rubber-soled shoes rendering him completely silent but for the occasional sound of his clothes as his legs brushed together when he walked. Everything he wore was selected for silence and ease of movement, but also to blend in and avoid drawing suspicion as he walked and drove through the streets of North London, dressed as he was in grey-flannel trousers, blue shirt and necktie, his padded black anorak zipped up against the cold. He'd noticed a lot more police cars in the area lately, and even some checkpoints stopping men in cars, although he was yet to be pulled over and questioned himself. He thought of the children he'd recently rescued – poor little Bailey, even her name was a joke, a thing of amusement and ridicule for all who cared to laugh at her. He almost wished he'd been able to take her siblings too, but his instructions had been clear and specific – *take only the girl*. In any case, even though the parents weren't deserving of any children, to take more than one would have been too cruel a punishment. He hoped that in losing one child the parents would be able to appreciate more the ones he'd left them with. In taking George and Bailey he'd saved their siblings too – just like he'd been told he would.

His gloved hand rested on the polished wooden bannister as he began to climb the stairs, slowly and purposefully. He reached the first floor and walked without hesitation past the children's playroom and the room their mother used as an office for the business she ran as a justification to abandon her children to be raised by a succession of full-time housekeepers and nannies – the latest of which was an economic refugee from some South-east Asian country who lived in the smallest of the top-floor bedrooms.

As he arrived at the second floor his heart rate increased, reaching dangerously high levels, momentarily threatening to trigger a panic attack. But the words of his guides came to him when he needed them most and calmed his fear, controlled his sudden urge to retreat back down the stairs and flee the house, leaving the family to wake as if nothing had ever happened. He was reminded of his cause, his resolve stiffened. Belief drove him forward, past the sleeping parents who he knew could never understand his reasons for doing what he must, and up the next flight of stairs to where the children of the house slept in two separate bedrooms, one opposite the other. Samuel and his younger brother, surrounded by all that money could provide, yet virtual strangers to their own parents. It was his duty to save them, to stop them growing up to love only money and status – to stop them from having more unloved children in their turn. But he could save only one, and it was Samuel who had been chosen for him, shown to him.

He came to the pristine white-panelled door, unmarked by the play of young children afraid to free their spirits for fear of damaging anything in the house and reaping the wrath of their overly house-proud mother. The boy waited on the other side, unaware that soon he would be in a better place, a place where he would be loved more than he could possibly conceive, with new brothers and sisters he could grow and mature with in a way that would ensure they became the special people they deserved to be – giving back to those around them, loving those around them, loving all mankind, even those who deserved no love.

He placed his small bag on the floor and took from it the thing that he knew was special to the boy. He stood and rested a gloved hand on the door, easing it open slowly on silent hinges, stepping into the room and seeing that everything was just as it had been before. Made-to-order dinosaur-print wallpaper, handcrafted wooden storage boxes for the toys Samuel wasn't allowed to make a mess with, built-in cupboards and wardrobes with shelving mounted on brushed chrome railings, all lined with exclusive, top-of-the-range soft toys – but all too high for Samuel to even reach. He felt his heart sink with sadness as he imagined the boy sitting alone in a room full of toys he wasn't allowed to love.

A smaller collection of soft toys littered the boy's bed – less expensive, less cared for, but more loved, scattered without order, the remnants of his night-time games, before sleep had finally taken him. Allen closed his eyes as a sense of calmness and happiness gently swept through his body, reassuring him of his right to be there – his right to take the boy. He gripped the precious thing tighter than ever and stepped into the room, moving slowly across the floor, watching the tiny child's entire body seem to rise and fall as he breathed peacefully in his sleep. He reached the boy's bedside and knelt down, his knees creaking, firing pain through his legs.

The drugs his doctor had prescribed for his advancing arthritis weren't the only ones he'd deliberately chosen not to take. He wasn't about to be turned into an automaton, like all the other soulless robots he saw wandering aimlessly, their pains and fears wiped clean by pharmaceutical cocktails prescribed by general practitioners too overworked and undertrained to do anything else. He'd rather live with the pain than live in the fog, even if the headaches were sometimes unbearable, rendering him almost unconscious at times. The drugs made the voices stop too, the voices that guided him, the voices that told him what to do and when to do it – the voices that kept him safe. The voices of those who loved him most. He wouldn't take the drugs and kill those he loved most.

The boy began to stir, sensing the presence next to him, chasing his dream away, or perhaps this was part of his dream – the voice of a man whispering softly – whispering words of kindness – whispering his name, gently drawing him from his sleep: 'Samuel. Samuel. I've brought you something – something special.' The boy rolled over to face him, still more asleep than awake, eyes merely flickering open a millimetre or two before closing tightly again – seduced by tiredness. 'Samuel, you need to open your eyes. It's time to wake up. Wake up, Samuel. Someone's come to see you – someone who's missed you very much.' The boy's pupils stopped dancing under his eyelids, his slightly sticky eyelashes the first things to part as he at last woke from his sleep and instantly stared at the man kneeling next to him, his face too close. Shock and fear involuntarily filling his lungs with air as he prepared to call out into the house, into the night, but a smothering hand clasped over his mouth before he could release any sound, and the man's other hand pushing something in front of his face, something it took him took a few seconds to recognize. But when he did, the recognition brought with it instant relief and joy, the fear in his eyes turning to happiness as he snatched the precious thing from the man's hand and the other hand was removed from his mouth.

'How did you . . .?' the boy tried to ask, but the man pressed a finger to his lips and one to the boy's.

'Sssssh. Don't speak,' he whispered. 'If they hear us, they won't let you come.'

'Come where?' Samuel asked, his voice still too loud in the night as he sat up in his bed, the duvet falling around his waist to reveal his blue-and-white dinosaur pyjamas. He clutched the precious thing in the crook of one arm while his other hand rubbed at his sleepy eyes.

'To a magic place,' Allen whispered, 'where only the best children get to go.'

'Where is it?'

'Not far, but we have to go straight away.'

'How do we get there?'

'Oh, you'll have to wait and see. It'll be a surprise.'

'Do I need to get ready first?' Samuel asked, still innocently blinking the sleep from his brown eyes.

'No. You can come as you are. Just pop on your dressing gown and slippers and we'll be gone. But we have to tiptoe very quietly down the stairs. We mustn't wake anyone.'

'Why?'

'Because they might try to stop us.'

'Why – have you done something wrong?'

'No,' he whispered, hiding his awkwardness behind a slight laugh, 'it's just they wouldn't . . . understand.'

'My mummy and daddy will be very cross with me if I go with you. They told me I should never go with strangers.'

'But I'm not a stranger,' Allen implored, his desperation growing – the others had been so simple, so straightforward, so willing. 'You know me – we've met before, remember?'

'I don't think I know you,' Samuel argued, his voice growing louder again.

'Of course you do. You remember me. You must remember me.'

'I don't want to get into trouble.'

'You won't,' Allen reassured the boy. 'I promise.'

'Can Tommy come too?'

'Of course,' Allen answered, relief spreading over him as he felt the boy weakening. 'Of course.'

'I suppose . . . I suppose I could come for a little bit.'

'That's right. That's right, and there are other children already there – waiting for you – waiting to be your friends.'

'Really?' Samuel asked, genuine excitement in his small voice.

'Really,' Allen confirmed. 'I wouldn't lie to you, Samuel. I'd never lie to you. Now quickly and quietly put your dressing gown and slippers on and we'll be off.'

'Is it like Neverland? Do we have to fly there?' Samuel asked as he slipped silently from his bed and searched for his slippers.

'Better,' Allen told him.

'Better?'

'Yes, better. Better because it's real.' He waited for the boy to tug his dressing gown on and took him by the hand, still kneeling on the floor. 'Now remember – we have to be totally silent and not wake anybody up. Do you understand?'

'Yes,' the boy answered, lowering his voice. 'I'll be very quiet, promise.'

'Good,' Allen told him and struggled to his feet, still holding the boy's hand. 'Now we need to go,' he continued and began to lead the boy to the bedroom door and out into the waiting hallway, all the time listening for the sounds he feared most – of a woken parent, a nanny or housekeeper come to challenge him, incapable of understanding why he had to take the children, instantly brandishing him a monster. But there were no such sounds, just the eerie, still silence of a sleeping house. 'Come on,' he told Samuel conspiratorially, as if they were on a great adventure together that had to remain a secret just between the two of them. The boy nodded his agreement, smiling nervously.

Together, hand-in-hand, they made their way down the flights of stairs, Allen steering the boy away from any creaking floorboards, pressing his finger to his lips whenever he felt the boy was about to speak and accidently betray them, until they were finally past the sleeping parents' room and halfway down the stairs that led to the first floor and comparative safety. But Samuel's growing concerns could wait no longer as he ignored Allen's signals to be silent and spoke – spoke too loudly.

'I don't think I should go,' he half-whispered. 'Mummy will be too cross with me.'

'You don't have to be afraid of Mummy any more,' Allen desperately whispered his reply, pulling the boy closer to him. 'She can't follow us to the magic place – no one can.'

'I don't want to go,' Samuel told him, the fear returning to his eyes. 'I don't want to go with you.'

'Yes you do,' Allen insisted, frantically looking back up the staircase, trying to hear the sounds of danger above his own words. 'Of course you do. Look,' he pleaded, 'Tommy wants to go.'

'No he doesn't,' Samuel answered, his voice dangerously loud now, but not loud enough to conceal the sound of voices coming from above – from the parents' room – voices growing ever more awake and alert.

'We have to go now,' Allen told the boy. But Samuel pulled away from him and slumped on the stairs, back against the wall, shaking his head in defiance, making Allen's already fluttering heart begin to pound out of control. The sheen of sweat across his brow turned to small drops that ran down the sides of his face, dampening his hair and sticking it to his skin. Footsteps now, on the ceiling above them, moving to the hallway and making him stop breathing until he realized they were heading upstairs towards the boy's room and away from them.

He only had a minute or two to escape at best. He looked down at the shivering boy, waiting to be told what to do – waiting for the voices in his head to return – but nobody spoke to him. Panic was his only guide now. He grabbed the boy up and smothered his mouth with a hand, pressing him against his body as he ran as silently as he could down the remaining stairs, trying not to drop the boy or his bag, hearing the increasing commotion above, wide-awake voices now, shouting to each other as he fumbled with the Yale lock, the boy beginning to kick and buck in his arms, his screams muffled by a gloved hand.

As soon as the front door opened he was hit by an unexpected rush of freezing air that stole his breath and almost pushed him back into the house where only danger waited. He forced himself through the opening and into the moonless night, fleeing along the deserted street, his footsteps almost totally silent as the rubber soles hit the pavement, adrenalin taking him halfway along the street, closer and closer to his waiting car and safety. But the boy grew heavier and heavier, while his own ageing body grew weary under the weight of him, arthritis robbing his joints of any spring as his run slowed to a jog and then to a walk. The freezing night air burned his lungs as he gulped at the oxygen, the realization dawning on him that he would never make it before the danger from the house hunted him down in the street.

Tears of pain and fear began to sting at his eyes that were already sore from the cold as they searched for a place to hide – a place where he could wait with the boy until the storm had passed. Quickly he looked over the railings of the nearest house and down into the basement area. He could see bins below. The gate wasn't locked and he knew he had no choice. Holding the boy as tightly as he could, his gloved hand still pressed over his mouth to keep him quiet, he skipped down the stairs and sat on the ground, pulling the bins carefully in front of them as silently as he could. He waited, trying to control his own frantic breathing, afraid the plumes of his frozen breath would betray him. Loud footsteps filled the street above, a man's voice calling into the night, desperate, bloodcurdling screams. Douglas Allen held the boy tighter than ever and squeezed his eyes shut, shivering and trying not to listen to the screams, the pain in his head beginning to hammer violently until at last the screaming and pounding footsteps passed by, fading as they headed further along the street. Time to go.

Lucy Hargrave slept soundly, her slightly too slim body lying some distance from her husband's in the super-king size bed. But invading voices jarred at her subconscious, stirring her from her sleep until finally her eyes twitched open. Was her mind playing cruel tricks on her? Could she hear *voices*? She sat up in bed, her silk night vest revealing her slim, muscular arms, neck and shoulders, pulled taut by the strain of listening, unsure if she was still asleep and dreaming. But then she heard them again, and she was sure. She snapped the duvet off and sprang from her bed, the sudden movement waking her husband.

'What's the matter?' he whispered.

'I heard something,' she hissed in reply. 'I think it's one of the kids – downstairs.'

'They wouldn't go downstairs,' he told her dismissively, throwing his legs out of the bed, yawning and scratching the back of his head. 'Check their bedrooms first. If they were downstairs they're probably back in their rooms by now.'

'We should have got the alarm fixed already,' Lucy said, genuine fear in her voice.

'They're doing it as soon as they can,' he assured her, 'and nobody's broken in. This house is like Fort Knox.'

'I definitely heard something.'

'Check their rooms then, but if it's Sam don't try and deal with it tonight – we'll speak to him in the morning.'

'Fine,' she answered, leaving him sitting on the edge of the bed as she headed into the hallway, more and more willing to accept her husband's reassuring conclusion that the sounds had merely been those of a mischievous child wandering in the night. She wearily climbed the stairs to the floor above and headed for the open door of her son Benjamin's room. Pale blue light leaked from within and already she was sure the three-year-old wasn't the one responsible for her broken sleep, but still she peered around the corner of the door at the tiny figure huddled at the top of an oversized bed that was low to the floor. He was sleeping soundly, his mouth slightly open, his head and body surrounded by his favourite cuddly toys, his breathing too perfect to be faked. She smiled a little and retreated from the room, taking the few steps towards Sam's room. Her heart beat quickening as she noticed that his door was far wider open than she remembered it being when she'd checked on him just before going to bed herself.

The sudden, undeniable realization that her worst nightmare could be coming true instantly knotted her stomach and began to induce a mild case of shock, the blood retreating from her non-vital organs, her stomach and intestines, rushing to keep her heart and brain protected, making her feel nauseous and light headed, turning her lips pale and skin white and clammy. She felt an almost overpowering urge to sit down and breathe deeply, but she pushed on, driven by a mother's instinct to protect her young at any cost.

The last two steps to Samuel's room seemed to take her for ever, her legs like lead weights, but reach the room she did, pushing the door fully open, wary of the dark shadows in the corners yet determined to press on, no matter what – no matter what danger she sensed. Then she saw the empty bed, the duvet rolled down, only the scent of the boy remaining in the room: the smell of fabric conditioner from his clean pyjamas, the bath oil for his dry skin, and Nivea cream. She felt the air rush from her lungs as if they'd been punctured by silent bullets, increasing levels of shock making her legs buckle, but she managed to stay upright, padding deeper into the room, her arms outstretched in front of her as if she was blind or searching in the pitch-black, not trusting her eyes, more willing to rely on her sense of touch. But she could neither see nor feel the boy. He was gone, somehow he was just gone, and she knew it. 'Samuel,' she whispered softly, afraid she might scare the boy from revealing himself, praying her intuition was wrong. 'No more games, Samuel – you need to come to Mummy now. You're not in trouble, I promise.' Her pleas were met with silence. She abandoned stealth and strode to the boy's bed, dragging the duvet aside, although she already knew he wasn't underneath. She dropped to her knees and peered into the gloom under the bed, her eyes needing to see what her heart already knew was true, her arm stretching underneath, feeling in the dark for a little boy she knew wasn't there, the sound of her own rushing blood deafening inside her head as she leapt to her feet and ran for the light switch, flooding the room with the harsh white light from the halogen spotlights set into the ceiling. Then she moved back across to the bed and on to the floor again, scanning underneath the bed, confirming her fears when she saw nothing but shadows. She sprang upright, her body beginning to burn with adrenalin as she spun around the room, opening every cupboard and drawer, no matter whether Samuel could have fitted inside or not, until she was as physically sure he was gone as she was psychologically, the memory of what had first broken her sleep, first electrified her body with fear, telling her where she needed to go. 'Downstairs,' she told herself, not caring who heard. 'He's gone downstairs, that's all.' But the vague, sleep affected memory of voices magnified her terror. *Why were there voices? Why wasn't it just Samuel's voice? How could there be someone else? How could someone else be in their home?*

'No,' she said through a thick panic like she'd never experienced in her entire life. 'No, Samuel, no,' she began to almost shout, her tears constricting her throat, making her voice break as she tried to speak. She ran from the room and down the stairs, tripping in the semi-darkness, her shoulder hitting the bannister hard, but she didn't feel the pain, springing back to her feet and clearing the remaining stairs, only for her husband to catch her as she made it to the landing. He wrapped one arm around her waist while the hand of the other covered her mouth as he put his lips to her ear.

'Ssssh,' he hissed. 'Can you feel it – the cold air?' She was suddenly aware of the freezing breeze drifting up the stairs and over her skin, making her hairs stand on end to trap the warmth of her body, her husband's heart beating through her back, holding her tightly until they conquered their fear enough to speak again. 'The front door is open,' he continued. 'Someone's down there.'

'Samuel,' she tried to call out, but fear strangled her words to nothing more than a faint plea. 'He's not in his room. He's gone.'

'He couldn't have opened the front door,' Henry told her. 'He can't reach.'

She tried to pull away from him, to run down into the cold darkness below, her only instinct to run to her child. 'Samuel,' she called out, louder than before, struggling against her husband's restraining grip. 'Let me go,' she shouted. 'Let me go. You don't understand – someone's taken him.'

'Wait,' he told her, his mind spinning. 'Wait. Go to our bedroom – call the police. I'll check downstairs.' He pulled her backwards to the bedroom, nodding wide-eyed at her to encourage her to make the call, before he headed to the stairs. He went as fast as he dared, peering into the corners where the shadows seemed to be constantly moving, trying to see into the dark recesses, listening like he'd never had to listen before. All the while the freezing stream of air invaded from outside, drawing him ever further down until he could see the yellow street-light pouring through the open door that should have been the firmest of barriers between the outside world and his family. Now it had been breached, and there was no denying the undeniable any more, the rising sense of panic covering his body in a thin layer of sweat despite the cold as he stepped off the last step on to the ground floor.

Eyes wide in the dimness he moved forward into the house that was still new enough to feel like a stranger's, every sound and sight unnerving him further. He pushed forward, feeling the wall until he found the light switch, flicking it on and flooding the hallway with brightness that temporarily blinded him. Drawing a long breath he blinked the blindness away and moved to the living room, flicking on every light switch he could find, hoping, praying to see Samuel cowering in a corner. *A noise downstairs had woken him and drawn him downstairs. He'd seen an intruder and been terrified, but the intruder had fled, leaving the boy who was now too scared to move or speak.* He had to believe, but the light only brought more silence and emptiness, his eyes scanning every inch of the room, refusing to accept he couldn't find his son.

'Samuel,' he called hoarsely, terror leaving his throat raw. He tried to consciously pump saliva into his mouth, swallowing the tiny amounts to lubricate his larynx. 'Samuel, you can come out now – there's no need to be afraid any more. It's Daddy – you can come out now.' Silence. No movement, except the tormenting breeze from the front door swirling around his ankles. He ran to the ground-floor study, his panic becoming intense. 'Samuel. Please, Samuel. You need to come out now. You need to come to Daddy now.' Nothing. He looked slowly over his shoulder at the open front door, as if it was a porthole to another world, a world he knew his boy had been taken to – a porthole that might slam shut any second, for ever separating them. Suddenly he found himself running towards it, its yellow light warm and inviting. But as he burst into the world beyond the door, the freezing air gripped his body, naked but for his pyjama bottoms.

He ran into the empty, silent street, looking frantically in both directions, standing in the middle of the road, desperately searching for a clue as to which direction to run in. 'Samuel,' he shouted into the night. But the night didn't answer, the only sound the distant rumble of the city traffic. 'Samuel,' he shouted again, allowing the boy's name to tail off slowly, eventually fading and dying into the night, a collapsing echo reverberating off the house fronts. 'Samuel.' Even louder this time, some lights beginning to flicker on in the windows of the other houses as the freezing air flooding his empty chest felt like toxic fumes. Again he span in the road, unsure which way to run, tears of frustration, anger and fear blurring his vision, the light from the street lamps star-bursting in his eyes, until his instinct told him that to do something was better than doing nothing, and he ran, he ran along the street, unwittingly heading in the same direction as Douglas Allen had, his naked feet hitting the road surface hard as he sprinted, ignoring the pain in his body, not even feeling it as he ran past the basement entrance where Allen cowered, and where his boy grew weaker and weaker, struggling to breathe through the hand clamped over his tiny mouth, his once wide brown eyes now only half-open as the pounding of his father's naked feet grew fainter and fainter, like his own breathing and heartbeat, until neither could be heard any more.

*　*　*

298

Once he finally turned into the street where his home was Allen turned off the headlights and coasted until he found a space close to his own front door. He was physically and mentally exhausted. The incident earlier and the constant need to watch for and avoid police patrols and roadblocks had drained him, but his guides had eventually seen him home safely. Although how much longer he could carry out his work living where he did he began to wonder. His dream of moving to the country might have to be moved forward. The patrols and roadblocks would surely only get worse – especially after tonight.

He checked the road ahead and behind before hauling himself from his car, quietly closing the door before again searching for signs of life in the eerily silent street. He moved to the rear passenger door only when he was satisfied he was unobserved, opening it soundlessly and peering in at the tiny figure of Samuel Hargrave lying still and silent under an old, tartan blanket, just the hair on top of his head visible. Allen leaned into the back of the car and gently rocked the little figure, but the boy didn't stir or make a single sound.

'Samuel,' he whispered, but the boy didn't move. 'Sam,' he tried again, but the boy didn't respond. A terrible feeling of dread began to sweep through Allen's own body – a feeling he hadn't had since two years ago when he'd finally had to accept that he was losing his beloved wife and that he'd be for ever alone. At least that's what he'd thought at the time, before the voices had begun – the comforting voices that offered him guidance. But now the voices had fallen silent. He swallowed hard to keep his throat from closing as the grief swelled, his lips beginning to tremble as he tried to pretend the unthinkable hadn't happened. He reached into the back seat and wrapped the lifeless little figure tightly in the blanket before pulling the boy through the doorway as gently as he could. He cradled the bundle to his chest, carrying it like a mother would a new-born baby, fighting back tears as he closed the car door with his foot and headed stealthily along the street holding the bundle ever tighter as he whispered comfortingly. 'Let's get you inside, Sam – out of the cold.'

Allen hurried to his front door and fumbled in his jacket pocket for the house keys, managing to keep hold of the boy's dead weight as he turned the locks and eased the door open. The sudden sound of the alarm-activated warning pushed panic into his chest as he stumbled into the darkness and found the keypad, entering the numbers carefully, terrified of making a mistake and shattering the silence of the night, bringing unwanted attention crashing down on him. Finally he pressed 'enter' and silenced the high-pitched warning. He stood motionless, barely breathing as he listened to the sounds from inside his own house, for the children who should be sleeping two floors above him. At last he allowed himself to exhale and closed the front door, locking it top and bottom. The weight of the boy still pressed to his torso began to tell, his knees creaking as he carried him across the main downstairs area that remained in almost complete darkness to a room at the back of the house that he used as an office. He closed the door before laying the boy on the small desk and turning on the old lamp that stood next to where the boy's head was, his hair still poking from the top of the blanket.

Awkwardly he began to unwrap the boy, his heart thundering with fear, but also with hope that he may yet be mistaken, that the boy might just be resting, rocked to sleep by the motion of the car. With increasing horror he realized the nightmare was coming true. The boy's body felt increasingly stiff and inflexible, his joints unwilling to do what they did so easily when he was alive. Finally he was free from the tartan blanket, lying in his blue pyjamas covered in prints of every dinosaur imaginable, one arm trapped under his back and his half open brown eyes still resonating with the lingering trace of life – not a bruise or mark on his tiny body, yet broken beyond repair all the same. Allen covered his mouth to quell his gasps of horror, staggering backwards away from the realization of what he'd done as the tears flowed unhindered from his eyes and down his ruddy cheeks.

He tried to move, but couldn't – frozen where he stood staring at the lifeless boy he'd thought he was saving from uncaring parents and an uncaring world. But now the boy was gone and by his hand – and who would understand it was an accident? They'd call him a monster, in those vile newspapers he saw but never read – on those lascivious news programmes he never watched. But he knew what they would start saying about him now – the lies they would tell. They'd call him a child murderer, a killer of children, a beast to be hunted down and slaughtered. There would be no let-up. The police patrols and roadblocks would be increased. They'd already visited all the houses and shops in the street, speaking to all the occupants and owners, even to him, but next they'd want to come inside and look around – their desperation would demand it. He needed to know what to do – he needed the voices, his guides, to tell him what to do, but still they remained silent, leaving him alone and afraid.

The pain in his head was only matched by the pain in his chest, a tightening and crushing that left him short of breath and dizzy, dropping him to his knees, his head in one hand while the other clutched and clawed at his chest, as if he was trying to rip out his own heart. 'Help me,' he whispered as he fell forwards. 'Help me.' He felt darkness and oblivion begin to drown him, the pounding in his head making his body want to escape into unconsciousness, but he fought against it, knowing that this was when the voices of his guides usually came, when the pain was as its worst, when he thought he could bear no more, when he thought he might have to surrender to the doctors' wishes and take the drugs they'd told him he must. That was when the voices came, and so they did now, quietly at first, but growing louder, comforting and reassuring, telling him he wasn't alone, giving him the strength to resist and accept the pain, guiding him to his feet and back towards the body of Samuel lying on his desk.

He wiped away his tears and stood next to the boy, crossing himself with the sign of a crucifix as he gathered his thoughts and listened to the voices' instructions. He nodded his head gently in approval and understanding, quietly speaking the words of the twenty-third psalm as he began to prepare the boy, untwisting his tiny arm from under his body and stroking his hair as neatly as he could with his hand:

The Lord is my shepherd: I shall not want.
He maketh me lie down in green pastures:
He leadeth me beside the still waters.
He restoreth my soul:
He leadeth me in the paths of righteousness for His name's
   sake.

Though I walk through the valley of the shadow of death,
I shall fear no evil: For thou art with me:
Thy rod and thy staff, they comfort me.
Thou preparest a table before me in the presence of mine
enemies:

Thou anointest my head with oil:
My cup runneth over.

Surely goodness and mercy shall follow me all the days of
   my life,
and I will dwell in the House of the Lord for ever.

He stretched the boy out carefully on his back, straight-ened out his blue pyjamas and closed his eyes fully, still listening to the voices as he opened the desk drawer and took out an antique wooden box and turned the small, ornate key to unlock it. Inside he could see the precious things that had belonged to his wife, things she had no one to pass on to: her engagement ring and wedding ring, a cameo brooch and other jewellery, although there was little of it. He brushed his fingers over the items lovingly until they rested on what he was looking for – the small silver crucifix with a tiny Christ sacrificed upon it. He lifted it from the box before speaking softly and quietly. 'Are you sure – are you sure he needs it?' He nodded his head slightly as he listened to the voice. 'I know,' he answered. 'I know you'll guide him to green pastures. I know you'll lead him to still waters.' He wiped the tears from his face with the back of his hand and pressed the crucifix into the boy's hand, crossing his arms over his still chest as his eyes fell upon the special thing he'd brought for the boy – the precious thing that had remained trapped in the blanket throughout. Allen pressed the palms of his hands across his eyes to stop the tears from returning, the sight of the thing so special to the boy almost overwhelming him – the thing he'd used to convince the boy he was a friend not a threat. He waited for the crushing sadness to ease before reaching for the special thing, lifting it from its resting place and tucking it under the boy's folded arms. He carefully wrapped the blanket once more around Samuel Hargrave, but this time left his face showing, as if he didn't want to suffocate him. Once the boy was prepared as well as he could be, Allen once again sank to his knees, this time not in pain, but to pray, not just for Samuel Hargrave, but for himself:

'Our Father who art in Heaven . . .'

10

Rush hour was beginning as Sean approached the Swain's Lane entrance to Highgate Cemetery, only a short walk away from where Bailey Fellowes had been taken from her own home. Whoever was taking these children had been successfully avoiding the random roadblocks and stop-checks the police had been conducting in the area. Or maybe he hadn't – maybe he'd been stopped, but allowed to go on his way. Sean pulled up behind the two marked and the two unmarked police cars parked across the entrance and took a few seconds before stepping out into the cold morning air, too preoccupied to register the chill. He took a long look around before heading to the lone uniform who guarded the taped off entrance – a young-looking constable who seemed more nervous than the usual, as if he was aware the scene would be of more interest to the world and its media than most, uncomfortable with being left alone to keep the journalists and TV crews at bay when they eventually arrived.

Sean showed the young constable his warrant card and ducked under the blue-and-white tape flapping in the breeze before speaking. 'DI Corrigan. Special Investigations. Where's the body?'

The constable cleared his throat before replying. 'If you just follow the path, sir, around to the left about seventy metres in you'll find the other detectives.'

Sean looked him up and down before indicating the two marked vehicles. 'Where are your colleagues?' he asked.

'Stationed at the other entrances to the cemetery, sir. Just in case.'

Sean nodded. 'OK. Good. Now call up your Control and have them get these marked cars out of the way – they're attracting too much attention.'

'Of course,' the constable nodded and immediately reached for his personal radio. Sean headed along the path to the scene of the body drop, the tranquillity of his surroundings allowing the chill to finally take hold of his consciousness as he pulled his thin raincoat tight to try and capture what warmth he could. He walked through the trees and past the gravestones, some modest, others huge testaments to the dead who lay below them. Donnelly had only told him the bare minimum over the phone, ever fearful of eavesdropping journalists and bloggers, and now Sean's lack of knowledge of the scene was allowing his imagination to run wild at what he might be about to see. Certainly Donnelly had sounded more disturbed than he was used to hearing, and it took a lot to knock him from his stride. Finally, with equal trepidation and relief he saw Donnelly and two other figures wrapped in raincoats up ahead, all standing quietly. It did not bode well. He noticed all three detectives stiffen as he grew near.

'Gentlemen,' Donnelly introduced him. 'This is DI Sean Corrigan.' Sean just nodded.

'DS Simon Rogers,' the older, greyer detective offered, holding out his hand. Sean accepted it briefly before turning to the other detective and his already outstretched hand.

'DC Martin McInerney, guv'nor.' Again Sean just nodded.

'Is it one of the missing children?' Sean asked.

'No,' Donnelly answered, his lips thinner and paler than usual. 'It's a boy, about four or five years old, but it's not George Bridgeman.'

'We're aware of your investigation into the missing children,' Rogers told him. 'Figured given the age of the victim and the location, you'd want to take a look.'

Sean looked over Rogers's shoulder at the rolled up tartan blanket lying on a shallow, grey slab of stone, the grave marked with a simple headstone that was too far away for Sean to be able to read. 'Yeah,' he answered remorsefully, 'I need to take a look.'

He walked between the two detectives and stepped slowly and carefully towards the rolled-up blanket, not speaking, examining the floor to avoid accidentally stepping on any potential evidence – a footprint or discarded food wrapper, a snagged clump of human hair or fabric – but he saw none.

The body was laid with its head pointing towards the tombstone: carefully arranged, not dropped in a panic, or dumped by someone who didn't care. *Did you pick this grave for some particular reason?* Sean asked silently. *Is there something special about it, here amongst thousands of others? Are you trying to tell me something – something about yourself – about what you're trying to do – why you're taking these children?* He twisted his head slightly over his shoulder to speak to the detectives behind him, although he avoided looking at them, their searching eyes examining him, watching for signs of weakness or uncertainty, ready to judge him. 'Any reports of missing children overnight?' he asked.

'Not in our borough,' Rogers told him, 'but we've put out a Met-wide request for everyone to check their overnight MISPER reports. Amount of publicity your investigation's been receiving, it shouldn't be long before we find out who the poor little sod is – or was.'

'No,' Sean agreed, 'I don't suppose it will.' Slowly he turned back to face the rolled-up blanket, inching forward until the boy's face began to come into his eyeline – just a little hair and the outline of a nose at first, but eventually his entire face confronted him, his eyes closed peacefully, his lips slightly parted, but no warm breath plumed into the cold morning air. Sean breathed in deeply and involuntarily found himself holding the air in his lungs as he leaned as close as he dared to the boy's porcelain face, the images of the dolls from Bailey Fellowes' bedroom flashing in his mind. He thanked God the boy's eyes were closed and prayed that this time, at this scene, he could make a connection with the man he hunted – the man who'd killed now, taken the life of a young child – the most heinous crime imaginable. If the missing children had caused a storm, then the discovery of a child's body would cause a hurricane and Sean knew he'd be at the centre of it.

He wondered if Addis already knew a child's body had been found. He tried to clear his head of all the irrelevant crap that weighed him down, cluttering his mind and strangling his instincts. He needed to make a breakthrough, the sort of breakthrough only he could make – a leap across the existing evidence, one single piece of unique insightfulness that would set off a chain reaction of realization and finally put Sean on to the scent of the child murderer.

At last he released his breath and began to examine the boy, his beautiful, peaceful innocence momentarily swamping him with deep sadness like only the death of a child could, violent or otherwise. He quickly built brick walls in his mind to stop thoughts of his own children invading and overwhelming him, allowing him to look beyond his grief and do his job, although he knew the sadness he'd suppressed would return sometime in the future – when he was alone late in his office, or perhaps when he tiptoed into his daughters' room to kiss them on the forehead.

He examined the blanket and the gravestone slab it lay upon, but could find no signs of blood, or even the slightest disturbance – nothing. Already he was sure the tartan blanket would have come from the killer's home and would be a treasure chest of forensic evidence, possibly enough alone to convict the killer. But it was probably next to useless in his search to find his quarry. And there was no telltale sign of old blood seeping through the blanket where the base of the boy's head lay. If he'd been hurriedly dumped on the stone or even thrown down, then the scalp would have probably split. He was convinced that the boy had been carefully placed on the stone, but why?

Look beyond what's staring you in the face, Sean told himself. *The killer's trying to tell you something, even if he doesn't know it himself.* He almost began to speak out loud before he remembered the detectives standing behind him, watching his every move without speaking, unwittingly interfering with his train of thought, their mere presence disturbing him. If only he could be alone. But he couldn't think of any logical reason to send them away and instead had to do his best to block them out – to pretend they didn't exist, that only he and the little broken body of whoever this was were in the cemetery together – alone.

So what are you trying to tell me? he asked, his eyes still fixed on the boy's face. *Is it something about the body, something you've done to the body that will lead me to you?* He could barely resist unwrapping the blanket and examining the body himself, right here and now, but the risk of losing invaluable forensic evidence stopped him. Besides, his instincts told him the body would be unharmed

– undamaged. But what if the killer had left something wrapped in the blanket – something he wanted Sean to find. How badly he wanted to unwrap that blanket, but with Donnelly and the others standing so close he daren't, no matter what. Best to unwrap it under controlled conditions in the morgue, remove each piece of evidence hair by hair, fibre by fibre. The body as it was told him nothing other than that the killer had cared about its disposal – had wanted to ensure the boy suffered no more – *had felt guilt for what he had done?*

You left him here, where you knew he would be found. Why? Because you couldn't bear to dump him where he might not be found – to bury him in a shallow grave or leave him in the woods at the mercy of scavenging animals. Why did you care what happened to him after death so much? Because you wanted to show the world you're not a monster? And why here, in a cemetery – so he could be with his own kind – the dead – to give him some peace?

Donnelly's voice all but collapsed the house of cards he was building in his mind. 'You found something, guv'nor?'

'No,' Sean snapped back before mellowing his tone, looking sheepishly at the detectives who were still strangers to him. 'Nothing yet.' He quickly turned away and tried to descend back into the world he'd just been dragged from – to be alone with the man he had to hunt. *In leaving the body here you've already told me so much, but there's more, isn't there? Something right here, right in front of me. But I can't see it, can I? For some reason I just can't . . .* He suddenly stopped his own thoughts, his head slowly turning towards the gravestone, as if some unseen force was twisting him towards it, opening his eyes for him, enabling him not just to look, but to see. He found himself reading the words carved into the pristine gravestone – yet the stone the body lay on was obviously over a hundred years old. 'The gravestone's new,'

Sean called to the others without looking away from the stone, 'but the grave's old.'

'I suppose the family had it replaced then,' Donnelly offered. Sean ignored him and continued to read.

'I know this name,' Sean said quietly. 'How could I know this name?'

'Maybe it just sounds familiar?' Donnelly unhelpfully suggested.

'I remember now,' Sean told them, still not looking away from the stone, reading the story of the grave's most decorated occupant. 'Robert Grant was awarded the Victoria Cross while serving in the British Army during the Indian Mutiny in 1857.'

'The Indian what?' McInerney asked. Everyone ignored him.

'He returned to Britain and joined the Met,' Sean continued. 'He was a cop for ten years before he died of TB and was quickly buried here along with seven others who died the same way in an effort to stop the spread of the disease. Just a few months ago the Commissioner at the time found out about Grant's story and had this new gravestone erected so others would know too.'

'Nice way to treat a hero,' Rogers pointed out, 'stick him in an unmarked grave with seven others, half of whom were probably local scum. How d'you hear about it anyway?'

'It was on the news. But why here – why specifically choose to leave the boy's body here – on this grave?'

'He clearly wanted us to find the body and now we have. Does the actual grave matter?'

'Yes,' Sean answered slowly. 'With this one it matters. It means something. It has to mean something.'

'So he felt guilty about murdering him and somehow, in his sick mind, leaving him where he could be found relatively quickly was his effort to . . .'

'Just,' Sean almost shouted at Rogers as he cut him off, 'just wait a minute – I just need a minute.'

Donnelly slightly raised his eyebrows and rolled his eyes a little at the other two detectives, his way of explaining that Sean was perhaps a little different from what they were used to, and that they needed to be patient.

Why here? Sean spoke to himself, no longer wanting or willing to share his thoughts with strangers or even Donnelly. They talked too much, continually breaking into his mindset, snapping any connection he was beginning to make with the man who'd taken the children – with the man who'd killed the boy. *You didn't just want us to find him, did you? You wanted to show me something – wanted to tell me something about yourself – something you want me to know.* Sean hurriedly began to search with his eyes, only his head moving as he scanned the area around the blanket holding the body, around the stone it lay on, the ground underneath and the inscription on the headstone, but he saw nothing he hadn't already. The sudden silence in his head was matched by the silence in the cemetery as he stared at the words on the headstone, an idea germinating slowly in his mind, like a shattered mirror reflecting a thousand different images, all different, but somehow part of the same picture, until at last they came together to form a solid pattern. *You wanted him to be protected, even in death. You wanted him to be cared for. So you sought out a protector. And what greater protector could you find than a police officer – one who'd been awarded the Victoria Cross. Did you believe he would guide the boy's soul to a better place?*

He turned to the waiting, watching detectives. 'He left the boy here not just to ensure he was found, he left him here because it's the grave of a cop. That was what was so important to him. That's why here.'

'Why does he care?' Donnelly asked.

'Because he wanted to leave the boy with someone who'd look after him.'

'He's dead,' Donnelly added coldly. 'Too late to care for him now.'

'But when he was alive,' Sean tried to explain, 'did he take him for the same reason? Is he trying to protect them?'

'Protect them from what?' Rogers joined in.

'I don't know,' Sean admitted. 'Some danger he thinks they're in.'

'Thinks or knows?' Rogers continued.

'If he knows, then he knows more than us,' Sean admitted. 'We checked out the families and found nothing of concern.'

'Something else then?' Rogers offered.

'The children weren't in any danger,' Donnelly interrupted. 'And if he wants to protect them he's got a funny way of showing it – snatching them from their beds and murdering them.'

'We don't know he's killed before,' Sean reminded him.

'Of course he has. We all know it. We just haven't found the bodies yet,' Donnelly insisted.

'No,' Sean told him calmly, assuredly. 'He hasn't killed before and I don't think he meant to here either.'

'Oh come on, guv'nor,' Donnelly could barely disguise his disgust. 'He's a child murderer and probably a paedophile too. The body hasn't even been examined properly yet – God knows what evidence of abuse we'll find.'

'Maybe we should take a look at the body now?' Rogers suggested. 'Just in case.'

'No,' Sean snapped, warning them all away from the body, as if they intended to snatch it from him. 'We unwrap the blanket out here we could lose whatever evidence is trapped inside. We wait until he's moved to the mortuary.'

'That could be hours – will be hours,' Donnelly argued. 'If we take a look now at least we'd know.'

'Maybe we would – maybe we wouldn't,' Sean half agreed, 'but I'm not going to risk losing critical evidence.'

'Maybe you just don't want to see?' Donnelly accused him, turning the atmosphere poisonous. Sean's dark anger rose in his throat like hot bile as he rounded on Donnelly, the sudden, shrill chirping of a mobile phone in the silent cemetery stopping him as he moved forward threateningly. Rogers searched himself until he recovered the phone from his raincoat pocket.

'DS Rogers speaking.' He listened for a second before interrupting. 'Let me hand you to the man in charge,' he told the caller as he stretched the phone out to Sean, who accepted it suspiciously. 'CID from Camden. You need to speak with them.'

'DI Corrigan, Special Investigations Unit,' Sean introduced himself before listening silently for what to the others seemed an age until he finally spoke again. 'I understand. Can you email the photo to this phone? Good. I'll be waiting for it.' He hung up, his face expressionless.

'Well?' Donnelly prompted him, reminding Sean they were there.

'A boy matching the description of our victim was apparently taken from his home a few hours ago – from Primrose Hill, not far from where we are now. The parents heard someone in the house, but by the time they realized what was happening the boy had already been taken.' Rogers's phone vibrated in his hand and he almost dropped it before he gathered himself and opened up the email without asking permission, the attachment revealing a picture of a young boy, smiling, dressed in his infant school uniform, his hair combed neatly for the photograph. Sean moved back to the body in the blanket and held the phone next to the lifeless face, the difference between the living and the dead as striking as it always was, making the boy, to the untrained eye, unrecognizable. Sean struggled to compare and match the features of the two, but ultimately came to the conclusion he'd already arrived at in his heart and gut – the boy in the cemetery was the boy taken from his home in Primrose Hill – Samuel Hargrave, only five years old. 'From the cradle to the grave,' Sean unconsciously whispered.

'What was that?' Rogers asked.

'This is him,' Sean answered. 'This is the missing boy from Primrose Hill: Samuel Hargrave.' He gave them all a few seconds to absorb the news – the name – before snapping them back into action. 'OK, make sure your local uniforms keep this place locked up nice and tight. No one in without clearing it with me or Dave first, and speak with the grounds-keeper – if the grave was selected as carefully as I think, then maybe our killer had been here before, maybe numerous times. Ask the groundskeeper if he's noticed anyone hanging around it more than usual.' Rogers nodded his acceptance. 'Dave – get hold of the local Murder Squad and tell them we need to borrow their Forensic Team.'

'What about Roddis's team?' Donnelly asked.

'I haven't sorted that yet,' Sean told him, 'and I don't have time now. We'll have to go with the one for this area. I'm sure they'll be fine. Get the body removed directly to the mortuary. I'll make sure Dr Canning knows it's on its way.'

'You want it taken to Guy's? That's out of this area's jurisdiction,' Donnelly reminded him.

'It doesn't matter,' Sean told him. 'It's still within the Metropolitan borders. If there's a problem I'll have Assistant Commissioner Addis sort it out.'

'If you say so,' Donnelly submitted.

Sean was already searching his mobile for the number. After six rings he heard the familiar voice at the other end.

'Hello, Dr Canning speaking. How can I help?'

* * *

315

Douglas Allen knelt in front of the old, inexpensive sideboard in his first-floor living room. It looked more like a shrine than a piece of furniture – a shrine to his dead wife and the God he believed she'd gone to the side of. Old photographs of his one and only love were neatly arranged on the tabletop, mostly of her alone, her eyes increasingly lifeless as age and then cancer took its toll – her inability to have children weighing her down, dragging her deeper into unhappiness. He only appeared in two of the pictures – a fading colour photograph of their wedding day, standing outside the church with the vicar, and a small gathering of mostly family and one or two like-minded friends, all dead or moved on now. But the centre of the table was reserved for something else: an ancient and almost worn-out postcard-sized print of Da Vinci's painting of the Head of Christ, the once vivid colours and tones now mere shadows of what they had been. Above the picture, hanging from the wall, the same Christ was displayed nailed to the cross on which he died to save mankind – to save Douglas Allen, so that he in turn could save others.

Allen whispered his prayers, his voice fast and intense, eyes squeezed tightly shut, palms pressed together, his lips barely parting. The pain in his head beat fiercely to the rhythm of his muttered words. 'Dear Lord, help me understand why the boy had to die. Why did you take the life of an innocent? Help me understand, Lord. *Even though I walk through the valley of the shadow of death, I will fear no evil, for you are with me.* But why the boy? I thought I was supposed to save him – isn't that what you wanted? *The Lord is my shepherd, I shall not be in want.* I've tried, dear God, tried to understand why you took the boy, but I . . . I . . . *He guides me in paths of righteousness for his name's sake.* Help me. Help me find the right path and do what is right.'

But he heard no reply, no answers to his questions. 'Iris,'

he whispered his dead wife's name. 'The Lord has forsaken me in my darkest hour. I need to know what to do. I need you to tell me what to do.' The pain in his head was beginning to make him feel nauseous and weak, close to passing out, until suddenly he heard her voice, soft and comforting, as if she was kneeling next to him, an arm around his shoulders, guiding his prayers. *Lead us not into temptation, but deliver us from evil. For thine is the kingdom, and the power, and the glory, for ever. Amen.* 'Iris? What should I do, Iris? I killed a child, Iris.' *It was an accident,* his dead wife reassured him. *You were trying to do the right thing. You were doing God's work.* 'But I killed a child – an innocent child.' *You were trying to save the child.* 'And now he's dead, by my hand.' *Not your hand. You are but a vessel – a tool to be wielded by the hand of the Lord.* 'But why? Why did he have to take the boy?' *Ours is not to question his will. Ours is not to doubt his grand design.* 'But they'll call me a murderer or worse.' *Because they don't understand you are doing God's work.* 'Why don't they understand?' *Because they serve another Lord. They have wandered from the flock and can't find their way back.* 'Are they my enemies? Should I fear them?' *Thou prepare a table for me in the presence of mine enemies; Thou anointest my head with oil; My cup runneth over.* 'Then I shouldn't fear them?' *The Lord will protect you and I will always be here, watching over you.* 'What should I do now?' *You must carry on with the work God has given you, blessed you with.* 'More children? I don't know if I can.' *You must. The Lord has chosen you to save them; Surely goodness and mercy shall follow me all the days of my life, and I will dwell in the House of the Lord forever.*

Tears flowed down his face and dripped on to his hands, tightly clenched in prayer under his chin. *The Lord is my shepherd and I shall not be in want.* 'Guide me, dear Father. Tell me what to do and it shall be done.' A sudden presence behind him made him spin around. George Bridgeman stood staring at him still dressed in his pyjamas, his tired eyes trying to blink away his sleepiness.

'Why are you crying?' he asked Allen matter-of-factly, as if the answer didn't really matter.

'Because,' Allen replied, 'because I'm so happy.'

'Why are you crying if you're happy?'

'Because I'm sad too.'

'Why are you sad?'

'Because something bad happened – something terrible.'

'What?'

'Nothing you need to know about,' Allen told him, drying the last of the tears with a crumpled tissue he'd pulled from his trouser pocket. 'Something the Lord will forgive me for. Now, come to the kitchen and have some breakfast.'

'Why aren't we allowed downstairs?' little George asked.

'But you are downstairs. Your bedroom is above us, is it not?'

'I meant down the other stairs – to the place where we can hear the voices coming from. Where we can hear you talking to other people.'

'Because it's not safe for you down there,' Allen warned him, his tone more serious and foreboding now. 'When I'm not here you must stay in your bedrooms. When I'm here you may come down here, but never try and go all the way downstairs. *Never*. Do you understand me, George?' The little boy nodded slowly, fear surging through his slight body as he imagined the terrible things that waited downstairs. 'Now – breakfast.'

'When can I go home?' George suddenly asked, unable to stop the question tumbling from his lips.

Allen looked at him with genuine puzzlement. 'But you are home, George, and we are your family now. You must forget the others, as if they never existed. It is God's will, George. It is God's will.'

* * *

Sean and Donnelly entered their new office in New Scotland Yard together having already made dozens of phone calls each on their way back from the scene in Highgate Cemetery. It seemed everyone in the world needed to know about the murder of Samuel Hargrave. Their job now was as much about coordination as investigation and it continued to weigh Sean down like a lead jacket, choking his instinct and insight. But as devastating as the recovery of the boy's body was, at least it had given him his first close look at the man he hunted – finally a chance to try and understand his motivation. To understand his mind.

He stopped in the middle of the office and threw his raincoat over a chair. Donnelly understood what was happening and did the same.

'All right. Listen up,' Sean barked above the sounds of conversation and typing, allowing the room to drift into silence before continuing. 'As most of you have probably heard by now, we have another victim, Samuel Hargrave, abducted last night from his home in Primrose Hill. The parents disturbed the intruder, but he managed to get away with the boy. Several hours later the boy's body was found in Highgate Cemetery, left where it would be easily found – on the grave of Robert Grant, who coincidentally was a Metropolitan Police Officer about a hundred and fifty years ago. He'd also won the Victoria Cross.'

'What does that mean?' DC Jesson asked. 'This is his third victim, but the first we've found. Is he getting sloppy about how he disposes of the bodies?'

Sean looked around the room before answering. His team looked tired and demoralized. So far they'd only been confronted with photographs of the victims smiling, happy and alive, but now they knew they'd soon be seeing cold, livid pictures of the body at the recovery location and, worse still, from the post-mortem. It was always so much worse when the victim was a child, especially for the detectives who had children of their own. It dragged everyone into melancholy and darkness, while at the same time stiffening their resolve to keep going, to leave nothing undone until they could finally stop the human monster, march him into the custody area handcuffed and defeated – not a thing to be feared any more – not even a man – just a broken wretch, promising to tell them anything they wanted to know in exchange for protection from the baying mob and some hope of clemency.

'No,' Sean finally answered Jesson's question. 'I don't think he's getting sloppy. The body was very deliberately left there for us to find. He wasn't trying to conceal it. He wanted us to find it.'

'Why?' Carlisle asked in her Geordie accent. 'Why would he want us to find this victim, but not the others?'

'Because the other victims are still alive,' Sean told her with a trace of confusion in his voice, a little surprised she hadn't worked it out herself yet.

'So why did he kill this victim, but not the others?' Carlisle continued, the expressions on the faces of the rest of the team telling Sean he was running ahead of them.

'Because it was an accident,' he told them. 'Because he didn't mean to.'

'Then manslaughter, not murder,' Jesson added.

'We treat it as murder until we know any different,' Sean reminded them. 'Assume nothing. Murder or manslaughter – that's the CPS's decision.'

'More's the pity,' Donnelly mumbled.

'We still have two missing children out there who I believe are still alive, so what do we know? What have we found out?' Sean asked the room.

'We've checked out the estate agents for both families, the removal companies, alarm companies, all workmen who've been through both houses and any other possible link they could have, but we're not finding anything,' Sally updated them.

'Then we're missing something,' Sean insisted. 'Go back and have all the people we've spoken to spoken to again. Somebody, somewhere missed something.'

'We've already done that,' Sally argued.

'Then do it again, and let's speed up the new inquiries, checking with their GPs, after-school clubs, holiday clubs, anything that could link them.'

'But—' Sally began before Sean cut her down.

'Have you got a better idea?'

Sally looked at the floor and swallowed her rising anger, Sean's rebuttal stinging her. 'No,' she admitted.

'That's what I thought,' Sean added cruelly. 'And now we have another family to cross-reference with the other two Maybe now the link between all the families will show up.'

'What if we're wrong?' Carlisle asked. 'What if there is no link? What if the suspect's victim selection is totally random and we're wasting our time looking for a link that isn't there?'

Sean felt the colour draining from his face, his empty stomach tightening and twisting, his usual certainty weakening in the face of Carlisle's questions. *Why was he so sure?* Was he wasting their time, looking for things that didn't exist? *No*, he told himself. *The evidence was there to be seen.* 'We're not wrong,' he assured the room. 'Don't forget what we already know: whoever's taken the children knew too much about them for it to be random: Where they lived. That their alarms weren't working. That there were no dogs in the houses, and God knows what else. These weren't random – they were planned, and he had insider knowledge of all three families and their homes. He couldn't have done it if he didn't.' He looked at the faces

321

of the detectives who stared back at him, relieved to see them largely nodding in agreement, seemingly convinced by hard, cold facts. 'So let's find out everything we can about the latest family and see if we can't hunt down this link. The link is the key.'

'What about the press conference?' Sally asked.

'It goes ahead as planned, but we make no mention of the third victim.'

'We won't be able to keep it a secret for long,' Donnelly told him.

'Long enough to get the conference out the way. Any more questions?'

'Why's he taking them?' Sally asked, her voice slightly raised, silencing the growing murmur in the room, her eyes fixed on Sean.

He hesitated a moment, his eyes flicking to Donnelly, remembering the reaction of the other detectives in the cemetery when he revealed his theory. 'I don't know yet,' he lied, relieved to see that Donnelly didn't react.

'What about the victim's body?' Sally continued. 'Were there any signs of injury or anything else?'

'The body was wrapped in a blanket. It was impossible to tell. I'm guessing the cause of death was asphyxiation, but we'll know more after the post-mortem.'

'You didn't examine the body at the scene?'

'No. Best to do it under lab conditions.'

Sally flicked her eyebrows, surprised that Sean had been able to resist at least an initial examination.

'I took some photographs at the scene, on my phone. I'll email them to everybody, with a brief report of what we know so far. Chase down everything – all leads, witnesses, information reports, door-to-door, anything you can, no matter how seemingly unimportant. We need to stop this one, because he will take more. Why he's doing it I don't know, but I'm certain he'll take more. Whatever's driving him won't just stop, and neither will he.'

It was late morning when Featherstone entered the office of Assistant Commissioner Addis, who was already standing behind his desk stuffing a selection of coloured files into his black briefcase. Featherstone knocked on the doorframe to attract his attention, not willing to step further across the threshold without permission. Addis looked up with an expression of distaste on his face. 'Ah. It's you,' he said.

'You wanted to see me, sir.'

'Yes, but I haven't got time to sit and chat. You'll have to walk with me.' Addis quickly closed and locked his briefcase before unceremoniously striding past Featherstone and into the corridors of power, walking at a pace Featherstone struggled to keep up with, talking as he went, fluently and without any signs of breathing hard despite the relentless pace, occasionally glancing at his watch. 'Clearly you know that a third victim has been found?'

'Yes, sir,' Featherstone answered. 'Corrigan sent me an email with some photos and a covering brief.'

'You mean he didn't bother to contact you in person?'

Featherstone reminded himself that talking to Addis was like walking through a minefield. 'I imagine he's been too busy with this new one.'

'Yes,' Addis sneered. 'The new one – only this one's not like the others, is it?'

'How so?'

'Because this one's dead, Superintendent.'

'Yes, sir. I know.' A degree of insolence leaked into Featherstone's tone. Addis stopped in his tracks and turned to face the older, junior man.

'Do you know where I'm on my way to now, Superintendent? I'm on my way to do the press conference with the parents

323

of the other two missing children, and after that I'm going to have to tell them that a third child has been taken, and then I'm going to have to tell them that that child was murdered. That's not going to be a very pleasant thing to have to do, is it?'

'No, sir,' Featherstone agreed before continuing, eager to move the conversation on. 'Did you get Corrigan's brief for the press conference?'

'I did.'

'And?'

'And it is entirely adequate.' High praise coming from Addis, and Featherstone knew it. 'A few interesting ideas,' Addis admitted before breaking back into his stride along the corridor, speaking over his shoulder at Featherstone who once more struggled to keep up. 'But I need more than interesting ideas for a press conference: I need this bastard caught, and quickly. I'd have been speaking to Corrigan myself this morning if I hadn't been so busy, but there's only so long he can go on dodging bullets. Some of my contacts in the media have already given fair warning that it won't be long before they turn on us. A bungled police investigation always makes for profitable headlines and those cunts at the BBC won't miss a chance to stick the knife in, especially after recent events. It's only a matter of time, Alan, mark my words – it's only a matter of time.'

'Corrigan will bring home the bacon soon enough,' Featherstone tried to assure him.

'I hope you're right. But if you're not, someone needs to take the fall – for all of us.'

'Corrigan?'

Addis came to another sudden stop. 'Maybe I – *we* – over-estimated Corrigan's . . . *talents*. Perhaps he's not as *insightful* as I was led to believe.'

'He's not a fortune-teller,' Featherstone tried to remind him. 'He's not a psychic. He just needs a little more time.'

'There are plenty of other competent DIs out there, Alan – more reliable ones – ones who respect the system, and the hierarchy of rank.'

'There are no others like Corrigan out there,' Featherstone argued, digging his heels in to protect his man, risking more than he wanted to.

'Maybe,' Addis conceded, 'but what's the point in having an attack dog if it can't be controlled?' Addis's lips spread into a thin, venomous smile. 'Do you know what a sheep farmer does with a dog they no longer trust, no matter how loyal it may have been in the past?'

'No,' Featherstone replied, although he feared he knew the answer.

'They shoot it. They take it out into the woods or the hills and they shoot it in the head. They kill it before it ever gets a chance to bite them. We do understand each other, don't we, Alan?'

Featherstone said nothing as Addis's grin grew ever broader before disappearing as quickly as it had arrived. Then the Assistant Commissioner turned abruptly and set off at pace along the corridors of the Yard. Featherstone had half expected him to click his heels together and give a Nazi salute before marching away, but if Addis was any sort of a joke then he was a killing joke. It was no secret he had his eye on becoming the next Commissioner of the metropolis and he couldn't afford any skeletons in his closet, not in this day and age. A failed high-profile murder investigation would be exactly that. Corrigan needed to pull something out of his hat, and soon, or heads would roll.

'Just a few more months to retirement,' Featherstone whispered to himself. 'Just a few more months.'

* * *

Sean sat in his office trying to concentrate on the ever-rising piles of paper and cardboard folders that grew like model skyscrapers on his desk, not to mention the hundreds of unopened emails he knew waited for him on the Met's internal system. But try as he might to conscientiously read through the reports and files he kept drifting back to the photographs that lurked in his phone – photographs of Samuel Hargrave lying on the cold stone in the cemetery. Sean scrolled to one showing the boy's face and enlarged it as much as he could without losing what detail there was – his pale blue lips indicating cause of death was asphyxiation, probably due to smothering, but possibly by strangulation. Or maybe he'd even died through simple hypothermia. No matter what had killed him, the photographs were haunting and distressing.

Sean tried to pull his eyes from the unreal-looking photographs on the small screen, but no matter how hard he tried he couldn't look away, his brain kept desperately trying to see something in the pictures – something that could put him right next to the man he hunted.

'You don't want me to find you, do you?' he softly spoke to himself. 'You want me to believe you're not a killer, but you don't want me to find you. Why not?' He held the phone in one hand, using the index finger of the other to press his upper lip into his teeth, as if pain would help bring the answers. 'So many killers want to be caught, so why don't you? They want to be caught because in their souls they know they are wrong. They don't . . . they don't believe in what they're doing. It's all about belief, isn't it? You believe in what you're doing. You believe what you're doing is right.'

A knock on his already open door made him jump and he looked up to see Sally staring at him from the doorway. He dropped the phone on his desk and pretended to casually push it away as if he hadn't been looking at anything important. Sally gave him a few seconds before speaking, knowing exactly what he'd been looking at and why.

'Press conference is about to start,' she warned him. 'We've got it on the telly in the main office if you want to watch.'

'Yeah, I suppose I should,' Sean answered, pushing himself to his feet without enthusiasm, the thought of watching the parents of the missing children going through their private torture less than appealing. 'See if they can all stick to the script.'

They made their way to the crowd of detectives surrounding the small TV, Sean waving away offers of a seat as he instead chose to stand and look over their heads and shoulders, more comfortable knowing his reactions to the parents' agony would not be observed.

He watched as the incessant flashing of cameras began to subside and the two sets of parents took their seats, the familiar shadow of Addis coming into view, sitting between the two couples, indicating it was time for the baying journalists to settle down before the conference began. Sally leaned close to Sean and spoke quietly. 'Word has it he's a shoo-in as a future commissioner – sooner rather than later too. You wouldn't want to be in his bad books.' Sean said nothing, concentrating on the spectacle unfolding in front of him as Addis gave a recap of the disappearances of George Bridgeman and Bailey Fellowes, explaining the purpose of the press conference, that it was an appeal to the public for help in catching the man who'd been taking the children of the wealthy and privileged of North London. Sean couldn't help wondering whether the parents' riches would generate or reduce sympathy with the general public.

He was pleased to see Addis sticking to the brief he'd provided him, handing over as quickly as possible to the parents: a high-ranking police officer wasn't going to create empathy with anyone. He wanted whoever had taken the children to see the result of his actions. He wanted them to see the parents' suffering and pain – wanted them to be overwhelmed with so much remorse that they might possibly release them unharmed. But he'd prepared the briefing before the body of Samuel Hargrave had been found – before the kidnapper had killed. Before they had crossed the ultimate line from which no one could return.

Samuel's death had changed everything – making the press conference as much of a risk as it was an effort to save the missing children. The media appeal might make him panic and kill the other children. One death, two deaths, three deaths – it made no difference, not once the line had been crossed. Better to get rid of any witnesses – bury the bodies where they'd never be found. Sean knew the risks, but had chosen to keep them to himself, the opportunity to finally put some pressure back on the man who'd snatched these children from their own homes too tempting to resist. If he panicked, he'd start making mistakes and Sean would be close by, ready to bring his fantasy world crashing down to reality. He only prayed he was right about Samuel, that his death had been an accident. Whether it was murder or manslaughter, the man he hunted was still dangerous – dangerous and irrational. Anything could set him off at any time as he grew more and more unstable with each passing day – each passing hour. Sean didn't have time to play safe. He had to take the risks and be prepared to live with the consequences – the guilt, the regrets, the nightmares.

The Bridgemans spoke first, keeping dutifully to the script he'd prepared for them, speaking directly into the cameras, explaining how much they loved and missed George – how much his sister missed him, that she was heartbroken without her little brother. Showing the gathered media photographs of the two playing together, telling the world what a wonderful and special child George was. 'Good,' Sean barely whispered. 'Keep it personal – show George's life with his family. Make George a person, not just a thing.'

Next they spoke about how they understood mistakes could happen – how someone *might* think they were doing the right thing taking a child, but that George was loved by his family, and that they as a family forgave each other their mistakes, they were forgiving people, they never dwelled on accidents or cried over spilt milk – all coded messages to the man who'd taken George that they would forgive him and forget, if he would just let George go, even if in reality no such thing could ever happen.

After they'd finished, Addis introduced Bailey Fellowes' parents. They followed the same tack, only it was Mrs Fellowes who did nearly all the talking while her husband tried to control his sobbing. She stuttered and faltered as she tried to control her own emotions, almost crushing the family photographs she was supposed to show the cameras in her hand. 'Talk,' Sean whispered again. 'Talk to him, damn it – talk to the man who has your child.' Sally looked at him out of the corner of her eye, straining to hear what he was saying as Jessica Fellowes struggled onwards, her words barely audible through her sobs. 'Jesus Christ,' Sean said loudly enough for everyone to hear. 'You have to be stronger than this. He won't let your child go out of pity. You have to prove yourself to him. You have to show him you're worth a second chance.'

'I just want my baby back,' Jessica cried into the cameras, the intensity of the flashbulbs reaching new levels. They had what they came for – the picture that would make all of tomorrow's front pages.

'Fuck it,' Sean cursed. 'You'd think they didn't want to see their child again.' He felt fingers curl around his forearm and give a slight squeeze. He looked at the hand first, his eyes rising to see it belonged to Sally.

'They're doing their best,' she told him with sadly. 'They don't understand, Sean. They don't understand like you do – not many people do.'

He tried to think of a reply, but she was already walking back to her office. He waited a few minutes, watching the end of the press conference without listening, waiting for his anger and frustration to fade before heading after Sally to offer something akin to an apology. But when he reached her office she was sitting at her desk with her back towards the door, something no cop would ever do willingly. It was enough to tell Sean something was wrong.

'You all right, Sally?' he asked gingerly.

'No,' she answered without looking at him. 'No I'm not.' Her voice was shaking and he could tell she was crying. He crossed the small office and rested a hand on one shoulder while looking over the other. He felt her recoil slightly from his touch – the ghost of Sebastian Gibran still haunted her more than she allowed people to know.

'Why did it have to be children?' she asked.

'We don't get to pick and choose,' Sean reminded her gently.

'Christ, those poor parents. What must they be thinking?'

'We can get the children back. We'll find them.'

'Do you really believe that? I mean really?'

'I have to.'

'But not Samuel Hargrave,' Sally told him, her words like a knife in his chest. 'We can't bring him back.'

'No,' he agreed sadly. 'No, we can't do that.'

'I thought I was ready,' Sally admitted, 'thought I was ready for just about anything, but I was wrong. I never thought we'd get something involving children. I don't know why – it just never crossed my mind.'

'You're not feeling anything everybody else isn't. This has nothing to do with what happened to you in the past. You'll be fine.'

'What about you?' Sally asked. 'It doesn't seem to have affected you.'

Sean breathed in a chestful of air before answering. 'I don't always react in . . . in . . .' He struggled to find the words.

'In the same way as everybody else?' Sally asked.

'I was going to say in the most appropriate way,' Sean told her. 'I can get obsessive at times – forget how the people around me might be feeling, how the victims' families might be feeling. I see only the offender, the person I have to find and stop. I guess I can be a bit of a bull in a china shop.'

'You don't say,' Sally said, a rueful laugh cutting through her tears.

'That's why I need you: to give me the occasional kick up the arse and keep me from getting myself into trouble.'

'I'll do my best,' she agreed, drying her eyes, her stuttering laughter replacing the crying.

'Good, because I'm going to have to piss a few more people off before I catch this one. I don't have time to tread softly if I'm going to catch him quickly. And that's what I have to do, because this one is beginning to really worry me. He's no Sebastian Gibran or Thomas Keller, but he's just as dangerous. He's living in some sort of fantasy world, and the moment that world starts to collapse around him, God only knows what he'll do.'

Donnelly watched the end of the press conference and then headed for the exit. He stepped between a couple of detectives who were blocking the way. 'Must visit the little boys room and point the python at Percy.' He walked the

331

rest of the way along the corridor to the toilet, whistling all the way, swinging the door to the bathroom open as if he was entering a saloon. He kept the whistling going until he was sure the room was empty, then entered a cubicle and silently locked it behind him, sitting his considerable frame on the toilet with the seat still down. He was fighting hard to push the images of the parents during the press conference away, but even as their anguished faces faded slightly, the face of Samuel Hargrave in the cemetery continued to haunt him, the boy's image burnt on to his mind. He pulled his warrant card from his jacket pocket and slipped a small photograph he carried of his family from inside. It had been taken a few years ago when the twins were only eight and his youngest, Joshua, only three. He tried to picture him alive, playing at home with his brothers and sisters, but the image of his son lying on the stone in the cemetery wouldn't leave his consciousness – his own boy's lips blue and his skin pale.

He felt his throat constricting with grief and squeezed a large palm tightly over his own mouth to stem any betraying noise as his vision became blurred by the gathering tears – tears that somehow he managed to stop from flooding his eyes. Dabbing at the corners of his eyes with the back of his hand, he struggled to bring his breathing under control, filling his lungs and holding his breath until the involuntary convulsions began to fade. He kissed the photograph of his family and carefully tucked it back into his warrant card before slipping it back into his jacket. He sniffed the mucus from his nose and cleared his throat before standing. If anyone asked about his red eyes, he'd say what he always said: 'Work hard, play hard. Life's not a bloody dress rehearsal.' It was what people expected from him and he saw no reason to challenge the image they were comfortable with. He flicked the cubicle lock open and stepped into the empty toilet, checking himself in the mirror before heading back to the main office, straightening his tie and smoothing his moustache. 'Kids. Why did it have to be bloody kids?'

11

It was late afternoon and already growing dark by the time Sean pulled up outside the tall, slim Georgian terrace in Primrose Hill, the scene of the latest and vilest crime committed by the man he needed to try and become if he was going to catch him. Sean knew the sooner he could start thinking like this one, the sooner he could catch him – no matter how uncomfortable it might be. He parked in one of the residents-only parking bays that unusually ran at ninety-degree angles to the pavement, rather than adjacent to it: a neat way of doubling the amount of parking spaces for the City bankers and their wives who dominated this area. The street seemed unnaturally quiet as Sean hauled his tired body from his out-of-place-looking Ford; a lull before the storm, he decided. The school runs were complete, but the husbands were still at work. He rolled the stiffness out of his neck, jerking it to release a series of cracks as he looked up at the empty, dark house.

The family had been moved away while their house was examined and the forensic team had packed up and gone home, as per Sean's instructions. They'd been working as covertly as they could for most of the day, doing everything within their power to avoid drawing attention. Even the usual uniformed guards had been dispensed with, replaced by surveillance units who watched from unseen positions close by. As well as keeping the scene nice and quiet, they'd also been briefed by Sean to watch for anybody who appeared to be taking an unnatural interest in the house, even if they just lingered outside for a few seconds. There was always the chance the offender would return to the scene. Sean didn't believe he would – this one didn't feel like that – but the possibility had to be taken into consideration. If there'd been an obvious sexual element to his crimes then the pull of revisiting the scene would have been much stronger.

Sean looked up the number of one of the surveillance team members who he knew would be looking at him right now and pressed call.

'Hello,' a female voice answered.

'DI Corrigan – about to enter the address,' was all he said.

'We have you,' the voice told him and hung up.

Sean pulled the house keys he'd borrowed from the forensic team from his coat pocket, rhythmically clenching and releasing his fist around them, feeling self-conscious, knowing the eyes of the surveillance team would be on him, watching his every move. Quickly he slid the key into the centre deadlock before suddenly freezing, looking down at the hand that held it – some instinct or some connection with the man who'd come in the night telling him his actions were wrong – out of sequence. In that second he forgot the surveillance team were watching and began to slip into his own dark world – the world he shared with only one other.

He pulled the key out without turning it and stepped back from the door, looking it slowly up and down. He noted that it had the same type of deadbolt security locks top and bottom, then a different type in the centre – the one he'd almost unlocked – with a Yale lock just below it for when the family needed to leave the door on the latch. Sean considered the report on possible points of entry. This scene was exactly same as the others – there was no possible way the suspect could have entered through anything other than the front door. All windows and rear doors of the three houses were fitted with security locks that could only be unfastened from the inside. As impenetrable as the front door looked, it was the only way he could have entered.

'Did it look daunting?' Sean found himself whispering. 'Standing here in the middle of the night, looking up at this door, all these locks – or didn't it bother you? No, you weren't afraid – you knew these locks would be child's play to you. You didn't stand here fumbling in the darkness – you came straight to this door, prepared your tools and opened the locks. But you didn't start in the centre of the door, did you? You wanted to control the movement of the door – you couldn't afford for it to pop open unexpectedly.' He scanned the door once more before sliding a different key into the top lock, one of a pair of identical deadlocks fitted top and bottom, opened by the same key, smoothly turning it to open. 'You did the top lock first,' Sean told the darkness, crouching down to slide the same key into the bottom lock, 'and then you did the bottom lock – the same type of lock, so you opened them one after the other using the same technique, the same tools.' After releasing the lower lock he stood and stared at the two remaining locks halfway up the door. 'Then you did the central deadlock,' he continued, again slipping the key into the hole, imitating the events of the night before. 'Did the excitement begin to rise – threaten to overtake you when you realized there was only one simple lock between you and the inside of the house? The family? The boy?

. . . No,' he eventually decided. 'No, you didn't come here for excitement, did you? Your cause is more serious – something you believe you have to do, even if sometimes you don't want to.'

He let the ideas fire around his mind for a while before finally slipping the Yale key into the last lock and turning it, the door immediately opening inwards with a click, the warm air from inside being sucked out into the cold evening, rushing past Sean and making him quickly close the door. 'No. You wouldn't have let the door open like that. You wouldn't have risked the noise, wouldn't have risked a breeze catching it and blowing it wide open.' He took hold of the door handle and pulled the door towards him, once again turning the key as he did so. This time the lock clicked open, but the door remained secure until he gently pushed in inwards and open, quickly and quietly stepping inside, closing the door behind him with another click as he leaned with his back to it, looking into the darkness of the house, listening for sounds of life. 'Did you wait here long, enjoying the warmth of the house after the cold of outside? Did you wait until the numbness in your hands and feet had gone before heading for the stairs?' Again Sean waited a few moments for the answers to come before daring to move. 'No, you didn't want to waste any time. You're no voyeur. You didn't want to spend time amongst the family's things – you didn't want to be a part of their lives. At the other two scenes you locked the doors behind you when you left because you didn't want to leave the families in any danger, exposed. You took no pleasure in the suffering you knew you were about to cause. You just came, took the child and tried to leave. Only this time something went wrong and you had to run and the boy died. But why are you taking these children in the first place? Why are you risking everything to take them?' No answer came.

He pushed himself off the front door and began to slowly walk along the hallway towards the stairs, the luminous light from the alarm system's control panel drawing his attention and reminding him of the other houses – the other scenes. 'All the houses have alarms, but somehow you know they're not working. How do you know that? Of all the houses in London, you pick three where the alarm isn't working – that can't possibly be by chance. You knew. You knew, but how? We need to check back further – check the . . . check the alarm-monitoring companies, the key-holders, the families who used to live in the houses. Were they once monitored by the police? Is it something about these alarms that somehow connects these families?' He froze for a second as he considered the dozens of lines of inquiry that such checks would throw up, but if they had to be done – so be it.

He left the alarm and headed for the stairs, climbing them steadily, his hand hovering above the bannister but careful not to touch it, talking to himself as he moved ever upwards, the street lamp outside providing the only light, just as he was sure it had the previous night. 'You're so damn comfortable in this house and the others, finding your way to the boy's bedroom in the dark – no accidental wandering into the wrong room. Damn it – I know you know these houses, but how? We've checked the estate agents, the removal companies, the alarm companies and everything else – nothing links the families, but you've been in these houses before – before you took the children, but when? What the fuck am I missing? What?'

He continued his climb to the third floor, briefly pausing outside the room he guessed the parents used as their bedroom, remembering the initial scene report: *parents on the second floor, children on the third*. The door was only slightly open, but he needed to see inside. He placed the knuckle of his index finger high on the door and pushed, acutely aware he wasn't wearing gloves of any kind. Touching the front door hadn't been a problem – he knew Forensics had completed their work there, but he couldn't be sure about the parents' room. Forensics would kill him if they knew he'd been in the scene without a full forensic suit, never mind without gloves, but he dare not put any type of barrier between himself and the house – between himself and the man who'd killed Samuel Hargrave. Not even a thin skin of latex.

As the door swung slowly open it made a slight creaking noise – the sort of noise that would go unnoticed during the daytime in a busy house full of noisy children. But in the dead of night the sound would have seemed a hundred times louder – potentially mysterious and terrifying. Sean quickly looked around the room before returning to the hallway, satisfied the room held nothing for him. As he climbed to the third floor and the children's bedrooms he noticed the creak of a stair, his heart beating faster and faster. Knowing an idea was about to reveal itself, he tried to clear his mind, to provide his thoughts with a blank canvas to paint their picture on – sure he was at last close to something, something case-changing.

He stepped on to the third-floor hallway and froze, every minute sound of the house echoing like church bells in his head until finally the idea showed itself. 'Fuck. Fuck. You know these houses in the night. You've been here before in the night. That's how you were able to enter and leave without a sound, wasn't it? Because you knew every sound the house could make to betray you.' But his elation was short-lived as a wave of other questions and doubts crashed over him, making his head begin to thump. 'You're good with locks, so you came in the same way – through the front doors. You looked around the houses, carefully noting everything – where the children slept, where the parents slept, which floorboards would creak – so when you came back for the children you would know everything you needed to. But . . . but why would you let yourself in, learn everything you needed to know and then leave without the child?'

Sean stood silent and still for what seemed an age, stuck in a trance-like state, bewildered by his own questions until his mind asked even more. 'And . . . and when you did come back, how did you take George Bridgeman and Bailey Fellowes without making a sound? Samuel fought and his noise betrayed you. If the others had fought they would have betrayed you too, but they didn't, did they? They went with you willingly, so they knew you, they must have known you or . . . or you had some . . . some special hold over them – something . . . magical . . . or you're a family friend . . . or you cased the houses when they were still empty, before the families even moved in . . . or . . . or . . . Jesus Christ, fuck it!' he suddenly swore, the frustration of the cascading, tumbling questions too much. He pulled a packet of ibuprofen from his coat pocket and popped a couple from the tin foil straight into his waiting mouth, swallowing them without water. He rubbed the sides of his head as he waited for the whirlwind of possibilities to subside.

After a minute or so the confusion settled and he could think again. 'You know all these families. We just haven't found the link yet. Something the families haven't told us yet. Something they're afraid of, or have maybe just forgotten – something they can't even conceive of as being relevant. Is that what you are – someone easily forgotten?' He walked along the corridor until he reached the two doors opposite to each other. He pushed open the door to his right, again using the point of his knuckle, staring into the room before daring to enter, trying to see into the dimness. He could make out little other than shadows and silhouettes, prompting him to search the wall for a switch and flood the bedroom with light.

After a few seconds of surveying the room from the doorway he stepped inside, scanning everything from the unmade bed to the toys that littered every corner and surface, seeing everything through different sets of eyes: the boy's, the killer's and his own, each giving him a different perspective of the crime. 'You didn't kill him here in this room, because the parents heard voices downstairs – so you wanted him alive. If you'd wanted to kill the boy in the house you would have done it in this room with the boy's own pillow, and nobody would have heard a thing. No,' he decided. 'You wanted the children alive and somehow you took them without a sound.' He was quiet for a while. 'Somehow you persuaded them to leave with you – to sneak out of their own homes and away from their own families. Only Sam changed his mind. You couldn't control him, couldn't make him be quiet, and when you heard the voices of his parents you panicked and ran. You panicked and smothered the boy and you killed him, and then you left him in the cemetery on the grave of Robert Grant as what . . . some sort of apology? Damn your apology and damn you too.'

He took a deep breath and one last look around the bedroom. It seemed as if each and every one of the large collection of soft toys were staring into Sean's eyes, trying to tell him what they had witnessed – lifeless eyes flickering and burning as they reflected the light – a hundred mirror images of himself looking back at him – accusing him. 'I'm sorry, Sam,' he told the room and flicked the light off, silencing the eyes of his accusers.

He made his way downstairs, moving quicker than he had when he'd arrived, satisfied the house held nothing more for him. It had convinced him the killer had been in the house during the night, possibly days, even weeks before taking Samuel Hargrave, but that was all he'd learned. Despite his initial feelings of excitement at this new revelation he was rapidly realizing it only posed more questions than it solved. *Come into the house in the middle of the night and leave without the children – why?* He shook his head at his own question, his mind turning to Mark McKenzie. *Was this still all part of a game McKenzie was playing? Was he working with a paedophile ring after all? Getting their kicks out of playing with the police as well as through doing unthinkable things with the children they were taking? John Conway and his sick followers had liked to play games. Could this yet be more of the same?* He doubted it, but he couldn't be sure, not yet.

He paused halfway down the flight of stairs leading from the second floor to the first – the place where both parents had said they'd heard voices. 'You stopped here, didn't you? The boy didn't want to go with you – he began to struggle, and you were afraid, weren't you? I can feel your fear – fear like you've never felt before. You had to stop him shouting so you did the first thing that came into your mind and pressed your hand over his mouth, but you covered his nose as well and he couldn't breathe.' He paused for a moment as he recreated the struggle in his mind – the boy fighting to escape as a panicking man overpowered him, gloved hands at first soft and warm on his skin, but then constricting and suffocating, an unbearable pressure crushing the boy's face. 'Did you mean to kill him? Did he make you angry – angry enough to make you want to kill him? Can you not bear the thought of facing up to what you really are – a murderer of children?' He let the rest of the scene play out behind his eyes, as clear as if he was watching a recording. The heavy, dark figure picking up the boy and hurrying down the stairs, afraid to look over his shoulder as he fumbled at the locks that only minutes earlier he'd opened from the outside with such skill and ease. Sean skipped down the remaining stairs, trying to catch up with the spectre of the man fleeing below.

Sean pulled the door open and walked quickly outside without closing it behind him, looking up and down the road just as Sam's father had, in some forlorn, desperate hope that even now, hours later, he might somehow see the man and boy under the yellow street lights. He found himself frozen to the spot, unable to decide which way to walk, waiting for some unseen power to direct him, turning one way then the other, squinting to try and tell which way to head, but nothing revealed itself. In the end he decided to walk in the direction where the road was longest, past the rows of parked SUVs and top-end estate cars, looking for a place where the man he hunted could have parked without disturbing the solitude of the street in the middle of the night. 'You didn't park here – didn't park close to the house, because if you had the father would have heard the slam of the car door, the engine starting – he would have seen you speeding away. So you were parked somewhere else – in the next street – at the end of the road and around the corner? But you couldn't have made it all the way to the end before he saw you – not while you were carrying the deadweight of the boy. The father said he couldn't see anyone – couldn't hear anything.' Sean stopped and looked around. 'So you hid – you hid with the boy, listening to his father running in the street, his footsteps little more than dull thuds as he searched for you in his bare feet. But the sound of those footsteps must have been terrifying while you cowered like a hunted animal, and you had to stop the boy calling out or making a sound – you had no choice – so you kept your hand pressed across his face, didn't you? You kept your hand pressed across his face until the footsteps disappeared, and then you ran – you took the boy to wherever your car was. But where did you hide?'

Again he searched the street. *Between the parked cars? No. Where then?* He walked to the closest house and peered over the iron railings into the basement, before moving to the next house and doing the same and then the next and the next. They were all the same – a mixture of chained-up bikes and wheelie bins, most in complete darkness, but not all. 'You hid down here, didn't you – like the coward you are. But which one, you bastard son-of-a-bitch?'

He kept moving along the street, looking into the basements, desperately searching for something that would tell him it was the one where the taker of children had hidden, but he could find nothing – feel nothing. 'Fuck,' he told the emptiness. Now he'd have to get Forensics to search every basement in the street. If he wasn't already Mr Unpopular, he soon would be. 'Damn you and damn me too,' he whispered. 'I don't know you yet, but I will find you. I just need more. I need something else. I need the post-mortem.'

Douglas Allen sat in his study that resembled a small work-shop on the first floor of his house, surrounded by his collection of clocks and mechanical toys. He wore a magnifying eye-scope over his right eye with his mini-potholing lamp strapped around his forehead, which was switched on despite the bright circle of light provided by the large flexible desk lamp he'd pulled close to where he worked. The rest of the room was in semi-darkness. He hummed along to the choral music that was quietly playing in the background as he selected a lock from his large collection and began to insert his delicate tools into the keyhole, reminding himself of where each pin and hole inside could be found – of every tiny sound they made as he gently manoeuvred them into exactly the right position to spring the device open. Within a few minutes he heard and felt the pins drop into their housings and the deadbolt suddenly retracted into the body of the lock. He put it to one side and reached for the next, only to be instantly frozen by a sound, real or imagined, coming from somewhere in the house. He cocked his head and listened intently, filtering out any sounds from beyond the house as he tried to allay or confirm his fears. Had one of the children wandered from their bedroom against his express wishes? He'd fed them, bathed them and put them to bed over two hours ago and checked on them since, finding them soundly asleep in their pristine pyjamas and bed linen. Maybe one of them had had a bad dream? After a few minutes he was satisfied the sound had been nothing and returned to his work, pulling the next lock into the circle of light before abandoning it just as quickly and reaching for a small, framed photograph of his wife, lifting it from the desktop and holding it close to his face, unclipping the eye-scope from his spectacles. The sadness of the previous night still hung over him like oppressive black clouds, haunting his every waking moment.

'What should I do, Iris?' he whispered, his voice trembling. 'I don't know what to do. If . . . if you were only here with me . . . I . . . I . . . I'd know what to do.' *You do know what to do.* 'Iris?' *You must carry on God's work.* 'I don't know, Iris – after what happened with . . . the last time.' *The Lord is thy shepherd.* 'Is this truly what God wants?' *He lets me rest in the meadow grass and leads me beside the quiet streams. He gives me new strength. He helps me do what honours him the most.* 'And do I honour him? Does doing what I do truly honour him?' *But Jesus said, Suffer little children, and forbid them not to come unto me: for of such is the kingdom of heaven.* 'Is Samuel with the Lord now?' *He lives with him for ever in his home now.* Allen choked back his joy and relief, but the tears still streamed down his face until he could taste the salt on his lips. *You must save as many as you can before it's too late. Time is always against us.*

He felt her fade away as suddenly as she'd arrived and the emptiness returned, tearing at his chest and pounding in his head, the pain making him dizzy and nauseous.

'God give me strength to carry on,' he called out, his eyes tightly closed, hands clamped to the side of his head, trying to squeeze the demons from inside his mind. 'God give me strength.' But the pain was unrelenting and merciless. With his eyes still firmly closed he clumsily felt around in the dark, fumbling at the small drawers of the desk until he believed he'd found the one he needed. He pulled it open and groped inside until his fingers coiled around the first small bottle as his other hand pulled at the lid, ripping it off and sending lilac pills cascading across the desk and on to the floor. 'God give me strength,' he begged again. 'God give me strength to bear my burden.' But the pain in his head had begun to exhaust his strength. *Just take the medication,* his doctors had told him, *just take the medication and you'll be fine – painless.* But the drugs took the voices away too – the voice of his wife, the voice of his Lord.

Blindly he gathered up a handful of the pills from the desktop, not looking to see how many he was about to swallow, weeping with pain and shame – shame that he was about to betray his own wife, the only person who'd ever really loved him. 'Please, God . . . please God, give me strength,' he begged one last time, his hand moving closer and closer to his mouth, as if it was controlled by the Devil himself, pushing the poison relentlessly nearer. But as his lips reluctantly began to part, the white pain suddenly broke like a giant wave over the shore, its energy spent and fading. His breathing began to return to normal, his eyes flickering open, still dazzled by the lamplight, but increasingly able to tolerate it. He rocked back on his knees and opened his clenched fist, allowing the lilac pills to trickle from his grip and fall to the floor. 'The Lord is my saviour – the Lord is my shepherd. The Lord is my saviour – the Lord is my shepherd.' He swayed back and forth as he chanted his allegiance. 'Lead us not into temptation, but deliver us from evil – Lead us not into temptation, but deliver us from evil.' Over and over he repeated the words of the Lord's Prayer, frantically at first, then more calmly, until he could feel only a trace of the pain that had threatened to defeat him.

Finally he was able to stand, pulling himself up and hauling himself into the chair, wiping the sweat from his brow with the sleeve of his shirt, his hands still trembling as he tugged open another drawer and took out an innocuous-looking blue notebook. He flicked through the pages until he found what he was looking for. A name – Victoria Varndell, age about five years old. Address: 2 Bayham Place, Mornington Crescent. 'Blessed are those who are persecuted because of righteousness, for theirs is the kingdom of heaven.' It was his duty to save the child, but not tonight – he couldn't save her tonight, not until he'd learned all he needed to know. But tomorrow he could save her. Tomorrow he would be able to save five-year-old Victoria Varndell.

Sean hadn't been able to bear the thought of returning to the Yard after visiting the house in Primrose Hill – returning to the piles of reports and emails that undoubtedly waited for him. The increasing list of missed calls on his mobile was evidence enough that he was much in demand, but he had nothing to say to anybody, nothing he wanted to share – not yet. Instead he'd driven to the other two scenes, parking as close as he could to the houses the children were taken from without being noticed, just sitting in the dark, his window down as he listened to and smelled the streets. It was the first time he had travelled from scene to scene and he was struck by their proximity to each other. But the area between them still meant there were hundreds, maybe even thousands, of streets to cover. No matter how many dozens of extra cops they put on the streets, it would still be an incredible stroke of luck if they were to stop the right man and bring to a halt what the media were increasingly referring to as his *reign of terror*. He tried to remember anyone getting that lucky before, but couldn't.

Eventually he had to face the fact that the scenes wouldn't speak to him and he headed home to East Dulwich. He needed at least a few hours' sleep, a shower and change of clothes – maybe even some food that wasn't processed or out of a vending machine. By the time he arrived it was late enough that most of the other occupants of the street were either already tucked up in bed or heading that way.

He enjoyed the short walk in the solitude of the empty road, his footsteps loud enough to create a slight echo, his warm breath forming great plumes of steam that died as quickly as they were born. During his time as a uniform constable he, like most cops, had learned to make the night his – its sounds and sights, smells and tones. He was familiar with and comfortable in night in a way most people would never understand. If he hadn't been so tired he would have walked further, and there was still a chance Kate would be awake. Usually, when he arrived home late, he preferred to be alone, his mind too crowded for small talk or even talk of his family, but tonight was different – he needed to see Kate, needed to speak to her. Anna was right – Kate and his family were his anchor. Without them he could easily begin to lose himself. Anna was a temptation, one he still hadn't dealt with, one that still inhabited his consciousness – but he had no doubt who he loved, who he couldn't live without, and he needed to see her tonight.

As he slid the key into the only lock securing the front door he couldn't help but wonder how long it would take the man he hunted to open and enter his own house, gliding up the stairs to where his daughters slept, his wife not hearing a thing as he slipped into their bedroom and chose one to take – *but which one would he choose?* Sean found himself asking, before shaking the ugly thought away and letting himself in, closing and locking the door behind him, kicking off his shoes and walking to the rear of the house where Kate and the kitchen waited. She looked up from her laptop and greeted him as if he was a normal man, returning from a normal job at a normal hour.

'Wasn't expecting to see you for a while.'

'Thought I'd grab a few hours at home while I can – not that the world and his wife aren't looking for me.'

'Trouble?'

'When is it ever anything else?'

'That's not what I meant. I mean are you in trouble – you specifically?'

'Not especially,' he half-lied. 'Powers that be want this one sorted as soon as possible. They're putting the pressure on a bit, like they do. You would think I didn't want to find whoever's taking these children. Fools.'

'Do you still think they're alive?'

'Not all of them,' he told her.

'You find something then?'

'Yeah. A body,' he answered coldly.

'I'm sorry,' she said, and meant it.

'So am I.'

'One of the children you were looking for?'

'No. Another one – only taken last night. Something went wrong and the boy ended up dead.'

'Jesus. How are you coping?'

'With what?'

'With the fact children are involved. It can't be easy.'

'No – it's not, but I'm fine.'

'Really?'

'If everyone would just leave me alone I'd be fine, but I've got Featherstone and Addis breathing down my neck, admin from floor to ceiling, multiple scenes to coordinate, forensic teams I don't know to deal with – deadlines, media spin – it's choking me. I can't think. It's killing my instincts. I'm looking – I'm looking and looking and looking, but I'm just not seeing it. Every time I think I'm getting close, someone draws the curtains. I've picked up a few bits and pieces, but nothing that's going to lead me to him, nothing anyone else couldn't have seen.'

'You sure about that?' Kate asked. 'Don't take anything you've seen for granted. Chances are, you're the only one who's seen it or even could see it.'

'Yeah – I'm not so sure. I feel like my instincts are being strangled. If I can't think the way I need to, then maybe I don't want this any more. The frustration would drive me insane.'

'What are you talking about, Sean?'

'I'm saying maybe I need to do something different. Another job in the Met, or quit altogether, look into New Zealand again.'

'Oh no,' Kate insisted. 'No one wants you off that murder squad more than me, but not like this – not frustrated and defeated. It would burn you up, Sean. It would kill you. At least finish this case before you make any final decisions.'

'Maybe.'

'No, Sean, not maybe – definitely.'

'I know, you're right. But why can't I get inside this one's head? Why can't I think like him? I don't have any instinct any more. I don't know what happened to it – I really don't.'

'Yes you do,' Kate reminded him. 'It just got buried under an avalanche of interference and administration. You've got so much crap on your mind you can't think freely. You need to dig yourself out from under all the rubbish.'

'Oh yeah, and how do I do that?'

'Christ, Sean, I don't know. Use your imagination – be creative. Do something you haven't done in a long time, or something you've never done, anything to set your mind free again. Go back down the boxing gym, ride a bike, climb a mountain or see a bloody priest – just do something.'

'OK. OK,' Sean surrendered. 'I'll do something. I haven't got a damn clue what, but I'll think of something.' He stood as if to leave.

'You off to bed?' Kate asked.

He shook his head slowly. 'No. I just thought I'd pop in and see the kids.'

'They're asleep,' she reminded him.

'I know. I'll be careful. I won't wake them. Promise.'

Kate saw the need in his eyes. 'I know you will.'

He smiled before turning away and heading for the stairs, tiptoeing into the semi-darkness, trying to think of nothing but looking upon his beautiful daughters, but finding it impossible not to draw comparisons between his movements and those of the man he sought, no matter how hard he tried not to. He silently cursed his own mind as he reached the landing and the soft blue light that leaked through a half-closed door. He slipped inside the room, moving almost silently to the beds where the tiny figures slept, just their heads visible from under the duvets. He walked between the two beds and dropped slowly to his knees as if he was about to pray, looking from Mandy to Louise and back again,

351

stretching out his arms and gently resting a hand on each of the sleeping children, their warmth, the rising and falling of their chests triggering emotions he struggled to control as his head fell forward on to his chest. He pushed the tears back before they could flow from his eyes, swallowing hard to stop himself from sobbing and waking his children. He kept his eyes tightly closed until he had composed himself, his head eventually lifting as he blinked them open, once more looking from child to child.

'If anything ever happens to you,' he whispered to the sleeping infants. 'If anyone ever . . .' He pushed the ugly, remorseless words back into the darkness they came from. They had no place here. He exhaled long and hard until his breathing was normal again. He adjusted his position until he was more comfortable, closed his eyes once more and allowed his head to fall forward.

12

Sean stood on the pavement looking up at the large ecclesiastical building on the opposite side of the road with its steeply angled roofs and tall stained-glass windows. A small bell in a painted white housing topped the apex on the front of the dark brick structure. He had vague memories of being dragged to St Thomas More Catholic church when he was a young boy, but little more. He'd certainly never been as a man, or to any other church, except for weddings and funerals. Even now, the thought of entering the church somehow filled him with dread, but try as he might he couldn't stop feeling drawn to it. He squared his shoulders and crossed the road, dodging the traffic to reach the other side, looking into the grand entrance as if it was the mouth of a leviathan waiting to swallow him whole.

As he pushed the heavy wooden doors open, the smell of old wood and leather rushed at him, triggering memories buried deep in his olfactory system, memories from his childhood – memories of feeling safe, at least for a while. He remembered how his drunken father would refuse to join the rest of the family when they went to church on Sundays and special occasions, cursing the clergy and all they represented.

His mother said he'd burn in hell for the things he'd said. *He's burning in hell, all right*, Sean thought, *but not for that*.

He headed deeper inside, relieved to see the church was empty. Early morning on a weekday had kept the worshippers and grovellers away. Only the truly desperate came at this hour. As he walked down the central aisle he kept looking from side to side, more and more able to see himself as a young boy at his mother's side, kneeling at one of the seemingly hundreds of altar tables as the priests chanted in a language he didn't understand.

In the far corner of the church he could just about make out the old confessional boxes, almost hidden in the gloom of the lightless space, intimidating and foreboding. Yet somehow he felt himself drawn to them, walking through the rays of light that streamed in through the stained-glass windows, the sound of his leather-soled, metal-tipped shoes clicking loudly on the parquet floor. He stopped a few feet away from the boxes and waited for something to happen, although he didn't know what. Suddenly he felt a presence behind him that made him spin around. His eyes struggled to cope with the brightness of the light that shone almost directly into them. He squinted until he could see well enough to make out a man in black, with a thin white collar around his neck.

'Can I help you?' the priest asked, stepping closer, making Sean step backwards.

Sean studied him before speaking, quickly processing the man's description: six foot tall, slim but athletic, about thirty-three or -four, black collar-length hair and startling blue eyes. His accent was neutral, but with a hint of south-east London.

'No,' Sean answered. 'I was just . . . I was just looking around.'

'A trip down memory lane, perhaps?'

'Something like that,' Sean told him and unconsciously looked towards the exit, telegraphing his intentions.

'Always my favourite time of day here,' the young priest explained. 'The calm before the storm, you might say.'

'The storm? I'm surprised you ever get enough people in here to amount to a storm.'

'Ah well, we do all right. I suppose we're in a good spot. Location, location, location – isn't that what they say?'

'Yeah,' Sean answered casually, still looking for an escape route, 'that's what they say. Still, I've wasted enough of your time. I'd better get back to work.'

'Is there something you wanted to talk about? Something you wanted to get off your chest, maybe? Only I saw you heading for these confessional boxes. Perhaps you'd be more comfortable discussing whatever's on your mind the old-fashioned way?'

'You mean inside one of those boxes?' Sean asked incredulously.

'If it suits you. I'm Father Jones, by the way.'

'Jones?' Sean asked with a slight smile. 'I assumed you'd have an Irish name.'

'Everybody does,' the priest smiled back. 'Welsh father, English mother. Sorry to disappoint. When was your last time?'

'Last time what?'

'At confession?'

'Jesus, I can't remember.'

'No blaspheming in church, please,' the priest said, his smile broadening.

'Sorry . . . Father.'

'Come on,' Father Jones encouraged, his hand gesturing to the confessional box closest to them. 'It might make you feel more at peace with yourself, and I could do with the practice.' He walked past Sean and into the box, closing the door without waiting for Sean to follow, leaving him alone in the church, looking from the box to the exit, Kate's words etched into his mind: *Do something you haven't done in a long time, or something you've never done.*

'Jesus Christ,' he muttered quietly and headed for the box where Father Jones waited for him, closing the door as quietly as he could behind him and searching the cramped surroundings until he had his bearings. Eventually he pulled the small, purple, velvet curtain open and could feel Father Jones on the other side. 'I can't remember what I'm supposed to do,' Sean admitted.

'Well, I believe you're supposed to say something like, Bless me, Father, for I have sinned.'

'Fine . . . Bless me, Father, for I have sinned.'

'How long since your last confession?'

'Years. Never . . . never since I was a man.'

'That's a long time. So you've either been living like a monk or you'll have a fair bit to get off your chest, I would imagine.'

'I'm a cop,' Sean told him, without knowing why.

'I know,' the priest answered with empathy.

'How d'you know?'

'I could tell. I suppose our jobs aren't that dissimilar: we both see and hear things most people will be lucky enough never to have to think about. After you've done this job for a few years you get to be able to tell a lot about people very quickly – the same way you do, no doubt.'

'I see,' Sean agreed, still a little suspicious.

'So, where would you like to begin?'

'Sorry?'

'Your confession.'

'I don't know where to begin.'

'The beginning, perhaps.'

'I'm not sure I know when the beginning was.'

'Ah. All a little overwhelming, is it?'

'What can I say? I've beaten men to get them to tell me the truth. I've lied under oath when that's what I had to do to get the right man sent to prison. I've planted evidence. I've had terrible thoughts, and I've been unfaithful to my wife.' He hadn't intended to confess the final sin and it silenced him.

'Well – you've got a lot on your plate there, but I sense it's only the last thing you mentioned that you're truly sorry for.'

'Maybe.'

'And when you say you were *unfaithful*, do you mean in the full biblical sense?'

'No, but I wanted it. I wanted to.'

'But you didn't?'

'Doesn't the bible say thinking it is as bad as doing it?'

'*I say unto you, that whosoever looketh on a woman to lust after her hath committed adultery with her already in his heart* – to be exact, part of Jesus's Sermon on the Mount. But I always thought that was a little harsh: we are flesh and blood at the end of the day. The important thing is that you didn't sleep with this other woman – you resisted.'

'More a case of she resisted,' Sean confessed.

'Either way, I'm sure the Lord has already forgiven you. As for the other things, there's nothing there a bit of good, hard praying couldn't fix, although perhaps you may want to consider following a different path in the future.'

'Praying? God? Those things have no part in my life any more. God abandoned me a long time ago. I used to pray to him, used to pray for him to save me, but he never did – never showed himself to me – when my own father was . . . he never came to me.'

'I'm sure he was there.'

'No. No, he wasn't.'

357

'It's not always easy to understand his plans for us. You suffered as a child, but maybe it was that which empowered you as a man. It's never an easy or smooth path we walk. I don't think it's supposed to be. I don't think that's what God wants. But it doesn't mean he's not always with us, watching over us. Guiding us through life.'

'Not me. He was never watching over me.'

'Did you hear the one about the guy caught in a flood?' the young priest suddenly asked.

'Excuse me?' Sean responded, caught off guard.

'There's this man gets caught in a terrible flood – a tsunami, let's say. So he takes refuge on the roof of his house. A few hours later a fella rows up to him in a boat and says, "Jump in and I'll row you to safety," and the man replies, "No thanks, for surely the Lord will save me." A few hours later another man pulls alongside in a great big speedboat and says, "Jump aboard and I'll get you to safety," but the man replies, "No thanks, for surely the Lord will save me." A few more hours pass and a helicopter appears over the man and calls down through a loudspeaker, "We'll lower a rope for you and winch you to safety," but again the man replies, "No thanks, for surely the Lord will save me," and the helicopter flies away. A few hours later the main tidal wave hits and the man is swept to his death. When he gets to heaven, he says to God, "Why did you forsake me, Lord? In my hour of need I thought you'd save me, but you deserted me." And God says, "Deserted you? I sent you a rowing boat, a speedboat and a helicopter."'

'What's your point?' Sean asked.

'I think the point is, sometimes we can't see the Lord standing right next to us, watching over us, because we're looking almost too hard. It's like we're looking so hard, we just can't see.' The priest felt Sean's silence, as if something he'd said had disturbed him. 'You all right?' he asked.

'What?' Sean replied, having missed the question.

'Are you all right?' the priest repeated.

'Yeah. I'm fine – it's just what you said, about looking but not seeing. I've heard that before – recently. Seems to be following me around.'

'Then maybe it means something? The path you should follow?'

'The path to perdition?' Sean asked, his tone slightly mocking – sarcastic.

'Or the road to redemption,' the young priest told him. 'If not for you, then perhaps for those around you – those closest to you.'

'And the man I'm looking for – an abductor and murderer of children – what about his redemption? Will he be forgiven too?'

'If that's the type of man you're looking for, then I pray you find him, and I'll pray for his soul too.'

'And the children – his victims?'

'I'll pray for them too. But most of all, I'll pray for you.'

'You need to eat your porridge while it's still warm,' Douglas Allen told the two young children sitting at his kitchen table. He sounded tired and strained, his usually ruddy skin looking grey and lifeless, his eyes sunken and circled with dark rings. Both his hands trembled and his head still felt numb after the severe headaches he'd suffered the previous night.

'I don't like porridge,' a bored-sounding Bailey Fellowes told him, tossing her spoon into the bowl and pushing it away. 'It's disgusting. I don't have to eat this rubbish at home. I want Coco Pops.'

Allen breathed in deeply to calm his rising anger and frustration. 'This is your home,' he told her, 'and porridge is what children in this house eat for breakfast.'

'It's disgusting and I'm sick of it,' she answered back,

staring him squarely in the eyes. He could feel his chest tightening and every muscle in his body tensing as the small slim girl dared to challenge his authority. *The devil is in the child,* he told himself. *Be patient, and the Lord will give me the strength to go on – to save the child.*

'And you, George,' he asked. 'Do you like the porridge?' But the small boy just shrugged and forced a small spoonful into his mouth. 'You see?' he told Bailey. 'The porridge is fine.'

'He's just scared,' Bailey snapped at him, her eyes never leaving his. 'He's too scared to say what he thinks.'

'Why is he scared?' Allen asked, genuinely confused and concerned. 'There's nothing to be afraid of. You're safe here.'

'I want to go home and so does he,' Bailey insisted. 'We don't like it here – there's nothing to do and the food's disgusting.'

'You shouldn't say those things,' he warned her, the tightening in his chest intensifying until his vision became blurred and his ears popped. 'They are hurtful things to say, Bailey.'

'My mum says the truth sometimes hurts.'

'I don't think your mother was a very good person.'

'You can't say that. You don't know anything about my mum.'

'I know enough, and I know you need to forget about her now. We won't talk of her again.'

'You can't tell me to do that. You can't tell me to do anything. I hate you and I hate this place.' She sunk her head into her hands and began to sob as Allen looked on, clueless what to do with the sobbing child. He considered punishing her, to teach her discipline and respect, and gratitude – gratitude for everything he was trying to do for her, everything he'd risked for her – but George's tiny voice distracted him.

'Are we going to school today? I think it's a school day.'

'No,' Allen told him, feeling the beginnings of another raging headache. 'No school today. We shall study together later, after I've finished work. Now eat your breakfast.' He closed his eyes tight against the gathering storms of pain and pressed hard at his temples, fighting the nausea and dizziness.

'When will we be going back to school?' George innocently asked, but his words ripped the hidden anger from Allen's heart.

'For the love of God,' he roared, 'I've told you, forget about school – forget about your cursed families. They're nothing to us now. It's God's will. How dare you question the will of God? How dare you question his judgment?' He fell backwards as he spoke, on to the nearby work-surface. The pain made him call out in anger before he steadied himself and forced his eyes open. The two children were cowering at the table, weeping uncontrollably, fear and loathing etched into their faces. 'I'm sorry,' he managed to say between painful swallows. 'Please forgive me.' Another shot of pain forced his eyes closed once more. 'God forgive me. Dear God, forgive me for what I've done.' He staggered across the kitchen looking for the doorway like a blind man in unfamiliar surroundings. 'I must leave you now,' he managed to say. 'I have to get ready for work. Finish your breakfast and return to your bedroom. We must forget what happened here and never talk about this morning ever again. Never again, you understand? Never again.'

Sean pushed open the large flexible rubber flaps that served as swing doors leading to the main body of the mortuary at Guy's Hospital in south-east London. Dr Canning was using an electrical surgical saw to cut through the sternum of an ancient-looking female body lying on the metal table in front of him. Sean waited for the noise of the sawing to relent before coughing to get the pathologist's attention. Canning looked up, smiled and pulled off his protective goggles, holding them up for Sean to inspect as he walked closer.

'Bloody useful bit of kit,' the pathologist told him. 'Bought them at my local hardware shop.' He indicated the body with a nod of his head. 'Sawing through old people's bones is always a bit of a hazard – so brittle, you see, splinter easy. Wouldn't want one in the eye.'

'No,' Sean agreed, looking around the mortuary at three other bodies, all covered with standard-issue green hospital sheets. One of them seemed tiny compared to the other two and he instantly realized who lay beneath the sheet. 'I don't suppose you would.' He turned back to Canning before speaking again. 'Busy this morning.'

'This poor old dear here was a sudden death brought in from one of the many surrounding council estates. Been dead a good few days, but the cold of her flat's preserved her rather well. No obvious cause of death and we can't find a GP for her, so, an autopsy it is, although I don't expect to find anything too exotic. There's a middle-aged male, no doubt a heart attack, but I'll have to check: he wasn't receiving any treatment. Over there I have a relatively young woman who died in her sleep – a bit of a mystery, that one. And finally we have your little problem. The death of a child – always a terrible thing, but especially when foul play is involved.'

'Have you taken a look yet?' Sean asked.

'No. He's exactly as he was when he arrived – still wrapped in the blanket. I thought it better to wait until you or one of yours was present. Will you be taking care of the exhibits yourself?'

'No,' Sean answered. 'We can have a preliminary look together now and I'll send you a competent DC over later to log anything you find.'

'Fair enough,' Canning agreed. 'Shall we make a start then?' he asked, tearing off his latex gloves and tossing them into a nearby biohazard bin, repeating the process with his only slightly bloodied and stained apron. 'Give me a moment to scrub up.' He headed for the nearby sink and taps. 'Wouldn't want to be accused of cross-contamination, would we?'

'No,' Sean answered, not really listening.

'Any good with a camera, are you, Inspector?'

'Excuse me?' Sean asked, the question knocking him out of his daydream.

'We need to document our findings photographically. I'd usually have my assistant do it, but he's got the day off. Typical. And I'm afraid I'm going to have my hands full. There's a digital camera over there,' Canning told him, pointing with a jut of his chin to a wheeled trolley covered in more green sheets, a collection of tools on top along with the camera.

'My wife never trusts me with a camera. She says I take terrible pictures.'

'You'll be good enough,' Canning assured him. 'Just pretend you're at one of your children's birthday parties.'

'I'd rather not,' Sean replied.

'Ah. Quite. Bad example, but just snap away – I'll sort the wheat from the chaff later,' Canning told him.

'Fine,' Sean agreed, recovering the camera from the trolley and switching it on, making it *whir* slightly. A light began to blink.

'Shall we?' Canning asked, moving to the side of the small shape under the green cover. Sean breathed in sharply through his nose and nodded. Canning took hold of the top of the sheet and slowly, carefully peeled it back, mindful there could be microscopic traces of evidence clinging inside. Inch by inch he revealed the body of Samuel Hargrave, still wrapped in the blanket he'd been found in. His face was even more devoid of life than when Sean had first seen him, the features that had defined him in life now all but gone – his tiny body looking like nothing more than an organic shell, almost unrecognizable as a person, a child. Canning gave a cough to bring Sean back, prompting him to lift the camera and take two quick photographs. 'Someone's gone to great care to wrap him in the blanket: it's extremely neat and tidy, almost like the sort of swaddling you sometimes see babies wrapped in. Almost as if they were trying to preserve any evidence there may be on the boy's clothes or body.'

'He wasn't thinking about evidence,' Sean told him. 'He wanted to make sure Samuel stayed warm: it was cold out that night.'

'So the boy was alive when he left him?'

'No. He was already dead. The blanket's an act of guilt, of shame – an attempt to *apologize* for what he'd done.'

'Then his death could have been an accident?' Canning suggested.

'Possibly, or he lost it and killed him deliberately. Too early to say, which is why we're here, isn't it?'

Canning didn't answer, but instead leaned in close over the boy's face.

'His lips are quite blue and his skin extremely pale, even for someone who's been dead for this length of time, so my immediate thoughts are suffocation or strangulation.'

'If it's suffocation then it could be an accident,' Sean considered, 'but if it's strangulation we'll know it's a straight murder, although there'll still be the CPS to convince.'

'Fortunately that's your job, not mine. Now, no doubt you've noticed the plastic?'

'I did,' Sean admitted, glancing at the large plastic sheet spread out under the metal stretcher the body had been placed on.

'If anything falls from the body or blanket the sheet should catch it. After we've had a look around I'll remove it for later examination.'

'Fine,' Sean agreed, grateful for Canning's professionalism, but eager to press on.

Canning scanned up and down the wrapping before speaking again. 'There doesn't appear to be any fastening or adhesive. The blanket seems to be held in place solely by the skill of the folding. Whoever did this has either done it many times before – a nanny or paediatric nurse perhaps – or they took great care to make it so.'

'The families used nannies, but we could find no links between them,' Sean explained. 'But it's still worth considering.'

'I'm going to open the blanket now,' Canning continued, 'see what we can find.' He rested his fingers on top of the blanket, close to the boy's face, pausing a moment before loosening it. He moved painstakingly slowly, examining each newly revealed section until he could clearly see the boy's neck and the clothing around it. 'There's no bruising around the neck area, but I can see the early signs of bruising developing around his face, particularly the mouth.'

'So he was smothered, not strangled?' Sean interrupted.

'It would appear so, but we'll have to wait until I examine his trachea – internally, that is.'

'I understand,' Sean replied, keen not to be around when Canning undertook the surgical aspect of the post-mortem.

'And he appears to be still in his pyjamas, unless these are something the killer dressed him in before or after he killed him.'

'Ever tried dressing a dead person, Doctor? Even with a child, it's almost impossible. These are the boy's own clothes. The more I see, the more I think he panicked – smothered the boy to try and shut him up, and accidentally killed him – as easily and quietly as that.'

Canning had dealt with more detectives than he could possibly remember, but none were quite like Sean. He sometimes envied Sean's insightfulness and other times was grateful he wasn't blessed with such a cursed gift.

Eventually Canning looked back to the boy and continued to loosen the blanket, revealing more and more of the boy's pyjama-clad torso, until he suddenly froze before taking a step away from the body. The boy had a small soft toy clutched to his chest – a blue dinosaur with a smiling face revealing only the top row of friendly teeth, its huge, over-sized eyes cheerfully staring at nothing.

Sean immediately recognized the unfamiliar look of confusion and disturbance on Canning's face. 'You find something?' he asked, stepping forward.

'What does this mean?' Canning replied, letting Sean discover the toy for himself. 'Is it some sort of ritual gesture?'

Sean's eyes fell on the toy, the sight of it and the questions it brought making him feel a little lightheaded as he tried to comprehend what it could mean: the small, blue dinosaur tucked neatly, precisely under the boy's arms as they lay folded across his chest. 'What are you all about, my friend?' Sean asked out loud, unconsciously lifting the camera and taking pictures. 'Why did you do this? Where did the toy come from? Did you give it to the boy after you'd killed him – after you'd suffocated him with your own hands? Were you trying to say sorry to him, like you're now trying to say sorry to the world?'

'Maybe he has children of his own?' Canning offered. 'After he killed the boy, he felt so guilty he wrapped the body with one of his own children's toys? As you said, as a gesture of his sorrow – his guilt?'

'No,' Sean answered. 'He doesn't have any children of his own.'

'How do you know?'

'Because—' he began, breaking off as he realized that he didn't know, at least not in a way he could explain to Canning or anyone else. 'Wait,' he suddenly changed tack. 'There's something in his hand – his right hand.' He bent as close as he dared, squinting to better see the edge of something shiny and metallic protruding from the boy's clenched fist. Sean's hand began to stretch out towards the shining object, but Canning caught it around the wrist, making Sean's head snap towards him, a momentary glare of anger in his eyes.

'Gloves,' Canning told him. 'You're not wearing gloves.' Sean looked at his unprotected hands and withdrew. 'I'll do it,' Canning continued, taking hold of the boy's fingers and trying to prise them open as the lifeless muscles and tendons resisted. Canning audibly strained until at last he bent the fingers back far enough to extricate the object from the boy's palm. 'Fascinating,' was all he said as he lifted the tiny metal crucifix towards the bright mortuary lights.

The visit he'd paid to the church that morning flashed in Sean's mind, and he remembered the words of the young priest: *we're looking so hard, but we can't see.* 'That's all I need,' he grumbled.

'Excuse me?' Canning queried.

'That's all I need,' Sean repeated. 'A religious nut running around London abducting kids. The press will bloody love this angle. Keep this on a need-to-know basis,' he told the pathologist. 'As in, only you and me.'

'I understand,' Canning reassured him. 'But this sort of behaviour, leaving religious artifacts, personal items with the body . . . Inspector, I've been doing this job long enough to know these are the hallmarks of a serial killer. Yet if I

367

understand you correctly, you believe the perpetrator killed the boy accidentally. It appears your man is becoming something of a contradiction.'

'Maybe I'm wrong.' Sean put down the camera, tried to gather his thoughts. 'Or he's becoming what you say, but doesn't know it.'

'In which case you need to find him and find him quickly. He still has two other children, does he not?'

'He does,' Sean confirmed with a sigh and a frown. 'And there'll be more – soon.'

'I can see there's something else bothering you, Inspector,' Canning added. 'Would you like to tell me?'

Sean sighed again, but knew he could speak to Canning more freely than most. 'The toy,' he confessed. 'The crucifix I understand – he placed it in the boy's hand after he realized he was dead, as an offering, a religious token, something to try and make himself feel better, to dull his own grief and guilt. But the toy, I . . .' He stalled, the thought that had seemed so clear only moments ago suddenly drifting away from him. All he could do was wait – if he tried to grab at the thought it could slip between the fingers of his consciousness and be lost for ever. Slowly it drifted back to him. 'He goes into their houses and he takes the children. They make no sound. They go with him silently – willingly. What's one way of pacifying a child – what would win a child's trust in the middle of the night?'

He looked at Canning as if the pathologist might mouth the answer for him, but he just shook his head slowly and with no small degree of concern, so Sean supplied the answer: 'You take them a gift – a present. Bastard takes them a toy – he took them all a toy. They wake up sleepily, not sure whether they're dreaming, and the first thing they see isn't a stranger in their bedroom but a beautiful new toy only inches away from their face. They reach out for it and he lets them take it, lets them begin to trust him before he even has to speak – that's how he does it. That's how he can take them so quietly. I should have thought of this earlier.'

'What if the toy's not something he brought with him?' Canning argued. 'What if he simply took the toy from the child's bed before waking them?'

Sean considered it, chewing his bottom lip. As plausible as Canning's suggestion was, his instinct wouldn't let him accept it. 'No,' he eventually said. 'No, because it could too easily backfire on him. If the child woke and saw a stranger holding his favourite soft toy he might think he was taking it. Instead of building trust it could destroy it. Our man's a thinker and planner. He wouldn't risk it. He couldn't take that chance. He has to have brought the toy with him. But we'll check back with the parents anyway.'

'I see,' Canning murmured. 'Shall we continue?'

Sean nodded and the pathologist continued to unwrap the blanket as carefully as he could, inch by inch, until it lay hanging underneath the boy like the dead petals from the head of a flower. Canning moved on to the blue dinosaur-print pyjamas and began to unbutton them. He moved the cloth aside as carefully as if the boy was a living, breathing patient, and revealed his tiny, slim chest and abdomen – the skin as pale and soft as milk.

'No obvious sign of injuries,' Canning announced, before rolling the body to one side to examine his back, then repeating the process on the other side. 'No apparent injuries or wounds to the back either.'

Sean watched, knowing they would find nothing, but also knowing they had to look anyway, the sombre, darkening mood of both men tangible.

Next Canning began to remove the boy's pyjama bottoms, folding each section meticulously to catch any tiny pieces of evidence as they came free from the body. He placed them in a medium-sized brown paper evidence bag that had a transparent cellophane window running down the full length of one side. All clothes were bagged this way: if they were placed in plastic evidence bags any organic evidence on the clothing could turn to mould by the time the item reached the lab. Paper allowed the evidence to breathe – keeping it alive as long as it took to betray its owner.

Canning turned to the victim's immature genitals and anus. Sean didn't expect him to find anything, but still he prayed he wouldn't, looking down at his feet while the pathologist completed his initial examination of the boy's most intimate places.

'No obvious signs of sexual assault either,' Canning announced, immediately qualifying his statement: 'Although I can't say with absolute certainty until I examine him more thoroughly.'

'But it doesn't look like he was . . . like he was *touched* in any way?' Sean asked.

'No,' Canning agreed. 'It doesn't appear so.'

'Thank God,' Sean murmured, then gave a start as his mobile rang. It took him a moment to disentangle it from his inside coat pocket and answer.

'Guv'nor, it's DS Noble. It's my forensic team that's been examining the scene at 10 Hawtrey Road.' The voice went quiet while he waited for some recognition. Eventually Sean realized he was talking about the home of the dead boy lying only inches away.

'Of course,' he managed to say as if he'd never been in doubt. 'What d'you have for me?'

'Not much, but enough. A couple of fibres and a couple of hairs from the boy's bedroom that are probably the suspect's. No fingerprints, so I'm thinking he wore gloves. The lab can work the hairs up for DNA. They'll convict him once we have him, but if he doesn't have previous convictions then they're not going to help us find him.'

'Make sure the lab compare your samples to any from the other two scenes. At least they might be able to confirm we're only looking for one man.'

'I'll make sure it's done,' Noble assured him.

'Let me know if you find anything else,' Sean told him, 'anything at all.' He hung up before Noble could answer.

'Everything all right?' Canning asked.

'No,' Sean answered, once more looking down on the broken little body. 'This man's crossed the line now – broken his last taboo. Next time it'll be easier for him to kill, and it'll take less to provoke him. It's always goes the same way.'

'I thought you said this was in all likelihood an accident,' Canning queried.

'It was,' Sean explained, 'but next time won't be. He takes children from their own homes in the middle of the night. Does that strike you as normal or rational behaviour? No matter how many promises he's made to himself that he won't hurt another child, he will – if they try and escape, or they talk back too much, or they don't meet whatever twisted standards he thinks they should, or when he gets bored of them. He'll kill again, he won't be able to stop himself, no matter what he may think.' The thought of standing in the mortuary a second longer suddenly made Sean feel sick. 'I need to be somewhere else,' he told Canning. 'Call me if anything changes. In fact, call me even if it doesn't.' He quickly turned and headed for the exit – Canning's eyes silently following him all the way until he could see him no more.

Assistant Commissioner Addis sat in the back of an unmarked jet-black police Range Rover furiously tapping away on his private high-spec laptop. He'd soon tired of the cheap rubbish the police had provided him with and had decided the personal expense for something decent was worth it to give him the edge on his competitors. His out-and-about bodyguard sat in the front with his regular driver, neither of whom could stand Addis, but both of whom liked the relatively cushy number that looking after him provided. Most senior officers of his rank would be permanently shadowed by an inspector or chief inspector who would be referred to as his bag-carrier, but Addis worked alone, too organized and efficient to admit he could possibly need a personal aide. He barely needed a secretary, and besides, as far as he was concerned the less people who knew his business the better. The mobile phone that lay on the table next to the laptop began to ring and he answered it without looking, his right hand still frantically typing some new guidelines he'd be expecting the Anti-Terrorist Team to follow without divergence.

'Robert,' a familiar and intimidating voice replied. 'It's been a while. Just thought I'd give you a ring and see how everything is going.'

'Everything?' Addis choked a little. 'If this is about the conduct of some of our Anti-Terrorist officers overseas, then I can assure you that the situation will be addressed in the very near future.'

'Who cares if the Anti-Terrorist boys have been getting a little too pally with the Pakistani Intelligence Service? You know as well as I do that torture gets results, and what the public don't know won't hurt them. No, my more pressing concern is this Special Investigations Unit of yours.'

'In particular?'

'In particular, DI Corrigan. You told me this unit could be relied upon for the occasional bit of good news – good news that would reflect well on the government. But that doesn't seem to be happening, and now we've got the TV and papers all over it in their usual fucking way. Word has it it's only a matter of time before they start asking the Home Secretary what she thinks about it – maybe even the PM himself, for Christ's sake. These missing kids aren't being snatched from teenage single mothers living on some shithole estate in Birmingham, Robert. These families have influence, and the people they work for have even more influence. Their gripes go up the food chain and eventually they reach me, and it's my job to deal with them. We understand each other, don't we, Robert?'

Addis cleared his throat before answering. 'We do.'

'Excellent,' the voice told him, then softened into a conciliatory tone: 'Look, Robert – we in the government all agree that what London needs is a mayor who's strong on law and order. Free bikes and a decent firework show at New Year's are all well and good, but they're hardly vote winners. People want to feel safe in their houses, and they don't want to be tripping over beggars and vagrants every time they go to a West End theatre. London needs a Giuliani. Your public profile has been much enhanced over the last year or two, Robert, but if this investigation drags on much longer it could be irreparably damaged, along with it any political ambitions you may harbour. I just thought you should know.'

Realizing that the caller had hung up, Addis tossed the phone on to the seat next to him, rubbing his chin pensively.

He'd be damned if Corrigan was going to drag him down with him. It had been a mistake to trust a career detective – he should have given the job to a Bramshill flyer, someone he could control. Who cared if they'd never actually investigated anything more serious than shoplifting, at least he wouldn't have to worry about having the wool pulled over his eyes at every turn. But he quickly reminded himself why he'd chosen to use Corrigan instead of a flyer – because Corrigan wouldn't be looking to make a name for himself.

He'd get the job done and move on to the next one. A flyer would be looking to take all the credit and steal all the headlines, and he couldn't have that. All the same, he couldn't afford to give Corrigan more than another forty-eight hours, if that. If the right man wasn't in custody by then, he'd have to go.

Sean strode into the main office at the Yard still feeling displaced and nauseous after witnessing the preliminary stages of Samuel Hargrave's post-mortem. He needed to launch himself back into the investigation to chase the images and memories away.

Having seen him arrive, Donnelly tailed him to his office, waiting until they were inside before speaking.

'How did the post-mortem go?'

'I didn't stay for the whole thing,' Sean admitted. 'Just long enough to all but confirm what happened.'

'Which is?'

'He was suffocated, not strangled. No other injuries to the body and no outward signs of sexual assault.'

'So all the usual things are missing,' Donnelly stated flatly. Receiving no answer, he continued: 'In which case, the question remains: why is he taking them?'

'I don't know,' Sean confessed. 'But whatever his motivation is, it isn't sexual.'

'And you're absolutely sure of that?' Donnelly checked, unhappy about letting something as straightforward as a sexual predator fall away as a possibility.

'I'm sure.'

'Where does that leave us then?' Donnelly asked as he and Sean both slumped into their chairs. 'We have no viable suspects; his motivation is a mystery; we've nothing from Forensics that could help identify him, and the media appeal's drawn a complete blank, except for the odd crank and lunatic.

Where do we go from here? We still have two missing kids out there, boss.'

'We keep looking for a link – we go over everything again until we find something, only . . .'

'Only what?'

'Only, we may have to consider the possibility there is no link between the victims and their families.'

'What do you mean? We've put in a lot of hours looking for this link and now you're saying there might not be one?' Donnelly looked at him in disbelief. 'There must be a link, because whoever's taking these kids knew everything he needed to know, including the layout and security systems of the houses. He could only do that if he'd been allowed into the houses and had a good look around.'

'New information's come to light,' Sean told him.

'What information?' Donnelly asked, his arms spread wide.

'He was in the houses at night.'

'We know that. How's that supp—'

'He went in beforehand, at night.'

'How?'

'It's simple, if you think about it. The same way he went in when he took them: he picked the locks.'

'Hold on,' Donnelly said, his arms folded, his tone challenging, 'let me get this straight. You're saying sometime before he abducts the child, he goes to the house, lets himself in by picking the locks, has a good look around and then just leaves?'

'That's about it, yes.'

'But why wouldn't he take the child? Why risk a second visit? It doesn't make sense.'

'Not to you or me or any sane person, but he's not like any sane person. I don't know why he does it, I wish I did. My best guess would be it helps elongate his fantasy. He sees the child sleeping; sees the parents sleeping; sees the brothers and sisters sleeping, and leaves, locking up behind him so no one ever realizes he was there. And then he goes away – he goes away and he thinks about nothing else for days, until he feels the time is right to return and claim his prize.'

'This is a fucking nightmare,' Donnelly decreed.

'It's our job to deal with nightmares,' Sean reminded him. 'But this could also help us, give us some new angles to look at.'

'Such as?'

'Such as, if this is how he finds out whether their alarms are working or even whether they set them at night, then he may have tried to enter other houses as well as the ones we know about. Get the door-to-door teams to revisit the areas near the scenes – ask the occupants if anyone has had an unexplained alarm activation in the middle of the night. Maybe they even found their front door ajar because he had to leave in a hurry. If we're lucky, someone might have looked out of a window and seen a man run off or a car pulling away. Who knows – maybe they can give us a description or, even better, a number plate.'

'You mean if we're very lucky?' Donnelly pointed out.

'Most cases like this are solved by a lucky break. We've just got to keep looking.'

'Fair enough,' Donnelly agreed half-heartedly, lifting his heavy frame from the chair with the ease of a much lighter, younger man. 'I'll get straight on it.'

'Good,' Sean thanked him. 'Oh, and one more thing: the boy – Samuel Hargrave – when we unwrapped the blanket we found he was holding a soft toy in his arms and a crucifix in his right hand.'

'Interesting combination.'

'The crucifix is probably old and no doubt all but untraceable, but the toy – we might be able to find out where it came from. Maybe a shopkeeper will remember selling it to someone who left an impression on them?'

'You mean a weirdo?'

'If you like.'

'And you think he gave the toy to the boy?'

'Makes sense: he takes toys with him when he goes to abduct the children.'

'To pacify them. To show them he's a friend.'

'Exactly.'

'But the toy could be the boy's? He could have just grabbed it when he was leaving?'

'It could be, but I doubt it. He wouldn't want the child to think he was trying to steal their favourite toy. Safer to take a new one. But check it out anyway.'

'I'll get Paulo to look into it,' Donnelly assured him.

'Good. Dr Canning has the details and photographs.'

'I'll let Paulo know. And by the way, you look like shit.'

'Thanks,' Sean winced.

He watched the grinning Donnelly head into the main office in search of DC Zukov, then removed a small mirror from one of his desk drawers. Donnelly was right: he did look like shit – exhausted hollow eyes and unhealthy pale skin. He tossed the mirror back into the drawer and slammed it shut, looking across his desk at the piles of memos and reports that were rapidly accumulating. Could the one tiny piece of information that would turn the entire case be hiding in that mountain of paper, or in amongst the seemingly endless sea of information now stored on the inquiry's computer databases? He knew it was entirely possible, even probable, but he couldn't stomach the thought of sifting through any of it right now – the image of Samuel's tiny body embracing the little plush dinosaur haunted his consciousness and stopped him thinking straight or concentrating. He needed to get out – get out and do something, anything that could give him the insight he needed to find the man he hunted and find him quickly. Find him before he took another child, or took another life. He jumped to his feet, stuffed his coat pocket full of the things he needed and headed for the exit.

Less than an hour later Sean pulled up outside number 7 Courthope Road – the scene of the first abduction. He checked the area for any sign of the media and was relieved to see so far they were sticking to their promise to leave the victims' families alone, so long as the police gave them regular updates. But he was still pretty sure that as soon as he stepped from the car he'd fall into the frame of a long lens hiding behind a window or on a rooftop not too far away.

He dragged himself from the car and to the front door, remembering the first time he'd been here – the poisonous atmosphere of desperation and mistrust. After ringing the doorbell he stepped back, listening to the sounds coming from inside the house – normal sounds that masked the truth of what had happened here. A minute or so later he was relieved to see the door opened by one of his own – DC Maggie O'Neil, who was still acting as the Family Liaison Officer for the Bridgemans.

'Sir,' she said with surprise. 'I wasn't expecting a visit.'

'I wasn't expecting to make one,' he answered, stepping inside without waiting to be invited. 'How've they been doing?' he whispered.

'OK,' Maggie told him. 'Closer, since the DNA results showed the dad was also the biological father.'

'Wonderful,' Sean said sarcastically. 'He finally has proof the boy is his, only now he's gone. Where are they?'

'Kitchen – having dinner, or at least trying to.'

Sean waited for Maggie to lead the way, gritting his teeth at the thought of having to speak to the family again.

As they entered, Maggie told the Bridgemans, 'Sorry to disturb your dinner, but DI Corrigan's here to see you.'

The parents looked up at him with abject fear in their eyes while their daughter merely glanced at him and kept eating.

Celia Bridgeman began to rise from her chair, swallowing hard before speaking, convinced they would be her last words before finding out her son was dead – before her world stopped for ever. 'Has something happened? Have you found George?'

'No,' Sean answered quickly, understanding the terror his mere presence had caused. 'Nothing like that. We're still looking, and we'll keep looking till we do find him, I promise you.'

'Then why are you here?' Stuart Bridgeman asked, his eyes still distrustful of Sean, suspicious of his intentions despite the fact that his gut instinct told him Sean was their only real chance of seeing George alive again.

'Standard procedure,' Sean half lied. 'We find it's often useful to go over things again a few days after the initial incident. Sometimes the subconscious recalls things that seemed irrelevant at the time.'

'Anything,' Celia jumped in before her husband could speak. 'We're happy to assist with anything if it'll help get George back.'

Sean sat on the opposite side of the kitchen table and looked at the faces of the three family members before beginning the process of trying to unlock some buried nugget of information they probably wouldn't even know was there – praying for a shard of light to illuminate the way forward. 'I have to consider that George was initially targeted far more randomly than we first thought. It may have been something as simple as a brief encounter in the street, outside his school or in the park. You may have been followed home without knowing it – that's how they knew where he lived – nothing more complicated than that.'

'You mean a stranger?' Celia asked.

'Probably,' Sean answered.

'Which would make it even more difficult for you to find him, wouldn't it?' Her voice grew more alarmed as the realization sunk in. 'I mean, if it was someone connected to both families then it would only be a matter of time before you worked it out. But if it's a stranger, if George has been taken by a stranger, then you've got nothing, have you? Otherwise you wouldn't be here.'

'There are always plenty of lines of inquiry in an investigation like this,' Sean lied. 'This is just one more, so I need you to think – can you remember anyone, anyone at all, who may have approached you, no matter how inconsequential it felt at the time? Someone who just seemed a little bit off to you – who paid a bit more attention to George than the norm – no matter how friendly they appeared?'

Celia pinched her forehead between her index finger and thumb, shaking her head in concentration, before slumping in her chair. 'I've been trying to think of someone like this for days – ever since George was taken, but there isn't anyone. Nothing like that happened.'

'Try,' Sean urged her, attempting not to let his own frustration show. 'A bus or taxi driver – a waiter or barman?'

'No,' Celia insisted. 'Nothing.'

'Had you been anywhere with George, in the days before he went missing – the cinema, a play-barn, a library?'

'I don't know . . . an indoor play centre maybe.'

'Where?'

'The one over in Collingwood, a horrible place.'

'When?'

'I can't remember – maybe two, three days before he was taken.'

'Did anything happen – anything out of the ordinary?'

'No. I met some girlfriends from my old antenatal group. We had coffee, the kids played together and I went home.'

'Where else did you go?' Sean kept it up, praying he could break her down and shake loose anything that could be locked in her memory.

'I don't know – this café, that café, this shop, that shop. What does it matter – you'll never find him like this.'

'It could matter,' Sean insisted before she silenced the room and froze everyone inside it like statues.

'Is he going to kill him?' she asked coldly. 'Is that why you're really here – because you think he's going to kill George?'

'No,' Sean forced himself to say. 'No, I don't know that.'

'But you believe it, don't you? You believe it because he already has, hasn't he? He's already killed a child?' Sean felt his brain grind to a halt as her words cut deeply into him, paralysing any thought he had of talking his way around her questions and accusations. 'But not George,' she continued. 'If it had been George you would have had to tell us. Then it must be the little girl – Bailey.'

'No,' Sean admitted with a long sigh. 'Not Bailey.'

'Then who?'

'He took another child,' Sean explained, never breaking eye contact with Celia. 'Something appears to have gone wrong during the abduction and a boy was killed.'

'How?' Celia demanded.

'I can't tell you that.'

'How?' she repeated, her voice louder.

Sean sighed again. 'He was suffocated – we believe.' Celia sat motionless, her eyes unblinking.

'You said something went wrong,' Stuart Bridgeman reminded them. 'So it could have been an accident. It doesn't mean the same is going to happen to George.' He constantly looked back and forth between his wife and Sean, whose eyes had remained locked on each other. 'It was an accident, for God's sake.'

'Don't you understand?' Celia asked. 'He's killed now. He's killed a child, whether by accident or not. He tried to abduct another child and ended up killing them. He's even more desperate now and capable of anything – isn't that right, Inspector? And he still has George.'

'Well, if you think of anything,' Sean changed the subject, 'just let DC O'Neil know and she'll pass it on to me. I have to get back to the office and check a few things out. But listen,' he told them, 'we're doing everything we possibly can to find George and we won't stop until we do – I can promise you that much.'

'Find my boy,' Celia told him as the tears began to escape her eyes, her fists clenching until the knuckles turned white. 'I'm begging you, find my boy alive. Bring him home to me. You're our only hope.'

'I'll find him,' he tried to assure them while feeling like a liar. 'There's still time, I know there is.' He stood to let them know he was leaving. 'Mrs Bridgeman. Mr Bridgeman.' Finally he broke eye contact with Celia and made his way slowly from the kitchen, heading for the front door with Maggie close behind him. He waited until he was out the front door and standing on the steps before speaking. 'Keep an eye on them,' he told her. 'What they're going through must be hell. Mrs Bridgeman isn't the weeping, wailing type, but that doesn't mean she's not on the edge.'

'I'll look after them,' Maggie promised.

'Call me if they remember anything,' he told her, then he turned and headed down the steps towards his car, stopping only when he heard the heavy door close behind him.

He looked up at the clear darkness in the sky. Late afternoon had turned into early evening and the moon was already

382

full and low above London as another day all too quickly slipped past, and still the case wouldn't break. How much time had he wasted on Mark McKenzie and then Hannah Richmond, and all for nothing more than discovering what sort of person he wasn't looking for. 'Time. Time. Time. Time,' he muttered to himself as he climbed into his car, the thought of returning to his office both oppressive and depressing. There were no answers there, no clues hiding in amongst the piles of documents, paper or otherwise. Whatever the answer was to the riddle he was sure he hadn't found it yet and he was sure it wasn't back in his office – it was out here, on the streets of North London, at the scenes of the crimes, or in the mortuary. He either hadn't found it yet, or he had and had missed it. He pulled away from the kerb and headed towards Highgate.

13

Helen Varndell's frustration was growing into genuine anger as she stormed around her converted mews home in Mornington Crescent, just south of Camden Town. She swept up the stairs feeling ever more agitated and into the bedroom of her five-year-old daughter who waited, sobbing quietly in her bed. 'Damn it, Vicky, where did you leave the bloody thing?' The overhead light in the child's room made Helen's attractive but slightly stern-looking face seem harsher than ever, her short, blonde hair cut well above the slim neck that flowed gracefully into her broad shoulders and tall, slender body. She stood with her hands on her hips staring down at her crying daughter.

'I don't know,' the little girl answered.

'Well when was the last time you had her?'

'This morning, before school.'

'And you haven't seen her since?'

'No. Maybe Kathy took her,' she offered, referring to her three-year-old sister.

'Kathy's already asleep,' her mother explained. 'I'm not going to wake her up looking around her room for Polly.'

'But I can't sleep without Polly,' Vicky pleaded.

The shadow of her father appeared in the frame of the doorway, shorter than his wife at only five foot six. 'What's with all the noise?' he demanded. 'I'm trying to work.'

'Vicky can't find Polly and it's her bedtime,' his wife explained.

'Not again,' Seth Varndell declared, sounding exasperated. 'Well, it's too late to look for her now. I'm sure Polly's just gone for a sleep-over party with all her rag-dolly friends and she'll be back in the morning. Now pick another dolly to cuddle tonight and Polly will be back tomorrow.'

'No. I want Polly,' the little girl wailed.

Seth sighed and stood with his legs apart and his hands on his hips, studying the distressed infant he was usually so proud to call his daughter. 'Are you sure you've looked everywhere?' he asked his wife in desperation.

'Yes, Seth,' she snapped back. 'I've looked bloody everywhere.'

'But she can't sleep without Polly.'

'Well, she's going to have to,' Helen told him and bent over her daughter, kissing her on the forehead and flicking the night-lamp on. 'Go to sleep now,' she ordered. 'We'll find Polly in the morning, but it's a school day tomorrow so you need to get to sleep.' With that she swept out of the room, turning the overhead light off as she went, leaving her husband and daughter alone in the pale glow.

'Get to sleep, sweetie,' Seth told the still tearful child. 'I'll keep looking for Polly, and if I find her I'll tuck her up in bed with you once you're asleep, OK?'

'But I love Polly,' was all the little girl could say, her pain a knife straight into his heart.

'I know, sweetie. I know,' he told her as he backed out of the room and closed the door until it was slightly ajar, before heading downstairs to begin his impossible search for the rag-doll.

The things he needed for the task that lay ahead were spread neatly on the desk in front of him, lined up like surgical instruments. He had asked for guidance and it had been given – it was God's will. One by one he carefully slipped the miniature tools into their suede roll-up case, wrapping them securely before placing them in his small holdall. Next he checked the head-torch was working correctly and tucked it in the bag with the tools. Finally he lifted the thing the little girl loved so much, looking down on it as it lay limp in his hand, causing images of Samuel Hargrave's still body to rush into his mind, the grief and sadness instantly making his head throb.

He stuffed the special thing into the bag as he talked quietly to himself. 'God forgive me,' he pleaded, but no sooner had he spoken than his wife's voice echoed inside his head, catching him by surprise, making him grab at his fluttering chest. *You have done nothing that you need ask God to forgive. You are doing his bidding*, she reminded him. 'But I can still see the boy,' he told her, his voice shaking with fright. 'I can still see his dead eyes, looking at me. I can still see the fear in his eyes.' *Even when walking through the dark valley of death I will not be afraid, for you are close beside me, guarding, guiding all the way*. 'What does that mean?' he begged her to take his doubt and confusion away. *It means maybe the boy lacked faith – lacked belief. He feared meeting the Lord when he should have been rejoicing.* 'So?' *So maybe he wasn't worthy.* 'I don't understand.' *Maybe he deserved to die.* 'But he was just a boy – how could he deserve to die?' *The servants of darkness are everywhere – trying to betray you.* 'Betray me?' *The Lord took him to save you, so you can save those worthy of saving.* 'But what if others try to betray me?' he asked his dead wife, his eyes darting around the room suspiciously before involuntarily looking up to the ceiling and bedroom above it where the two children slept silently. *Who?* 'The girl can be . . . difficult. Ungrateful.' *Then the Lord will punish her.* 'How?' *He will guide your hand, as he did before. Ours is not to question why, but to trust in his divine judgement. The Lord will guide your hands.* 'But she's just a child. It'll take time for her to change, that's all.' *Then everything will be fine.*

His wife's voice fell silent, leaving him standing alone in the study, listening for its return – listening for sounds of the children, just as he'd done an hour earlier, standing with his ear pressed to their bedroom door, listening to them crying themselves to sleep, each calling for their mother through their quiet, mournful sobbing. He'd listened until finally they had fallen silent, sneaking back into the room to check they were asleep. He looked down on the tiny shapes under their blankets and sheets, watching their chests gently rise and fall to assure himself he hadn't done anything during one of his moments of blackness. He shook the memory away with a jolt of his head and packed the last few things he needed, then sat at the old desk chair where he would wait for hours, the holdall on his lap, before heading into the night. His voice was barely audible as he repeated the same line over and over: 'Because the Lord is my shepherd, I have everything I need. Because the Lord is my shepherd, I have everything I need . . .'

Sean sat alone in his office, having returned from revisiting the three abduction scenes, although the home of George Bridgeman was the only one he'd been inside. He'd sat and stared at the victims' houses, looking for some similarity between them, but he could find none other than that they were all reasonably large family houses. He'd walked the leafy affluent streets, but nothing new leapt out at him. In the end he had driven away from the final scene, the home of Samuel Hargrave, frustrated and angry with himself. The thought of going home, so far from the scenes, so far from the missing children, so far from the man he sought, was unbearable.

He looked into the half-empty main office, where detectives either hammered away at computer keyboards or talked urgently into phones, chasing down leads and possible witnesses. The rest of the team were out, following his instructions to repeat door-to-door inquiries, this time asking about any overnight alarm activations. They, like Sean, knew it was only clutching at straws, but they'd do it anyway. They'd all worked on cases before where freakish good luck had brought an investigation to a swift and satisfactory conclusion.

Sally was keeping everybody hard at it, wandering from detective to detective, offering words of advice and instructions, but Donnelly was nowhere to be seen.

I need to try something, Sean told himself, *something we haven't done yet – something to shake this bastard out of his tree – knock him out of his comfort zone. So what have we got?* He allowed himself to think for a moment, concentrating on the things he believed he could all but guarantee. *All the victims were taken from within a few miles of each other, so either you know this area well because you visit it a lot or you were brought up there, or you still live there – hiding right in the middle of the place where we're looking hardest – looking, but not seeing.* He tapped his pen on the open page of his journal before beginning to write down his thoughts and ideas. *We start searching houses – all of them, starting with the ones closest to the scenes, and spread outwards. Do it as overtly as possible – let the world see what we're doing. We don't have time to get hundreds, thousands of search warrants – wouldn't get them anyway – but we don't need them. As soon as the occupiers know what we're looking for, they'll let us do it anyway. Those who don't become suspects. Let's light a fire under this scorpion and get him running in circles instead of us.*

He looked out into the main office and saw the pictures of the three missing children stuck to one of the many whiteboards. *What do you have in common? You don't look the same. You're not the same age and you're not all the same gender. All your families are wealthy beyond most people's imagination, but what does that mean – why's that relevant?* He rocked back in his chair while he reviewed everything he'd learned about the families – what he had been told and what he had seen for himself. *All the families employed nannies or au pairs, even those where the mother wasn't working. Nannies and au pairs to take the children to and from school, to look after them at weekends and during the holidays – to cook for them, dress them, bathe them, put them to bed? But what does any of this have to do with you? Did you know that the parents had entrusted their children's upbringing to someone else?* He bit hard enough on his bottom lip to make it bleed, but didn't even notice. *Of course you did. You knew it all – knew everything you needed to know about these families. Was that it – was that the flame that drew you? The fact the parents didn't seem to care – didn't seem to . . . to love them – not like you would. You always choose families that had more than one child because you wanted to leave them with at least one – one who now you've taught them a lesson you believe they'll love in the way they should, in the way that's acceptable to you . . .*

Sean rolled his head and cracked the stiffness out of his neck, trying to organize his random thoughts, convinced he was right. But still something wasn't making sense. He closed his eyes and pinched his temples between the fingertips of both hands, elbows resting on his desk. *I know you're a man – the Hargraves heard a man's voice. But these thoughts you have, these . . . judgements, are more the thoughts and judgements of a woman. . .* Again he paused for a few seconds. *You're not like Mark McKenzie and you're not like Hannah Richmond, so what are you? Both? Something in between? You take the children because a woman tells you to? You snatch them and take them home to your loving wife to raise as your own?* His eyes opened as he suddenly stood and almost knocked over his chair, the frustration enough to make him want to sweep everything from his desk. 'No,' he told himself. 'No. That's wrong. There's no woman waiting for you to bring them to her. Your motivation is female, yet your actions are male. Taking the body to a cemetery, leaving it on the grave of a war hero and a cop were the actions of a man. Why can't I see? Why can't I understand you?'

The words of the priest began to snake around his mind, drowning out everything else: *We look, but we can't see. We look, but we can't see.*

He could feel them as soon as he entered the house – waiting upstairs for him to come while he stood feeling the warmth of the house chasing the chill from his muscles. He remembered the strange layout of the house, with its living room, kitchen and main bathroom all on the ground level where he was now. Two short flights of steep, narrow stairs led to the second floor and the bedroom of the little girl he'd come take. But now he was here, safely inside the silent, sleeping house, his legs refused to move. Doubts and fears swept through his mind, the harrowing memory of Samuel's lifeless body lying across his desk robbing him of the will to continue, evaporating his strength.

The pain in his head returned in a rush as he dropped on to one knee. 'God give me strength,' he begged in a whisper. 'The Lord is my shepherd. He will answer my prayers and offer me guidance.' He squeezed his eyes shut and clamped his head between the palms of his hands, waiting for God to speak to him. But there was only darkness. 'Iris,' he pleaded to his dead wife. 'The Lord has forsaken me. He has abandoned me.' *No*, she answered, making his eyes flash open. *He is with you now – he is always with you, and so am I, my love*. 'But he doesn't speak to me. He doesn't tell me what I should do,' he whispered. *He speaks through me. He tells me what to tell you*. 'But what if he's wrong? What if he's wrong about the parents? What if we're taking children from parents who love them?' His wife's usually calm voice grew angry, like the time they'd had *that* argument, when they were told they'd never have children. When she'd blamed him and called him all those terrible names. *Our God is a vengeful god*, she warned him, *and his word is not to be questioned by man, or they will feel his wrath*. 'I'm sorry,' he implored her, on both knees now, his voice growing dangerously loud in the darkness. 'I'm a weak man, and my faith grows weak inside me.' *You must take the girl. God wills it*. 'I can't,' he told her. 'No more. I won't do it any more.' *God wills it*. 'No more.' *God wills it*. 'Please. No more. Leave me alone. I won't take the girl.' *Our God is a vengeful god*. 'No.' *They will feel his wrath*. 'Please.' *You must save her from the darkness*, his wife's tone softened. 'What?' *Only you can save her from the darkness*. 'The darkness?' *Yes. Only you can save her. You must take her*. 'I'm saving her?' *Yes. Yes. Only you can save her. If you leave her here, the darkness will take her*. 'No. No. The darkness can't have her. I won't let the darkness take her.' He felt the strength seeping back into his body and mind. *Then save her. Go to her and save her*.

He hauled himself back to his feet and wiped the tears from his face with his gloved hands, placing one foot on the first stair. *God has made you strong again*. 'God give me strength.' *God will guide you*. 'The Lord is my shepherd.' *He will protect you*. 'He gives me new strength. He helps me to do what honours him most.' His other foot moved to the next step and pushed him forward, upwards towards the sleeping girl, his wife's voice fading as she repeated her last words over and over: *Let the little children come to me, and do not hinder them, for the kingdom of heaven belongs to such as these.*

He climbed the first flight of stairs and reached the floor where he knew the parents' bedroom was, drifting past it silently, staying to the right side where he knew the floor-boards were less worn and made no noise. He tried to ignore the scents of the sleeping man and woman, blanking them out of his mind, convincing himself that at this moment in time they didn't exist. He was afraid his fragile resolve might be affected if he started to feel sympathy towards them. Over and over he reminded himself that they'd had their chance, been given the gift he and his wife never had, and that they had chosen to hand the child to the care of strangers, passing her from one carer to the next: nannies, au pairs, child-minders, so they could pursue their careers and petty pastimes – to live their lives as if they'd never been blessed with children at all. No. They'd had their chance. She was a child of God and needed to be treated as one. He must stay strong – for her sake.

As if coming out of a deep daydream he suddenly found himself standing outside the little girl's bedroom, a moment of panic spreading in his chest as he tried to remember how he'd got there. He remembered being outside the parents' room and now he was here, looking at the pale light from a child's night-lamp seeping through the slightly ajar door. The moments of blackness were becoming increasingly frequent, and thoughts of what he might have done during them had grown increasingly troubling since he'd accidentally killed the boy. He looked at his trembling hands and listened to the sounds of the house, trying to detect any change in atmosphere, any sign that something terrible might have happened during the blackness, but he felt nothing.

'The Lord is my shepherd,' he whispered as he pushed the door open slowly, inch by inch, allowing the light from within to gradually intrude into the darkness of the hallway, casting a shadow behind him that crept across the floor and climbed the wall opposite – grey tendrils creeping through the gaps in the door opposite that led to the younger sister of the one he'd come to save – to give a better life to – until finally the door was all but fully open and he could see clearly inside, the pale light more than enough for eyes that had already adjusted to the dark. He stood frozen, unable to cross the threshold into her room. The scent of her rushed his senses, making him fill his lungs through his nose until he felt his chest would rupture. He could feel her warmth, but the beauty of her life made him stall – begin to lose faith. The doubts urged him to run from the house and keep running to somewhere far, far away where the voices couldn't find him. But in his soul he knew there was no such place. The voices would always find him. they were a part of him.

He crouched down and placed his bag carefully on the floor and unzipped it with only the faintest sound, both his hands sliding slowly inside before reappearing holding the small, inanimate thing that he knew would be so special to the girl that he would instantly have her trust. He held it as if it was a new-born life. She wanted it more than almost anything in the world and only he could make that happen. That knowledge gave him strength – the strength to stand, the special thing in one hand, the bag in the other, and to

393

walk into the room, moving closer and closer to the tiny figure huddled under the duvet.

The next thing he knew he was standing at her bedside, looming over her like a malevolent cloud, still clutching the special thing.

'The Lord is my shepherd,' he whispered softly as he crouched at the little girl's bedside, placing the bag on the floor as he held the special thing towards her face – her beautiful porcelain face, pale blue in the night light, eyes still closed peacefully as she breathed softly through her slightly pursed lips. He could just make out the bottom of her two front teeth. 'Let the children come to him and do not hinder them, for to such belongs the kingdom of heaven.' Her long eyelashes began to flicker, her lips parted further as she drew a waking breath. 'Victoria – time to wake up, Victoria,' he gently told her, brushing blonde curls from her face as he spoke, her innocent beauty tearing at his chest, the pressure inside his head becoming almost unbearable as he struggled to suppress the growing dam of tears he felt swelling behind his eyes. His strength and belief deserted him, and he momentarily closed his eyes, bracing himself to rise and flee from the room before the voices could come and persuade him otherwise. But when he opened them again he saw that her penetrating green eyes were now wide open, staring in disbelief, her pink lips spreading into a wide smile as she was suddenly completely awake.

'Polly,' she called out loudly enough to be heard beyond the bedroom, replacing his doubts with fear and panic. 'Where have you been, you naughty dolly?'

'Sssh,' he tried to hush her, watching her eyes focus beyond the rag-doll and on to him for the first time. 'We need to be very quiet now. We could get in trouble if we wake anyone else up.'

'You found Polly,' she told him excitedly with no fear or apprehension.

'Yes, and I brought her back to you. But we need to be quiet now, or they may take Polly away again.'

'Who? Who wants to take her away again?'

'Bad people,' he lied to her. 'People who don't understand things.'

'What things?'

'Just things,' he answered, his fear subsiding.

'But where has Polly been? Mummy and Daddy looked everywhere for her, but they couldn't find her.'

'Ahh, she's been to a very special place. A place where only the best toys ever get to go, and where only the best boys and girls ever get to see.'

'How do you know?' she asked, her face the picture of childish confusion and intrigue.

'Because I live there. I live there with all the special things and all the special boys and girls.'

'Is it a magic place?'

'The most magical,' he told her, choking back his tears. 'The most magical place you've ever seen.'

'Can I see it?'

'No,' he answered sadly. 'I should love to show you, but I think it's best you stay here with your family.'

'But I want to see it. I want you to show me.'

'Really?' he questioned, confused and disorientated by the child's insistence.

'Can I bring Polly?' the little girl asked.

'I think . . . I think Polly would rather stay here with all her friends.'

'No,' the little girl told him firmly. 'Polly wants to go back to the magic world. She doesn't like the other dolls here; they're mean to her.'

'Oh,' he queried. 'Why are they mean to her?'

'Because she's my favourite. They're jealous. Dolls are like people: sometimes they just like being mean.'

He looked at the door, trying to force himself away from her bedside without speaking with her any more, but she enchanted him. 'Are . . . is someone being mean to you?' he asked, afraid of what the answer may be. 'Is someone . . . hurting you?'

'No,' she answered almost flippantly, looking at Polly the whole time. 'Not hurting me, but they are mean to me.'

'Who?' he asked urgently.

'The children at my school. Mummy says they're mean to me because they must be jealous of me, but she says I have to stay there because she's too busy to look after me. She has to work very hard, so I have to go to the school.'

God has given you a sign, his wife's voice told him, spinning his mind into ever-deeper confusion. *You must believe – the child wants you to take her, wants you to save her. It is God's will.* 'No,' he argued. 'No more. Enough. I won't take her.' He closed his eyes tight trying to resist the voice – to silence his dead wife – until a tiny warm hand rested on his forearm and eased them open again.

'Who are you talking to?'

'No one,' he lied. 'I was just remembering something – someone I used to know.'

'You look really sad,' she told him. 'I think you must be very lonely. If me and Polly come with you then you won't be sad any more and neither will me or Polly.'

The girl is a sign – a sign that what you are doing is right, is God's will. He brushed the tears from his eyes and quietly coughed his throat clear. *You must do as God wills you to do – you must.*

'Very well,' he surrendered. 'You can come with me – come with me to somewhere where we'll never be treated badly. Somewhere no one will ever be mean to us again.

You and I, and the other children will all go together – to where there are green pastures and quiet streams – where only the righteous and the innocent are allowed – to live in eternal peace together. Would you like that, Victoria?'

'Can Polly come too?'

'Yes. Polly too.'

'And Mummy and Daddy, and Katherine?'

'Well, maybe one day they'll meet us there, but not just yet, I don't think. Not just yet.'

14

He stood in the corner, unable to move – unable even to look away as the dark silhouette of the man grew closer and closer to the boy sitting on the edge of the bed. He could hear the man's whispers of encouragement, although he couldn't make out exactly what he was saying. He had to watch helplessly as the faceless man sat next to the boy, his attempts to cry out, to warn the boy to run, trapped in his throat, as the shadow man started to gently stroke the boy's hair. He knew what was about to happen and desperately tried to scream out loud as the hand suddenly gripped the boy tightly by the scruff of his neck and bent him painfully backwards, twisting him so he could now see his face – his own face, when he was a boy. The man's features became clear too and he recognized his father, smiling, but snarling at the same time. Even in the dream Sean could smell the alcohol on his father's breath as his face moved closer and closer to the boy that Sean used to be. But he still couldn't move or even call out, despite knowing the horror of what was about to happen.

With every ounce of strength he could summon he managed to force his eyes shut, but he couldn't shut out his father's threats and the boy's painful, tearful pleas, sounds that stirred the deep rage that lurked in his very being, the rage that always sought to escape, the rage gave him strength – strength to open his eyes and scream *No*. But the man had already turned back into a faceless phantom and the boy was now sitting up in the bed, the sheets pulled up to his waist, his face impossible to recognize.

He watched as the phantom offered his hand to the boy – a hand the boy accepted, slipping from the bed and walking slowly and silently towards the bedroom door. *Don't go with him*, Sean begged the boy, but he didn't seem to hear him. *Please don't go with him*, he called out louder, but still the figures ignored him. *Please, stay here with me. I can protect you. I promise you'll be safe. Don't go.* The boy and the man suddenly stopped, the boy turning slowly towards him, making Sean gasp with relief and start to smile, until the boy's face began to clear and become recognizable. It was the face of Samuel Hargrave, but not as he'd been when he was alive – it was his face from the mortuary – pale white skin and blue lips, eyes almost completely closed – the dead, unmoving face looking straight at him, ripping away all hope. *I'm sorry*, Sean told him. *I'm sorry*. The boy turned away and was led from the bedroom by the man.

With a jolt Sean woke from the nightmare in the same position he'd fallen asleep, with his head resting on his folded arms across his desk. He straightened carefully, worried his compromised sleeping position would cause a muscle to pull or a joint to lock. Once he was sure nothing was about to rupture in his body, he stretched away as much stiffness as he could and stood gingerly, waiting for the dizziness to subside before deciding on his next move. It dawned on him that he probably smelled and looked as rough as he felt, so he grabbed a clean shirt he kept hanging on the back of his door and an emergency wash kit he kept in his drawer, then headed for the gym where he knew he'd find a shower.

Sean's tiredness kept him in a dream-like state as he walked the almost deserted corridors of the Yard, passing only the occasional bleary-eyed detective who'd also been trapped overnight by some investigation and looked as exhausted and haunted as he felt. After he'd showered and dressed, Sean headed into the streets outside in search of decent coffee and fresh air. This early in the morning he found both, even in Victoria, but the build up of traffic, cars, taxis and double-decker buses would soon turn the air foul.

He sat in the window of Starbucks, staring at the road outside and trying to clear his mind while he waited for it to be a respectable enough hour to call Kate. As he wondered whether he could stomach anything to eat yet his phone began to chirp and vibrate. He snatched it up before any of the other early morning customers were disturbed, the caller ID telling him who it was.

'Sally,' he answered.

'Guv'nor,' she acknowledged. 'You close by?'

'Close enough: Starbucks, over the road. Trouble?'

'ACC Addis is in your office with a face like a volcano. Won't say what he wants, just that he's waiting for you.'

'Why doesn't he just call me?'

'I don't know. Says he'd rather wait to see you in person.'

'Fuck,' he told her. 'All right. Get down to SO10 on the fifth floor – tell them I sent you and you need to borrow a phone. They'll look after you and they'll keep it quiet too. Start making phone calls and try and find out what the fuck's happened. Forewarned is forearmed. Don't let him see you leave. Call me when you find something.'

'And you?'

'I'm already on my way back,' he answered, 'but call me the minute you have news.'

He took his time gathering his things and thoughts, strolling from the café and across the now treacherous road, along the street and through the revolving security doors at the Yard, flashing his warrant card as he passed the security scanners. A few minutes later he entered the main office and walked as casually as he could to where Addis stood like a heron waiting to strike at a fish. Sean tried to act as surprised as he could to find him in his office.

'Morning, sir,' he greeted him, pausing to empty his pockets and hang up his coat before sitting behind his desk, further firing the fury in the Assistant Commissioner's eyes. 'Is there something I can help you with?'

'I saw DS Jones leaving the room a few minutes ago,' Addis began. 'I assume she's gone to do your bidding?'

Sean shrugged. 'I don't know what you mean.'

'Oh, I'm sure you do,' Addis told him, tapping the file he held across his chest with his thumb. 'But let me save her the bother. This . . . this, Inspector, is why I'm here.' He tossed the pink file marked *Confidential* on to Sean's desk.

Sean tentatively opened it, holding his breath. The first thing he saw was a MISPER report with the photograph of a smiling little girl attached to it with a paperclip.

'Fuck,' Sean barely whispered, but Addis heard him clearly enough.

'Fuck indeed, Inspector. More precisely, what the *fuck* is happening with this investigation? Another child taken – Victoria Varndell, five years old, snatched from her home in Mornington Crescent . . .'

Sean ignored the vitriolic tone, tuning out Addis's presence as he speed-read the file. He didn't know the area, but was pretty sure it was reasonably close to the other sites.

'. . . Four children taken – one killed, for Christ's sake – and the media all over it, all over us . . .'

Taken in the middle of the night – no sign of forced entry and nobody heard anything, except for the mother, who now thinks she may have heard whispering voices, but she thought she'd just been dreaming.

'. . . made any progress at all? Do we have anything for those media bastards, or are you still flying blind, blundering . . .'

The family, seemingly wealthy, live in a converted mews. Father a merchant banker, mother a fashion designer with her own label.

'. . . brought you here to solve high-profile cases quickly, not to make us look like incompetent, bungling idiots. I was told, wrongly as it turns out, that you were one of the best in the business. That you could make the connections . . .'

There was another child in the house at the time – the missing girl's three-year-old sister, Katherine, who doesn't appear to have been touched.

'. . . state of you, and your office: a bloody mess, like this investigation. And look at the state of your team: they look like shit. They're a disgrace. You're a . . .'

The house was alarmed, but the alarm wasn't activated at night for fear of the children setting it off if they went wandering.

'. . . sorry, Inspector Corrigan, but I'm going to have to remove you from the investigation, effective immediately. The people of London want to see the police taking action. Replacing you with someone more suited to this investigation will hopefully at the very least buy us time.'

Sean finally looked up from the file, not having heard a word Addis had said. Something told him he needed to get to the scene as fast as he could – that the answers were there. He needed to see it while he was still in a semi-exhausted, dreamlike state – while his mind was too tired to be cluttered with the irrelevant vines that clung to all major investigations, and too tired to be even slightly affected by Addis's sermon.

'It'll be done quietly,' Addis continued, 'you have my word on that. As soon as it can be arranged you'll be moved back to a borough that'll suit where you live. You should be grateful for the chance to work some sensible hours and see a bit more of your family.'

Sean stood and began to pull his coat on, still doing his best to ignore Addis, although he'd heard his last words.

'Where the hell do you think you're going?' Addis demanded.

'Out,' Sean replied without emotion.

'Out? Out where?'

'To clear my head,' Sean lied. 'If I'm not needed here any more, I might as well be somewhere else. You'll have my Handover Report by the end of the day.'

'Fine,' Addis stuttered as Sean brushed past him on his way out of the office. 'And I'll need you to clear your desk and vacate by tonight. Take some gardening leave until I find you a new posting.'

Sean stopped directly in front of him and fixed him with his cold, pale blue eyes. 'Before I go, tell me one thing – were you ever a cop – a real cop?'

There was a slight pause before Addis answered, his eyes narrowing menacingly. 'Once,' he answered. 'A long time ago. Can't say I liked it very much.'

'That's what I thought,' Sean told him, the disgust on his face barely disguised as he headed for the exit.

He would usually have been up by now, showered, shaved and dressed just as always, but this morning the pain in his head was debilitating, keeping him virtually paralysed in his bed, the usually neat sheets crumpled around his writhing limbs as his head twisted from side to side, a permanent grimace of agony etched into his grey, sweat-coated face. 'Make the pain stop,' he begged. 'Please make the pain stop.' But it only grew more intense. He jolted under its intensity, struggling to control his bladder and bowels.

All the while he could hear the pounding of the children's feet on the ceiling as they ran around in the room above. Their voices penetrated his pain as they chattered and laughed – conspiratorial voices mocking him, mocking his kindness. 'Please, tell me what to do. Help me know what to do. I don't know what to do,' he panted, his fingers clawing at the sheets, but the voices had abandoned him, leaving him nothing but pain and confusion. 'Dear God, help me. The Lord is my shepherd.' Even his prayers went unanswered. 'Why have you betrayed me – in my time of need?' He braced himself against the pain and rolled on to his side, shuffling forward, eyes still tightly closed, until he felt his feet hanging over the edge of the bed. 'God give me strength,' he pleaded. He pushed himself from the bed, his knees landing hard as he crashed to the floor, his upper body slumped over the bed. 'Have I not done everything you've asked of me? Why do you punish me? Tell me why.'

His eyes began to flicker open, the weak morning light seeping through the curtains serving to increase the hammering inside his head. Eventually he was able to turn his head and look up towards the footsteps pounding on the ceiling above. 'Have I made a mistake? Have I not chosen carefully enough? Is one of them a Judas?' His narrowed eyes slid from side to side, old, familiar feelings of paranoia spreading like creeping, strangulating vines through the roots of his mind. 'Is it the girl?' he asked. 'The one who will never do as she is told?' The pain faded as his delusions took hold, helping him grow stronger and stronger.

'I understand,' he told the voices crowding inside his head. 'I hear you,' he assured them as he pulled himself from the floor and tentatively stood without holding, his pyjamas clinging to his body, damp with sweat. Once he was sure his legs could support his body he began to head towards the bedroom door – slowly at first, but as the pain continued to subside and his strength returned, his shuffle turned into an unsteady walk and then into a purposeful, steady stride.

He walked into the hallway and stared up the stairs as he began to recite from Christ's sermon on the mount. 'And if thy right hand offend thee, cut it off and cast it from thee.' The words made it clear to him what he needed to do next. He placed a foot on the first stair and began to climb. 'For it is profitable that one of thy members should perish, and not that thy whole body should be cast into hell.'

The door was opened by a tall, slim, flat-chested woman in her mid-thirties wearing a two-piece grey suit, white blouse and long, straight brown hair. Sean immediately recognized her as one of his own. She looked him up and down suspiciously before speaking, making him wonder for a second whether Addis had warned her to expect him and prevent him entering the scene. 'Can I help you?' she asked sternly.

He tugged his warrant card from his coat pocket and let it fall open for her to see. 'DI Corrigan. Special Investigations Unit.'

Her face visibly relaxed. 'Thank God for that,' she whispered. 'Thought you were a bloody reporter. I was told they might come creeping around.'

'And you are . . .?' Sean asked with a false smile.

'Sorry,' she apologized, holding out her hand. 'DC

Amanda Haitink, local CID – Sapphire Unit, to be more precise. I was briefed to stay with the family till someone from Special Investigations got here, and to keep an eye out for reporters.'

'It's a little early for reporters,' he reassured her. 'No one knows about this yet, and that's the way we need to keep it – for now.'

'I understand,' she agreed, still guarding the entrance to the house. 'Sorry,' she said, finally standing aside. 'I suppose you want to come in.'

He walked past Haitink and into the hallway, leaving her to close the door. The inside of the converted stable-block was dark and quiet, the atmosphere oppressive.

He quickly looked around and found his bearings. It was a large and luxurious home, the old features of the building perfectly blended with the contemporary interior design. Any pleasure he might have taken in the beauty of his surroundings had already been crushed by the presence he had sensed as soon as he entered the house. He knew the man he hunted had been here: the fact the family were obviously wealthy, the age of the missing child, the time and method of abduction, the fact there was another child left at the house – it all led him to the same conclusion. But aside from the logical arguments linking this case to the others, for the first time he could *feel* the man's presence. His exhaustion, his conversation with the priest and Addis leaving him nothing to lose had at last freed his mind from the confusing clutter. He knew beyond doubt that there was something here, at this scene; something crucial that would finally lead him to the man he'd been so fruitlessly hunting. He could feel it with such certainty that his heart-rate began to rise and stomach tighten. Now all he had to do was find it, and find it before Addis had a moment of clarity and realized that he wasn't about to just walk away from his quarry and three missing children, not when he knew he was still their best chance.

'Any idea how they make their money?' he asked, still looking for any link between the families.

'He's an investment banker in the City, but apart from that he seems all right, and she owns and runs a clothing boutique or something,' Haitink explained.

'Where are they now?'

Haitink grimaced and kept her voice low. 'Dad's in the kitchen at the moment, although he can't sit still: keeps walking from room to room. Understandable, really. He's not too enamoured with the police right now – he knows all about the other abductions, wants to know how we could have let this happen.'

'I'll talk to him,' Sean promised. 'And the mother?'

'Not doing too good. I've tried to talk to her – just sit with her – but she wants to be on her own. Won't even talk to her husband.'

'Where is she now?'

'The missing girl's bedroom.' Sean fired her a look of concern, and she knew why. 'I know – I should have preserved it for Forensics, but . . . I just didn't have the heart. If you'd seen her . . .'

'It's all right,' Sean stopped her. 'I understand. Besides, she must have been in the room a thousand times: she won't affect its forensic state much now.'

'Thousands of times?' Haitink questioned. 'I don't think so. They only moved here a few weeks ago.'

Sean almost smiled at his own forgetfulness. 'Of course,' he told her. 'Of course they did.'

'Does that mean something?' Haitink asked.

'Only one man can tell us that for sure,' he answered.

'And who would that be?'

'The man who's taking them.'

407

Haitink studied him for a while before speaking again. 'Kitchen's through here,' she told him and headed towards it knowing Sean would follow.

As soon as they entered Seth Varndell rounded on them. 'Who are you?' he demanded, looking at Sean.

'DI Sean Corrigan – Special Investigations Unit. It's my job to find your daughter,' he told him, trying not to think of Addis and what he'd do if he knew Sean was here now.

'Then maybe you can start by telling me what the hell's going on?' Varndell's short, stocky frame was taut with tension, his almost invisible spectacles magnifying terrified eyes. 'We reported Victoria missing hours ago and nothing seems to have happened. Where are the forensic people? Why aren't the streets full of cops searching for her? And what about search dogs and helicopters? Why isn't anything happening?'

'That all takes time to organize,' Sean tried to explain, 'but it will all be done, trust me.'

'Time to organize,' Varndell mocked. 'No wonder you haven't caught him yet. Why's he doing this? Is he some sort of pervert, or has he got a grudge against people working in the City? Is this a revenge attack? How could you let him do this?'

Sean fought hard to resist the temptation to bite back. 'Unfortunately these abductions aren't the only bad thing happening in London right now and I don't have a limitless supply of people, but I can assure you we're putting as many resources as we possibly can into finding the man responsible, and getting the children back safely.'

'Safely?' Varndell questioned. 'Safely? Isn't it already too late for one of the children? I haven't just arrived from another planet,' he continued. 'I saw it on the news last night. You found a boy in Highgate Cemetery – right? Dead – and you think he was taken by the same man who's—'

He suddenly stopped himself, his hands searching for something to support him as his legs suddenly could no longer bear his weight. Sean sprang forward and managed to get both arms around Varndell's chest and manoeuvre him into one of the chairs at the kitchen table.

'You all right?' Sean asked with genuine sympathy.

'Yes,' Varndell answered, but he looked deathly pale and clammy. 'Thank you, and I'm sorry – I just can't believe this is really happening – not to us.'

'I understand,' Sean told him, still checking for signs that Varndell wasn't about to faint. 'Have you eaten anything, or had a drink?'

'No,' he admitted.

'You need to try,' Sean insisted. 'DC Haitink here will fix you something – a cup of sweet tea at least.' Sean looked to her for backup.

'Of course I will,' she told Varndell pleasantly. 'The DI's right – you need to take care of yourself if you're to help us find Victoria.'

'I'll try,' Varndell promised.

'Good.' Sean patted the man's shoulder. 'And while you do that, I need to speak with your wife.'

'Helen?' he asked, filling his lungs to combat the dizziness. 'Good luck there, Inspector. She doesn't seem to want to speak to anyone at the moment – not yet, anyway. Maybe you could give her a little time?'

'Sorry,' Sean explained. 'Time is one thing I don't have.'

'In that case you'll find her in Victoria's bedroom – on the second floor.'

Sean immediately headed for the stairs, telling Haitink: 'I'll be back in a few minutes.' She gave a single nod before turning her attention to Varndell.

'OK, Mr Varndell, where d'you keep the tea and sugar?' Sean heard her asking as he made his way up the steep staircase towards the bedroom where hours before Victoria Varndell had been sleeping only a matter of feet from her parents.

'There's something here,' Sean whispered to himself as he climbed the stairs. 'Something here for me to find, but I need to see, not just look. All I've been doing is looking, but now I need to see – need to see like you see. You left something for me at George Bridgeman's house, didn't you? But I didn't see it. I looked, but I didn't see it. And you left something for me at Bailey Fellowes' house too, but I didn't see that either. So you left Samuel Hargrave in the cemetery for me so I would see what you are.' He climbed the remaining stairs in silence until he reached the almost fully closed door of Victoria's bedroom, the quiet crying inside telling him he was in the right place. He knocked on the frame and waited, but Helen Varndell either hadn't heard or she wasn't ready to share her pain. Sean knocked again, easing the door open when he received no reply, peering inside where he could see Helen Varndell sitting on the end of the bed with her back to him, surrounded by dolls and soft toys, her body as still as if she'd been frozen in stone, her anguished yet gentle sobbing continuing unabated.

'Mrs Varndell,' Sean almost whispered, but she didn't respond. 'Mrs Varndell,' he persisted, louder this time, slowly entering the room, just as *he* had. He was sure that if Mrs Varndell hadn't been in the room he could have smelt the scent of desperation the man he hunted had left behind, but as it was he couldn't be sure it didn't belong to the mother. 'Mrs Varndell. I'm sorry to disturb you, but I'm Detective Inspector Sean Corrigan. I need to speak with you, if I can.'

Still she didn't respond. He walked deeper into the room until he was level with her. 'I understand you want to be alone, I would too, but I have to speak to you. I need to know what happened here.'

Her head snapped towards him, almost making him jump.

'Someone took my baby,' she told him clearly, despite the tears that slid down her cheeks. 'He came in here and he took her – the same man who took those other children. The same man who killed that boy.'

'Samuel Hargrave,' Sean explained. 'His name was Samuel Hargrave.'

'I didn't know that,' she answered. 'I wasn't paying that much attention when I saw it on the news. For a second I thought, God, how terrible that must be for the parents, then I didn't think about it again until this morning, when I went to get Victoria and saw she was gone. And I knew – I just knew straight away that she'd been taken. I – I remembered seeing it on the television, but I still couldn't remember the boy's name.'

'It's understandable,' Sean tried to comfort her. 'We never think these things will happen to us.'

'We have an alarm,' she told him, pain and guilt shining in her eyes, the thought of actions not taken haunting every line of her face. 'When we saw it on the news I said to Seth, I said we should set the alarm at night, but we forgot, we just forgot, and now Victoria is gone.'

'No,' Sean insisted. 'That's not why she's gone. She's gone because someone took her. That has nothing to do with anything you did or didn't do. This man is like . . . like a bolt of lightning. Who knows why lightning misses a million people standing in the open, but then hits one man as soon as he steps outside. Some things we just can't predict, and we can't live our lives always fearing the worst or we would have no life. I see these things almost every day, but do I make my wife and kids live their lives in some sort of protective bubble? Of course I don't, and I never would, no matter what.'

'Maybe,' she told him, 'but if something happens to her I'll never forgive myself – I'll be dead inside. I'll always be dead inside.'

Sean sat next to her on the unmade bed, unable to think of anything else to say – exhausted by the effort of being understanding and trying not to absorb her pain, until for the first time he noticed she was holding a small toy in her hands, almost concealed between her palms. 'Is that her favourite toy?' he asked, remembering the toy placed so caringly under Samuel Hargrave's dead arms and making a mental note to check what progress Zukov had made in tracing the toy's origins.

Mrs Varndell looked down at the toy she was caressing, then answered with a resigned shrug. 'This thing? God, no.' She opened her hands and Sean saw that the toy looked more like an antique from the Victorian age than a child's plaything – a monkey with a grinning porcelain face, dressed in a red soldier's uniform with a little red cap perched at an angle on its head while each hand grasped a miniature brass cymbal. 'I never wanted her to have it, but she insisted. Horrible-looking thing. Scary. I don't know why I even picked it up – perhaps because it was one of the last things I bought for her.'

Her words made Sean rise to his feet, staring down at the toy monkey still in the woman's hands, thoughts rushing at him too quickly to be processed. He was terrified that they might all melt away before he could form the whole picture in his mind. The words of the young priest came back to him. *It's like we're looking so hard, but we just can't see.* 'This isn't her favourite toy?' he asked her, his instinct telling him to keep asking questions, any that came into his mind. Just ask the questions and hope to decipher the answers when they came.

'No,' she told him. 'Victoria has only ever had one special toy – Polly the rag-doll. Sometimes I think she loves that doll more than she loves anyone alive. But all children have one special toy, don't they? One that they love above all others – the one they can't sleep without – the one that all parents are afraid of losing. Even if you give them an identical replacement, they know it's not the real one.'

'Yes, yes they do,' Sean agreed, thinking of his own daughters and their special soft toys – the ones they'd had since the day they were born. Never the largest or most expensive, but somehow the ones that each particular child formed a seemingly unbreakable bond with. 'So where is Polly now? Is she still here?'

'No,' she answered, 'or at least I don't know.'

'Have you looked?'

'Everywhere, but we can't seem to find her.'

'Then it's possible that whoever took her also took the doll,' Sean thought of the soft blue dinosaur in Samuel's arms, and realized that the killer hadn't brought it with him. It had always belonged to the boy and he'd taken it at the same time . . .

But Mrs Varndell hadn't finished yet.

'No,' she contradicted him. 'He couldn't have done that.'

'I don't understand,' Sean admitted, his eyes growing narrow with strain. 'Why couldn't he?'

'Because Polly didn't go missing last night – she went missing the night before.' She continued talking, but Sean wasn't listening any more as the significance of her words began to sink into his strained mind and settle into a composite picture he could finally understand. He'd had all the pieces of the puzzle he needed right from the first scene, but only now was he able to put them together – only now was he able to realize the significance and importance of each separate piece. 'We looked everywhere, but we couldn't find her, so he couldn't have taken Polly at the same time as he took Victoria, because Polly wasn't here.'

Sean staggered backwards a step, the weight of the unravelling truth making him dizzy as he began to speak out loud, not caring who heard or what he sounded like – he just needed to say the words that were racing through his head before they were lost: 'He knows the houses – knows everything about them, because he's been inside them before, during the night. And the children never cry or call out because he brings them something – something special, something more special to them than almost anything else.'

He paused for a second as the final picture took shape behind his eyes and at last solidified. 'Jesus Christ – he was in the house the night before he took the child. He was in all the houses the night before he took the children. He let himself in, checked everything he needed to check and then he went to the children's rooms and he saw which toys they were holding tightest. He knew they would be the ones he needed and he took them – and then he left as silently as he came, locking the door behind him so no one even knew he'd been. And when he came back the following night, he came with the toy. That's how he kept them quiet, by giving them back the thing they wanted more than anything – the thing they loved.'

'Oh my God,' Mrs Varndell said through her distress, covering her mouth with one hand as if she was going to start retching. 'Oh my God, he's been here before – walking around inside my house. Oh my God.'

Sean ignored her because he had to. He was too close to the final answer to let anything stand in the way. 'But that's not enough. Not for this one. He plans – everything is planned. If he went to the bedroom and the child wasn't holding the toy, then all the other parts of his plan would collapse, and he wouldn't risk that, so . . . so he already knew which were their favourite toys – the bastard already knew. But how – how did he know that?' He looked down at the sobbing figure of Mrs Varndell and the toy monkey in her hand, its porcelain face staring straight at him, just as the doll with the porcelain face had done when he stood in the bedroom of Bailey Fellowes – toys from a bygone era, out of place in the rooms of young children nowadays. He was seeing more and more as he dropped to his knees in front of Mrs Varndell, grabbing the hand that held the toy. 'Listen to me,' he pleaded. 'It's vitally important you listen to me.' She blinked away her tears and tried to focus on his face. 'I need you to tell me where you bought this toy. I need you to tell me right now.'

She shook her head, dazed and confused, her mind struggling to function properly. 'A toyshop,' she stuttered. 'A toyshop somewhere.'

'Where?' Sean demanded.

'I can't remember,' she told him. 'I'm confused. I . . . I.'

'Think,' he pushed her.

'In Hampstead, I think.'

Sean rocked back on his heels. Hampstead – right in the middle of the abduction sites.

'Where in Hampstead?'

'I don't remember. I don't know Hampstead very well. We just went for a wander, and we came across this toyshop, and it looked quite interesting – more interesting than usual – so we went in.'

'In what way more interesting?' he asked.

'It was old fashioned, I suppose. It didn't have many modern toys in it, mostly strange, old things, and lots of handmade clockwork toys. God knows who'd buy clockwork toys nowadays.'

'Clockwork?' Sean snapped his question, the picture of a man stooped over a desk piecing together a clockwork toy jumping into his mind – small, delicate tools in the man's nimble, practised fingers, tools like the ones used to pick locks.

415

'Yes,' she answered. 'They were everywhere. He told us he made them himself.'

'Who did? Who told you that?'

'The shopkeeper,' she told him, shaking her head in surprise that the answer hadn't been obvious to him.

'What was it called?' he asked, his heart thumping against his chest wall. 'I need to know the name of the shop.'

'I can't remember,' she told him. 'I don't understand. Do you think the man from the toyshop could have taken Victoria?' Sean's silence answered her question. 'No,' she pleaded, suddenly tossing the toy monkey to the ground as if it had magically transformed into a poisonous snake, kicking it away with her feet. 'He picked that for her,' she told him, staring disgustedly at the discarded toy. 'Took it off the shelf and gave it to her. He touched it with his hands and now he's touching my . . .'

'The shop?' Sean stopped her. 'I need the name of the shop.'

'I can't,' she begged him. 'I just can't.'

'OK,' he relented with a sigh. He hurriedly pulled his phone from a coat pocket and searched it for Sally's number, pacing the bedroom while he waited for her to answer.

'Sean,' she snapped at him. 'What's going on? I'm hearing all kinds of rumours back here and none of them good. I'm hearing you're off the case. I'm hearing you're off the team, Sean.'

'Never mind that now,' he told her. 'I need you to do something.'

'Of course, but where are you?'

'Mornington Crescent – at the fourth abduction site.'

'Bloody hell, Sean! If Addis finds out he'll go fucking spare.'

'Not if I get the children back first,' he explained.

'What?' Sally asked, barely believing what she was hearing. 'You know where the children are?'

'Almost, but I need your help.'

'What d'you want me to do?'

'We still have Family Liaison Officers with the other three families, right?'

'As far as I know.'

'Good. Get them all lined up on a conference call and make sure they have the parents of the children with them, then call me back fast.'

'Even the Hargraves?'

Sean paused for a second before answering. 'Yes,' he told her. 'I understand where you're coming from, but I can't take the chance of leaving them out. They may be the only ones who can tie this all up. I need them on the call.'

'OK,' Sally told him. 'I'll get it sorted and call you back.'

Sean hung up and turned his attention back to Helen Varndell. 'Is it possible the man from the shop could have followed you home?'

'I don't see how,' she answered. 'When we left the shop he was busy serving other customers.'

'What about someone else? Did anyone else follow you from the shop?'

'I don't . . . I can't remember.'

'He knew where you lived,' Sean told her brutally, 'so either he followed you or he had you followed . . . or,' he stuttered for a second as another thought entered the maze of his mind, 'or you told him your address.'

'Why would we have done that?'

'I don't know,' Sean admitted. 'Maybe you filled something out in the shop – some kind of form. Something you wrote your name and address on?'

Her eyes darted in all directions as she struggled to

remember, not wanting to rush her recall and scare her memories away. 'My husband – he filled something in. The shopkeeper said it was for a competition.'

'So he knew where you lived? You told him where you lived?'

'Yes,' she confessed, 'but how could we possibly have known?'

'You couldn't,' he replied softly.

For a few seconds they stood in silence, each trying to comprehend. Then his vibrating, ringing phone broke the trance.

'Sally?'

'I have the Family Liaison Officers standing by,' Sally told him. 'What d'you need to know?'

Sean took a breath and steadied himself. 'I need you to ask whether any of them have recently been to a toyshop in Hampstead.'

'A toyshop?' Sally quizzed.

'Please, Sally,' he snapped, 'just ask.'

He listened as she put the question to the Family Liaison Officers on the conference call, and then he waited in silence for the answer. He heard Sally breathing into the phone before she spoke and already knew he had his man.

'Jesus Christ, Sean – how did you know?'

'Long story,' he answered, unwilling and unable to dwell on his success. 'You need to ask if any of them can remember the name of the shop. Mrs Varndell was in it too, but she can't remember what it's called. Can any of them remember?'

'Hold on . . .'

Again he could hear Sally repeating the question into the other phone. This time there was a longer pause, each second making him fear the worst, before Sally came back on the line. 'Sorry, no. None of them can remember its name.'

'Damn it,' Sean answered, before recovering his optimism. 'Never mind. We know it's an old-fashioned toyshop in Hampstead – it can't be too difficult to find.'

'Sean, wait!' Suddenly Sally was back on the line, cutting across him. He listened to more voices, straining without success to follow the conversation. Then Sally returned. 'Mrs Fellowes says it's called the Rocking Horse and it's in Heysham Lane, Hampstead. She bought a doll from there for Bailey. She says you know which one.' Sean's mind filled with the picture of the ornate doll he'd lifted from amongst Bailey's other toys. 'Sean?' Sally prompted him.

'It was there all the time,' he told her. 'In Bailey's bedroom – the answer was always there. I held it in my hand, Sally – I held the answer in my hand, but I missed it.'

'We all did,' she reminded him, 'but you've put it together now. I don't know how, but I know nobody else could have. Question is – what d'you want to do next? Surveillance? Have the TSG take him out?'

'No. This one's no Thomas Keller. He's no danger to me.'

'And the children?'

'They'll be close. He'll be keeping them close.'

'But if he sees us coming?'

'If he sees us coming I'm not sure what he'll do – so we don't let that happen.'

'How can we—'

'Meet me in Heysham Lane as soon as you can. Just you, Donnelly and one other. Travel in two cars and park out of sight at either end of the road, and then wait for me. Tell nobody where you're going or what you're doing. Understand?'

'I understand. I'll update you with his description en route,' she assured him. 'Travelling time from the Yard,' were her last words before she hung up, leaving him alone once more with Helen Varndell.

'Have you found him?' she asked as soon as he lowered the phone from his ear. 'Have you found Victoria?'

'I can't promise that.' Sean's voice was shaking in the effort to suppress his excitement, he was almost beside himself, wanting nothing more than to get to his car and attach the magnetic blue light to its roof, parting the late-morning traffic like a wolf cutting through a flock of sheep. 'But I promise I'll do everything I can to bring her back to you – whatever it takes.'

15

Sean walked slowly along Heysham Lane, his collar turned up against the persistent cold, one more local businessman late for work or on his way to a meeting. He walked straight past the Rocking Horse toyshop with barely a glance inside, but it was enough. He found Donnelly's unmarked car behind a van and tapped twice on the window before jumping in the passenger seat.

'What took you?' Donnelly asked.

'Been walking the area a bit,' Sean told him.

'And?'

'And we're in the right place.'

'You sure?'

'I'm sure,' Sean assured him. 'He's skilled enough to make clockwork toys. Not much of a stretch from that to picking locks. He lives in the right area, he knew all their addresses and he understands children and toys. Last but not least, he's the only thing that connects all four families. He feels right. He just feels right.'

'How did he get their addresses?'

'Had them fill in some forms for a bogus competition.

Everything he needed to know, the families gave him themselves.'

'You know they all did this?' Donnelly asked.

'Yeah, I confirmed it on the way here. The bastard broke into their homes the night before he took the children and stole their favourite soft toy or doll – learned all he needed to know about the inside of the house, then the next night he comes back, with the same toy – gives it back to the kid and makes himself an instant hero. No wonder they went with him so easily – so quietly.'

'Fuck me,' Donnelly answered, trying to understand the mind of a man who would do such things. 'So what now? Surveillance?'

'No. Won't tell us anything.'

'Could tell us if the children are here, assuming they're—'

'They're here,' Sean insisted. 'I know they're here.'

'Maybe he keeps them somewhere else,' Donnelly suggested. 'Just in case anyone comes sniffing around the shop. Maybe he lives somewhere else himself?'

'No,' Sean told him. 'Zukov checked the local retailers' register. The same man who owns the shop is shown as owning and living in the residential property above it: Douglas Allen, male, white, fifty-eight years old. He's our man.'

'But why?' Donnelly asked. 'Why take these children if he's no paedophile or child-pedlar?'

'That's what I intend to ask him,' Sean told him while looking in the wing mirror of the car until he saw what he was waiting for – a mother entering the shop with her two young children. 'That's what I intend to ask him right now.' He tried to spring from the car, but a heavy arm from Donnelly stopped him.

'Last time you took one of these psychos on alone it didn't end too well, I seem to remember.'

'This is different,' Sean insisted.

'All the same, I think I'll tag along with you.'

'No,' Sean ordered. 'I need to see him alone with a family. Once I've seen that, I'll call you straight away. I promise.'

Donnelly released his arm and sank back into the seat, resigned to Sean's intentions. 'Just . . . just don't push your luck, guv'nor. OK?'

Sean looked him in the eyes for a brief moment. 'Don't worry about me. I'll be fine.'

Donnelly's quiet reply was lost to him as he opened the door. 'Aye. Of course you will. Of course you will.'

Sean moved quickly along the pavement, clocking Sally and Zukov parked at the other end of the street. He reached the Rocking Horse and entered, scanning the shop without making eye contact with anybody – he wanted to get his bearings and settle his mind before engaging anyone in any way. He ignored the displays of ornate, traditional and clock-work toys and headed for a corner of the shop seemingly set aside for the more modern – Lego, Duplo, Airfix and even Action Man. There was a distinct lack of anything computer-based.

Once he felt comfortable in his surroundings Sean began to covertly look around the shop, his attention closing in on a short, stocky man dressed in grey flannel trousers with a maroon V-neck jumper pulled tight over a white shirt and red tie. The man had to be at least fifty-five, with a small gut, but he looked nimble and strong, although Sean noticed he was stooping slightly. As he talked to the mother and her two young children the shopkeeper maintained a constant smile, but his face wore a troubled expression, as if he was bearing some great burden. Sean knew what it was. *Douglas Allen*, he spoke silently inside his mind, *I've come to take you away, my friend. It's time to go. It's time to end this ugly game*.

He listened in to their conversation, watching every move

Allen made, waiting for him to turn round and see him standing there, instinctively aware of who he was. But Allen was no Sebastian Gibran or John Conway – ready and willing to kill at the drop of a hat to save his own skin. This was an individual who was broken inside and confused about the world around him. Nevertheless it was Sean's job to bring that world crashing down.

'These are very popular,' Allen told the tall, well-spoken woman who held on to her children as they tried to pull away from her. He held out a porcelain-faced doll in a lace dress. 'I import them from Paris. They're handmade – their faces painted by true craftsmen, so each has its own expression and personality.'

'A bit like a Cabbage Patch Doll,' the mother told him unwisely, wiping the thin smile from Allen's face.

'Quite.' He bent down to show the doll to the eldest girl, who Sean guessed could only be five or six. 'And what do you think?' he asked her. 'Do you like this dolly?'

'I think she's beautiful,' the little girl answered, her wide smile revealing perfect white milk teeth as her blue eyes sparkled with happiness.

'Yes, she is, isn't she – almost as beautiful as if she was alive. But who's this we have here?' Allen asked, gently touching the small, beige teddy bear, almost squashed flat through years of being held too tightly by the little girl.

'That's Mr Teddy,' the mother answered for her with arching eyebrows. 'Mr Teddy goes everywhere.'

'Then he must be very special?' Allen asked.

'Mr Teddy's the most special,' the little girl told him.

'Of course he is, but I bet you'd like this doll?' he suggested.

'I'm not sure,' the mother interceded. 'It looks very expensive, for a young child's toy.'

'You can't put a value on quality,' Allen argued. 'You can't compare these beautiful Parisian dolls to the cheap rubbish they mass produce in Taiwan, or China I suppose it is now. These dolls were made to last a lifetime.'

'So long as they're never played with,' the mother joked, but Allen wasn't laughing.

'Please, Mummy,' the little girl pleaded, tugging at her mother's coat. 'Please can you get her?'

'No, darling,' the mother insisted. 'It's not even a toy. It's more like an ornament. Pick something you can play with. Look – they've got Lego over there.'

'Yes. Yes,' Allen agreed, carefully placing the doll back on its shelf. 'We have some Lego. In fact, we're having a little competition at the moment. First prize is quite a collection of Lego, or you could always choose the doll as a prize.'

'Mummy, Mummy, I want to win the dolly,' the little girl chirped excitedly.

'Wait. Wait,' the mother told her. 'Fine. How do we enter? What do I have to do?'

'Just fill in this form.' Allen held out a piece of paper, but the mother stopped him.

'I really don't have time to start filling in forms. I've kind of got my hands full here.'

'Of course. Then please allow me to fill it in for you,' he offered, hurrying behind the counter to retrieve a pen. He looked at Sean for the first time since he'd entered the shop. 'I'll be with you in one moment, sir.'

Sean nodded turning away to examine the Lego, allowing Allen to focus on the mother.

'Now, if I could just take your name, Mrs . . .?'

She barely paused before answering. 'Mrs Orwin – Carine Orwin.'

'And the names of your children?'

'This is Anarra,' she told him, pointing to the older girl. 'She's almost six. And this is Lucy. She's still only three.'

'And your address?'

'Nassington Road, next to the Heath.'

'A beautiful street,' he added. 'Your husband must have a wonderful job?'

Her pride overcame her suspicions. 'He works in the City.'

'A banker?'

'No,' she answered, keen to avoid the stigma of being associated with that profession. 'He's a trader.'

'I never can work out the difference,' Allen admitted with a smile before moving on. 'And your telephone number? Home number will be fine.'

'Sure – it's 0207 151 3728. Do you want the email address too?'

'No. No. I'm not much of a one for email. I'm sure I'll be able to get hold of you if you win. Nassington Road's so close I could always drop it in to you.'

'Always best to call first,' the mother told him. 'We're out and about a lot.'

'I'm sure you are, although I've never seen you in here before – are you new to the area?'

'No,' she answered casually. 'We've lived here for a few years now.'

'And what a wonderful place to live,' Allen replied, 'although one always has to guard against break-ins in an area like this.'

'I'm sorry, I don't. . .' the mother began, a little confused.

'A wealthy area such as this will always attract an unsavoury element, I'm afraid. It pays to have a good security system, don't you agree?'

'I suppose so. My husband takes care of all that. He's very security conscious – state-of-the-art this, state-of-the-art that. I can hardly step out of the bedroom without setting something off.'

'I see,' he told her. 'Well, has anything caught your eye today?'

426

'Er, we'll have a think about it and maybe pop back later,' the mother told him, ignoring the five-year-old tugging at her coat, trying to pull her in the direction of the Parisian doll.

'Of course,' he replied with a forced smile, opening the door for the tangled jumble of legs and arms that left the shop looking like a single, multi-limbed creature. 'Have a nice day,' he told them, closing the door on the mother's struggle and instantly turning to Sean. 'Are you looking for anything in particular, sir?'

Sean looked long and hard into his eyes for the first time – the eyes of Samuel Hargrave's killer, and the abductor of at least three other young children. He made the effort to swallow his loathing and sorrow for the man, but he couldn't manage a smile as he looked into Allen's dead eyes – like the glass eyes of the dolls and figures that stared lifelessly down on their impending duel. He desperately wanted to arrest him without waiting another second – handcuff him to a radiator and run through the house looking for the missing children. But he needed to speak to Allen first, to be absolutely sure that this was the man he'd been searching for – to wash away any last lingering doubts at the end of an investigation that had been plagued by so many.

'Not really,' Sean told him. 'I was just looking for something for the kids.'

'Boys or girls, sir?'

'Two girls,' Sean answered, instantly regretting bringing any truth about himself into the charade. 'Six and three.'

'Is it a special occasion?'

'No. We've just moved into the area and I was hoping to buy them a little house-warming present, you know.'

'Of course. Maybe you could tell me what sort of things they like?'

'Just normal girls' stuff – dolls and dresses.'

427

'Perhaps these then,' Allen suggested, sweeping his hand to take in the porcelain-faced dolls. 'I'm sure they would look quite at home in your girls' new bedrooms.'

'Maybe.' Sean could tell Allen was trying hard to conceal his contempt at his lack of appreciation for the beautiful dolls. If this had been any other toyshop on any other day he'd have bought his girls the dolls in a heartbeat.

'What road did you say you'd moved into?' Allen changed the subject.

'Cannon Place,' Sean volunteered, using the name he'd memorized on the way from Mornington Crescent.

'A beautiful street,' Allen told him. 'Very expensive nowadays, I would imagine.'

'I got a good bonus,' Sean lied.

'Ahh. Another banker.' Sean just shrugged. 'Seems the whole area's been overtaken by bankers and traders, whatever that is. Eastern European, most of them.'

'Is that a bad thing?' Sean asked.

'No. Except it drives the house prices to levels that no normal people, no normal families can afford.'

'Good for you,' Sean told him, looking around the shop as if he was admiring its potential value, taking in the door behind the counter that he assumed would lead upstairs to the rest of the house, 'if you own this place.'

'I do,' Allen almost snapped at him. 'I've lived here for years.'

'Then you know the area well?'

'Of course.'

'And what about Highgate and Primrose Hill? Mornington Crescent?'

'Well,' Allen staggered a little, his lifeless eyes narrowing with fear and suspicion, 'I know them a little, but Hampstead is my home.'

Sean let the oppression hang in the air before speaking

428

again. 'Well, I'd better get going – give the nanny a break from the kids.'

'The nanny?'

'Yeah,' Sean told him casually. 'My wife's at the gym and then lunch with her friends, then no doubt a bit of shopping. You know how women are.'

'Quite,' Allen lied.

'I've got the guy from the alarm company coming sometime this afternoon, so I might as well give the nanny a couple of hours off before her late shift.'

'Alarm?' Allen asked, his eyes opening wider.

'Yeah. New house – old alarm system. I'm getting it upgraded. Can't be too careful. Like I heard you telling that woman who was just in here – areas like Hampstead can be targets. Should be sorted in a few days.'

'Indeed.'

'So, anyway – I was wondering if you have any electronic games – computer games, that sort of thing? Something to keep the kids busy, and not to mention quiet?'

'Computer games?'

'Yeah. Anything, so long as it means I don't have to play with them.'

Allen cleared his throat before speaking. 'No. No, I'm afraid I wouldn't have anything like that. Perhaps you'd like to bring your girls to the shop, so they can choose for themselves? It's always a pleasure to meet young children. You could bring them this afternoon, after your alarm man's been. I'll still be open.'

'Maybe.'

'And while you're here, perhaps you'd like to enter our competition?'

'What do I win?'

'I would let your children choose the prize for themselves.'

'Which children?'

'I . . . your children, of course.'

'But what about . . . the other children? Don't they get to choose?'

'I . . . I don't understand. If you're referring to the other children who enter the competition, then of course, they get to . . .'

'That's not what I mean,' Sean stopped him, slipping his warrant card from his coat pocket and letting it fall open for Allen to see. 'Detective Inspector Corrigan – Special— Metropolitan Police.'

'I . . . I don't understand. You said you were a banker.'

'You understand, Mr Allen – Douglas Allen. That is your name, isn't it?' Sean watched as Allen took a couple of steps backwards. 'There's nowhere to go, Douglas. It's over. I know you took them.'

'No, I . . . I don't know what you're talking about.'

'That's not true, Douglas. We both know that's not true. I need to make sure the children are all right. I need to see if you've hurt them.'

'I . . . I would never hurt them,' Allen told him, glancing from side to side, as if an escape route might suddenly open up for him. 'I wanted to protect them – to give them a better life. It's God's will.'

'Jesus Christ,' Sean accused him. 'You did this because you thought God told you to? You did this in the name of God?'

'Let the little children come to me, and do not hinder them,' he breathlessly tried to explain, 'for the kingdom of heaven belongs to such as these.'

Sean realized Allen was slipping away from him. Slipping away from any grasp on reality. The killer and taker of children – the man who great swathes of the population would now want executed – the man the media would accuse of being a paedophile – the man whose fellow prison inmates would go to great lengths to try to maim and kill – was nothing more than a broken-down, lonely, ageing man who thought he'd heard the voice of God.

'Where are they?' Sean demanded, not expecting an answer, his eyes drifting towards the door behind the counter. 'They're here, aren't they? Through that door.'

Allen's downcast eyes, the utter defeat in his posture, told Sean everything he needed to know. He moved to the door, his heart rate beginning to rise with expectation and the sense of victory, when suddenly the shop door flew open, the frame filled by a familiar sight.

'Everything all right in here?' Donnelly asked.

Sean looked from Donnelly to the broken figure standing by the counter. 'Stay with him.'

'And the children?'

'Upstairs,' Sean told him.

'Are they all right?' Donnelly asked, trying to work out what could have happened between the two men before he arrived.

'I don't know,' Sean answered without emotion, confusing Donnelly all the more.

'D'you want me to check it out?'

'No,' Sean insisted. 'I'll go.' He walked past Allen, who was sliding to the floor, eyes staring straight ahead, fixed on the rows of porcelain-faced dolls, as the tears ran down his cheeks. 'Arrest him, for abduction and murder.'

'One thing,' Allen suddenly blurted out. 'Just one thing – how did you find me? How did you know it was me?'

'God brought me here,' Sean told him without really knowing why. 'Your God brought me here.' For a moment he thought he saw a burning light of hatred in Allen's eyes as he hurried past him and behind the counter to the door. He turned the large metal key and the door opened outwards, the scent of the house beyond unexpectedly rushing him, making him step backwards before he caught himself and pushed forward, through the porthole into the other part of Allen's life.

Sean could see there was a door immediately on his right and a short flight of stairs with another door at the top. He turned the handle on the door to his right and pushed it wide open, the small windows inside providing enough light for him to see clearly as he stepped just inside the doorway.

'Anything?' Donnelly called after him.

'Looks like an office,' Sean answered. as he unknowingly surveyed the desk where only days ago Allen had laid out the body of Samuel Hargrave. 'We'll search it properly later, but right now I need to find these children. Wait here.'

'You're the boss,' Donnelly told him as Sean leapt up the stairs to the other door. Images of Samuel Hargrave, in the cemetery and the mortuary, filled Sean's mind and mingled with the memories of other scenes he'd witnessed where children had been the victims. Was that what waited for him on the other side of the door? He forced the fear deep inside himself and moved on, turning the key and pushing the door open. The atmosphere beyond was starkly different to the quaint charm of the shop below. Here he could smell fear, anxiety and desperation, and not just Allen's or the children's. He sensed an oppression that seemed to have been consuming the house and all who lived in it for years. Some deep sadness from which Allen had been trying to escape. Only for him there had been no escape, and there never would be.

Sean moved steadily along the corridor, pausing for a few seconds to draw his telescopic metal baton, palming it in his hand without extending it, its weight and coldness reassuring him as he ventured deeper into the house. He imagined the three tiny bodies neatly lined up, lying on their beds, each wrapped tightly in a tartan blanket, crucifix

432

in hand and their special toys clutched to their non-breathing chests – their non-seeing eyes waiting to fall upon him when he finally entered the room where they silently waited. He could feel the coldness and texture of their skin as he saw himself pushing his fingers into their throats, searching fruitlessly for their pulses, only admitting it was too late once it was utterly pointless to pretend otherwise. He thought of Kate, the times she'd come home from work visibly upset, and he knew without asking that she'd had to deal with an infant death – not just having to face the lifeless body of a child, but having to tell the parents that their child was gone – gone for ever.

There were five doors leading to what he assumed were five separate rooms on the first floor. He hurried along the corridor and entered the first room on the left. Quickly he scanned the corners of the room for any signs of danger, but saw nothing. Now that he'd confronted Allen, looked into his sad eyes, Sean was increasingly sure he'd worked alone. Wasn't that ultimately the point of his crimes – so he didn't have to be alone? But instinct made Sean check for danger before proceeding to the next floor.

As he looked around the unnaturally ordered room, his eyes fell on the small dressing table pushed up against the wall and the things laid out on it – photographs and pictures, a shrine. A place where Allen could worship the woman who appeared in all the photographs and the God whose son hung on the crucifix nailed to the wall. Even from the doorway he could see the optimism in the faces of the young couple in the photographs, fading as they aged until pictures of Mrs Allen showed her suffering from the ravages of illness, leaving him in little doubt she was gone now and had been for some time. He wondered whether she was buried in Highgate Cemetery. Sean sighed deeply, feeling he understood Allen more and more.

Leaving the altar, he headed back into the hallway, comforted by the sound of Donnelly's voice coming from downstairs as he spoke to the silent Allen. But he knew soon there would be other voices downstairs – Sally's and Zukov's, and then there'd be heavy footsteps on the stairs as they ran to join him. He needed to be in the house alone, needed to find the children alone, no matter *how* Allen had left them – to bring a suitable end to what had increasingly felt like a lonely journey back to himself, back to the gifts that he knew separated him from most other detectives. Gifts he'd feared had been lost, until the moment Helen Varndell told him that the toy she held wasn't little Victoria's favourite.

He hurried across the hallway and stood in the doorway of the kitchen. It looked as if it had been frozen in time, a reminder of the kitchen his mother had seemed to permanently inhabit in the council house he grew up in, only this was far more ordered. At least that's how Allen had tried to keep it, but there were signs he was struggling to maintain the illusion: the tea-towels were neatly folded and hanging from the oven, but Sean could see that they were filthy; glasses had been placed back on the shelves, but looked stained and greasy, and the fruit that filled the bowl in the centre of the kitchen table was beginning to rot. Clearly Allen had been descending into a world of denial and fantasy for some time. In the sink Sean could see the evidence of more than one meal having been prepared and eaten – dirty plates piled up with cups, pots, pans and even used glasses. The last meals of the children? In Allen's collapsing mind, had he felt it was the kind thing to do – feed them before he killed them? Prepared to end their lives, but not prepared to see them suffer in life?

Sean feared the worst as he walked back into the hall without having set foot in the kitchen. He didn't have time to dwell. As much as his dark instinct wanted to move slowly through the house, examining every aspect of Allen's life, absorbing his very existence, he couldn't – not while the children were still to be found. He checked the other first-floor rooms as quickly as he could. Allen's bedroom was next. The curtains were drawn and the stale smell told him the windows hadn't been opened in a while.

He entered the room and opened the curtains, but the light revealed no tiny bodies. Sean exhaled with relief before glancing around one last time and heading back into the hallway and across to the bathroom. The towels were folded neatly, but foul smelling, the laundry basket overflowing. He noticed something else too: next to the bath, almost hidden amongst the things an adult would need, he saw children's bath soaps and lotion, flannels and sponges. The thought of Allen washing the children, even just watching them bathe, made him shudder. His eyes moved to the sink, instantly finding what he was looking for – three little coloured toothbrushes nestling in a filthy glass along with toothpaste for milk-teeth. There was no doubting it – the children had at the very least been kept here. But where were they now? Still he hadn't heard any sound coming from the rooms he searched or from above. The dead made no noise. Leaving the bathroom behind, he headed for the last of the first-floor rooms, his pace increasing.

As soon as he entered the final room on the floor he knew it was evidentially the most important. 'Fuck me,' he whispered as his eyes came to rest on a large desk that was being used as a workbench. He took in the assorted half-assembled clocks, watches and mechanical toys, the fine tools needed for Allen's trade spread amongst them and abandoned where they'd last been used. Without entering he scanned every surface until he found what he was looking for, all but hidden under the clockwork toys: disembodied locks, three or four of them, dissected as if they'd undergone a mechanical autopsy. 'Jesus Christ. What was going through your mind?'

He walked away from the room to resume his search. Somewhere in the house the children waited for him, and there was only one place they could possibly be.

For a split second he was tempted to run up the stairs shouting *Police, Police*, but it didn't feel right somehow. If the children were alive it would be best not to terrify them more than they already were by charging around shouting. And if they were already dead – if he was too late – he didn't want to hurtle into a room and immediately be confronted by his worst nightmare. All he could do was silently pray as he climbed the stairs to the top of the house, pushing himself forward as fast as he dared.

When he reached the landing he could see there were only two doors leading off it – both closed. But he could see no locks or even keyholes, so either they were unlocked or they were locked from the other side. Allen hadn't kept the children as prisoners in one of these rooms, they'd been allowed to roam the upper section of the house. He'd wanted them to treat his house as their new home – to come and go between rooms as they pleased, so long as they didn't come down to the shop – so long as they remained quiet. A secret. But what if they hadn't remained silent? What would he have done to them if they threatened to reveal their existence?

Sean pushed the questions away and turned the handle of the first door. Bright sunlight flooded through the windows inside, spilling on to the landing as he slowly swung the door open. He peered inside, holding his breath and squinting against the light that made his eyes slightly watery, blinking them clear until he could see the room in front of him and everything in it. Empty. The room was empty, except for some simple ivory-coloured furniture and two single beds, both with wooden headboards – one still immaculately made, with a porcelain-faced doll lying on the pillow, while the other had clearly been slept in and remained unmade. As he grew used to the brightness he could see the entire room had been lovingly prepared for the use of children, with clouds and rainbows, stars and moons covering the walls. Mobiles with unicorns, lions and birds hung from the ceiling, their intricate shadows gently dancing on the walls and floors. Some old-fashioned toys – a spinning top, clockwork train and a Jack-in-a-box – lay in the middle of the room, played with before being abandoned. Others looked on from the shelves of the seemingly idyllic children's bedroom. But no amount of toys and furnishings could hide the atmosphere of fear Sean sensed in the room, stained deep into the walls. He shivered at the prospect of what may have happened in this place, the lack of any signs of violent struggle doing nothing to ease his fears as he remembered Samuel Hargrave's barely touched body. He only had one more room to check.

Sean crossed the landing, resting his hand on the door handle, taking several deep breaths before almost reluctantly turning the knob and opening the door by no more than an inch, waiting for the scent of death to give him fair warning of what he was about to see. But he could smell no such thing. He began to push the door open slowly, confused by the lack of sunshine. This room was in semi-darkness, telling him the curtains or blinds were still drawn and no lights had been turned on. He took it as a bad sign and braced himself for what he would find, filling his lungs so he'd have something to exhale when his eyes fell upon the scene of horror.

When the door was finally open he peered inside, trying to adjust his eyes to the dimness. The main body of the room was around to his left. All he could see from the doorway was the wall to his right. As he walked further into the room, the scent of children, of living children, washed over him, increasing the rate of his already thundering heart – his heart that was suddenly full of hope. He rounded the door and looked into the twilight, wondering if his eyes were playing tricks on him as he looked down at the floor where three small figures sat silently facing each other. They looked up at him, neither smiling or crying, just staring expressionless, eyes wide open with wariness – the faces from the photographs he'd first seen pinned to the Missing Person's Reports what seemed like a lifetime ago. And yet, here they were – real, living children.

Instinctively he stepped towards them, but sensing they were ready to scurry away like frightened mice, he froze where he was. He almost reached for his warrant card before realizing it would be a futile act – showing children something they would neither recognize or understand. Finally he opted simply to speak, crouching down low to appear as unthreatening as possible, slowly stretching out his upturned palm. But when he tried to speak the words stuck in his dry, tight throat. He swallowed hard and tried again. 'It's all right,' he told them, his voice raspy and unpleasant. 'I'm a policeman. You don't have to be afraid any more. The man who brought you here is gone now.' He waited for a response from the children, but they said nothing, looking away from him and turning to each other, as if they were communicating telepathically. Sean watched them as he tried to think of something else to say until finally the tiny figure of George Bridgeman got to his feet and faced him, apparently without fear.

'Have you come to take us home?' he asked, looking down at his fellow captives as if seeking assurance he'd asked the right question. Sean had to stifle a laugh born of relief and elation.

'Yes,' he answered. 'Yes, I have. I've come to take you home.'

Sean stood to the side of the elevated desks that were the focal point of the custody suite at Kentish Town Police Station. Two uniformed sergeants surveyed all they controlled from on high, behind the huge booking-in desk with its built-in computers. Oblivious to the hustle and bustle going on around him, Sean read each page of Douglas Allen's custody record, focusing on the summary of the Mental Health Team's findings. Already he could foresee a plea of not guilty on the grounds of diminished responsibility due to mental illness. 'Why didn't you just take the damn pills?' Sean asked out loud. 'You could have saved a lot of people a lot of pain – yourself too.'

A brash voice snapped him back to the real world.

'Talking to yourself again?' barked Donnelly. 'First sign of madness, apparently. Speaking of which, the search team's found a shitload of drugs in the house – as in medicinal drugs, not the fun stuff. Nothing I'm particularly familiar with, so I ran a few of the names past the local police surgeon. It appears they're for the treatment of depression and schizophrenia.'

Sean didn't mention he'd already seen the drugs during his hunt for the children; instead he handed the custody record to Donnelly. 'There's an entry in there from the Mental Health Team,' he explained. 'They've managed to speak to Allen's GP, or should I say GPs – he swapped whenever he got one who told him what he didn't want to hear. They all say he has treatable depression with schizophrenic overtones – also treatable, but only if he took his medication.'

'Which he wasn't doing,' Donnelly finished for him.

'He was home alone,' Sean continued. 'He didn't have anyone to make sure he took the drugs – so he stopped taking them, preferring to listen to the voices in his head. Same fucking sad story we've seen before, and will see again.'

'Care in the Community,' Donnelly spat. 'You've got to fucking love it.'

Sean felt the phone vibrating before he heard it, pulling it from his inside jacket pocket and checking the caller ID: anonymous. Not unusual on a detective's phone, but always a cause for concern. He answered it anyway. 'Sean Corrigan.'

'Detective Inspector Corrigan,' Addis's voice leaked from the phone. 'I hear congratulations are in order.'

'Sir.'

'Although I seem to recall dismissing you from this investigation?'

'You did, but I remembered something – something I felt was crucial and that needed to be acted on immediately. Turned out that something was right.' He waited for the response.

'You're sure he's our man?' Addis eventually asked.

'Found the children in his house, and so far he's not denying it.'

'And he was working alone?'

'As far as I can tell. It looks like he has mental health issues – probably depression and schizophrenia. There's nothing to suggest he was working with anyone.'

'The children – where are they now?'

'Already back with their families.'

'Have they been interviewed yet?'

'No. That can wait. I'll have SOITs start interviewing them tomorrow.'

'SOITs?' Addis queried anxiously, the fact Sean wanted to use officers trained in Sexual Offences Interview Techniques giving him cause for concern. 'Do you think they've been sexually assaulted?'

'No,' Sean answered, 'but I want to be sure.'

440

'Very well,' Addis agreed. 'I want a full report on my desk by tomorrow morning – first thing.'

'Isn't that for my replacement to do?' Sean asked, hungry for his pound of flesh. 'I'm still waiting for them to arrive here at Kentish Town so they can take over.'

'Don't play games with me, Inspector,' Addis warned. 'You know full well no one's on their way to take over anything. You saved yourself – though only just. *I* have decided to leave you in your current position – for now. Your report – my desk – tomorrow – first thing.' The line went dead.

'Problem?' Donnelly asked.

'Nothing I can't handle.'

The door to the interview room opened and a head popped around the corner, searching for Sean.

'We're ready when you are, Inspector,' the appointed duty solicitor announced, struggling to conceal his delight at landing such a high-profile case.

'Shall we?' Sean asked Donnelly, and headed to the interview room without waiting for a reply.

Sean hurried through the legal requirements he needed to complete before the interview could begin, speaking as quickly as he could without betraying his impatience, relieved to get the legal ramblings out of the way so he could start with the questions and answers.

'Douglas, I need to ask you some questions. Do you understand?'

'Yes,' Allen confirmed, 'but why is she here?' he asked, looking at the woman sitting next to him. 'I don't need an appropriate adult. There's nothing wrong with me.'

'Law says different,' Sean told him. 'Leane's a trained psychiatric nurse. She needs to be present before I can interview you.'

'I see,' Allen agreed suspiciously.

'Douglas,' Sean began, focusing intently on him, as if they were the only two people in the interview room. 'Do you know why you're here?'

'I . . .'

'Because you've been arrested for the murder of Samuel Hargrave and the abduction of George Bridgeman, Bailey Fellowes and Victoria Varndell. Do you understand?'

'I didn't murder him,' he almost gasped. 'It was . . . it was an accident.'

Sean said nothing, hoping the oppressiveness of silence would encourage Allen to say more. It worked.

'It's just . . . it's just he was making a lot of noise and . . . and I was afraid.'

'Afraid of what?' Sean asked gently.

'Afraid they would hear us.'

'Who?'

'His parents.'

'This was when you were inside the boy's house – Samuel's house?'

'Yes.'

'So what did you do?'

'I put my hand over his mouth.'

'And?'

'That's all, I swear.'

'But you must have had to restrain him – hold his arms still?'

'Yes, but . . .'

'Otherwise he could have pulled your hand away.'

'No . . . he couldn't have done that.'

'Why not? If his hands were free?'

'Because I was pressing . . .'

'You were pressing what?' Sean pushed him. 'You were pressing down on his mouth too hard?'

'Excuse me, Inspector,' Leane Kerry intervened, 'but do

442

you think this style of questioning is appropriate, given Douglas's mental health issues? With the right treatment he'll be fine, but the medication takes several weeks before it's up to speed. At this time he's effectively untreated.'

'Thank you – I read the custody record.'

'Then maybe you could go a bit easier?'

'And in the custody record it says you've come to the decision he's fit to be interviewed.'

'That's true, but—'

'Then maybe it would be better for all of us if you'd let me get on with it,' Sean rebuked her, but then eased off. 'I'll bear in mind your . . . suggestions.' He turned back to Allen. 'So, Douglas – were you pressing down too hard, so hard that not only was Samuel unable to call out, he couldn't breathe?'

'I told you,' Allen replied, more scared and panicked than angry, 'it was an accident.'

'There's no such thing as an accident,' Sean told him calmly but firmly. 'It's always someone's fault. If you hadn't been in the house trying to abduct the boy, you wouldn't have had to clamp your hand so tightly over his mouth that he couldn't breathe, and he'd be here today – alive. You killed him, Douglas. Whether you like it or not, you killed him.'

'No! No!' Allen raised his voice, tears welling in his eyes. 'It was an accident. Why won't you believe me?'

'Because we call those sort of accidents murder,' Sean told him. 'At the very least, manslaughter – although in this case, child-slaughter would seem more fitting.'

'Inspector, please,' Leane appealed to him.

'OK, OK,' Sean relented. 'Let me ask you something simple, Douglas: why did you take them? Why did you take these children?'

'To give them a better life – better than the life they had.'

443

'These were children from privileged backgrounds – wealthy parents, beautiful houses, good schools, exclusive areas of London – what could you give them that would make their lives better?'

'Love,' Allen answered without hesitation. 'I could give them love. Their parents didn't care – not really. Nannies, au pairs, child-minders, toys to keep them quiet, computer games to keep them distracted. Their parents would do anything for them except spend time with them – nurture them and love them. They didn't deserve children. Iris and I tried for years, but the Lord never saw fit to bless us with a child, even though we would have given it all the love in the world.'

'Iris?' Sean asked. 'Your wife?'

'She died.' Allen told him what he already knew. 'More than two years ago. Cancer. She deserved better. *We* deserved better. I only took the children who I could see weren't loved. And I would have loved them, loved them as if they were our own.'

'Must have made you pretty angry – seeing these parents with beautiful children, blessed by God when they didn't deserve to be, while he left you with nothing: no children and your wife taken from you?'

'Not angry – determined. Determined to save the children from a loveless childhood.'

'That wasn't for you to decide,' Sean snapped at him. 'That wasn't your judgement to make.'

'Not my judgement,' Allen agreed. 'God's. It was God's judgement. He blessed them with children and they forsook his blessing, they ignored and took for granted the gift of all gifts they had been given. God passed his judgement on them and gave me the strength and guidance to do his work.'

'To take the children?' Sean asked. 'You're telling me that God told you to take the children?'

444

'The Lord is my shepherd.'

'And how did he tell you to do these things?'

'He spoke to me – in my mind – his voice as clear and distinct as yours is now. The voice of Our Lord and the voice of my wife guiding me, always guiding me – telling me what I must do.'

'You heard your wife's voice too?' Donnelly asked.

'Yes – giving me the strength to go on, even in the darkest of hours.'

'Given Douglas's medical history,' Leane interrupted, 'there's no reason to doubt what he's saying.'

'No,' Sean agreed. 'I don't suppose there is. But I need to know, Douglas, why didn't you just take your medication?'

'And silence the voice of God, and lose my wife for ever? Is that what you would have done?' Allen asked. 'Do you think yourself more important than God?'

'No,' Sean answered. 'No, I do not, but I'm not the one being interviewed, am I? You are.'

Allen's mouth fell open as if he was about to say something, but then it slowly closed. Sean sensed he might be going into lock-down and knew he needed to keep him talking, at least until he had enough to be sure Allen wasn't a far more darkly dangerous animal than appearances would suggest. That his medical history wasn't just something he'd created and nurtured so that he could hide behind it if he ever got caught.

'What did it feel like,' he asked, 'when you let yourself into their houses? What did that feel like?' For the briefest of moments he thought he'd detected the slightest glimmer in Allen's eyes. 'It was cold out at night. Inside the house must have felt warm – warm and safe. Did it make you feel like you belonged there?'

'I don't understand,' Allen told him.

'Did it make you feel in control? Did it make you feel like the God you say you serve?'

'It didn't feel like anything. I was only there for the child – for the sake of the child.'

'Come on, Douglas – it must have felt special, knowing the house was yours – standing alone while the family slept – knowing exactly where the child you'd come to take waited for you. Did it make you feel powerful?' Allen said nothing, his eyes never leaving Sean's. 'Because you knew everything about the house, didn't you, Douglas? You'd been there before. You'd been there the night you took the child's most prized possession – the thing you knew they loved more than anything – the thing you knew you could use to win their trust when you went to take them. That sounds like a man in complete control to me – not someone listening to voices inside his head.'

'I did it so they wouldn't be scared,' Allen tried to explain. 'I went to them the night before and I took their special toys so they wouldn't be scared when it was time to come for them. I didn't want them to be afraid, that's all. I couldn't stand it when they were afraid. They looked so . . . so alone.'

'And when *you* were alone with them, what did you do to them? When you stood next to their beds in the middle of the night, did you touch them? Did your hand slide under their blankets and *touch* them?'

'No! Never! You're completely wrong. You don't under-stand – I'd never . . . hurt them. I'd never do anything like that. I just wanted to love them.'

'Love them? But when Samuel became too much trouble, you killed him.'

'I told you – that was an accident.'

'What about the others, Douglas? What were you going to do when they became too much *trouble*? Were you going to kill them as well?'

'No, no!' Allen spluttered, burying his head in his hands.

'Get rid of them like the rubbish they were?'

446

'No! I just did what the voices told me to do. I just did what the Lord told me to do – what Iris said I should do. They would never tell me to harm the children.'

'There are no voices in your head,' Sean accused, his voice rising. 'No one's telling you what to do. You took the children because you wanted to. You killed Samuel Hargrave because you wanted to – because it made you feel good.'

'No!' Allen fought back. 'It tore me apart. The guilt was unbearable.'

'Inspector,' the solicitor interrupted. 'I have to point out that, given my client's medical history, it is entirely possible, even probable, that he has been hearing voices telling him what to do.'

'If his medical background's real, if it's not something he's created to hide behind. Manslaughter on the grounds of diminished responsibility sounds a lot better than murder – doesn't it, Douglas?'

'I didn't murder anyone, I swear.'

'You murdered Samuel Hargrave. And it was only a matter of time before you murdered the other children as well.'

'That's a lie!'

'One by one you'd have taken them from the room you kept them in and you'd have—'

'No.'

'You'd have pressed your hand over their mouths and held them—'

'No! Stop this!'

'Held them until they weren't struggling any more.'

'No.'

'And then you'd have taken them to some place and left them for us to find. Some place you thought was special – some place where leaving them there made you feel less like the cold-blooded murderer of children you are.'

'No!' Allen shouted, tears, mucus and saliva mixing together and making his face shiny and wet. 'No. No. No.'

'I think that's enough,' Leane stepped in, but Sean was finished anyway.

'All right,' he told Allen, his voice calm and normal again. 'All right, Douglas. That'll be enough for now. Have a chat with your solicitor and Leane, then get some rest. We'll talk again later, or maybe tomorrow.' He stopped the recording, took the tapes out and began to seal one in its case.

'When can I go home?' Allen's quiet voice broke the silence.

Sean looked up slowly. 'Excuse me?'

'When can I go back to my shop? I need to get back to the shop.'

'I don't think that'll be happening for a very long time, Douglas. I'm sorry.'

'But I was only doing God's work,' Allen explained. 'I was doing what he willed me to do.'

Sean sighed deeply before answering, remembering the pitiful sight of Samuel Hargrave in the mortuary – his tiny broken body clutching his favourite soft toy, trying to equate that terrible scene with the shadow of a man who sat in front of him now. 'It wasn't God's work, Douglas,' he told him, 'and it wasn't God's will either. One day I hope you can see that – I really do.' He gathered his files and the tapes and stood to leave, looking from Leane to the solicitor. 'Take as long as you need. Just let the jailer know when you're done.'

He left the room as quickly as he'd arrived, Donnelly trailing in his wake. They stopped at the oversized custody suite desk to book the master-tape in as evidence.

'Well, you certainly went for him,' said Donnelly accusingly.

'I had to know,' Sean told him. 'I had to know for sure.'

'Know what?'

'Whether he would have killed the other children – eventually.'

'I see,' Donnelly replied. 'So what d'you want to do now?'

'Let's see how the search teams and Forensics get on. Let him rest. We'll interview him again tomorrow in more detail. See if he can remember the when, where and how stuff.'

'And then?'

'Talk to the CPS – see what they want to do. It's their decision.'

'Fine,' Donnelly agreed. 'But what do you think?'

'About what?'

'About whether he would have killed the other children?'

Sean looked into Donnelly's grey eyes. 'That depends.'

'On what?'

'On what God told him to do,' Sean answered, his face serious and still. 'But then you might say it was God who saved them – in the end.'

'God?' Donnelly questioned. 'I thought it was you who saved them.'

'Whatever,' Sean said, continuing to log the tape. 'None of that really matters now. The main thing is, this show's over – for now, at least.' He closed the logbook and tossed the master-copy tape on top of it before looking back to Donnelly. 'Drink?' he asked.

'Constantly.'

Five Days Later

Sean crawled around on his hands and knees collecting dozens of treacherous pieces of Lego from the living-room floor. He could hear the voices of his wife and daughters one floor above as Kate struggled first to get them into the bath and then struggled even more to get them out. A couple of days' rest had made him feel almost like a different person. Normal. He allowed himself a smile as he listened to Kate's toil, glad to be left in charge of the downstairs tidying up. It was almost the first time he'd let the children out of his sight since coming home after seeing Douglas Allen being led away on remand to await his possible trial. He tossed the last of the Lego pieces into the box and stood, still feeling stiff and sore after surviving the investigation with close to no sleep or proper rest. At least he still had another couple of days off before going back to work. When and what the next case would be, God alone knew the answer.

He made his way to the kitchen and poured himself and Kate a glass of inexpensive Chianti, sitting contentedly at the dining table to wait for her to reappear before he got on with cooking dinner – something he hadn't done in quite a while. He hoped the distraction would stop his mind from wandering back to Douglas Allen and all the others before him. He didn't want to return to that world, not just yet. Kate had pushed him for details about the investigation, but as usual he'd kept it vague – even more so than usual. No details.

Kate's hurried footsteps down the stairs broke his tranquillity and warned him something was wrong. A few seconds later she burst into the kitchen looking agitated.

'What's the matter?' he asked, getting to his feet.

'I can't find Louise's Froggy.'

Sean knew his daughter wouldn't sleep without the floppy green toy she'd had since birth.

'What d'you mean, you can't find it?'

'I mean I don't know where it is.'

'Can she remember where she left it?'

'If she could do that it wouldn't be lost, would it?'

'When did you last see it?' he asked, his voice urgent and anxious.

'When did I last see it?'

'Yes,' he snapped at her. 'When did you last see it?'

'I don't know.'

'Think,' he pushed her. 'Did you see it this morning?' *Allen had been working alone, hadn't he? There couldn't be – another?*

'I . . . I can't remember,' she answered, growing increasingly concerned as she watched him frantically move around the kitchen, searching in every cupboard and drawer, under the table and every chair.

'I haven't seen it today,' he told her over her shoulder. 'If I had, I would have remembered. Did she have it last night?'

'Yes,' Kate replied. 'She definitely had it last night.'

'But you can't remember seeing it this morning?'

'No.'

'What about when you made her bed?'

'I can't remember.'

'But I thought you always put it on her pillow?'

'Not always. Sometimes she keeps it with her. What's this about, Sean? You're beginning to scare me.'

'Like you said – she won't go to sleep without it.'

'No – something else. There's something else you're not telling me.'

He walked past her and headed back towards the relatively tidy living room, certain he hadn't come across the prized toy when he'd cleaned up.

'Sean,' Kate asked as she followed him into the room. 'Why are you so worried about this bloody toy?'

'I'm not,' he lied. 'Just help me find it – please.'

She shook her head and without another word began to help him search the room. Sean pulled toys from the shelves and dropped them on the floor, emptying out boxes of Duplo and anything else that could be concealing the thing he desperately searched for. His eyes fell upon the sofa the children had not long ago been curled up on, watching cartoons before bath and bed. He grabbed handfuls of loose cushions and threw them aside, pulling off the covering blanket they used to try and preserve the sofa covers and hurling it to the side until only the main cushions remained. He drew a breath and said a fast, silent prayer before tossing them aside, dropping to his knees with relief as a huge weight suddenly lifted from his mind and body. He held the small green frog in both hands, breathing out and smiling slightly as he stared into its stitched eyes.

'Jesus Christ, Sean,' Kate asked. 'What's the matter with you?'

'Nothing,' he replied, never looking away from the toy. 'Nothing at all.'

452

ACKNOWLEDGEMENTS

Again I'd like to thank my agent, Simon Trewin at WME and my publishers, HarperCollins for making this third book possible – in particular Kate Elton, my editor Sarah Hodgson, my line editor Anne O'Brien, Kiwi Kate and the Killer Reads team as well as the sales team who did a great job getting the second book – *The Keeper* – into many important outlets. Thank you all.

I'd also like to say a big thanks to some of the people who encouraged me long before agents and publishers ever became involved, and persuaded me my first book – *Cold Killing* – had real potential. Unfortunately I can't always use their real names for security reasons. Firstly, thanks to my two great detective buddies, McGoo, who I've known since training school and is one of the funniest and bravest men I know, and Grim – a hardcore, old school detective who had the villains running scared and once famously said on TV – *'We'll hunt them down like the dogs they are'*. They know who they are.

I'd like to thank another cop buddie, Bin and his wife Sal, who loved *Cold Killing* from the start and really encouraged me to keep going, as did our dear friend Tans and not forgetting SH who took the time out of her own busy writing schedule to not only read *Cold Killing*, but to put me in touch with Simon Trewin, which turned out to be the single biggest break I've ever had.

To you all. Thanks a million.

LD